Lauren realized that deep down she was seeking a reason, any reason not to do what she planned to do. Shivers darted up and down her spine.

"Why do you continue to risk your life, and your crew's and your ship?"

Adrian's grin was lazy and wicked, all seriousness gone now as though he'd given away enough today. "A game," he confirmed. "An exciting, profitable game."

He moved back in his chair, grinding it against the floor. "And I'd better return to my duties to make sure it remains that way."

Adrian moved with the restless grace that always fascinated her. He reached her, then bent down. "I may not have another chance tonight to do this."

His lips met hers, and they fused in sudden, fierce desperation.

Lauren was saying goodbye. Understand, she suddenly, silently demanded of him. You have to understand. And then she was standing up, propelled by his hands, until she merged into his body. His hands caressed the nape of her neck, and his tongue played along her teeth until she opened her mouth, and it darted in, moving, teasing, seducing.

Sweetness and violence. They were both there . . . and it aroused a hunger so strong she thought she would explode from it.

LIGHTNING

PATRICIA POTTER

BANTAM

NEW YORK LONDON TORONTO SYDNEY AUCKLAND

LIGHTNING

A Bantam Fanfare Book/Published by arrangement with Doubleday
PUBLISHING HISTORY
Doubleday edition published May 1992
Bantam edition / August 1992

ISBN 0-553-29070-3

Published simultaneously in the United States and Canada

PRINTED IN THE UNITED STATES OF AMERICA

RAD   0 9 8 7 6 5 4 3 2 1

With love and appreciation
to Richard Swanson and Sara Fountain,
for their friendship and support throughout the years
and for always being there.

LIGHTNING

PROLOGUE

Lauren woke to her own scream, an excruciating pain filling her, terrifying her.

Her bed was bathed in sweat, her body and hair sticky with it, as she heard what sounded like the boom of cannon. Almost against her will, she opened her eyes.

The window was open in the hot, humid night, and the curtains were blowing wildly; fat raindrops splashed onto the pale green rug. A vivid streak of lightning lit up the room, then the thunder roared again, its fury every bit as intense as the cannon she'd thought she heard in the nightmare.

Please God, let it be a nightmare.

But the pain became even more intense, swelling until it seemed to consume her body. Then, suddenly, it vanished, leaving her drained. Empty.

But the relief was no relief at all, for in its wake the pain left a blackness that was worse than the agony.

"Larry!" she screamed in a cottage empty of any life but her own.

Another roll of thunder drowned the name as she hurled herself from the bed. For a moment she almost fell. She grabbed the poster of the bed, holding on to it as she turned her eyes once more to the storm raging outside.

"Larry," she cried again, but this time in a whisper as despair overcame her. "Larry," she called again and again, but it was as if a huge gray dark cloud had enveloped her, stealing a part of her soul. She felt pain again, this time so strong that she fell on the bed and lay panting there.

And she knew, with a soul-searing certainty, that Larry, her twin, was dying. Somewhere, in a storm like this, his life was draining from him. She'd felt his pain before, as he had hers. They'd wondered at their enduring each other's illnesses and accidents, and felt it a curse.

No more. She knew that too. The weakness was growing, the emptiness swelling until it seemed to suck her into a vortex of blackness.

Another flash of lightning illuminated the room, and she almost believed she saw Larry again, grinning mischievously, his hand extended toward her. And then he was fading; the light was gone, and she was alone.

Completely alone.

Their father had once said Larry was like the first bright glow of sun in the morning, and Lauren like the gentle twilight of evening. Both so different, yet parts of a whole. But he was gone now too.

Lauren held out a hand in the darkness. "Don't go," she whispered, but she knew there was no one to hear her cry.

And she wondered how could she endure days with no mornings.

CHAPTER 1

Charleston, April 1863

"Patrol boat at starboard."

The soft whisper was barely intelligible in the fog-shrouded night. It was passed from man to man by lips that barely moved. Sound carried in this still, humid night.

Adrian Cabot winced at the dull, throbbing sound of the engines and the slightly audible slap of the paddle blades turning slowly through the water.

The *Specter* was only crawling now, feeling its way between the gunboats of the Union Navy that sat like great vultures just beyond the entrance to the Charleston Harbor. The open sea, and freedom, were minutes away.

Standing at the wheel of his own ship, his pilot beside him whispering guidance, Adrian felt a familiar mixture of anxiety and exhilaration. He had never experienced anything quite as intoxicating as running the Union blockade.

It seemed luck was with them tonight. The moon was only a slice, but even that was blacked out by the fog that had settled around Charleston in the first early hours of the morning. The *Specter* had already glided, unnoticed, past one Union gunboat, and then another. Now, on the starboard side, still another ship appeared out of nowhere.

Adrian said a brief seaman's prayer. He knew his ship was difficult to see, particularly in this fog. He had designed her himself and took pride in her speed and maneuverability as well as her sharp, sleek lines that blended into night. The *Specter* was painted pearl gray, even its sails, and its hull rose only slightly out of the water. Only the most alert of sentries would find him tonight.

His hands tightened on the wheel. He needed this run. This one, and eight more like it. They represented the one opportunity to buy back his heritage, to redeem the honor of his family.

He took one more cautious look around the heavily laden ship. No light shone anywhere. Tarpaulins covered all the hatchways. Any light at all was cause for the severest discipline.

The Union ship on the left disappeared from view, and Adrian held the course steady, depending on the pilot's knowledge to steer him away from dangerous shallows, sandbars, and shipwrecks. Johnny was endowed with the ability to see at night, and knew these waters better than anyone Adrian had met. Adrian complied without question with the instructions that Johnny delivered in a soft, unexcited voice, but he still felt like a blind man in the dark fog, and he could never quite accept his own lack of control.

He was just going to give orders to increase speed when a flare suddenly split the sky. He heard an explosion from starboard, and shot whistled through the rigging.

"Full speed ahead," Adrian called, no longer caring who heard.

Another shot crashed into a bale of cotton to his left, sending white fragments everywhere and igniting several nearby bales. The smell of burning cotton assaulted his nostrils, but before he could say anything, sailors were dousing the cargo with pails of water.

Adrian felt a choking sensation from the sudden smoke that billowed up. He turned to Johnny. "How far to deep water?"

"We're almost there, Captain."

Another shot whistled overhead, this time missing the ship altogether.

"The smoke. They're losing us in the smoke," Adrian said with satisfaction as one of his men appeared out of the thick, soupy mixture of fog and smoke.

"The fire's out, sir."

"And the smoke will keep them blind until we're out at sea," Adrian said, grinning. "We ought to send them a message of thanks."

"Bloody Yanks," said the man who had just reported that the fire was doused. "Wish we could fire back."

Adrian chuckled. "I wouldn't mind that either, Sinclair. Now I know how a damn fox feels."

Another flare went up, but it was behind him, and only faintly visible in murky darkness. They had lost their hound, temporarily anyway.

A glorious release filled him, the exhilaration supplying him with energy and confidence. They were past the worst of it, past the main strength of the blockaders.

He stayed at the wheel until dawn broke. They spotted another blockader, an ironclad that Adrian had no trouble outrunning, even with his heavy cargo.

He took inventory. No one had been injured, although he found a bad burn on his arm from a piece of flaming cotton; the damage to the ship was minimal, and they had lost only a small amount of cotton. They had another two and a half days' travel before reaching Nassau, but he was elated. He had sufficient coal, and he knew the *Specter* could outrun nearly anything the Union Navy had.

More than twenty runs now. And this one was the most profitable so far. Adrian wondered briefly how Socrates was faring in his cabin, yet he dared not leave the wheel—not until they were much farther from the coast. The Union

Navy had greatly reenforced the coastal blockade now that Charleston, Wilmington, and Galveston were the only Southern ports open.

"Go to bed, Johnny," Adrian told the young pilot. "You've done your job. And bloody well, too."

"Thank you, sir," Johnny replied, a note of pride in his voice. "Good night, Captain."

Adrian watched his pilot disappear down the hatch, then he looked back out over the ocean. The shore was no longer visible, and the fog had entirely dissipated. The morning was clear, the sun a rising ball of fire in the east. Warm satisfaction flooded him. It was good to win. And it was a damned fine day to be alive!

Five hours later, Adrian turned the wheel over to his first mate and descended the stairs to his cabin, hesitating before he entered. He never quite knew what to expect, and now that the danger had lessened, fatigue crept into every corner of his body. He'd had no sleep in two days.

Peace, he knew immediately upon opening the door, was going to elude him. With resignation he ruefully surveyed the wreckage of his cabin.

In addition to the broken mirror that now lay in shards across the floor, pages of a book were torn and strewn on his bed, and his favorite shirt was wadded into a bundle.

He sighed as he saw black eyes studying him with what he supposed was glee. All because he hadn't had time to soothe the creature after the bombardment this morning.

Adrian couldn't decide whether his greatest regret stemmed from the loss of his mirror or the book. Books were precious to him at sea. They were the one escape from wild fluctuations between extreme boredom and extreme danger, and he was only half through this one.

And the mirror. He needed it for shaving, and now he would have to borrow one from one of his crew. He had, after all, he thought wryly, a certain reputation to uphold, which often helped him get the best crew members and his ship the fastest repairs.

Wincing, Adrian looked down at his hand. In addition

to the recent burn, there were other, tiny little marks up and down his hands and wrists. He was used to sharp little bites now.

There was not a crew member aboard who didn't wonder why he didn't get rid of Socrates.

Sometimes he, too, wondered. There had never been a more ill-tempered, cantankerous creature than the one squatting down in front of him, looking insufferably pleased with himself for the damage he had wrought.

But it was that very independence that appealed to Adrian. He was fascinated that the monkey dared to bite the hand that had saved and then fed him.

His often-irreverent first mate, Wade, said the two of them, Captain Adrian Cabot, also known as Lord Ridgely, and the monkey Socrates were very much alike.

Adrian knew he could be ill-tempered and that he sometimes lashed out and snapped at friends. But he always felt remorse and tried to compensate. Socrates did not.

And the mirror! Bloody hell.

Adrian was not a superstitious man. Yet the broken mirror sent ripples of apprehension up his spine.

He shook his head at his own absurdity. A man made his own luck. Those who depended on fate were headed for disaster.

But he was too tired to think of it anymore. He pushed the glass to one side with his boot, and then found a package of crackers for Socrates. Shortly he lay down and, within minutes, was asleep.

As they approached the Bahamas, Adrian gave one more disgusted look at his disordered cabin. He had no cabin boy, not wanting a youngster under fire, and his crew had better things to do than clean up after an errant pet. As usual, he would have someone in Nassau clean the room and do his laundry.

He went out on deck. They would be approaching Nassau soon, and this run had been an uncommonly profitable one. He wanted nothing to interfere now, although he had little fear of the Union blockaders around Nassau. His ship could outrun any of them, and they dared not venture too close to the islands and risk British wrath. Britain was supposedly neutral, and prohibited any aggression within its territorial waters. Both Union and Confederate ships, in fact, visited Nassau for supplies and repairs, an oddity that resulted in numerous fights both on streets and in taverns.

Adrian grinned as he saw Wade trying to maneuver around the bales of cotton piled all over the deck. Every spare inch of space was taken, and he had heard any number of curses and complaints. They were good-natured, however, since each man would share in the profits of this voyage, and they would be substantial. Rum and women were readily available for a price, and his men would be knee-deep in both tonight.

He made his way through the cotton bales and leaned on the railing, staring at the dot growing larger in the horizon. A day of sleep, and then negotiations for a new shipment and another run through the blockade to Charleston. He had no time for women, nor was he willing to spend his money on them. Ridgely was all that mattered now. His family's estate for nearly seven hundred years, until his older brother gambled it away and then put a gun to his head and killed himself.

The American Civil War was giving Adrian a chance to buy it back. Another year of successful runs, and he would be a wealthy man.

If only the war would last . . .

As the ship neared New Providence Island and its capital city of Nassau, he thought again of the mirror and once more felt that unfamiliar twinge of . . . not fear, but a kind of foreboding.

Nonsense, he told himself. If only the war continued, he would have everything he'd ever wanted.

On the main deck of the American clipper *Marilee*, Lauren Bradley felt alone and hollow and uncharacteristically unsure of herself. She'd always had a place before, duties she understood, people she loved. Now she had none of those, and was embarked on a mission she found frightening and, in many ways, unprincipled.

She had become more and more uncertain of her ability to lie and pretend during the months of training in both Washington and England, but she had committed herself and was determined to do her best. She owed that much, and more, to her brother, Laurence. He had given his life for his country. Surely she could give several months of her time and relinquish a few principles for a better cause—or at least so she kept telling herself.

Her gaze lifted from the water to the distance, where she spied a gray ship. Barely visible, the vessel appeared uncommonly graceful, even with the chimney and sidewheels, as it moved swiftly through the water.

She heard a sound beside her and turned to the captain, who had just approached her. "I've never seen a ship like that," she remarked.

"That's the *Specter*," he said admiringly. "It's probably the most successful blockade runner on the seas."

Lauren felt her stomach lurch. So that was Captain Cabot's ship. She turned around and smiled at the captain, who had taken her under his wing during the three-week voyage. "Tell me about it." *Tell me about the man who killed my brother. Tell me about the man who helps prolong this terrible war.*

Captain Harry Taggert was only too pleased to do so. Lauren Bradley had a way about her. She smiled frequently, although there was a hint of sadness in her eyes.

She was a Marylander, she'd told him privately, and both her father and brother had been killed in the war. She didn't say which army they'd fought for, and he hadn't asked. It was enough that she was in mourning. She said her uncle in Nassau had invited her to come to the island and, needing a change, she had agreed.

And now she wanted to know about the man who fascinated Taggert above all others. Cabot aided the enemy, but Captain Taggert appreciated his seamanship.

"He has the luck of the very devil," Taggert remarked. "He's completed more runs than any other captain." With the awe many Americans held for English nobility, he added, "And he's an English lord."

Lauren looked at her informant with surprise. Mr. Phillips had not mentioned that fact—she wondered why.

"An English lord?" she echoed.

"Lord Ridgely." Captain Taggert smiled through broken teeth. "He's a viscount."

"Why would a British aristocrat involve himself in our war?" Lauren wondered.

"Why, for the money, of course," Taggert said. "There's a large number of English firms and crews involved in running the blockade. Enormous profits involved, you understand."

"Why would Lord Ridgely need money?" Lauren inquired.

Taggert shrugged. "No one knows," he said. "No one even knew he was a viscount until the arrival of a government official who knew his family. But," he added with an appreciative smile as he thought of something that might amuse his charming passenger, "he does have one well-known peculiarity. He has a monkey he takes everyplace," Taggert said triumphantly, pleased to see the question in her eyes replaced by astonishment.

"A monkey?"

"A monkey he calls Socrates," confirmed Taggert. "Bad-tempered beast. Bit me once—bites most everyone."

"A monkey named Socrates," Lauren said aloud, wondering at a man who would choose such an affectation. What kind of a man would use a helpless animal that way.

One who cared nothing about life, about morality, who would profit from war, from death. The bitterness in the pit of her stomach grew. She forced a smile back on her lips. "Your Captain Cabot sounds very interesting."

Captain Taggert was startled to hear an edge in her voice, but then he thought he might have only imagined it. Regretfully, he knew he had to leave her. He wanted to be at the wheel as they approached Nassau.

"I'll miss you, Miss Bradley," he said.

"You've been very kind, Captain," she replied, with a warm smile.

"Perhaps I'll see you in Nassau?"

"I'm sure you will," Lauren said. "My uncle's shop is on Bay Street, and I'll be helping him."

"I'll be by," he said, with a smile, and touched his hand to his forehead in respect. Then he left her to gaze at the island which was taking more substantial form as the ship neared.

She turned and again looked back out toward the sea, and saw that the blockade runner was following them in. Luck? Fortune? The steamer was closer now, and she squinted in an effort to see more, to try to make out figures on the deck. But the distance was too great.

Captain Adrian Cabot was aboard that ship. He was, most probably, on deck. Adrian Cabot . . . she remembered the first time she heard his name. It was in a small, nondescript office in Washington, D.C., and a large, bulky man had regarded her carefully. "I'm sorry about your brother, Miss Bradley," he said.

"Thank you," she heard herself say tonelessly. The last few months had been a nightmare. First her father, then her brother. They had both been doctors, healers. Her father had died of a fever contracted from a patient two months before her twin brother had been killed on a Union ship where he served as a doctor.

Lauren had received a visitor three days after her premonition of Larry's death, officially informing her of her twin's demise. She had traveled to Washington and made a nuisance of herself trying to discover what had happened, but no one had any information, or would give her any. Finally, a visitor came to the hotel where she was staying; he said he had some additional details about her brother, if she would accompany him to a government office. Thirty minutes later, she was sitting in front of a man named E. J. Phillips, feeling strangely uncertain as he stared at her with searching eyes. Phillips had told her there perhaps was something she could do for her country; she had grasped at the opportunity.

"Your brother was killed," he said slowly, "by one of our own ships."

Lauren bowed her head. Of all things she had expected, this explanation was the most painful. "How . . . ?"

"Your brother's ship was chasing a blockade runner in the dead of night. There was another patrol ship in the vicinity. The blockade runner apparently knew our signals, and gave the second ship the coordinates of the one chasing the runner." The big man slouched down in his chair. "There was a direct hit."

Lauren absorbed the information painfully. "The blockade runner?"

"Got away free."

"You're sure it wasn't the blockade runner that fired?" Somehow the pain would be less if Larry died by the enemy's hands.

Phillips's hands played with some papers on his desk. "Few blockade runners carry guns, Miss Bradley. They're too heavy, for one thing, and take space reserved for cargo. For another, their crews could be charged with piracy if they attacked a Union ship. Especially this particular blockade runner."

"Why this one?" Lauren asked, sensing quickly that Phillips's words had special meaning.

"This captain is English. He would not have the protection of a Confederate uniform. The damn—excuse me, ma'am—the . . . Brits are supposed to be neutral, but they're financing blockade runners as well as building ships for the Confederate Navy."

"But why?"

"Money," he said contemptuously. "Unlike with the Southern captains, no patriotism is involved, only huge profits at the expense of the North and in violation of their own country's neutrality."

Lauren had felt anger—deep, deadly anger. Her brother had died for gold, her dear, good brother who had wanted only to make people well.

She noticed that Phillips was watching her closely, and she wondered why. The answer came quickly.

"You might be able to help us, Miss Bradley."

"What can I do?" she said quietly.

"If we can cut off the Southern supply line, the war could end months, perhaps even years, earlier." He continued for a long time. The blockade runners had almost no Southern ports remaining to them. New Orleans had been captured, Mobile was effectively closed; so was Savannah. Charleston, Wilmington, and Galveston were the only ports remaining open to any degree.

"We don't have enough ships to completely block these ports, and seventy-five percent of the blockade runs are successful. And blockade runners can expect profits of a hundred thousand or more on a run," Phillips said. He added, perhaps unnecessarily, "It's more than sufficient incentive to keep open the lifeline of the Confederacy."

He had paused, assessing her, and Lauren had waited for him to continue.

"We have to make it unprofitable," Phillips explained. "These captains are wily, and none more so than the captain of the *Specter*. He always seems to know our signals, and often he disappears along the coast when we sight him. It's obvious he knows some waterways we're not aware of."

"What happens if you capture him?"

Phillips looked disgusted. "Damned little—beg your pardon, miss. We can confiscate his ship and cargo, of course, but because he's English, a neutral, we can't hold him any longer than it takes to hold a prize court. And he makes enough money from one run to purchase a new ship. But," he added, "that will take him time, time which will hurt the Rebs."

Lauren was horrified that a captain could be responsible for the destruction of an American ship—for her own brother's death—and still be considered a neutral. "After destroying one of our ships . . . ?"

"Remember," her visitor said, "he doesn't carry guns . . . It was one of our own which fired the shell."

Lauren frowned. "But I still don't understand what I can do."

"The blockade captains have a real eye for the ladies,"

Mr. Phillips said. "We have spies in Nassau, of course, but none of them has been able to get close enough to Cabot to give us any help."

Lauren's eyes widened, and a flush crept up her face.

"No, no," the man opposite said hurriedly. "We're not asking you to do anything improper. We have a man there, a merchant. We can send you there as his niece, and you will come in contact with the blockade runners. Some men say more to a lady. They like to . . . boast a little. If we can learn his schedule, the rivers or inlets where he sometimes hides, then we can have ships waiting for him."

Lauren's gaze questioned him, and he shifted uncomfortably in his seat. "There's another possibility," he said.

Lauren straightened in her chair.

"If something . . . were to happen to the ship when approaching Charleston, Cabot would have no choice but to surrender."

"What?" she asked suspiciously.

"We have men who can show you ways . . . some sand in an engine or one of the shafts . . . several possibilities. I have men who can train you."

"But how?"

"The blockade runners often carry passengers."

Lauren was silent.

"Believe me, Miss Bradley, there could be no greater service for your country . . . or your brother. Many lives can be saved."

Despite her reluctance, the last words convinced her. If she could save lives, then perhaps Larry wouldn't have died in vain. There was certainly nothing to keep her at home. The small house in Dover was altogether too empty; there were only echoes of her father and brother, the two people who had filled it with life and laughter and compassion.

Her father's medical practice had died when he had. She had helped both him and her brother, and her father had often said her medical knowledge was nearly as great as their own; but no one took a woman seriously. She had thus merely assisted the two of them, yet had been happy to do so. But now that they both were gone, there were no patients who would trust her alone.

Her father had left a little money—not much, but enough to live on for a while. She'd tried to volunteer at several military hospitals, but none would accept a young, unmarried woman.

Now Mr. Phillips was giving her a chance to do something for her country, something to avenge her brother . . .

A gull swooped down into the water, startling Lauren from her memories. Revenge. Would Larry have really wanted that?

She doubted it. She even questioned her own motives. She had never sought revenge before, had thought it a most base objective. But Mr. Phillips had given her a cause, a purpose.

Lauren knew she was irretrievably committed, but she also realized she wasn't entirely comfortable with the role she was to play. She had been coached extensively at a small house in Washington, taught how to signal, how to sabotage a ship, even how to flirt. It had taken several months, months in which to think, to consider whether she was capable of such deceit.

But she did owe her brother. And, according to Mr. Phillips, nothing really frightful would happen. The worst that could confront Adrian Cabot was loss of his ship and a short imprisonment, nothing nearly as terrible as what had happened to Larry. And she could help shorten the war. Anything was worth that.

Wasn't it?

The gray ship that Captain Taggert had identified as the *Specter* drew closer to the clipper ship. The blockade runner wasn't nearly as pretty as the clipper, Lauren thought with prejudice. Her gaze found a stocky blond figure at the wheel. She also saw bales piled everywhere. Contraband. Cotton. Then, as the ship moved past, she saw a tall figure with reddish-brown hair, who was talking intently to the shorter blond man at the wheel. He suddenly lifted his head as a breeze ruffled through his hair, met her gaze, gave her an almost breathtaking smile, then bowed slightly.

And why shouldn't he be exultant? she thought, as her own glance raked the crowded decks of his ship. He'd obviously had another successful run.

Under any other circumstances she might have smiled back, dazzled by the pure charm of his smile, but she suddenly remembered Larry—Laurence Bradley II—who once also had a smile that made women melt . . . and who had it no more.

According to her training, she should smile back across the short span of bay, but suddenly she could not.

Instead, she turned her back and went down the short corridor to her room. Everything was already packed and ready to go, although she knew most of her clothes would not be suitable for this hot climate or her purpose. She did have some money Mr. Phillips had given her for clothes—he'd said she must discard her black dress and look gay and bright and even a bit flighty. She didn't quite know if she could—she had always, until now, been eminently competent and sensible—so sensible, in fact, that she had scared off practically every suitor. She was twenty-four—some would say an old maid. But she had never considered her value dependent on a husband.

Now she had made a commitment, and she must follow through on it. It could all be for naught, anyway, she thought. While she'd had suitors, none of them had been mad with despair at her lack of interest. She knew she was not plain, but neither was she breathtakingly pretty.

So why might the infamous captain pay her any mind?

Lauren entered her room, taking one last look to see that she had everything together. She then stopped by the mirror, peering at herself critically.

Mr. Phillips, if that really was his name, had said the captain was a womanizer. But Captain Taggert had intimated that he was a loner. Which was he? Or could he be both?

Lauren reviewed her assets, and pitted them against her liabilities. Her eyes were probably her best feature. They were wide and expressive, a soft hazel that changed in color according to her clothes and her mood.

Her hair was her curse. It was much too curly, and tendrils were always unraveling from whatever hairstyle she tried. Neither was she pleased about the color, which was something between blond and brown. Her mouth was too wide for beauty, and her chin too firm. It was a mismatched face, she judged critically for yet another time. Why Mr. Phillips believed she might appeal to an English lord, she could not determine.

She wondered briefly why he had not told her more about Captain Cabot, that he was a member of the English nobility. Perhaps he thought that might intimidate her.

Well, it did. She'd had doubts from the beginning about her ability to flirt, let alone enflame a man to where he would tell secrets, and now the notion seemed more ludicrous than ever.

She felt the soft bang of the clipper against the wharf and wondered whether Jeremy Case would be waiting there for her, he and his wife, Corinne. Fear slowly invaded her, fear of what she was being asked to do, of what was expected of her.

Lauren thought of the man who had smiled at her, then bowed. She had come to think of Captain Adrian Cabot as ruthless and evil. Yet he smiled like an angel—if indeed that had been Adrian Cabot on deck. She hoped with all her being it was not.

Lauren found a bonnet, tied the bow under her chin, and went back up on deck. Captain Taggert had said he would see that her luggage was delivered later.

The deck was bustling now, the other passengers all staring out at the busy wharf where crates of goods were stacked. She heard a man's loud voice from where she stood; an auction of some kind was being held somewhere below her. She had been told to wear this particular bonnet, and now she saw that someone was staring at her, at the hat. He raised his arm in greeting, and she did the same. He was, after all, supposed to be her uncle.

In her role, she would run down the gangplank to him.

Her gaze moved toward the ship that had just docked on the other side of the long wooden pier. The blockade runner.

Suddenly it was very important that she leave the ship before she saw the man she'd glimpsed minutes earlier, and she hurried toward the gangplank.

As she moved down the shaky planks, she became conscious of a man in a blue coat and white trousers striding easily across the boards of the pier. She hesitated a fraction of a second, then moved again, stumbling slightly. Just as she was about to reach the pier herself, a furry animal streaked toward her, and she stepped back, one of her heels catching in an opening between planks as the animal seemed poised to attack. She tried to jerk her foot loose and move back another step, but the sudden freedom of her heel sent her lurching forward instead, and she was falling, her hands reaching out for a hold that wasn't there.

Fleetingly, she thought of the irony of her situation. She was supposed to make an impression. She would! Right into the water.

And then there were arms around her, impossibly strong arms that righted her. Intuitively, she knew it was the man on the blockade runner, and she looked up slowly, very slowly, until her gaze found the deepest blue eyes she'd ever seen.

CHAPTER 2

No one was more surprised than Adrian to find a woman in his arms, especially one who had turned her back on him earlier, an unusual occurrence that had both puzzled and interested him.

Her eyes were wide, startled, as they stared back at him.

She felt good, too good, and he found he didn't want to take his hands away, even when she was standing straight again. He justified his failure to release her on a barely perceptible trembling of her body.

He flashed her the smile that usually garnered him a quick and favorable response. "Are you all right, miss?"

She stiffened and moved away, causing his arm to let go of her. "Yes, thank you," she said in a soft accent he couldn't immediately identify.

"My pleasure," he said slowly, meaning it. She was a small thing, slender but not without attractive curves. Her plain gray dress did nothing for her coloring, but her eyes flashed with a kind of golden fire as they regarded him solemnly. "Miss . . . ?"

She hesitated, a captivating blush stealing into her cheeks, and again he felt a certain surprise and fascination. He couldn't remember ever being rebuffed by a woman, possibly, he admitted to himself, because he knew when, and when not, to make advances. Yet he had offered no insult, only assistance and good will, and this woman was regarding him as more villain than savior.

"Bradley," she finally said softly. "Lauren Bradley."

"A fetching name for a pretty lady," he said with his most practiced charm. He was determined to get a smile, at least.

But there was none. She stepped back, her eyes meeting his, and suddenly he felt as if a gale were brewing somewhere deep inside her. Their eyes held, seemingly unable to part, as vivid but indefinable emotions passed through hers, like stormclouds before a hurricane. She took another step backward, bumping into a departing passenger from the clipper and trapping herself between the other passengers and Adrian. And he had no intention of moving back, not until she yielded some of her stiffness.

He bowed slightly. "I'm Adrian Cabot," he said, and took her elbow. "I would dislike your first visit to our island to be an unhappy one, and I believe your near disaster is all my fault. I hope you'll accept my apologies."

"Your fault?" She had wrenched her eyes away from his face, and her voice held a slight tremble.

Adrian looked several feet away, to where a monkey perched, an innocent expression on his face. He was wearing a pair of sailor's trousers and a mate's hat. "That little scamp belongs to me. He apparently escaped my cabin. He likes to hide under wide skirts, and apparently he saw yours."

He braced himself for anger, but it didn't come. Instead, those fascinating eyes suddenly, unexpectedly, twinkled. "I can honestly say it was a unique welcome, Mr. Cabot."

Adrian was thoroughly charmed. He'd believed he was beyond being charmed by a woman, but her now-sparkling eyes conveyed a sudden infectious and guileless delight that stunned him. "This *is* your first visit, isn't it? I haven't seen you before."

"And do you see everything?" she asked as her eyes caught his and became serious once more. It was almost as if she regretted her brief laughter.

"I try," he said, his hand firming on her elbow as he still felt resistance. "Everything that's important, anyway."

He knew he was giving her no choice. She was obviously alone; there was no gentleman from the ship rushing to her aid, and unless she planned to block the gangplank all day, she would have to accompany him.

Her eyes told him that she recognized what he was doing and didn't like it, and he grew even more intrigued. There was control in her face now, although she couldn't hide the blush in her cheeks. She was tense, and he didn't understand why. His interest heightened, and he almost forcibly led her down the remaining few steps to the pier, where they stood aside to allow the other passengers to finally disembark.

There was a flurry and chattering behind him, and he turned around. Socrates had moved; deciding, apparently, that he was forgiven, he now wanted attention. The small monkey stood like a wizened little man, his eyes blinking at Lauren Bradley. Adrian stiffened, wondering whether another attack was imminent, when Socrates made a little bow to Lauren and offered a gnarled hand with crooked little fingers.

To Adrian's stunned surprise, she laughed and stooped to take the small hand, totally unafraid of and unawed by the monkey. Women, he had discovered, often to his disgust, usually giggled nervously or backed fearfully away when confronted by his furry companion. He sometimes wondered if that was why he often took Socrates with him.

But Lauren Bradley accepted the small hand and curtsied to the monkey's bow with such fanciful enjoyment that Adrian was captivated even as he noted that she reacted with much more warmth toward his monkey than she had toward him.

"Socrates," he interrupted with a rakish smile, "this is Miss Bradley."

Both appeared to ignore him. Socrates chattered happily if unintelligibly, and Miss Bradley stooped to Socrates's level and tipped her head as if trying to understand. He had never seen Socrates take so readily to anyone, and Lauren Bradley's smile was now full and open and completely enchanting as she glanced up at Adrian with delight. And then the delight quickly vanished, as if she were a small child caught doing something wrong.

She stood again, and as she glanced around him, her smile reappeared. He turned and saw a familiar figure hurrying toward them.

"Uncle Jeremy," the girl said, and Adrian watched as the two embraced warmly before the newcomer turned to Adrian and stretched out his hand. "Captain Cabot, my thanks. I saw you save my niece from an unexpected swim."

"Your niece?" Adrian replied with some surprise. He had often frequented Jeremy Case's shop on Bay Street. It carried the finest goods, including high-quality cloth, the best cigars in Nassau, and gift items such as music boxes and porcelain. He liked Case, who was unfailingly fair and courteous in his dealings. "Then I'm especially pleased to be of service."

"You have been indeed, Captain Cabot. Perhaps we can repay you with supper." Jeremy smiled. "You and your small friend here."

Adrian grinned. "He's not often included in invitations."

Jeremy's smile grew wider. "I think your Socrates is quite smitten with my niece."

"As am I," Adrian replied gallantly. "We would be delighted."

"How long will you be in Nassau this time?"

Adrian hesitated. There were any number of spies in Nassau, some with signaling abilities. He didn't want any leak as to when he might leave, which would assure he'd have Union boats waiting for him. "I haven't decided," he said. "I have to sell this cargo and find a new one."

Jeremy gestured with his hand to the crates lining the docks. "You'll have no trouble finding goods. There's far more cargo available than ships to carry it."

Adrian looked appreciatively at the sight. "Aye, that's true, and there are fewer ships all the time. The risks are getting too great."

"But not for you?"

"The danger's part of the attraction, Jeremy, you know that. We've spoken of it before."

"I leave that to you, Captain," Jeremy said with a smile. "In the meantime, in the peace of Nassau, why don't you join us for dinner tomorrow evening?"

Adrian's gaze went to the woman's face. It was guarded now, her pleasure from Socrates's unprecedented courtesy gone. But despite the quiet gown, the reserved look, she still held a certain appeal, no, more than that. A bit of mystery, perhaps. And challenge. He felt a peculiar stirring inside, even as, for a flash of a second, he remembered the mirror and that odd sense of foreboding.

Yet his hand still felt warm from touching her, and there had been a moment, when their eyes met, that something flashed between them, something so different and arousing and . . . stimulating . . . that he'd been hard-pressed not to tighten his hold and lean down and . . .

He forced his thoughts to behave. "I would be delighted," he said. "So would, I expect, my mischievous friend." He nodded to Lauren Bradley. "Until tomorrow then."

Her eyes stared solemnly up at him, and he wondered what was behind them. "Thank you again, Captain," she said in an attractive low voice.

"My pleasure." He grinned, his eyes studying her carefully before he turned and strode down the pier with the rolling gait she had noticed in other seamen.

Jeremy Case interrupted her inspection. "Very well done, my dear. I'd not expected such fast work."

Startled, Lauren turned to him. He was an older man,

tall and thin but saved from austerity by the twinkle in his light blue eyes. His face was weathered, lines reaching out from his eyes and mouth in crinkles that gave his face character and substance. She liked him instantly.

"I didn't plan that fall," she admitted wryly.

"Then Providence is our accomplice," he replied with a quick smile. "I'm Jeremy Case," he said, "and my wife and I are delighted to have you staying with us."

"Does she know why I'm here?"

"No. She really believes you are my niece."

She was moving along with him now, their voices low. She was curious. How could Mr. Case's wife not know about her husband's relatives?

His hand went to her elbow as they came to a stone step. "I've . . . been estranged from my family for some time. Corinne knows I dislike talking about the past, but she was delighted when I told her you needed a home for a while. She . . . we . . . have always wanted a daughter, but God never blessed us in that way."

Lauren heard the quiet resignation in his voice. She cast a quick glance his way and tried to guess his age, but she couldn't. The eyes were youthful, and the lines could be the result of grief and trouble as well as age.

He hurried them along, past carriages lined up along the wharf, through a square filled with peddlers hawking fish and fruits to a narrow street lined with neat pastel-colored storefronts.

"This is Bay Street," Jeremy explained. "We live over the store." He stopped a moment and searched her face. "It's not very elegant."

Lauren smiled back warmly. "I'm a doctor's daughter, and my father cared little whether he was paid for his services. It looks very grand to me."

A slow smile spread over his face, and it was obvious he had been as apprehensive as she about their arrangement. She wondered briefly exactly what he had expected. Or, for that matter, what she had. She had tried to guess what a spy might look like. Had he also?

A spy? The prospect had seemed so right in Washington, so . . . noble when her grief at Larry's death was new and fresh, when she had no real prospects of her own, when she'd wanted desperately to do something for her country. Once she'd had time to think, she'd silently questioned that reaction, and now that she had met the man she was to trick and betray, she had even more doubts.

It wasn't that she was attracted to him. He was much too bold and arrogant for her tastes. She detested everything he was, everything he did, yet he had saved her from a humiliating fall, from injury.

She felt Jeremy Case's hand on her shoulder. "Call me Uncle Jeremy," he warned. "You are the daughter of my sister, Abigail."

Lauren nodded. She had been told this earlier, in sessions with the mysterious Mr. Phillips, and she had memorized it all. They had decided on Maryland as her residence, since she knew it well, and the state was filled with Southern sympathizers. The two of them had worked out a story, step by step, that she could use. But now she felt uncomfortable with the deceit.

"We're here," her companion said, and she looked with interest, then admiration, at the neat shop with its content of treasures. Inside, a woman turned as they entered, and Lauren warmed at the instant welcome in the woman's face.

"My poor dear," the woman said, moving quickly toward her and putting her arms gently around Lauren. She was all pillowy curves—not exactly fat, but comfortably padded. Impressions crowded Lauren's mind: a clean, flowery scent that pleased the senses, a warmth that had nothing false about it.

Lauren allowed the embrace, although it felt odd from a stranger. She had not known a mother; her own had died in birthing Laurence and herself, and there'd not been any family other than her father.

And now it felt good to be hugged like this, to be swept into someone's arms in such unwary and unabashed fashion.

The arms fell away, and Mrs. Case studied her in sympathetic concern. "You must be hungry, and want a bath, and perhaps some rest. Jeremy can take care of the store. You must call me Corinne. Now just follow me. I hope you'll be happy with us." The words were all jumbled together, requiring no answer, and Lauren was grateful.

She followed Corinne up some steps at the side of the store and into a hallway. Corinne opened one door to a large living area that looked out over the harbor. Opposite that room was a large kitchen dominated by a brick fireplace for cooking and blessed with a number of windows that sent fresh sea breezes through the room.

Lauren continued to trail Corinne down the hall until her hostess opened a door and stepped back, allowing Lauren to enter first.

She stood at the entrance, her gaze moving from the contents of the obviously newly decorated room to the windows through which she could see the harbor. It was a beautiful view, with sailing vessels and the sleek new steamships speckling the clear turquoise of the water. She swallowed painfully. These ships were so beautiful, yet Laurence was dead because of them. She felt the familiar loneliness welling up inside.

"I'll have Mary bring some water for a bath," Corinne interrupted her thoughts.

"Mary?"

"Our maid . . . and friend," Corinne said. "She takes care of all of us."

Lauren smiled. "A bath sounds wonderful." She hadn't realized how grimy she felt until a bath was mentioned.

Corinne came over and hugged her again. "I'm so glad you're with us," she murmured, and then she was gone.

Lauren turned back to the window. She had done everything wrong today. She bit her lip, thinking she made a poor spy indeed. Her mission was to befriend the English captain, not to snub or avoid him, but every time she looked at him, she thought of Larry.

No one would have suspected she and her brother were twins. He had been tall while she was short, merry while she was serious, sweetly teasing while she tended to believe everything. She had been his perfect foil when they were young, but he had never been mean to her, merely mischievous.

Larry had been serious about only one thing: medicine. Her father, from whom she had inherited her own serious nature, had always said that Larry used charm, if traditional methods didn't work, to heal his patients. And so he did. Everyone had loved Larry as soon as they met him, and both she and her father swore some cures came about because Larry's patients just wouldn't disappoint him.

And now he was gone, his body buried at sea rather than in the pleasant wood-shaded cemetery where their mother and father both rested. That fact caused a continuing hurt, an ache that never quite went away.

She had always liked the sea before. But now, when she looked at it, she saw night and fire and shot. She saw her brother's body slide under the waves. The last male Bradley. Her eyes found the *Specter*, still tied to the wharf for unloading; when completed, it would join the other ships anchored in the harbor until ready to sail.

Ready to sail and deliver more deadly cargo to the South, more guns and more ammunition.

She saw movement around the deck of the ship, although she couldn't see specific figures. She wondered if the captain had returned, he and his curious and charming little monkey.

Lauren was usually very good at judging people, but the English captain—English lord—confounded her, or perhaps it had been her own reactions to him that clouded her mind.

When Captain Taggert had mentioned a monkey, she had immediately conjured an image of a chained animal, not the seemingly free and curious creature she had encountered. Nor had she missed the obvious affection in the captain's voice as he introduced Socrates.

Socrates.

It was a whimsical name, and Captain Adrian Cabot appeared anything but a whimsical man. Despite his surface charm, she had immediately sensed something hard and unyielding about him. And certainly there was nothing whimsical about selling guns for profit. She recalled every moment of their conversation, searching for a weakness. "The danger's part of the attraction," he had told Jeremy. Words to remember.

And Jeremy Case, the man she was to call uncle. Who was he? She detected the slightest of Southern accents, but she wasn't sure.

Most of those living in Nassau, Mr. Phillips had said, were Southern sympathizers, many of them descendants of Tories and royalists during the Revolutionary War. They had migrated here mostly from the South after the American victory, and those ties had persisted through generations. And then, she thought bitterly, there was profit. Nassau was obviously flourishing as the base of blockade runners.

Why, then, was Jeremy Case a Northern sympathizer?

There was a knock at the door, and she turned to open it for the maid who was to prepare her bath. She wished she could wash away the misgivings she was suddenly feeling. She was beyond her depth in this mission, and she knew it.

But she had promised, and she had never reneged on a promise.

Yet she couldn't block the image of the English captain from her mind. She saw him again as he had been on the pier, the breeze ruffling his thick chestnut-colored hair streaked by rich veins of copper, the face strongly featured, and the eyes a piercing blue that seemed to see straight into her soul.

And she knew she was in trouble. Far more than she had ever contemplated.

Adrian strode quickly to the Royal Victoria Hotel, where he maintained a suite of rooms. Socrates rode on his shoulder, scolding about some imagined wrong.

They were greeted every step of the way by fellow runners, each congratulating Adrian on a successful trip and asking about the run into and out of Charleston. How many ships guarded the port? How much trouble did he have? What prices had he obtained for his goods? How much had he paid for cotton?

Nassau would be full of runners for the next few days. The moon was growing fuller and brighter. Few others would risk any but the one trip every twenty days when the moon was only a sliver in the sky. But Adrian always took more risks than the others. He had more reason than most, who spent their money as fast as they earned it. Champagne ran in the streets of Nassau. And he wished he had only a small percentage of the money wasted at gaming tables.

As he had once wasted it, years ago.

He sighed. He had told Case that he ran the blockade in part for the danger. That was true. But it was a very minor part. Money was the real reason.

There would be a celebration at the Royal Victoria tonight. There was always one when a run was completed successfully. It was another excuse for a party, not that one was really needed. Nassau never quite stopped celebrating, even when the news from the South was dismal. The city didn't seem to understand that its wealth would end with the war, as would Adrian's income.

"You look lost in thought."

Adrian turned quickly to see Clay Harding, who was probably the closest thing to a friend Adrian had among the blockade runners. Clay was a Virginian, a former Union naval officer who now commanded a Confederate blockade runner.

He was grinning at Adrian now. "I see you still have that little rascal. I keep hoping you'll lose him on one of these trips."

Socrates exploded into scolding chatter, and Adrian chuckled. "Sometimes I swear he knows everything we're saying or else he just plain dislikes you."

"He dislikes everybody."

"Not so," Adrian countered.

Clay raised a curious eyebrow.

"We just met a young lady, and Socrates was very polite."

Clay's lazy expression became more interested. "A young lady? New?"

"New," Adrian confirmed.

"Pretty?"

"Why else would Socrates be polite?"

"Damned if I know. But damned if I even know why you keep him."

"He keeps me humble." The amused drawl, however, belied the words.

Clay chuckled. "Now that is an acceptable reason. Especially for your friends. Your damned *Specter* makes us all look lazy. But tell me more about this lady."

Adrian's smile grew wider. Clay, for all his competence at sea, was a notorious womanizer. "She's staying with Jeremy Case. His niece."

"Unmarried?"

"Since when has that made a difference to you?"

Clay looked uncomfortable. "Since last time I almost got caught by a husband."

Now it was Adrian's turn to look interested. "And what happened?"

"I made it out the window."

Adrian's imagination supplied the details. "With or without clothes?"

"Well, I had a coat," Clay said defensively.

Adrian's laugh boomed out over the street. "And the lady?"

Clay grinned. "I imagine she has a trunkful of various male clothes." He paused, not quite yet diverted from his original question. "Now tell me about the lady who bewitched Socrates. Not planning to keep her for yourself, are you? She must be spectacular."

"No," Adrian said thoughtfully. "Not spectacular. But . . . pleasant-looking."

"Pleasant?" Clay's eyebrow arched again in amusement.

"Not your usual style at all," Adrian countered as he wondered over his unexpected irritation.

"Every woman's my style," Clay chuckled as he noticed a frown on Adrian's face. "I think I need some more cigars from Jeremy's store."

Adrian felt himself tense without understanding why. He merely shrugged. "I doubt you'll have any luck."

"Want to make a small wager?" Clay's eyes gleamed with competitive spirit.

Why not? Adrian was irritated with both Clay and himself—mostly himself, for making more than necessary of the brief meeting with Lauren Bradley. He had no idea why he now felt protective about her. He nodded.

"The stakes?" They both knew, without saying it, that the bet concerned seduction.

Adrian's face tightened, although he meant to smile. He tried to avoid gambling, except for these damned ridiculous wagers between captains that had become tradition. They had simple wagers on everything from how many ships would make the run in one week to whom Socrates would bite next. "Name it," he said, confident that any attempt to seduce Lauren Bradley was doomed to failure. If there was one type of female he could usually fathom, it was a virgin, and one who meant to stay that way. And there was something else, an effort, he supposed, to deny his own unaccountable attraction to her.

"A night's drinking for my crew against one for yours."

"Done."

"Good. Now tell me about your run."

Adrian shrugged. "About as usual. I think there were more gunboats, though. They sighted us coming out, and one shot hit a bale of cotton. It was a blessing in disguise. The smoke allowed us to escape."

"You should start thinking about Wilmington."

"My pilot knows Charleston."

"If you decide to go to Wilmington, I'll loan you my pilot, and he could teach Johnny. I know how damn good they both are."

Adrian considered the offer. It was a generous one. Captains held on to their pilots as Adrian held his gold. But Clay had reason. He was not a private businessman like

Adrian, but a Confederate naval officer, and his principal interest was in getting as many supplies to the South as possible. As captain, the Southerner received no profit from the runs, although his crew did.

Despite Clay's often irreverent comments and observations, he was fiercely loyal to the Confederacy, and Adrian respected both his dedication and seamanship, especially since Clay often made light of both.

"Thank you," he said sincerely. "I'll talk to Johnny about it."

"Do that," Clay replied. "When do you intend to go out again?"

"Two days if I can get the cargo unloaded and new cargo loaded quickly enough."

"Risky."

Adrian grinned. "No more than usual. It will only be a half moon."

"Bright enough for Yankees to see."

"Ah, but they won't expect us for that very reason. They're getting lazy and spoiled, working only several nights a month."

Clay shook his head at what he considered foolhardiness.

"And right now, I need a bath," Adrian said.

"Aye, you do," Clay agreed, wrinkling his nose. "Tonight? There's a party at the Royal Victoria. Kenyon and Talley came in yesterday too."

"Were any ships lost?"

"Abbott isn't back. He should have been here yesterday."

"Damn," Adrian exclaimed. Cal Abbott was a Southerner and captained a ship owned by Southern-owned Fraser, Trenholm & Company, one of the largest blockade-running firms in the business. Though not exactly a close friend of Adrian's, Abbott was well liked among them all.

"The odds are getting stiffer, my friend," Clay said. "Get your bath, Adrian. I'll see you later." His eyes went to Socrates, who had scampered off Adrian's shoulder and now tugged impatiently at his hand. "I think your . . . friend is hungry."

"He's always hungry," Adrian said with resignation.

"Bring him along tonight. We have a new captain."

Adrian chuckled. It had become a game of sorts, springing Socrates on newcomers. There was always an elaborate charade prepared, one Socrates usually, but not always, cooperated with.

"What time?"

"We'll bring him in at exactly eight."

"Good enough," Adrian agreed. God knew there was little enough diversion on Nassau.

"Till tonight then."

Adrian nodded and resumed his walk to the Royal Victoria. Reviewing the conversation, he wondered why his thoughts lingered disconcertingly over the part about Lauren Bradley.

CHAPTER 3

The bath was deucedly uncomfortable. As Adrian descended into the small tub, he thought it could double as an instrument of torture for his tall form.

He leaned back as much as possible, his knees almost to his chin, and cursed his size. But the warm water felt good. His cabin aboard the *Specter* was little more than a hole, containing only a narrow bed and a desk. His crew's quarters were equally as sparse, but that was the way he had designed the ship, maximizing every inch for cargo.

There was certainly no room for bathtubs or, for that matter, extra water.

When he had been a young officer with Her Majesty's Navy, he had envied the captain his elegant and spacious cabin and had longed for the day he would occupy one, even though he'd known the chances were slight. He had been poor, and rebellious, and an insubordinate officer, according to most captains, until he served under Giles Gray.

Captain Gray had seen what no one else had taken the time to see: Adrian was a born seaman who detested incompetence. Under Gray, he had flourished, had even distinguished himself in the Crimean War.

And he had been happy for a time . . . until Captain Gray had been promoted into the Admiralty, and Adrian became first officer under a man he considered a thorough incompetent and a coward to boot. He had said as much in public and found himself ejected from the Navy. Two months later, his older brother shot himself in the fashionable town house the Cabot family had owned for several generations. John Cabot, the viscount of Ridgely, had gambled away the last of the Ridgely estate, an estate that had been in the family since the Norman conquest. Adrian became a viscount, but one without an estate or money.

Adrian had vowed then never to gamble more than he could afford to lose. He also vowed to get Ridgely back . . . if he had to steal or cheat to do it.

The American Civil War had made the goal possible sooner than he'd ever thought possible. Adrian was second mate on a commercial clipper when he received a summons from Giles Gray. One of Giles's friends was looking for captains to assume command of ships to run cargoes to the Southern states. The "friend" was particularly searching for British naval officers. Would Adrian be interested?

Adrian didn't need time to think. Not when he heard the sum being paid the captain: $5,000 for each trip. He accepted and was given command of one of the first blockade runners built by a group of English investors. It was an odd-looking ship, particularly compared to the sailing ships he knew so well, but he quickly mastered the essentials of a steamship. He had a larger cabin then, and he filled it with goods of his own that he sold on the side. In nine months, he had made enough to commission his own ship. Unlike the other captains, he wasted little of his salary and profits on gambling or women.

And now he had nearly a quarter of a million pounds in a London bank. As the total mounted, he knew that he might, just possibly might, be able to regain Ridgely. It was his only goal.

Other than to live long enough to accomplish it.

The water in the tub was growing cold, and he rose, feeling the warm breeze that flowed through the window. Socrates was in the corner, nibbling on a bowl of fruit Adrian had ordered. The monkey wanted nothing whatsoever to do with water, and Adrian grinned at the malevolent stares he had received while in the tub.

He stretched, then started pulling on clothes: a pair of dark blue trousers, a shirt of fine linen, and a light blue waistcoat. They were all well-tailored and of good cloth, in keeping with an image he often used to charm and cajole buyers and sellers of cargo. This was one time that his title proved useful. He had not used it when he first came to Nassau, but when an acquaintance made it known, he had been amazed at the doors it opened. The merchants of Nassau and Charleston were apparently impressed with a viscount, even a landless one. It made little sense to him, but he was practical enough to take advantage of it.

The title, however, did not seem to impress Jeremy Case, who never came down on prices or fawned over Adrian as some others did. He grinned suddenly as he thought that the man's niece was more than a little like her uncle.

He recalled Clay's interest and the damnable bet he'd just made and wondered why in bloody hell he'd agreed to it. But he had been confoundedly irritated by Clay's interest, and even more vexed with himself for feeling that way. He was quite sure that the detached and reserved Miss Bradley wouldn't succumb even to Clay's noted charm, but it had been a low thing to do, and he already regretted it.

Adrian spent much of the day supervising the unloading of cargo and the purchase of coal and goods bound for the South. The Confederacy paid dearly for ammunition and guns and medicines, although luxury goods brought an even higher profit. He divided his new cargo among the two, selecting enough of the former to keep the goodwill of the Confederate Government, which, after all, provided protection when sailing into Charleston. There had been attempts to regulate all blockade runners, forcing them to use at least 50 percent of cargo space for government supplies, but so far all such attempts had failed. Adrian did not wish to test the government's patience.

Several times during the afternoon, he'd cast a look toward the upper level of Jeremy Case's mercantile store, where he knew the merchant lived with his wife, but there was only a stillness. He wished he understood exactly why he was so newly interested in the store.

He finally left the unloading with his first mate and started to return to the Royal Victoria for dinner. Adrian fetched Socrates, who'd been staying on the ship while he saw to business, and decided to take a detour. It damned well didn't make sense, but nonetheless he found himself in front of Jeremy's store.

Well, damn it, he could use some cheroots, and Jeremy had the best.

But he found his eyes searching for something other than tobacco when he reached the interior of the store. Jeremy was getting ready to close; and the merchant's eyes seem to twinkle knowingly as Adrian approached him.

"Captain?"

For one of the few times in his life, Adrian was disconcerted. "Some cheroots," he said briskly.

"How many?"

Adrian hesitated, drawing out the visit as his eyes went to the stairs he knew led upward. "A dozen," he said finally.

Jeremy nodded, and reached inside a humidor, extracting the long, thin cigars. "And a peppermint for your friend? A gift from me?"

Adrian nodded. Something else that ran in the family, he thought. Jeremy, too, inexplicably liked Socrates, a rarity in Adrian's circle of acquaintances.

Socrates chattered happily, as if he understood that the piece of candy being added to the cigars was meant for him. Adrian's eyes moved from the stairs to his small companion. "Say thank you," he instructed, and Socrates bowed quite nicely, taking off his cap as he did so.

Adrian heard laughter then, a soft chuckle that somehow warmed him deep inside. He looked up and saw Lauren Bradley descend the steps. She looked different now, the somber gray dress replaced with an equally modest one, but of a green color that caught flashes in emerald in her eyes, and her hair was down, tumbling in damp waves as if she'd just washed and brushed it nearly dry. He felt himself tensing in a rare way, his senses responding to her as they had not responded to another woman in a very long time, and a warning bell exploded in his head.

He nodded his head and bowed, much as Socrates had, and he saw her smile broaden for just a moment before something happened to it, and the smile became stiff and forced. He felt suddenly confused. Confused, disappointed, and strangely bereft.

"Captain," she acknowledged, before turning to Jeremy, "I was sent to fetch you for dinner."

Adrian watched her turn and flee upstairs, and he wondered why she seemed to avoid him, to be so on her guard with him when she was so open with Socrates—just the opposite of other women's reactions to them.

But perhaps he could melt some of her reserve tomorrow at dinner. He quickly paid Jeremy, swung Socrates up onto his arm, and left for the Royal Victoria. It was time to ready Socrates for the standard welcoming of newcomers to the circle of blockade runners.

A table of eight was awaiting them in the Royal Victoria's dining room. Four other blockaders rose when Adrian appeared with Socrates, who was now adorned with a small captain's cap and a pair of small shoes. Adrian accepted congratulations on the successful run and joined the others for a glass of champagne, trying to dismiss Lauren Bradley from his thoughts.

"To cotton," toasted one of the men.

"And England, which buys it," said another.

"And the Yankee blockade that keeps the price high," said the third.

It was a traditional toast, oft repeated in the Royal Victoria Dining Room, much to the discomfort of the occasional Union seaman who wandered into the hotel on leave.

David Beauregard, a Charlestonian and probably the most experienced blockade runner among them, looked at his watch. "Nearly eight," he observed.

Grins broke out on the faces of Adrian's companions as he urged Socrates under the table. Sometimes Socrates cooperated; sometimes he did not.

But he'd been on his good behavior most of the day, and now he appeared predisposed to participate in this traditional game. He disappeared under the table.

Exactly at eight, Clay entered the dining room with a man dressed in a gray uniform, and all five men at the table stood, welcoming the newcomer to their midst. Once more, they repeated the traditional toast.

A waiter approached and asked their pleasure. The newcomer, who had been introduced as Reid Cooper, looked curiously at the one empty chair. "Perhaps we should wait on the eighth person," he said.

"Ah no," David said, with an exasperated smile. "No sense waiting for him. It's the pilot of Cabot here, our English lord," he teased. "The rascal is always getting into one thing or another. Fine pilot, but totally lacking in any kind of manners."

"Pilot?" Reid Cooper's eyes brightened. "I've heard you have one of the best. Perhaps you can help me find a capable man."

Just then, a shoe stuck out from under the table.

Adrian grinned. "I might . . . just might . . . be persuaded to part with mine. He's getting a bit restless."

Cooper smiled. "I would be grateful."

Prompted by Adrian's foot, the shoe from under the table stuck out a bit farther, and the newcomer noticed it. "Some . . . someone's under the table."

Clay raised his eyes toward the ceiling. "Not again,

Adrian. You simply have to keep better control of your . . ."

"Pilot," chimed in Davis, as the new captain's expression changed from confusion to sudden dismay.

"Your . . . pilot?" Reid Cooper repeated, his eyes studying the awkward position of the shoe.

Adrian shook his head sadly. "He's a little eccentric," he said solemnly. "And shy."

Puzzlement covered the newcomer's face as he quickly reevaluated Adrian's earlier offer. The others looked around innocently, although devilment danced in six pairs of eyes.

Slowly the shoe moved farther out from under the table, revealing a very hairy ankle. Another leg emerged as the Confederate captain moved back, almost tipping over his chair as chuckles filled the air. Then a hairy arm was revealed, and finally a head, as Socrates scampered up and took his place on the chair, looking very pleased with himself. One of his hands clutched his hat, and he pulled it on his head, and then doffed it toward Reid Cooper.

"Your pilot," Adrian explained graciously as chuckles grew louder.

The new blockade captain stared in horror as Socrates calmly sat in the chair, looking hungrily at the empty plate. Slowly, comprehension dawned as Reid Cooper's gaze moved from man to man, each one trying to stifle laughter in his own way, and finally Cooper's own mouth stretched into a wide, appreciative smile.

Lauren would have enjoyed dinner thoroughly if it had not been for the lingering thoughts of Adrian Cabot and disgust at her own earlier behavior. She didn't understand why she'd been assaulted by such confusion when she saw him, nor why the rhythm of her heart had suddenly quickened.

She tried to dismiss those thoughts and give all her attention to her current companions, and when she could indeed banish Captain Cabot from her mind for a while, she relaxed in a way she hadn't in months.

Until this moment, Lauren hadn't completely realized how lonely the past weeks and months had been. She had retreated from everyone, nursing her wounds until she had met with the mysterious Mr. Phillips.

And although purpose had fired her anew, the loneliness remained, deeper even than before because she was so entirely alone.

But she felt drawn to Jeremy and Corinne Case. Their natural warmth reached out to her without demand or invasion.

Jeremy had said Corinne did not know about his activities for the Union, but she must guess. The couple appeared to be too close to keep anything secret for long.

It was not, she knew, that Jeremy would be in danger of arrest or imprisonment. Nassau was neutral, and men in gray and blue both walked the streets. But being known as a Union spy, or even sympathizer, would hurt his business, if not ruin him. Although the people of Nassau tolerated the Union soldiers on leave, they made no secret as to their sympathies. The Union consul in the city was often snubbed and taunted in the streets; he was even attacked once, according to Jeremy and Corinne, who told her even more of the blockade runners and their activities.

In the name of amusement, Jeremy said, the blockade runners did some very strange things. They spent the better part of each month in port, waiting for the new moon, and their restlessness was legendary. Some would sit in windows with bags of shillings and throw handfuls of the coins to crowds of loafers in the street to see them scrambling. Others remained drunk on champagne during most of their time in Nassau.

"Doesn't that affect their abilities?" Lauren asked, her mind going back to the clear blue eyes of Adrian Cabot.

"It doesn't seem to," Jeremy grimaced, confirming what Phillips had told her.

"You shouldn't concern yourself with all that, anyway," Corinne said. "I hope you just enjoy Nassau. I don't expect your father would have wanted you to be unhappy."

"I would like to help Uncle Jeremy in the store," she said.

"Good gracious, no. You're our guest."

Lauren looked over at Jeremy again for help.

"I think Lauren would like something to do. Why don't we try it for a few days?"

Corinne looked doubtful. "I've already planned a tea for the day after tomorrow for a few friends . . . and their daughters."

"And Captain Cabot is coming for dinner tomorrow night," Jeremy said.

Corinne looked askance at that. She, like every woman in Nassau, had been charmed by the English captain, but there was something about him that radiated danger.

"He did Lauren a service today," Jeremy said quietly. "I could do nothing less."

Corinne's eyes turned to Lauren with curiosity.

"I . . . stumbled and fell. I fear I would have gone straight into the water were it not for the captain." Lauren was aware of an unwanted blush creeping up her cheek, and she didn't quite understand why.

"And that little companion of Cabot's took a shine to her," Jeremy said with amused understatement.

"The monkey?"

"Aye, I invited him too. So you'd best serve some fruit."

Corinne looked at her husband as if he were mad. Jeremy had always been friendly to the blockade runners who patronized their store, but he'd never invited any into their home. She had sensed that he disapproved of them, although he'd never said anything about it. She did know, however, that he abhorred slavery. When the subject was mentioned, his eyes went cold. Now, however, his eyes were sparkling with life, and Corinne was grateful. Entertaining Captain Cabot and his monkey was small-enough price for such. She smiled her assent.

Lauren looked from one to the other, envying the Cases' closeness, the way they looked at each other. It was a tragedy, she thought, that they had not had children. And she felt the ache of aloneness again.

It was as if Jeremy understood. "Would you care to visit the garden?" he said, as Mary started to clean the table.

Lauren smiled her assent. Nassau had looked fascinating from the ship with its colorful buildings sitting in the sun. It appeared pleasantly exotic, and she had never been short of curiosity.

While the front of Jeremy's building faced Bay Street, the back faced the wharf area. A colorful garden, surrounded by a neat white fence, buffered the house from the busy docks. Unfamiliar but lovely blossoms flourished. There was a certain haphazard design in the vivid garden of colors that delighted the senses.

"But it's beautiful!" she exclaimed, and Jeremy smiled in pride.

"Corinne can make anything grow," he said, with a tender smile.

They went out a gate in back and walked around the front to Bay Street. Most of the shops were closed now, but Jeremy pointed out a tailor, a hat shop, a dressmaker's establishment, a confectioner's shop. They heard the sound of faraway noise, and Lauren looked questioningly at Jeremy.

"The taverns and grogshops," he explained.

"Where do the blockade runners go?"

"The officers usually stay at the Royal Victoria," Jeremy explained as he studied her carefully. She was not at all what he had expected. When he'd received word a woman spy was coming, he had been wary at first, reluctant to bring a stranger into his home. But he had been assured she would fit in quite nicely. And she did. She appeared the kind of girl anyone would welcome as a niece or daughter.

Jeremy could not imagine her as a seductress. Yet, strangely enough, she had caught Captain Cabot's attention immediately. Jeremy had not missed the spark of interest in the blockade runner's eyes. Perhaps Phillips was far more astute than he'd believed.

"It was a stroke of luck . . . your fall today."

Lauren was surprised to feel herself blushing again.

She'd never blushed much before, and yet she had done so several times already today. "It was an accident."

"So it appeared."

They returned to the garden, taking a seat on a wooden bench. Lauren looked out toward the bay, which was sparkling in the soft light of a quarter moon. Activity still continued around the *Specter*, though she didn't see the tall figure of its captain. "It's a lovely ship." Her voice was wistful, uncertain.

"And could be very useful to the Union," Jeremy said, his voice soft but passionate.

She turned and studied his face, now harsh and determined. "Why . . . ?" She hesitated, reluctant suddenly to intrude on private reasons.

"Why do I care?" he finished for her.

Lauren nodded.

Jeremy was silent for a moment, considering an answer. They would be working together, but there were some things that he could not tell anyone. Not even Corinne.

"I dislike slavery," he said simply.

There was steel in his voice. Steel, and passion, and commitment.

She wanted to ask more, but his expression was closed, and she sensed intuitively that he would not elaborate. She understood. She didn't want to talk about Laurence either; the pain was still too raw. She merely nodded, accepting the short explanation.

Jeremy rose. "I have some paperwork to do tonight."

"I think I'd like to stay in the garden for a little while," Lauren said. She needed time to think, to absorb all that had happened this day; and the garden, in this fine, clear night, seemed to be the best place to do it.

"Of course," he said. "Please consider this your home as long as you stay."

"Thank you," she said, spontaneously reaching out to put a soft hand on his arm for just a second, and earning a quick smile in return as he turned and left.

The garden smelled wonderful, the scent of sweet flowers mixing with the aromatic sea air. Unlike the cold coastal winds of Delaware, the breeze teased and seduced her, the moist warmth fondling her skin, and rustling her hair and making her feel languorous and lazy and . . . wistful.

She wondered why she'd had so few reservations when she had undertaken this task and now had so many. When she had learned that Adrian Cabot was from the English nobility, she had expected a haughty, lordly person, not a man with teasing eyes and a monkey as companion.

Lauren suddenly realized that fulfilling her duty involved betraying this man, betraying him and lying, two actions she had always despised in others.

But you owe it to your country, her mind told her. And to your brother.

She unlatched the garden gate and started walking restlessly. She had always kept busy, and she'd grown weary of days of enforced idleness during the past three weeks on the clipper. She thought sadly of her busy days in Dover, days in which she had been useful and of service.

The Bradley family had never had a servant. Her father often took a chicken in payment, or no payment at all, and her brother's education had consumed what little savings they had. Lauren had kept house and cooked and often helped in her father's office, both with patients and with what books and accounts there were. She had become very independent, used to doing things for herself.

And she'd had a measure of freedom unusual for young ladies. She'd had no mother, no female authority, and her father had been too preoccupied with medicine to worry about proprieties. She had often taken long walks alone in Dover, enjoying the seasons. She had also accompanied her brother on trips to the bay; Lauren had always loved the water.

Now she felt a need to rid herself of energy and doubts she knew would keep her from sleep. Lauren felt no fear of Nassau; the lovely island wove a spell of its own. The noise of celebrating sailors was well away, and she was used to going where she wanted. She was a modern woman, and self-sufficient. Hadn't she traveled successfully to Washington, then to England, and finally to Nassau, all without chaperones? She was twenty-four, and more than able to take care of herself.

She didn't know how long she walked along the now nearly deserted dock, her gaze continually turning to the eight blockade-running ships anchored in the harbor along with large merchant ships from England and small, frail fishing skiffs. Three ships, including Captain Cabot's blockade runner, were still tied to the wharf, but even his ship was relatively quiet. She wondered whether he was on board.

Then she shook the thought from her mind. She was thinking entirely too much about the man. She looked away, toward the dock area. The waterfront now seemed ghostly, lined with many crates but little or no movement other than shadows. She wondered about guards. There must be some, but none were in sight. She felt an unexpected tremor of fear, and she started to turn back.

"Hey, lookee there." The voice seemed to come from nowhere.

"A purty lay-dy," a second voice added, delight in the drunken tones.

"Let's gi' 'er a drink."

Lauren turned, ready to defend herself, although with what she didn't know. She suddenly realized she had nothing but her wits.

She drew herself up to her tallest height, which wasn't very tall, and with a look that had often quelled unruly patients glared at the four roughly dressed men before her.

But the look seemed to have no effect whatsoever. The men moved closer, and one reached out and grabbed her arm.

"Wha's yer name, darlin'?"

She jerked away to laughter as three of the men jeered at the one just rebuffed. "She sure don't cotton to ya, Luke."

Luke grinned. "Ah, she's jest playin' hard to git."

"Mebbe you're jest too ugly. Wha' 'bout me, sweetheart?"

An arm went around her, holding tight, and she could smell the whiskey and foul breath as her captor pressed his mouth against hers.

She bit—hard—and he cursed, his hand going to her hair, which was neatly pinned into a bun at the nape of her neck. She felt the hair tear loose, and his hand knot around it, jerking her head back. Her face was forced upward, and his lips descended once more as she heard raucous cheering behind them.

"You bite agin, and I'll pull out yer hair," her attacker said just before his mouth covered hers with punishing violence. Her hands fought back furiously, but she was no match for his strength and anger. She couldn't even call out with his mouth gagging her own.

Lauren felt sick to her stomach, sick and terrified. She realized he and the others didn't intend to stop with a kiss, and remembered what her brother had once told her about a man's most vulnerable spot. She stopped struggling, letting her body relax, and when her attacker did the same, she kneed him in the groin as hard as she could.

She heard him grunt, then she was free, and she started to run, but one of the other men caught her. "Feisty little thing, ain't she? But you ain't goin' anyplace, sweetie. We ain't through."

Lauren opened her mouth to scream, but a hand clamped over her face, and the man started dragging her toward an alley. Stark terror filled her, terror and something like self-disgust for putting herself in this situation.

Where was everyone? Why hadn't anyone heard her scream?

But everything was fading, even fear, as she sought desperately to breathe air that wasn't there.

"I don't believe the lady wishes to go with you."

Somewhere deep in a mind going black, the words registered. A new voice. A cultured voice.

The hand slipped from her nose and mouth, and she thankfully sucked in air.

"This ain't none of yer business . . . it's between this doxy and me friends."

"Take your hands off her."

Lauren's rebounding senses noted that the voice was familiar. She wriggled against the rough hands holding her; it was easier now that her captor's attention was elsewhere.

"I said it ain't none of yer business." Lauren heard the sound of feet moving, and she fought hard to see, but the man held her tight, one hand still twisted in her hair, forcing her head away from the would-be rescuer. Lauren felt new fear, not only for herself now but for the newcomer. There was only one voice speaking up for her, and there were four ruffians.

"Git 'im," she heard one of the attackers say, and she listened to the dull thud of skin against skin. There was a grunt of pain, some curses, then the man holding her yelped, and she was suddenly free.

She felt something else touch her, something furry, and she looked down. The monkey she'd met earlier was avoiding a kick from the man who had just been holding her. A dark red was staining the man's already soiled trousers, and Lauren realized the monkey had bitten him.

Lauren pushed back her hair to see better. Captain Cabot was fighting two men at once, moving agilely away from heavy blows, and then striking back hard. A third man was on the ground, and her own attacker was going after Socrates.

Lauren stuck out her foot to trip him, and he went down heavily, Socrates pouncing on him and biting his ear. Lauren screamed and then screamed again, until finally she heard shouts and the sound of running feet.

The attackers also heard them, but it was too late. They were surrounded by a crowd of sailors, a number of them seizing the arms of the man attacked by Socrates, another setting his foot on a man already supine, apparently made so by Adrian Cabot.

They did nothing, however, to stop the ongoing fight between the captain and two remaining ruffians.

"Do something," she demanded.

A small man with straw-colored hair grinned. "The captain would never forgive us, ma'am. He has it under control." But Lauren didn't think so. Already, one of the captain's eyes was swollen and discolored, and blood was dripping from the side of his lips. But he dodged a blow readily enough and delivered one solidly to an opponent's stomach. The man went down.

Now there was only one man left, and he was backing away, eyeing the growing number of onlookers warily, but not nearly as warily as the man crouched in a fighting position before him. "We're jest having a piece of fun," he whined.

"I don't think the lady agreed," Captain Cabot said coldly, and gestured for two of the onlookers to take the man still standing. "Take them to the jail."

"Aye, sir," one of the men said, and Lauren realized that these men must be part of the crew of the *Specter*.

Lauren watched as the captain's attention turned to her and his eyes widened with recognition. Nervously, she pushed back her hair and looked down. Her modest dress was torn so it no longer was modest. The ripped bodice opened to show the swell of her breasts, and she clutched her arms over them.

Reaction settled in, and she felt herself tremble. "Thank you," she whispered miserably, realizing that for the second time in one day she'd made an idiot out of herself in front of Captain Adrian Cabot.

"What in bloody hell are you doing out here alone?" he asked roughly. "Nassau's no place for a woman alone."

"I . . . I needed a walk." Why, oh why, did she get so tongue-tied with him? Her legs trembled even more, and her body swayed ever so slightly. She wondered if she was going to fall.

But then he was next to her, strong, sure hands steadying her once again, just as they had hours earlier. "I'll see you back," he said.

Lauren wanted to say no. At least the sensible part of her wanted to say no. But the fear was still with her. She could still hear the obscenities of her attackers, still feel the rough hand over her mouth and nose.

"Are you all right?" His tone was softer now, more concerned than angry, and she looked up at his battered face.

She tried to smile. "Better than you, I believe."

He frowned slightly. "It's nothing." He looked around and found Socrates, who was sitting on his haunches, patting his head as if congratulating himself. He, at least, certainly looked none the worse for the confrontation.

"He was a hero," Lauren offered tentatively to break the uneasy silence.

"But I wasn't?" The question was offered with wry humor. She seemed singularly unimpressed with his own assistance. "I believe you need a keeper, Miss Bradley."

She flushed. "I know you probably don't believe it, but I'm usually quite able to take care of myself."

His stern mouth quirked upward at the corners. "I saw you trip that man. You didn't do so badly." But then his lips firmed again. "Except for coming out here in the first place. Didn't Jeremy warn you never to walk alone at night?"

"He thought . . . I was in the garden. I didn't realize . . . everything seemed so peaceful . . ." Her voice trailed off. Nothing was going according to Mr. Phillips's plan.

She looked up. Her gaze found the piercing blue eyes of her rescuer, and she struggled against the startling magnetism between them, the comforting sense of safety she felt around him, the unexpected pleasure that flooded her. Excitement that sent her blood racing.

Don't, she told herself. Don't. Remember, he's a blockade runner. Remember, he's the man who caused Laurence's death. Remember . . . remember . . . remember.

His hand was warm as it clasped her arm and steered her toward Jeremy Case's store. When they reached it, she turned and gave him a small, solemn smile. "I would appreciate it if you said nothing to Uncle Jeremy about this. I don't want him to worry."

"Your testimony will be needed against those men."

"I . . . I'd rather just let it go."

His eyes fastened on hers for several seconds. "If you wish."

He turned to leave.

"Captain!" At her word, he turned back, one of his eyebrows arched in question. "You *are* a hero."

He grinned, a look that made the hard features look endearingly youthful. "Good night, Miss Bradley."

"Good night, Captain." But he was gone, and the words were so soft, only she heard them. She didn't understand why they made her so infinitely sad.

CHAPTER 4

Lauren lay awake all night long. She had been able to reach her room without seeing either Jeremy or Corinne, and she'd silently mumbled her thanks. She didn't want them to know how careless she had been.

She'd closed her eyes, but then she felt the dirty fist over her face again. Even worse, she kept seeing concerned blue eyes in a battered face. Battered because of her foolishness.

She thought about Jeremy's words when she first met Captain Cabot: "Stroke of luck," he'd said.

It wasn't a stroke of luck at all; it was more a curse.

Captain Cabot was nothing like what she expected.

She had to make herself think of Larry . . . of the last time she had seen him.

His eyes were green, much more vivid than her hazel ones, but then everything about Larry had been vivid and glowing. She had adored him, followed him, imitated him.

Lauren had always been Button Nose to him, and since so many followed his lead, she'd become Button to everyone in their acquaintance. Laurence and Lauren were all too alike in sound, and she'd been the only one to call him Larry.

The years he was away at school had been misery, but she had worked with her father, helping with dressings and splints and assisting with operations. She took great satisfaction in knowing that soon all three of them would work together.

When he had finished his medical studies, the war was in its second year, and Larry felt bound to offer his services. He had always loved the sea, and had often said that if medicine weren't in his blood, he would have plied the China trade. So it wasn't surprising that he chose the Navy. Lauren had been pleased, believing the sea far safer than the bloody battlefields down South.

He had looked so grand that last day, tall and strong and excited about his new adventure. Everything was an adventure to him, and this was to be the greatest one of all . . .

Lauren turned over in the bed. Button. How she wished she could hear him say it again. Once more. A dozen times more. A hundred times more, as long as she was wishing.

But he never would, because of Adrian Cabot. Blue eyes and a handsome face couldn't compensate for that loss. Neither could a rescue.

She closed her eyes tightly against Captain Cabot's invasive interruption of her rest. Part of her wished for sleep, but another part feared it, feared the nightmare that had recurred since the night Larry died. Feared the pain that struck her as it must have struck Larry.

And she knew she would do anything she had to do . . . to see justice done.

Adrian gingerly washed the cut on his lip and placed some very expensive ice on the discolored skin around his eye. He looked like bloody hell.

Socrates had jumped up on the bureau and was likewise

peering in the mirror, first at himself with a deplorable lack of modesty, then up at Adrian, chattering fiercely.

God, but he was exhausted, as well as hurting. He had left the dinner to check on the continuing unloading of the ship when he had heard Lauren Bradley's cry and ran to the rescue.

He winced as his hand touched another sore spot. He must be getting old, or else he'd forgotten how damned painful a fight could be.

But it had been worth it, he'd decided, for the moment of seeing Lauren Bradley without all the defenses he'd noticed in her. He had been strangely attracted to her earlier in the day, though he hadn't known exactly why. Perhaps it had been the fire in those lovely eyes, or perhaps the almost hostile attitude that piqued his interest. But even then, except for the eyes, she had appeared quite unremarkable in the modest gray dress with the high neck and severe hairstyle.

But that evening, she had been extremely fascinating, especially when she'd so ably tripped one of those louts instead of fainting as so many of the women he knew would. And she was very appealing with her hair flowing in wild curls halfway down her back, and her dress ripped to show at firsthand her deliciously feminine curves. Even in the dark, he had seen the blush creep up her face as she had said her last words, and he had been amazed at the surge of warmth he felt when she had so grudgingly thanked him.

Lauren Bradley was very different from any other woman he'd ever met, and he wondered if perhaps that was why he was so interested. She mystified him with her hostility, attracted him with the secret fire in those amber-green eyes, and challenged him in a way he hadn't been challenged in years.

It could also be, he thought a bit wryly, that she did not behave in the ways other women of his acquaintance usually did. She was so different from Sylvia, the first love in his life and, he had vowed, the last . . .

Sylvia had been what his peers called a diamond of the

first water—or at least her beauty was. Adrian had been in London with his brother John during her season, and they both attended the first great ball.

Sylvia Clairmont was the daughter of a minor baron, and Adrian had been warned that her family was looking for a major alliance for her, in both title and wealth. But that fact had little meaning for him as they danced, and she looked up with teasing blue eyes and an invitation on her lips.

Adrian had always been successful with women, with almost everyone, in fact, except his father. Even as a boy, he'd charmed the cook and maids into extra favors with a smile that one neighboring girl told him put the sun to shame.

It was a smile that he had retained, despite some very bitter years. He used it to cover disappointments and losses, and even bewilderment. It had, in fact, become almost automatic, a tool, and seldom did the smile stretch to his eyes, and never now to the heart.

But then, at nineteen, when he had seen Sylvia, his heart had responded, and he'd wanted her as he had wanted few other things in his life. His only other obsession was Ridgely, and he knew, by then, he would never have it, as he had never had his father's love. That had all been reserved for John, and even with his brother it had been sparingly given.

Adrian had fallen in love, totally, blindly in love with Sylvia. He was attending Cambridge, but made it back to London at every opportunity. He knew he was only one of many admirers, but she allowed him to believe he was the one she wanted. They would disappear into the gardens, behind some sheltering tree, and she allowed him liberties that led him more and more to believe that he was the chosen one, fortune or not.

And it was not as if he didn't have prospects. He had an inheritance from his grandfather, and if he wasn't completely sure as to what he would do after Cambridge, he had friends aplenty and many opportunities to make his fortune.

It came, then, as an abrupt shock when Sylvia announced her engagement to a marquess nearly three times her age. She quickly assured Adrian, however, that she would continue to be available to him.

For Adrian, who had suffered through a marriage of convenience between his mother and father, the disillusionment was immense. He remembered the terrible arguments between his parents, and the violence directed toward his brother and himself. When there wasn't anger, there was coldness, a chill that froze everyone around the Cabot family. He used to escape to the glades of Ridgely, to the bank of the river that wandered merrily through the property, to the small houses of the tenants who, though poor, had more love in their dwellings than he had in his. And they had cared more for the boy, and the man he was, than his family had.

Despite the discord in his family, however, Adrian had always loved the heartbeat of Ridgely. He felt its life when he looked at the grand portraits of his ancestors, as he traveled halls that had been trod hundreds of years earlier. He explored the underground dungeons and wondered how it must have felt to be confined in their inky blackness, as his family's enemies had been, even one of their own blood during the Wars of the Roses. He had studied the history and read the personal journals, and knew more about its people than his father or brother. Yet he had no claim to it, and he could only watch his father's mismanagement and realize his brother's disinterest, even hatred of the place.

And Sylvia had wanted him to do the same with her . . . to lose the whole and accept leftover crumbs.

Bitterness, and a sense of hopelessness, had gnawed at him. He'd left Cambridge and started drinking and inhabiting gambling clubs, where he recklessly lost his inheritance from his grandfather, and more. Annoyed by his son's insistent creditors, Adrian's father offered to buy him a naval commission, and announced he would then be through with him. Adrian, with few options other than debtor's prison, accepted. A year later his father was dead, and John owned Ridgely . . .

Much to his surprise, Adrian had liked the sea, although he didn't like naval discipline. Not even his smile helped there. But gradually he'd adjusted and learned everything he could. He had been happy enough until his last tour of duty. The captain was both a martinet and a fool, and Adrian's hot temper destroyed his career. And then John had lost Ridgely after a long series of losses at the gambling tables.

Adrian had felt hollow at hearing the news, as if a vital part of him had been torn away, and he realized then that he had always expected to return. And now a man named Rhys Redding, whose sole talent was gambling, owned Ridgely, and there wasn't a damn thing he could do about it—until the American Civil War erupted and created opportunities for quick wealth.

But in those years during his childhood, his courtship of Sylvia, and the final betrayal by his brother, he had lost any trust he'd ever had in others. And since Sylvia, he'd had no serious thoughts for women.

So why did Lauren Bradley haunt him so?

Socrates sat in front of him, his head positioned on his hands like a little wise man, as if surveying a mystery.

Or a fool.

Lauren dressed carefully the next evening. She felt the strangest combination of dread and excitement, and she didn't understand the tingling inside her body. She should feel nothing but loathing for the Englishman.

Yet there had been something about him the previous night—the wry, crestfallen charm when she had called Socrates a hero, then the bright, shining smile when she had amended the compliment to include him. She had not been able to dismiss either expression from her thoughts.

She had spent much of the day with Jeremy in his shop. It had not taken long to learn there were few secrets in Nassau. The first customer, a gentleman involved in the shipping business, remarked on her "unfortunate incident," and later Lauren felt her cheeks glow brightly as she explained to Jeremy what had happened.

"It was really nothing," Lauren tried to assure him. "I didn't want to bother or worry you."

His forehead furrowed with concern. "Tell me everything that happened."

"The night was so pretty. I was feeling restless, so I took a short walk. I often walked in the evening in Dover," she explained.

He raised a thick gray eyebrow. "I'm afraid Nassau isn't Dover," he said quietly. "It's safe enough on some streets in the daytime, but you shouldn't go anywhere alone at night. I should have warned you."

Lauren knew he thought he shouldn't have to warn her. It had been a careless thing to do, and she realized he probably now had doubts about her competence. But she had needed that time to think.

"Continue," he prodded gently.

"Four sailors," she told him. "They were drunk and thought . . ."

"I can imagine what they thought," he interrupted curtly.

"I would have been in a great deal of trouble if Captain Cabot and his monkey hadn't happened along."

Jeremy's eyebrow rose higher. "Cabot?"

She nodded. "And Socrates. He bit one of them."

Jeremy smiled as he shook his head. "Someone seems to be on our side."

Lauren frowned slightly in question.

"There's no quicker way to a man's heart than to bring out the protective side of him."

Lauren's hand went to the side of her skirt, and her fingers clutched the material. "It's going to be more difficult . . ."

His voice gentled. "Phillips thought you could handle it, and you can. You must think of the good you're doing for your country, the lives you can save."

They spoke no more about the incident, and at Lauren's insistence, Jeremy had spent much of the rest of the day showing her the stock. She needed to be busy, to be helpful.

All the while he talked about the island of New Providence, and Lauren realized he was trying to divert her attention from her obviously growing doubts about her mission. He told her how pirates once roamed the seas, how English seamen used Nassau as a base to raid Spanish ships, and the Spanish, in turn, sacked and burned the city.

The Bahamas had a bold and adventurous history, he'd said, but had settled down to a peaceful and quiet existence until the Civil War. Sunday, he said, he would take her to see the governor's mansion and some old houses, as well as the Royal Victoria Hotel where Captain Cabot and the other blockade runners stayed. The mention of the captain cast a shadow over the afternoon as Lauren thought again of the lies she would tell that night, the false pretenses, the deceit.

And yet she still felt so expectant . . .

She looked at herself in the mirror. She was wearing a dark green silk dress with puffed sleeves and a high neckline decorated with lace. It was a modest dress, but flattering, and the color made her face appear more vibrant, her eyes deeper, more mysterious.

Even from her upstairs room, Lauren heard an authoritative knock at the front door, and the rich sound of Captain Cabot's English-accented greeting as the door was opened. She bit her lips to make them red, and pinched her cheeks for color, but then they flushed naturally as she realized how much she cared what he thought of her appearance.

Taking a deep breath, she left her room and walked to the parlor.

There she saw Adrian Cabot standing, listening to Jeremy speak. When the captain turned around, she winced guiltily at his black eye and bruised cheeks. But he merely shrugged and flashed a teasing smile that seemed to share a secret with her. Socrates, dressed in his usual sailor pants, looked up and chattered happily as he started toward her and held out his arms to be picked up.

Lauren did so, unable to resist the grin on the monkey's

face. Socrates hid his head behind her neck, jiggling up and down with pleasure.

"It's clear you've won a heart," his master said. "And believe me, it's a difficult heart to take."

Lauren's gaze moved from Socrates to Adrian Cabot. His voice was amused, his eyes inscrutable. She felt confusion dart through her, and an unexpected warmth.

"What about you? Haven't you also won it?" she asked, afraid that her voice was a bit shaky.

"Me?" he said with surprise. "I think he considers me an archenemy at times. You should see the chaos he creates in my cabin, not to mention several rather painful bites he's given me."

"Why do you keep him if he bites you?"

"It's become a challenge, trying to civilize him."

"And you're civilized, Captain?"

"What makes you think I'm not?"

"The way you seem to enjoy war."

"I don't think 'enjoy' is the word for it. I'm merely taking advantage of something that exists."

"But you also enjoy it. I remember your telling Jeremy that . . . yesterday."

He grinned suddenly, caught by his own words. "I suppose I'm stimulated by the excitement. Perhaps we all are. If you ever ran the blockade, I think you would understand."

"I'll never understand violence."

"Running the blockade is not violent, Miss Bradley. We don't even carry armament. It's more a matter of skill."

"But people get hurt, don't they? They die?"

"Every man knows the chances he takes. He does it willingly."

"For money?"

"For money," he confirmed. "It's as worthy a cause as any."

"That's a cynical statement."

He raked a hand through his hair. "Everyone has a reason for going to war. Patriotism, money, fear. The reason doesn't make anyone less dead."

"No," she said in a small voice, some of the challenge lost in the sadness of the word.

He studied her face. He had enjoyed the exchange, but now he hesitated to continue. "You've lost someone?"

"A father. A brother."

"How?" he asked quietly.

Lauren looked around for Jeremy, but he had disappeared. She knew it was for the purpose of leaving her and the captain alone together. Corinne was in the kitchen, supervising the meal.

Lauren swallowed. She had said more than she had meant to say, and now she had to lie. She hadn't realized how difficult it would be. Especially when his eyes held sympathy.

Desperation must have shown in her eyes, because he suddenly backed away. "I'm sorry," he said. "I didn't mean to revive sad memories."

The quiet compassion in his voice surprised her. But then everything about him surprised her, and frightened her because she was finding she *liked* him. And she couldn't. If she wasn't going to start fulfilling her task now, she never would. She knew that just as she knew the sun rose every morning.

"It's all right," she said, looking up and meeting his eyes. "They both died in Virginia."

"Confederate?"

"Yes." There it was—the first lie, bold and ugly. Lauren hated how easily the words flowed from her mouth. Mr. Phillips had done his job well, selecting her, and the thought did not please her.

He was silent, and she was relieved he offered no additional condolences.

"How did you happen to come to Nassau?" he asked instead.

"My home was in Maryland. Many of our neighbors were Unionists. It grew . . . awkward, and Uncle Jeremy asked me to stay a few months. It seemed . . . best."

His blue eyes, those startling dark blue eyes, probed hers

for several moments. "It must have been difficult leaving everything you knew, your home."

A depth of understanding flowed in his voice, and it struck her as odd in a man who made the sea his home.

"Yes," she said simply. "And your home?"

His face clouded. "I have none at the moment."

"Except your ship?"

"Except my ship," he confirmed.

"And family?"

"None."

"Except for Socrates?"

"Except for Socrates," he confirmed again with that slight wry smile. "But I don't think he accepts that relationship."

"I think he does," she said, more softly than she intended. She found that they were staring at each other, as if in a trance. Tension radiated between them, and a growing excitement stiffened their faces, made their eyes wary as they felt something extraordinary happening, something neither wanted.

"Family resemblance?" Adrian grinned suddenly, and she knew he was trying to break that strange sense of time-lessness that had unexpectedly shrouded them.

Her gaze swept over him, over the light blue jacket that flawlessly covered broad shoulders and the dark blue trousers that hugged well-formed long legs. His hair, the rich red brown of a sun-ripened chestnut, was thick. It curled slightly, crisply, over his forehead and at his neck, emphasizing strong, clean features. The forehead was broad and broken by dark eyebrows that arched naturally in a perpetually quizzical expression. His cheekbones were high, and his mouth wide, the lips set above a square jaw. Even with a black eye and bruises, it was a handsome face. If she had not known differently, she would believe it a face of character.

But you do know better. The unspoken words jerked her back to her duty. He was an opportunist, an adventurer. Yet when he smiled . . . dear God, she forgot everything else.

"Now that you mention it, there is the slightest similarity," she said, forgetting everything but the almost mesmerizing charm of that smile.

"I think Socrates would resent that observation," he said, his eyes twinkling, coaxing an unwilling smile from her. Socrates appeared to know he was the center of attention and swung down from Lauren's arms. Squatting on the floor, he clapped his hands together.

Lauren looked at the grinning Socrates and then up at Adrian. "No, I think he's rather pleased."

"He's pleased with you and the attention," Adrian corrected.

Relieved that some of the tension was eased by Socrates's antics, Lauren smiled. "How long have you had him?"

"Nearly two years now."

"And where did you find him?"

"A port in Spain."

Lauren looked down at the monkey, who seemed perfectly content at the moment. She needed to look away from eyes that scrutinized and a smile that beguiled. "How—"

They were interrupted by Jeremy, who announced that dinner was ready and ushered them into the small dining room, where a table gleamed with silver and fine glassware.

Adrian offered his arm with a regal formality that Lauren sensed came from experience in court and with nobility. It daunted her until his hand touched hers, and she felt heat spark there and creep up her arm. His grip was firm, even possessive, and from the way his hand tightened around hers she knew that he was feeling the same uneasy attraction that assaulted her.

Dinner was a pleasant affair. Jeremy talked easily about politics and literature, and Lauren was impressed by Adrian Cabot's range and breadth of knowledge.

The subject turned inevitably to the war. As Mary refilled the wineglasses, Jeremy leaned back and looked at Adrian. "How long do you think you can continue running the blockade?"

"As long as I have the *Specter*, and Johnny," Adrian

replied lightly. He turned to Lauren. "Johnny's my pilot, and he knows every inlet, every river, every sandbar, and every wreck in the Charleston Harbor."

"Is the blockade so ineffective then?" she asked.

Adrian's tone turned serious. "No. A ship was lost this last week, and three the week before, and it looks as if Charleston might soon be closed. The Federals are attempting to take Morris Island, and if they do . . ."

"Will you stop then?" Lauren fought to keep a hopeful note from her voice.

Adrian shook his head. "I'll move to Wilmington. Its Confederate coastal defenses are very strong. Once we get within their guns, we're safe."

"But won't there be more Union ships then?"

"Yes," he said. "But they cannot cover every inch of sea, and if there's a fog bank or dark night, we can sneak through."

"But how do you know there will be fog?"

Adrian grinned. "We pray a lot."

Lauren wanted to retort, but she held her tongue. Jeremy, as if reading her mind, asked another question.

"You've had exceedingly good luck, Captain. How many runs now?"

"A few more than twenty," he replied, "but I don't like to talk about luck."

"Tempting fate?" Lauren asked.

"Something like that."

"Are you superstitious, Captain?"

It was as if no one else was in the room. Their eyes were fixed on each other, her words a bit breathless and his a bit puzzled as he tried to decipher the singular, almost magical, aura that enveloped them.

"All sailors are superstitious, Miss Bradley."

"Even those who are English lords?"

"I can't speak for English lords. I haven't been one that long, and I fear I have little in common with most."

"But how does one come to our shores?"

"Not all of us are wealthy, Miss Bradley." His voice was curt, as if he wished the topic to end. "We, too, must earn our way. And," he added quietly but firmly, "how do you like our island?"

The spell was broken. Her eyes dropped from his. "It's beautiful. I've never seen water like this before."

"No one has," he said softly, then, with affection, added, "though it's treacherous as blazes."

"Why?"

Again their eyes caught. She asked more questions than any woman he'd ever met. He found it both intriguing and flattering since his experience had shown him that most women seemed to enjoy talking more about themselves. He was surprised at how much he was enjoying her.

"Reefs, shallows, wreckers."

"Wreckers?"

The corner of his mouth turned up in a quizzical smile. "Are you really interested, Miss Bradley?"

The question took her by surprise. "Why shouldn't I be?"

"Most women aren't."

"And you've met most women?"

The challenge was there again, the challenge she continued to throw at him. His smile widened. "Most women in my acquaintance," he amended carefully, his eyes twinkling.

"Then you have a very limited circle of acquaintances," she said primly, but her mouth twitched with mischief. Adrian's fascination deepened. She was very direct and very honest, and he liked both qualities. He found he liked them very much.

"Is it that much different in Maryland?" he asked.

"Do women have brains in Maryland, you mean?" Her lips were twitching even more, as if she were delighted at the prospect of trapping him.

Adrian looked over at Jeremy, who returned the glance sympathetically. "I have the highest respect for the intelligence of women," Adrian finally said, trying to think of a graceful way out. "It's just . . ."

She tipped her head with curiosity. "Just what?"

"Interests are different," he said triumphantly.

"I'm very interested in what you do," she retorted.

"And I'm interested in you," he countered as a becoming blush started up her face.

Jeremy cleared his throat, and Adrian was reminded that it was not only he and Lauren Bradley at the table.

Corinne was looking at them with an intrigued expression on her face, and Jeremy looked amused. "A cigar?" he asked Adrian as he pushed back his chair.

Adrian leaned back, wondering at the speed with which the evening was passing. He looked over at Socrates, who had been given a bowl of fruit and was now sprawled asleep on a chair. He had been extraordinarily well mannered that night, and Adrian was relieved. He wondered if it was because of Lauren Bradley; he'd never seen Socrates take to anyone so rapidly, and his little imp had been on good behavior ever since.

He watched as Lauren's gaze also went to the animal and her face softened. She was a curious mixture, full of contradictions. Direct one moment, vulnerable the next. He remembered how she'd tripped one of her assailants when most women would have fainted—or pretended to do so. But then Lauren had trembled like a leaf in the wind, and she had seemed to welcome his touch, even while wariness was apparent in her eyes.

He nodded his assent to Jeremy's question. They would disappear into another room, and he would have time to assess the effect Miss Bradley had on him. Lauren. It was a musical name.

He pushed back his chair. "Perhaps I could show you Nassau tomorrow," he said to her.

Lauren looked toward Jeremy and Corinne. Jeremy nodded.

"I would like that," she answered.

"Tomorrow at noon?" He was surprised at his own eagerness.

She nodded, startled by the anticipation the invitation caused to swell in the pit of her stomach. Anticipation and foreboding.

And fear.

CHAPTER 5

The small skiff skimmed through the water.

Lauren took turns between looking at the man at the tiller and the impossibly clear water that reflected every shade of blue and green. They were equally fascinating.

She had hesitated before agreeing to a short sailing trip around the island, but Jeremy and Corinne had both assented, saying no man was a better, or safer, sailor. Society on the island was more accepting than in many other places, and here a sail was no more eyebrow-raising than a daytime carriage ride. Besides, she was at an age where one could do what one wanted.

Lauren knew Jeremy had ulterior motives, even if Corinne didn't. They were both, Lauren and Jeremy, doing exactly what was demanded of them.

But Lauren had decided she wasn't going to think about that now. She was going to enjoy this brilliant day, and the glorious water that melded from aquamarine to turquoise to the deepest emerald. She felt she could reach down and touch the bottom of the ocean even when Adrian said it was twenty feet deep.

He was "Adrian" now, just as she was "Lauren." She heard her name on his lips with a sense of sadness and regret. Somehow, it seemed to make him a friend. But how could he ever be that? How could he ever be anything other than an enemy?

Yet his touch still sparked new sensations, and her heart reeled crazily whenever she saw his reckless grin.

He had, this day, left Socrates with Johnny, the pilot, the only man, he said, who would tolerate the beast. He added, with that quick, devilish smile, that he wanted no chaperon that chattered incessantly.

Lauren, for her part, would have preferred the imp's presence. She would have preferred anything other than being alone with a man she would be forced to betray. But now she refused to think of it, and merely took pleasure in the sun and the breeze and the lovely water, and the striking man who so confidently handled the sail and tiller.

There was something incredibly appealing about him, as he stood and moved so agilely among the sails. Once on the boat, he had given her an apologetic smile and pulled off some very polished black boots and stood happily, like a small boy, on bare feet. He was wearing a pair of snug trousers and a loose flowing shirt, its sleeves rolled up to his elbows, revealing strong, tanned arms. The wind whipped the thick chestnut hair, and the sun made it flame with reddish gold as he moved with quick elegance and grace, and occasionally threw her a glance of pure delight for a lovely day. He seemed nothing like an English lord, or, she corrected herself, as she had imagined one to look. Except, possibly, for that proud set of his chin and the attractive, precise speech that would always single him out.

Lauren tried not to look at him, to look instead at the depths of the sea, at the fish she could see, and the sand, and the rocks and the coral. She tried not to sense the restlessness that ruled his body or the runaway attraction that was ruling her mind.

She leaned back against the side of the boat, occasionally following his instructions to lean this way or that, without knowing exactly why but trusting him explicitly. Corinne had chosen this dress from her small wardrobe, and Lauren had protested at first but was now pleased. It was a dress she had purchased before her father's death, an extravagance, but when she had seen the light green muslin material, she hadn't been able to resist, and she had made the dress herself. Like all her clothes, it was modest in cut, but it seemed to float when she walked, and the dark green ribbons around the neckline made her eyes wider and deeper. She had not worn it since her father's death nearly eight months earlier.

Lauren tried to tell herself that the flash of appreciation in Adrian's eyes meant little to her, but in her heart she knew it meant a good deal. She had never really cared that much before, because she had never met a man who had really attracted her. She had, in fact, sometimes even questioned her womanliness. But now she knew it had just been lurking inside, ready to reveal itself at the worst possible time.

"Lean forward," he said, and she did as the small craft turned, spraying cool water on her, and she felt like laughing with the pure joy of movement and warmth and beauty.

A beach spread out before her, a lovely wide white beach washed by aquamarine water. He guided the craft almost to water's edge and lowered the anchor, jumping out with such loose grace that the movement appeared effortless. The water came to above his knees, but he seemed indifferent, as he held out his arms for her.

Lauren hesitated, remembering the effect of his touch as he had helped her into the boat earlier, but neither did she wish to ruin her favorite dress or seem childish. Nonsense, she scolded herself. She had already been in his arms twice in as many days—not exactly voluntarily, but there, nonetheless.

He grinned as if he knew exactly what she was thinking. "Only Socrates bites," he said. "You're safe with me."

Lauren pretended to consider his words. "Somehow, I question that."

"Now you know Jeremy and Corinne wouldn't allow you to come with me if I weren't completely honorable."

"I've heard quite different stories about English lords," Lauren countered.

"That's all in the past," he said, the smile spreading to his eyes. "Queen Victoria makes us behave these days."

"All of you?"

"Every last one," he promised, his lips twitching.

"And you always tell the truth?"

"Always," he swore.

The tongue-in-cheek teasing was infectious, and she felt her own face crease into a smile as she surrendered and allowed him to carry her to the beach. She had never felt so naturally comfortable with a man, so at ease, even though she knew that was the last thing she should feel. There was no censure of her impertinence, no impatience of her outspoken questions and curiosity, and she knew that under any other circumstances she would enjoy every second of his company. It was odd, so very odd, and she had to force herself to think of Larry. She couldn't allow herself to forget why she was here, to allow Adrian's easy charm to divert her.

"A halfpence for your thoughts," he said, as he set her down on sugary sand.

"You put little value on them," she retorted.

"A pound then? You looked so serious, perhaps they are worth that vast sum."

"A thought is only valuable to its possessor."

"I think not," he said, looking at her intently. "I believe your thoughts would be most interesting."

"And yours?" she returned.

"Do you always answer a question with another question?"

"When I have no intention of answering."

Adrian leaned back and laughed. "An honest woman."

Lauren felt what was now becoming a familiar ache. "Is honesty so important to you?"

His face changed quickly, the smile and laughter gone, and hard lines taking their place as his eyes bored into hers. "Yes," he said simply, and the ache in Lauren deepened. There was pain in that face now, something she hadn't seen before, or expected.

But then the lines eased and the smile was back in place, and she wondered whether she had imagined pain at all.

He went back to the small sailing craft and returned with a basket and a rug, spreading the latter over the sand and then helping her down.

"What would you have done with the picnic if I'd said no?" she asked curiously. He had not broached the subject of a sail until he'd come to pick her up this morning.

"I would have found a shady tree someplace, but I did want you to see this water. There's none like it in the world, not in England or Maryland or South Carolina."

"And you've been all over the world?"

"Questions again? You should have been a solicitor."

"You avoid as many as I ask."

"No," he denied. "But it's very unfair. I'll make you a bargain. If I answer one, then you must."

She leaned back on her hands, which were firmly positioned in the sand. Her fingers curled around the grains that leaked from them, and she thought how fragile and tenuous they were. Like the truth.

"All right," she said finally. "But I go first."

"Agreed."

"How does it feel to be a viscount?"

His smile faded a bit. "I haven't been one very long," he answered slowly, "and most of the time I've been out of the country."

"At sea?"

"Aye," he responded. "First with the English Navy, and then with a trader."

"And you've sailed around the world?"

"Almost."

"And what is the most beautiful place you've been?"

"England." The answer came swiftly and as a surprise to Lauren.

"Then why do you leave it?"

"I think I've counted five questions," he said. "And now I have one."

She grimaced, but she couldn't deny the bargain. "All right."

His hand went up and brushed a honey-colored curl from the side of her face. "Why is such a lovely young lady alone?"

"There's a war," she replied simply.

"And before?"

"I . . . I took care of my father and brother."

"And there's no young man?"

"No," she answered stiffly.

"I didn't know Americans were such fools."

Lauren took her eyes from his steady gaze and devastating smile. She almost felt as if he were reaching inside her, grabbing for something that should be hers alone. It had been a mistake, coming here with him. She had known it when she'd agreed, but she had thought she could keep her senses in control, that she could remember Larry and remain immune. But now her heart fluttered at his words, her blood moved faster, and her hands trembled where they hid in the sand.

"I'm considered," she said at last, "a bit eccentric."

"And why is that?"

"That's your last question," she said. "Now it's my turn again."

"But not until you answer. Why were you considered eccentric?"

"Because there was no one I wished to marry."

"But I think that's very wise of you, not eccentric."

"I've always wanted to do things. A wife seldom can," she observed. It was something she had never admitted, even to her father.

"What things?" The question was soft, even gentle.

I wanted to be a doctor like them, like my father and my

brother. Like my dead brother. But that would be saying too much. "Perhaps sail to China."

"It's overrated," Adrian said with a chuckle. "Five months on a ship can become very dull."

"But you said you liked it."

"Did I?" he asked, with an arched eyebrow, and she searched her memory for his exact words.

"Don't you?"

"Still questioning, and it's not even your turn."

"I've lost count," she said.

"Ah, and I thought you were honest."

"Perhaps not always."

His hand covered hers, and she felt heat radiating from it. She looked up and saw his eyes, eyes that were so impossibly deep, and that didn't always smile when his mouth did. For a moment, there were no more bantering words. She knew, and knew that he did, that they were both protecting parts of themselves, that because of the very strength of the attraction between them they needed that protection. She knew her reasons. She wondered about his.

He rose and drew her up with him. "Come walk with me."

She stood and took several steps before her shoes filled with sand. She looked enviously at his bare feet.

"Take them off," he suggested.

It was a highly improper suggestion, but being here at all was rather improper, she told herself. Indeed, everything she had done in the past few years had been improper: working in her father's practice, going to Washington alone, and then sailing alone to England and Nassau. One improper step led very easily to the next, she was learning. And the sand did look very inviting. She had never seen any so powdery, so soft.

"I'll help," he said enticingly, and she knew consent was in her face if not in her words.

The last thing Lauren wanted was to feel his hands on her legs, her ankles. The light touch of his hand on her hand was dangerous enough. She looked longingly at the water and sand, and then at the skirts that covered her shoes. Longing warred with propriety, with worse than propriety, with a sense of sinking into quicksand.

She looked up. He was watching her internal war with fascinated relish, with a dare in his eyes and a challenge on his lips.

Devil take it, she finally decided, and sat down. In for a penny, in for a pound. Turning away from his amused eyes, she unbuttoned the black shoes and rolled down her silk stockings. Her toes automatically curled up in the sand, relishing the feel of it, and she experienced a sudden joyous freedom, as if she were a child again.

She stood once more, digging her feet in the sand, feeling the sea breeze, hearing his soft, deep chuckle that was, to her, a siren's call to forget everything but this day and this minute.

When he held out his hand, she took it, lost in the exploration of sensation, of stimulation, of the sensuality of the sun and sea and sand.

And Adrian Cabot.

He stepped closer, and she could smell his scent, a rich mixture of bay and some other spice she couldn't identify. Nor did she have time to think about it, for his lips were touching hers, lightly as if not to frighten, but still intoxicatingly.

She started to respond, and then a deeper instinct made her jerk away.

He let her go, his head cocked slightly at an angle as if studying her. "You're enchanting, you know," he said.

She had never been called enchanting before. Just as she had never been called lovely. Pretty, yes. But even that had come from her brother and father, and they were certainly prejudiced. But now she felt enchanting, and enchanted, and she also felt shivery and shaken and altogether confused.

"Come," he said, taking her hand as if the kiss had never happened.

And she did, almost without will, with purpose forgotten. He took her to a tidal pool and showed her a multicolored crab that was trying to find its way back to the sea. Crystal water reflected each of its shades, as well as the tiny fish that darted like colorful streaks of energy. A little farther on, he discovered a conch shell; he washed its dead interior with seawater and held it to her ear so she could hear its special ocean music.

Lauren listened with fascinated wonder. She had always had a curiosity and hunger about the world, which was too often left unsatisfied by those who thought a woman should have no such interests. Even her father, so busy with his practice, had little time to sit and explain, and her brother was more amused than helpful. Her suitors had never wished to discuss politics with her, or new scientific discoveries, and few of them read the books she treasured.

She looked up at the man beside her. While he'd shown amusement when she'd divested herself of her footwear, there was none as he shared his knowledge of the island and the sea. His voice, deep and so attractively accented, held its special appeal, an authority and power that made her heart quicken. She could well imagine his presence on a ship, his orders quick and sure as he evaded the blockade, as he falsely ordered rockets, as he . . .

Lauren shook her head, and tried to bring his words back in focus.

"I'm losing your attention." The rebuke was rather like that of a disappointed schoolteacher, and she wondered for a moment at the different sides she had seen of him: owner of a wayward monkey, rescuer, English lord, rakish captain, teacher, war profiteer. Which one was the real Adrian Cabot? It didn't matter, though. There was only one aspect she could consider—the latter one. But she liked the others. It scared her how much she liked the others.

"I'm hungry," she answered, but not quite quickly enough to escape his searching gaze.

"Is that all? You seemed hundreds of miles away."

"I was . . . thinking of home. My brother used to take me to the ocean."

She felt his hand tighten on hers. "I'm sorry."

There was regret in his voice, and she wished she didn't

feel that familiar ache inside, the ache and guilt. "Do you have a brother?"

His face tightened again in that rare, unexpected way. "I did."

Lauren knew from his expression she shouldn't intrude, but she couldn't help herself. "What happened?"

It was an intrusive question, and she half-expected him to ignore it, but instead he looked away at the sea as he answered very quietly, "He shot himself."

She closed her eyes. So he had known loss too. She should have felt a tiny speck of satisfaction, but she didn't. Only compassion, for he said it with a kind of sad aloneness.

"There's no . . . other family?"

"A few distant cousins."

Her hand unaccountably squeezed his, and his eyes searched her face. "You're a very unusual woman, Lauren Bradley."

"A hungry one, at least," she said, knowing she had to do something to break this mood that made them one, rather than two separate people with two distinctly opposed goals.

"There's no romance in your soul, Miss Bradley," he said, but his voice was again light, as if he, too, knew they had been entering uncharted waters.

The meal would have been wonderful if Lauren had not lost her appetite. But since she had mentioned hunger, she forced herself to eat, to keep her eyes on the roast chicken and fresh bread and fruit. When she did look toward him, his eyes were on her, their contents hooded, but his mouth smiling. Each time, she felt something inside her respond in ways that were treacherous. She wanted to reach out and touch him. She hungered for contact, but she knew she could not risk it.

"When will you be . . . making another run?"

"I leave on the tide tonight," he said.

"But I thought—" She stopped abruptly.

"You thought what?"

"That you waited until the moon wanes."

"Some captains do," he said. "Certainly the most activity takes place then, but I can't wait that long. And it's only half moon. With luck we'll have fog going into Charleston."

"Aren't you afraid of bad luck?"

He shrugged. "It's something you can't control, so I don't worry about it. I only worry about things I *can* control, like having the best bloody crew and the fastest ship."

The reply was so sure, even arrogant, that she felt the old resentment rise, the knowledge that his luck and skill had killed her brother. She nibbled at a piece of fruit she didn't recognize; it was tangy rather than sweet. Sipping a glass of light wine, she looked out over the water. The sun was tracing patterns over its surface, making the variations of colors even more complex.

"How . . . how long will you be gone?"

"About ten days. I'll wait in Charleston for the full moon to pass."

"Do you ever take passengers?"

"No." The answer was flat.

"But I've heard . . ."

"Some ships do take passengers. I don't. The *Specter* isn't equipped to carry them. We have no extra cabins, only cargo space."

"But . . ."

"If I have to worry about women and children or even civilian men, I might make a mistake, Lauren. I may not take risks which are sometimes necessary. Every man who sails with me knows the danger, and the odds, and they accept them, but I'm not willing to assume the responsibility for more lives."

Lauren stared at him with surprise. He had always before spoken of the blockade with such light disregard. "But I thought you enjoyed it."

"Part of me does," he admitted. "There are few thrills like successfully running the blockade, of knowing you've outwitted one of the best navies afloat, but I don't want anyone else to pay the price for my perverse pleasure." He was quiet for several seconds. "You aren't thinking of running the blockade?"

"Perhaps," she said.

"But why?"

"I have friends in Charleston, and . . . perhaps I could do something for the war effort . . . nursing perhaps." She swallowed hard at the lie. Why had she ever thought this could be easy?

Adrian stilled. "Nursing?"

"My father was a doctor. I used to help him."

"Have you ever nursed a man torn apart by a cannonball?" His voice was intentionally rough.

"No."

"I've seen war wounds, Lauren," he said, his voice harsh. "They're a lot different from illness."

"When?" The word was barely a whisper.

"Not here. The Crimean War. My ship rescued survivors from another ship. It was hell."

Lauren digested the words, the feeling in them. Adrian Cabot did not take death lightly. But still he played with it. Still he had killed Laurence. She shivered, and knew he saw it as his mouth gentled once more. "I'm sorry," he said. "But you don't want to go to Charleston."

His assumption angered her. "That's my decision."

His steady gaze didn't change, but he nodded without argument, and several minutes later they were back in the small sailing skiff. Some afternoon clouds appeared, and some of the brightness left the day, as if imitating Lauren's own fogged senses.

They arrived back at the wharf in late afternoon. What intimacy had been between them was broken, and Lauren knew Adrian also realized that some indefinable barrier had been erected, though his puzzled look told her he had no idea why.

But at the private back door of Jeremy's, he took her hand and held it a moment, the warmth of the sun passing from one to another, warmth from the sun and warmth from their bodies, and warmth from . . .

"It's been a pleasure," he said, his voice low and beguiling, full of promise. "May I call on you when I return?"

Lauren felt a sizzling heat race through her blood, knew a dizziness that had nothing to do with the usual causes of such impairment. She looked up at him, into the eyes that regarded her steadily with a befuddlement of their own, and she wanted to reach out to him, to touch. To touch and to preserve.

"Don't go," she said, suddenly desperate without knowing why.

He looked even more puzzled.

"Don't run the blockade!"

His mouth relaxed. "I'll be safe enough."

She swallowed a protest, suppressed her fear, although she didn't know for whom she feared. She nodded and watched as he turned and strode quickly toward the wharf and his ship.

Her room overlooked the harbor and his ship. She hadn't been able to eat any dinner, claiming that the picnic had been more than sufficient. She had often found Jeremy's gaze on her, but he hadn't had a chance to speak with her privately.

She retired early, pleading a headache from the sun, and she sat at the window, watching the activity around the *Specter*. As dusk fell, lights glowed from the ship, and as its gray shape melded into evening twilight, the twinkling lights seemed to come from nowhere.

Lauren continued to sit there, to watch as the lights moved slowly away and grew dim, and then disappeared into the night.

CHAPTER 6

The run into Charleston was one of the easiest Adrian had experienced. Few runners tried the run during this phase of the moon, and the Union lookouts were lazy. The *Specter* had glided unnoticed past two visible ships before coming under the protection of the guns of forts Moultrie and Sumter.

The tide was high as they crossed over the bar into the harbor, the cannon of Fort Moultrie signaling their arrival. By the time the *Specter* reached the wharf, there would be numerous agents gathered to inquire about his cargo, despite the early hour. Later in the day, the commercial cargo would be auctioned off to Charleston merchants, and Adrian would probably spend the rest of the day bargaining with Confederate agents for the remaining cargo—munitions, guns, and medicines.

Each arrival of a blockade runner was reason for celebration in Charleston, and he knew there would be several invitations this morning for dinners and dances. Charleston was determinedly gay, even in face of the growing shortages. It had become, he knew, a matter of pride for the city's residents to maintain appearances.

But this night he would decline them all and get some badly needed rest, for he'd had little in the last several days. He never slept well during the passages, knowing they could be sighted at any moment by Union warships, but this trip had been even more disturbing than usual, for he had not been able to erase the hazel-eyed Miss Bradley from his mind.

Nearly seventeen years ago, he had learned that women were basically untrustworthy and deceptive. He knew if he ever regained Ridgely he would marry, but simply to acquire heirs, nothing more. If he didn't regain Ridgely, then he'd decided to remain unencumbered and free.

And, he told himself, Lauren Bradley was not, in any way, his usual cup of tea. She was, apparently, a bluestocking, a type he usually avoided. Yet he had been intrigued by her endless curiosity and intelligence, and, at times, the ability to stay quiet when she had nothing to say. That, he thought cynically, was the most unusual thing about her. She had said damned little on the sail back around the island several days ago, and he'd been surprised at how much he'd enjoyed just having her there.

She was not as beautiful as most women he'd squired. She was pretty enough, but it was only during those rare times that she truly smiled that she became really beautiful. More than beautiful. He thought how altogether irresistible she'd looked when she was trying to decide whether to divest herself of shoes—the small unsure looks she'd darted at him; the pleasure on her face as she'd surrendered and buried her feet in the sand. He'd thought his heart would drop straight to the sand.

He hadn't even known he'd had a heart left.

Disgusted with his thoughts, he turned the wheel over to his first mate. Wade gave him a careful smile, and he knew he had been as short-tempered as Socrates on this trip.

Adrian went to his cabin to see whether it needed cleaning before the agents arrived, but Socrates had disturbed nothing. He had been so subdued on this run, Adrian had worried, but the monkey had eaten well enough. Adrian wondered if perhaps the small animal didn't miss Lauren Bradley too. Not that he himself had missed her.

Socrates padded over to him, although Adrian knew better than to touch him unless the monkey made the first move. Socrates had been badly mistreated by his former owner, and sometimes struck out in confusion and fear if someone came too close. Two years had passed since Adrian had acquired the animal, but there were still moments of distrust.

Adrian sometimes wished heartily he could rid himself of Socrates, but then the monkey would come and look at him with its tipped head and sad, wise expression, and pat his hand as if to thank him, or console him, and Adrian would remember that day when the bloodied monkey fled to him for help. His owner had been drunk, and Socrates was on a chain, a collar around his neck, and utterly helpless as the man threw him against a box and beat him. The man had let go of the leash for a moment, and the monkey ran in pain and confusion toward Adrian.

In that moment, Adrian had remembered another small creature beaten so many years ago. Rage, lying fallow for thirty years, exploded. He'd nearly killed the man, throwing down a wad of notes that was probably thirty times the value of the monkey.

Adrian soon discovered he had purchased trouble. He hadn't known anything about monkeys, and the first thing he'd learned was their overwhelming lack of gratitude. The second was a complete lack of modesty in their personal habits. He had threatened to maroon Socrates, to return him to his former owner, to toss him overboard, but the bloody monkey was unimpressed with all his threats and blandishments and bribes. Secretly, Adrian had rather enjoyed the battle of wills and even the sometimes reluctant companionship. He was aware that part of his fondness or attachment probably stemmed from loneliness, from having no family of his own or even anyone who cared a tinker's cuss except for his crew, and that, he suspected dryly, was because he had made most of them bloody rich.

But now Socrates was in one of his more mellow moods, as he viewed Adrian with a beady but sympathetic gaze, his hand resting on Adrian's knee. Adrian felt he was in a sorry fix indeed when he incurred the pity of a monkey. He stirred himself and dressed for company, for though it was just past dawn, he knew he would soon be besieged with visitors.

The day passed quickly. He sold his commercial cargo for even more than he'd anticipated. Apparently there was still a vigorous market for fine brandy and silks, as well as more practical items such as sewing kits, nails, toothbrushes, and corsets. The latter had been requested several runs ago by a group of ladies, and he had ordered them from England, although he knew the ladies of Charleston needed corsets less and less as food became scarcer. Adrian had a growing admiration for the underdog South, for the pride and stubbornness of its people. That admiration was one reason he earmarked half of his cargo for war necessities, rather than wholly for luxury goods as did many of the other English captains.

He met with the Confederate agents in the afternoon, and after agreeing on a price for the present cargo, they discussed the next shipment. Of specific interest were English-made cannon. The South would make it well worth his while to bring them; he was one of the few blockade runners with whom they'd entrust the precious cargo.

Adrian didn't hesitate, although he knew word would spread, and his ship would become an even greater target for the Federal Navy. There was already a bounty on the *Specter*.

"Twenty-five thousand pounds," he said. "In gold. Deposited to my account in England."

"On delivery," the agent agreed.

They shook hands, and the agent asked Adrian to join him for dinner.

"I've still some business," Adrian said. "And I'm damnably tired."

"How long will you be here?"

Adrian shrugged. "I'll load cotton and wait until a dense fog or a new moon."

"We need the cannon as quickly as possible."

"Is it in Nassau?"

"It will be within ten days, no longer."

"Anyone know about it?"

The agent shrugged. "It's being crated as furniture, but there are spies everywhere. In London as well as in Richmond and Nassau."

"I'll bring it in," Adrian said.

The agent smiled. Captain Cabot was one of three captains the War Department had insisted upon. One of the other three had wrecked coming into Charleston three days ago; the ship was torched so Union forces wouldn't obtain the cargo. The other was Clay Harding, but Harding was already scheduled to bring in essential rifles and ammunition, a cargo as important as the cannon.

"If you need anything, Captain, please call on me."

"A dense fog."

The agent's smile grew wider. "I'll see what I can do."

Adrian spent the rest of the afternoon with cotton brokers. The wharfs were piled with it; the surplus had already filled all the warehouse space, and the price was cheap. He purchased a total of thirteen hundred bales of cotton, knowing it would fill nearly every inch of available space up to the gunwales, and he made arrangements for its loading.

By nightfall, he was exhausted. Most of the crew had gone ashore. The blockade runners had become the heroes of Charleston, and there wasn't a door unopened to them. There was even a pretty widow, whom he occasionally visited, but the idea seemed singularly unappealing now, and he was too tired to wonder why.

Adrian extinguished the oil lamp and stretched out on the bed. The cotton should be loaded in two days, maybe less; since there were no other blockade runners in port, he would receive maximum attention. Usually he enjoyed staying in Charleston, but now he felt restless and wanted to get back to Nassau. He decided not to ask himself exactly why.

Jeremy eyed Lauren quizzically. She had said little in the past two days since Captain Cabot had been gone, and he'd hesitated to ask.

He liked Lauren. The last woman Phillips had sent to Nassau had been flashy and bold, the type to catch a man's eyes. She'd been in Nassau months without ever learning anything, although Jeremy was sure she'd shared her bed with several of the blockaders. She'd never, however, been able to attract Captain Cabot, and had finally been called back to Washington.

Jeremy had been amazed at Cabot's interest in Lauren, and conceded that perhaps Phillips was more astute than he'd believed when he first met Lauren. He wasn't told why Lauren had agreed to the plan, and he wondered about her motives now because there was uncertainty in Lauren's eyes. Uncertainty and doubt and confusion.

Lauren was helping him with inventory, but frequently Jeremy would see her eyes cloud and know that her mind was wandering.

"Captain Cabot?" he asked when she failed to respond to one of his questions.

A book in her hands dropped, and she leaned to pick it up, her eyes seeking the floor rather than Jeremy's. She had not been able to keep Adrian Cabot from her thoughts. She knew she should wish his capture, but she couldn't. She was afraid for him, and that made her afraid for herself.

"You don't have to go through with this," Jeremy said gently.

She hesitated. "I don't even know if I can. He said he doesn't take passengers."

"And if he did agree to take you?"

Lauren looked miserable. "I don't know. He's . . . not what I expected."

"What did you expect?"

"Someone . . . who didn't care about anything or anyone."

Jeremy sighed. He had wondered from the beginning whether his guest was too gentle for what was expected of her. "He's very likable," he said cautiously.

The door opened then, and a customer entered. Lauren didn't look up as Jeremy greeted the newcomer. "Captain Harding, what can I do for you?"

Lauren looked toward the customer. She had heard Jeremy mention the name before as one of the more successful blockade runners and a friend of Adrian Cabot's.

"Some cigars," Captain Harding said, his drawl very pronounced, very Southern, as his gaze swept around the store and settled on Lauren. This was the third time in as many days that he had made an excuse to stop at Jeremy Case's store. It was the first time that the girl Adrian had mentioned had been there.

Jeremy saw the Southerner's dark eyes find Lauren, saw the small smile form on his mouth. "Lauren, this is Captain Clay Harding," he said, "and this is my niece, Lauren."

Clay Harding bowed with a courtliness that was obviously meant to charm. "My pleasure, Miss . . ."

"Bradley," she replied, thinking that he, too, was a very attractive man. She had always thought of sea captains like Captain Taggert, older and bearded and salt-tongued, but Clay Harding reminded her of Adrian with his clean good looks and devilish eyes. Yet there the resemblance ended. There was something boyish about Clay Harding, and there was nothing boyish about Adrian Cabot.

"Our island is richer for your arrival," he said, and she had to smile at the extravagant compliment.

"Thank you," she said solemnly but with a slight smile, "and which of the Southern states is poorer for your absence?"

There was the slightest playfulness in the words, so small, in fact, that Clay wondered whether he imagined it. "South Carolina, ma'am," he said as he studied her more carefully. At first glance, she was most attractive, certainly pretty enough to spice his bet with Adrian, and then she'd smiled, and he'd wanted to smile with her.

"Here you are, Captain," Jeremy said, handing a box to his customer, who quickly looked around the store.

"Perhaps," Clay started, seeking to delay his departure, "some . . . ah . . ." He noticed a book in Lauren's hands. "A book," he said triumphantly.

"This one, Captain?" Lauren asked, the smile on her face growing.

"Anything," he said.

"I'll wrap it for you," she said, and disappeared into a side room.

When Lauren reappeared, the book was wrapped carefully, and she handed it to the South Carolinian.

"Thank you. There's a dance at the Governor's House on Friday evening," Clay found himself saying. "May I have the honor of escorting you?"

Lauren looked quickly over to Jeremy, who nodded. "We've received an invitation today, and I thought you might enjoy attending."

"Yes," she said softly. "I would like that." Friday was six days away, and Adrian wouldn't be back yet. And she had been asked to discover what information she could about any of the blockade runners. And perhaps, just perhaps, Clay Harding could take her mind off Adrian, and the *Specter*.

In the next several days, Lauren accustomed herself to the pace of Nassau. Clay Harding stopped in nearly every day, and once asked her to tea at the Royal Victoria, the new fine hotel that sat on a hill, overlooking the bay. Curious about him and the other blockade runners, she accepted.

Clay called for her later that day in a carriage, although the Royal Victoria was only a small walk away. The hotel was magnificent, with verandas and balconies overlooking elaborate gardens. The building hummed with vitality and energy, and despite Lauren's antipathy for the blockade trade, she couldn't stifle excitement that was contagious.

Lauren was astonished as she went inside. Ladies in extravagant gowns and lower than proper necklines eyed both her and Clay curiously, as did lounging men in both uniform and civilian dress. Several men intercepted them, obviously waiting for an introduction that was reluctantly made. Lauren tried to remember names, but there were so many of them, and so many faces, some leering, some appreciative, some frankly admiring, some curious.

And then they were finally seated, and Lauren knew she probably appeared stunned, but he chuckled. "It must be overwhelming."

"They are all blockade runners?"

"Most of them. There're seventeen ships in port now, waiting for the new moon. But there're also some merchant ship captains."

Lauren looked at her escort. He was wearing a Confederate Navy uniform and looked daring and distinguished. His hair was blond, almost the color of wheat, and his eyes were gray. He was a handsome man, but while Adrian Cabot stirred confusing emotions in her, this man did not. She thought she could like him if she'd allowed herself, but nothing about him made her knees weak or her tongue to lose power.

"How many runs have you made, Captain?"

He shrugged. "Fifteen or so."

"Tell me about it. How does it feel to have ships firing at you?" She shuddered slightly.

He stared at her intently. "It's scary as hell, sometimes."

She had to smile. "I didn't think men ever admitted they are scared."

"Then they are liars."

"It's really dangerous, then? I was told . . ."

"War," he said frankly, "is, by definition, a deadly business. But I don't suppose blockade running is any more dangerous than any other duty," he said easily. "You wouldn't be worried about someone?"

Her gaze met his, and she saw the question in it. He too then knew about the afternoon she'd spent with Adrian. Did nothing go unnoticed on the island? "No," she lied.

"Good." The one word held any number of implications, and Lauren knew an unexpected, and unusual, surge of excitement that still another man apparently found her appealing. She wondered if it was those hateful lessons in Washington where she was instructed on how best to dress and wear her hair, and how to flirt. She did look better, she knew, with her hair framing her face rather than drawn severely back, and her clothes were more suited to display her figure. It wasn't that she had tried to be unattractive before so much as not having a mother to guide her, or the time to experiment. Her beaux had usually been lifelong friends who'd never claimed everlasting passion for her but thought instead that it was time for marriage and that they would be "compatible." "Compatible" had never seemed very interesting to her.

So she hadn't really understood why Mr. Phillips thought she would be an effective spy, and she was still partially stunned that she had been sought out by two such attractive men. She was even more confounded by her own reactions, both her confusion and the odd but compelling attraction of Adrian Cabot and now the pleasant warmth of Clay Harding.

Lauren's attention was suddenly diverted by a tall man dressed in civilian clothes who had just entered the dining room. His gaze went almost immediately to her companion, and the two men nodded warily. "Is he a blockade runner?" she asked curiously as Clay's face tensed.

Clay was slow in answering. "He's a Union officer. His ship came in for repairs. A confrontation, I heard, with one of our privateers."

"But he's not in uniform."

"He's wise. There's a lot of anti-Union feeling here."

Lauren was confused. "But you know each other."

"We went to the Naval Academy together," he said simply.

"You were friends?"

"Very good ones."

"And now?"

"He'd blow my ship out of the water if he could." The

words were spoken lightly, but Lauren detected pain in them.

"It must be very difficult," she said slowly, "to find yourself torn between loyalties." She was beginning to know a little of how it felt.

"Yes," he said simply. "But that always happens during a civil war. It's one of the inherent tragedies."

Lauren knew something about that. Much of Delaware had been divided over the war, although her part of the state had been mostly pro-Union. But she knew no one personally who had decided to fight for the South. Until now.

Lauren looked back to the Union officer. "It must seem strange to eat in the same room as your enemy."

He grinned, the twinkle back in his eyes. "You'll discover many strange things about Nassau, Miss Bradley. It's an anomaly, a neutral port which is not neutral at all, and fortunes made in a day and thrown away as quickly."

"Is that what Captain Cabot does?"

"Must we talk about him?" Clay said.

"No," she said, both relieved and yet oddly disappointed at his response. She had wanted to know so much more about the English captain.

The subjects of war and Adrian Cabot were avoided during the next half hour, and Lauren found Clay Harding a charming and amusing companion, who kept her smiling even as he drove her back to Jeremy's store.

"The book you sold me," he said, with a lopsided smile, as they left, "was most interesting."

"You read it from cover to cover?"

"Of course."

"You can knit now?" she questioned.

"Exquisitely," he replied solemnly.

Lauren couldn't help giggling. The image of Clay Harding knitting was an irresistibly amusing one.

He feigned a look of injury before smiling again. "Next time I'll look before I buy."

"Only," she added mischievously, "when you have an unscrupulous clerk."

"I like unscrupulous clerks. Pretty ones, at least," he amended.

But then they were back before she could answer. He handed her down and smiled. "I'll see you Saturday evening. Good day, Miss Bradley."

"Thank you for a lovely afternoon," she replied, surprised that she really meant it.

Later, Lauren noted Jeremy's speculative look as she told him about her afternoon, of Clay Harding and the Union captain, and wondered aloud at the sadness in Clay's voice as he'd talked about it. They had gone out to the garden after closing the store, and were completely alone.

"You didn't expect to care, did you?" he observed gently.

"Mr. Phillips . . . he made them all sound . . . so mercenary. At least Captain Harding's doing something he believes in."

"And Captain Cabot isn't?"

Lauren nodded miserably.

"Does that make Captain Harding any less effective?"

"No."

"Nothing is black and white, Lauren. I suppose Adrian Cabot has his own reasons for running the blockade. Perhaps he even believes in the Confederacy. He could certainly make a greater profit by running more luxuries than he does."

"Are you taking his side?"

He shook his head. "I just want you to realize there are two sides to everything. You can't make rational decisions without understanding that, or everything will collapse." He hesitated. "Why did you decide to come?"

Lauren was silent for a moment. But she needed a friend, someone in whom to confide. "My brother . . . was killed five months ago on a Union patrol boat near Charleston. He was a doctor."

There was more, and Jeremy knew it. He hesitated to ask. But he didn't have to.

"Mr. Phillips said he died because of Captain Cabot,

that . . . Captain Cabot tricked one Union boat into firing on another one."

"It seemed so easy in Washington, didn't it?" Jeremy asked, and she nodded.

"Not easy, exactly," she admitted. "But it seemed . . . right."

"And now . . . ?"

She nodded slowly. "I still think it's right, but I hate lying . . ."

"I can write Phillips," he said, "and ask him to send someone else. You can be on your way home on the next ship."

"Nothing important is easy," she said in a soft voice. "I'll stay."

He merely nodded, approval in his eyes.

But as they went inside, she wondered whether she might lose her soul in following her conscience. The irony did not escape her.

CHAPTER 7

The ball was glittering, and Lauren felt like Cinderella. She had never attended such an elegant event before.

She knew how to dance, of course. Her brother had taught her well, and she had attended small parties. But she had never even imagined anything quite as grand as this.

The Government House was ablaze with lights, with lanterns on the grounds and great chandeliers inside. Never had Lauren seen such elegant gowns and such a myriad of uniforms, or heard laughter so gay or conversation so vibrant.

Everything appeared larger than life. There was a humming sense of vitality, of danger, of immediacy, that both fascinated and repelled her. Repelled her because she knew it resulted from war.

Clay's hand tightened on her arm as they walked through the receiving line, then to the huge ballroom that seemed to move itself with whirling figures. She knew she looked better tonight than she had ever appeared, and part of her enjoyed the admiring glances thrown her way.

Her gown was simple and not overly expensive, but the moss-green silk suited her coloring perfectly, making the swirling colors in her hazel eyes soft and mysterious. Purchased ready-made at one of the shops, it had required only a few alterations by Mary.

And her hair. Mary and Corinne had labored hours over her hair, washing it first in perfumed water, and brushing as it dried before taming the curls into a French braid laced with flowers. Mary applied just the least amount of color to her cheeks, and when Lauren was finally allowed to see herself in the mirror, she felt she was regarding a stranger. A lovely stranger, an unfamiliar shell that hid the real Lauren Bradley.

The fairy tale continued as Clay arrived. Dressed in the dashing formal uniform of a Confederate naval officer, he looked much like a prince with his golden hair and blue eyes that blazed with admiration when he saw her.

That look frightened her, and so did this new knowledge that she could inspire such a look. She didn't like the sense of suddenly not knowing what and who she was.

But there was also an underlying excitement, such as she felt when she traveled to Washington, when she explored London. Neither grief nor loneliness had completely squashed the adventurous part of her, and neither could uncertainty now.

The feeling of unreality persisted as they arrived at the ball, and Lauren was assaulted by any number of uniformed men. Men in red, blue, gray, and even green uniforms, until she could keep none of them straight. They all clamored for dances, but Clay warded them off, claiming the first dance, a waltz.

Lauren was nervous at first. Corinne and Jeremy planned to come later—he'd had some business to take care of—but they'd urged her to go ahead with Clay.

Now she felt alone and uncertain. She had previously danced only with her brother and boys she'd known all her life. But Clay was a wonderful dancer, and her nervousness gave way to pleasure as they moved in sure, graceful steps across the dance floor.

Held lightly in Clay's arms, she felt nothing of the electric attraction she felt toward Adrian Cabot, and she wondered why not. She knew instinctively it would be easier to like, even love, a man like Clay Harding than one like Adrian Cabot. Despite Adrian's easy smile and courtesy, there was something very private, very alone, about him.

Which was total nonsense. She couldn't, wouldn't, allow herself to think that way about either of them. She had a job to do, nothing more.

The dance ended, and once more men started for her. Clay took her arm and deftly led her out through French doors to a wide porch, guiding her to a shadowed corner.

"A glass of champagne?"

Lauren nodded. She wanted to be alone for a few moments.

Clay disappeared, and she looked out over the lush, elaborate gardens of Government House. Adrian had expected to be gone for several more days, yet every morning she had risen expectantly from her bed and looked out the window. Each day, the harbor grew more crowded as runners waited out the bright night sky. Her eyes would travel over each of the newly arrived ships, and she felt an inexplicable disappointment when none was the *Specter*. It didn't, she knew, make sense; yet her body trembled with fear for him. She wanted, needed, craved, to see those deep blue eyes, experience the energy she felt around him, even, God help her, to know his touch again. She had seen him four times, and already he filled her mind.

It was so terribly wrong, so unfair. Why Adrian Cabot? Of all the men in the world, why the man who had caused Larry's death, who traded in death?

And yet no one had treated her as he had that day on the island, laughing with and teasing her, sharing with her his knowledge and pleasure. He'd touched her with hands that burned and branded, that made her long for something more, so much more.

Clay returned and handed her a glass of champagne. "I just saw Jeremy and his wife come in," he said. "I thought you would like to know."

"Thank you."

She knew his eyes were on her, but she looked away, toward the lanterns that lit the flower beds. A delicious fresh smell from the gardens mingled with the aroma of rich foods and desserts. Above, a full bright orange moon hung high in the sky. A moon to fear, according to most of those present tonight. Beautiful and treacherous—and Adrian Cabot was out there somewhere. Out there and hunted.

She shivered.

"Would you like to go in?"

Lauren turned back to her escort. "It's so beautiful tonight."

"It always is during this phase of the moon."

She looked at him curiously. "Is that why the ball is tonight? Because so many of you are in port?"

"Smart girl," he said. "The governor usually plans his affairs during the full moon."

The rest of the evening moved quickly. After several more dances with Clay, she saw Corinne talking with some other women and stopped to be introduced. She conscientiously tried to remember everyone's name, but her thoughts kept straying to the moon, and the danger she knew Adrian was facing.

Trying to listen, Lauren was suddenly aware that everyone was turning toward the door, a ripple of surprise passing through the room like a breeze on a fall day at home. She, too, turned, and was startled to see Adrian Cabot standing in the entryway. His blue eyes swept over the crowd, lingering slightly on her before passing on.

He was magnificent in evening clothes, every inch the English aristocrat. He wore dark blue superbly tailored trousers, which hugged his deeply muscled legs, a lighter blue waistcoat with a snowy-white cravat, and a midnight-blue formal jacket that darkened the deep, now slightly clouded, blue of his eyes. Socrates was not in evidence, but then she thought quickly that not even Adrian would dare bring an unruly monkey to the Governor's Ball.

Trying to subdue the relief, the inexplicable joy, that flooded her, she bit her lip in confusion, hiding her trembly smile. He was alive. And safe.

As if he read her mind, even as he still stood in the doorway, apparently enjoying his entrance, he smiled endearingly, and then his glance dropped to the empty space next to him, as if noticing with her the absence of Socrates. He shrugged briefly, as if wryly admitting concession to occasional propriety. She knew her smile was growing wider, and she could do nothing about it, for he looked amusingly like a wayward schoolboy caught in some mischievous act.

The glances between them were potent, filled with understanding and even a trace of wit, and Lauren realized suddenly that others were looking at them, from one to another, with obvious interest. She dropped her eyes and turned back to Corinne as a crowd of men surrounded Adrian, their congratulations noisy even in the large room. In a room filled with reckless, attractive men, Adrian Cabot dominated, radiating an aura of energy and power that dwarfed the others—even Clay Harding, who now made his way over to her possessively.

He stood at her side as Adrian fielded dozens of questions with rapid, short answers, his gaze continually returning to her and his eyebrows furrowing as he saw Clay place his hand on her elbow and lean over to whisper an invitation to dance.

Lauren didn't really want to dance. Her body felt like a mass of quivering nerves, anticipating, wanting, needing in ways she'd never imagined. She still felt extreme pleasure that he was safe, that his eyes had sought her out and lingered on her when there were other more attractive women in the room. She also knew hunger and guilt and anticipation and so many more warring emotions that her hand trembled when Clay took it and led her onto the middle of the floor where a reel was beginning.

Now she was grateful for the music, for the concentration required for the dance, for the need to flash a smile that had little meaning. She was both sorry and grateful when it ended, for she instinctively knew Captain Cabot would be standing there, waiting.

And he was. As Clay led her off the floor, his arm lightly around her waist, again in an almost annoyingly possessive way, they ended up in front of Adrian.

"Miss Bradley," he said. "May I hope to have the next dance?"

There was an undercurrent of amusement in the question, as if his request was no request at all but a foregone conclusion, one that neither she nor Clay could deny.

It surprised her that she felt no resentment about the presumption, only a joyful jump of her senses. But Clay frowned slightly before saying evenly, "If the lady agrees."

Lauren nodded. She'd been given a dance card, but Clay had deftly deflected all candidates and filled in each dance with his own name.

Adrian took her gloved hand, and she wondered at her reaction to his touch, and why only he caused a current of fire to rage through her. His hand, too, was gloved, and despite two layers of cloth, she knew once more the tingling of skin, the white-hot heat that moved up her arms to the core of her body.

The dance was a waltz, for which she was simultaneously grateful, because it brought him near to her, and fearful, because of the trembling his proximity caused. Although Clay had been a fine dancer, Adrian was even better, graceful and masterful, his light but sure movements taking her from earth to the sky, to dance in the heavens, stars as her companions.

She leaned back in his arms, feeling protected and secure as she looked at his distinctive face, at the eyes that smiled down at her. His fingers tightened ever so slightly on her hand as his other hand drew her closer to him. They dipped and swirled and marveled at the magic between them, a magic that hadn't disappeared during his absence but had only grown stronger.

His eyes locked on hers, as if he, too, was trying to

decipher what was happening between them, as if he also feared feelings so openly volatile.

Lauren forced words, to try to dispel some of the tension between them. "You returned early, Captain."

"There was a very opportune fog, and, besides, I had a special incentive," he replied, making it quite clear he meant her. "I didn't expect you to be with Clay."

There was a note of inquiry in his voice, and something else. Something like jealousy, or disappointment. Lauren didn't know which, but the thought of the latter hurt.

Lauren met his eyes. "He thought I might enjoy it."

"He thought *he* might enjoy it," Adrian retorted.

Lauren lowered her gaze to his shoulders. She wished momentarily that she were better at flirting, but then she really didn't want to flirt with him. They were, in some way, beyond that. She knew that. She also knew how dangerous that realization was.

"I've never been to a ball like this," she said finally, feeling a bit guilty about having come with Clay although she knew she really had no reason to feel that way.

Adrian had been scowling ever so slightly, and now his expression lightened. "Then I'm sorry I wasn't the first to bring you. You look exceedingly lovely, you know. Much too lovely for Clay."

"Are you friends?"

"Once upon a time," he answered, after a slight hesitation.

"And now?"

"I'm thinking about it," he replied, with that amused smile that disguised what he was really thinking.

There was meaning in the words that Lauren didn't want to probe. She changed the subject. "Was it a successful trip?"

"Yes," he said, but Lauren felt him hesitate for the briefest moment.

Lauren felt a tightening inside, her emotions in conflict. She felt pleasure that he was safe, yet also an almost sickening sense of failure.

"When did you get in?"

"Two hours ago."

"And you came right here?"

"I went to Jeremy's first. I had this very odd compulsion to see a young lady."

"Odd?"

"Odd," he confirmed.

Lauren swallowed deeply, wanting her heart to slow its frantic pace. She wished the dance would end—and she wanted it to go on forever.

She wasn't sure how she felt when the former wish was granted. The music stopped, and Adrian bowed regally to her. "Must I return you to Clay?"

"You must." The voice came from behind her, and Lauren didn't miss the edge of irritation in the usually soft, pleasant drawl of Clay Harding. "And congratulations. I take it you didn't have any difficulties."

"None going in. There was dense fog, and they obviously weren't expecting anyone."

"And coming out?"

He shrugged. The silence told Clay there had been trouble, but it wasn't to be discussed in front of a lady.

Adrian gave them both a wry smile and excused himself. "I see some friends."

Lauren's gaze followed him as he strode over to several men in the corner and took a glass from a tray held by one of the many waiters. Despite his straight back, he looked tired, strained, and she wondered exactly how difficult the run had actually been.

The rest of the evening was a blur. Adrian departed the dance shortly after he'd joined the group of men, and with him went the enchantment of the evening. Lauren merely went through the motions of talking and smiling, every minute wishing she were with Adrian, yet knowing that such wishes were folly in the extreme.

Adrian walked to the Royal Victoria from Government House. He maintained rooms there, as did his first mate and pilot, on a permanent basis. Many of the other crew members used rooming houses around town.

He quickly changed clothes and berated himself for a fool for stopping at the ball. He had known about it for several weeks but had not planned to attend. Adrian usually hated such affairs, but when he had stopped by the Cases' home and was told everyone was at the ball, he didn't stop to think. He had—damn it—just wanted to see her. He hadn't stopped to think she might be with another man—particularly Clay Harding.

Adrian remembered the bet and cursed himself for making it. If he hadn't been so damned tired that day . . .

As he was now. But he wanted to stop by the hospital and see how Terrence was faring. On arrival in Nassau, he had seen to the man's delivery to the small island hospital, and had heard the verdict: Terrence would probably lose his left leg. Adrian had comforted the man, who had been with him over a year, and had assured him that he would have enough money to establish a small tavern in England. It had been the man's dream, and now it would become true, but at a terrible price.

He stopped at the hospital. Terrence had been given morphine and was asleep. Adrian stood by the man's bed for several moments before cursing silently to himself. One of his fellow captains had once compared blockade running to riding the lightning. This time, the lightning had burned.

He left the hospital and strode to the *Specter*, which was tied to the wharf and was already being unloaded. New ships with cargo would arrive on the morrow: goods from England, France, Spain. All destined for a supply-hungry South. He wondered idly when the cannon would arrive.

The ship was alive with lights, and many of his crew members were still aboard. He stopped at his cabin and retrieved an irate Socrates, then found Wade.

"Terrence?" his first mate asked him.

"The doctor says he'll probably lose that leg. I asked him to wait a few days, and he agreed, but at the first sign of infection, he'll go ahead and amputate."

"We'll need two more men."

"I know."

"It shouldn't be any problem. There's not a sailor in Nassau who wouldn't prefer to serve with you."

"After getting one man killed and making another a cripple?" The question was bitter.

"Don't blame yourself, Captain. It was just damned bad luck."

"I shouldn't have tried a run at this time."

Moodily, Adrian leaned against the smokestack, and thought idly what an oddity it was. Designed specifically for blockade runners, the smokestack was retractable, just as the masts were short, to keep the ship's silhouette as invisible as possible.

His glance swept over the rest of the cargo-laden ship, past the spots on deck that had been cleansed of blood to the splintered railings. They would be repaired in the next several days. But Terrence's leg could not be so easily fixed, nor could John Green be brought back from the dead.

Wade remained silent. He had been with Adrian a long time, originally as second mate on the trader when Adrian was first mate. Then he'd followed Adrian to blockade running and had become his first officer. And he trusted Adrian as he trusted no other man. Perhaps, he thought as he looked at Adrian's tortured face, because the captain cared about his men as no other captain he'd ever sailed with.

The captain was a strange one, though. He would allow people to get so close, and no further. The crew all liked him, and he often drank with them and kidded with individual members, but there was always a part of him that remained secret, a dark, brooding part that remained alone and separate.

As he was now.

And there was, Wade knew, nothing he could say to break that mood.

"I'll start looking for new men tomorrow," he said.

Adrian nodded.

"I'll narrow them down to a few," Wade continued. Adrian always made the final selection. It was imperative that the twenty-four-man crew be cohesive, that all members work easily together in those tense hours of running the blockade.

Adrian merely nodded again, and Wade left, knowing he could offer little comfort.

Minutes later, Wade watched as his captain, shoulders slightly slumped, and Socrates descended the gangplank. His captain, Wade reflected, had many friends, an easy manner, a way with people . . . and yet sometimes Adrian Cabot, Lord Ridgely, seemed like the most solitary man Wade had ever met.

Lauren felt curiously empty after Clay took her home from the dance.

The Cinderella feeling, like the carriage and gown in the fairy tale, had disappeared. While she had at first enjoyed the adventure and color of the event, she had been filled with desolation from the moment Adrian had left the ball.

There had been, she recalled, a certain disappointment in his eyes when he'd realized she had been with Clay Harding. She couldn't help but feel he was disappointed in her, and that she had lost something important.

It was ridiculous, of course. He was her enemy. She was sent here to betray him. He had killed her brother. He was prolonging the war. He was a danger to everything in which she believed.

And yet her mind had separated the two so thoroughly —the handsome, enigmatic, sometimes gentle man who had possibly saved her life and certainly her virtue and the man Mr. Phillips had portrayed to her as an unprincipled war profiteer—that they no longer were the same person.

She had hated the latter. She had lost her heart to the former . . . in a matter of days. In a matter of hours on a crystalline beach that haunted her in its recurring images.

It made no sense, but both facts were true, and Adrian's barely disguised disappointment in her hurt . . . and in a way that few other opinions ever had.

Larry. What should I do? What can I do?

But there was no answer. There would never be an answer again. There would never be a teasing pair of eyes regarding her fondly as he said, "Button, you'll work it out. You always do."

Clay Harding made the Case store one of his first calls the next day. He was not quite sure what had happened last night, but something sure as hell had, and he didn't like thinking it might have been Adrian's brief appearance. But some of Lauren Bradley's brightness had faded after Adrian's departure, and it hadn't returned.

As he entered Jeremy's store, he was delighted to see her there, rather than her uncle. But his delight faded when he failed to see the same light in her eyes that he'd noticed last night when she was dancing with Adrian.

Still, her voice was warmly pleasant as she asked how she could help him.

"Some cheroots," he said, watching her move gracefully to a cabinet. She was wearing a modest gray dress, and her hair was gathered in a neat knot at the base of her neck. She looked subdued and . . . sad.

"And supper tonight?"

She looked up at the offer, her eyes meeting his. "I can help you with the first, but not the second," she said. "Aunt Corinne is planning a tea this afternoon."

"And after?"

A sudden smile lifted the sides of her lips. "And then I think I need some rest. Maryland isn't nearly as gay as Nassau."

"But you did enjoy the dance last night?"

"Yes," she said softly. "I did enjoy it, Captain, and I thank you."

"Tomorrow then?"

She raised her eyes, and they were full of wistfulness that hurt, since he knew it wasn't for him. "No, thank you," she said simply. "I think I should spend some time with my aunt and uncle."

Clay knew then that Adrian, as usual, had won their bet. With resignation, he surrendered halfheartedly. "Some other time, then?"

She nodded absently, which did nothing to appease his ego. "When will you be leaving?" She didn't want to ask the question, but it popped out. Adrian might be leaving at the same time. The harbor was filled with ships now. She wondered how even one more could find room in the protective harbor that lay between New Providence Island and Hog Island.

"A few days. Wish me luck?"

After so much soul-searching, Lauren couldn't bring herself to lie. Even if she wasn't sure it was a lie. She didn't want to see Clay hurt, but neither did she wish the blockade runners success. "I don't think you need it. Nor Captain Cabot." She couldn't keep the words from her mouth.

Cabot again. He shrugged. "I wouldn't agree completely with that. Adrian lost one of his men this last run, and another wounded."

"Oh no!" she exclaimed.

Clay shrugged. "It's not the first time he's been hit. But he always manages to escape."

"But not always those around him?" she asked, a trace of bitterness in her voice that he didn't understand.

"No, not always." He hesitated. He liked her. He liked her a lot, despite her obvious preference for Adrian. "Your uncle said you might be returning to the South. If you need passage . . . I'll take you."

She smiled, a strange sad smile. "Thank you," she said. "I'll remember that."

Blaming business, he left then, after some final pleasantries, and Lauren stood watching his retreating steps. She always said more than she meant to say, but her mind and thoughts were so full of conflicting emotions that they demanded some kind of release, wise or not.

The tea Corinne had planned was an ordeal. Lauren had always been different from other girls. She'd grown up with responsibility, with her father's expectation that she study hard, that she help with his practice. Her companions had been her brother and her brother's friends. She did the womanly tasks required of her, but she'd never enjoyed them, nor had she simpered with other girls about boys, and how best to ensnare them.

And that was all this group talked about. She tried to make the proper responses, but she was profoundly grateful when it was over. All she could think of was Clay's words: Adrian's ship had been hit, members of his crew injured. He had left Charleston during the full moon because of an "incentive," he'd said. Had he really meant her? Had he really risked so much to be with her?

Lauren excused herself from dinner, saying she was tired from the dance. She went to her room and again stared out at the lights below, at the *Specter*, brooding about the man who captained her.

Adrian got drunk that night. Very, very drunk.

He'd had to. He kept hearing Terrence's screams, the sound of the saw as it cut through flesh and bone. He had gone to the hospital that morning and had known immediately that surgery was necessary. His second mate was feverish, sweat dripping down his face.

"Gangrene," the doctor said without preamble. "We have to amputate."

"No," Terrence said. "Don't let 'em, Capt'n."

The plea was heartfelt, and Adrian understood. He didn't know if he himself would want to live with one leg. He leaned over. "Think of your wife, Mary, and the children."

"I am," Terrence cried. "I can't go back 'alf a man."

"A whole man, Terrence. You'll always be a whole man. And you'll have that tavern you always wanted. I'll make sure of it. You can grow old and fat and irascible."

Terrence's pain-filled, terrified eyes closed briefly as he struggled against his fears. A cripple. He would always be a cripple now.

"I don't know, Capt'n."

The doubt, the fear, the pain, stabbed Adrian to the core. He had seen dead and wounded before, during the Crimean War. But they hadn't been "his" men then. They hadn't looked at him with such bloody trust. He forced strength in his voice. "Your family needs you," he said simply. "Don't abandon them." *Like mine abandoned me.*

"Will you stay with me?" Adrian heard the surrender in Terrence's voice.

"Aye," he said.

"If anything . . . 'appens, you'll see to Mary and the children?"

"I will. I swear."

Terrence forced a smile. "It's been an honor serving wi' you, my lordship."

Adrian's brows furrowed together. "I thought we'd dispensed with that long ago, you Irish brigand."

The exchange between them was ritual, almost from the moment they'd met. Terrence Dugan was a superb seaman, but he hated the English. Adrian had tolerated the disrespect, just as he had Socrates's ungratefulness, because he'd admired Terrence's ability, independence, and leadership potential. They had, after a year, reached a point of mutual respect, if not total liking.

"I'm ready, then," Terrence said.

Adrian had stayed. There was morphine, but even that hadn't been enough to prevent the agonized groans. The barely human cries clashed with the terrible grating sound of the saw in a hellish symphony. Adrian had watched from the corner, his hands clenched behind him.

He remained throughout the day, until Terrence had regained consciousness and looked at the flat place under the sheet where his leg should be and wept.

It was past dark when Adrian left, and the only thing he wanted was a bottle and a bottomless glass. He fetched Socrates, who had been left with Johnny on the ship, and visited a small tavern near the Royal Victoria. He also found Clay Harding, the last person he wanted to see.

Adrian was angry. Angry and hostile, as he'd been last night at the dance when he'd discovered Clay with Lauren. The events of this day had done nothing to improve his disposition, and now he glared at Clay.

But Clay was as morose as he was, and barely greeted him as Adrian sat down. Clay glowered at both Adrian and

Socrates, who looked offended and chattered threateningly, before climbing on a chair and looking expectantly at the empty space before him.

A barmaid, who'd confronted Socrates before, approached cautiously, keeping one eye on the beast while trying to smile bewitchingly at Clay.

"Rum," Adrian ordered, "and some fruit."

Socrates started bouncing up and down on the chair, and the girl disappeared quickly. Usually Socrates amused Clay, but now the frown remained set on his face. "Obnoxious beast," he observed.

So Clay hadn't been successful with Lauren. Adrian started cheering up. "Consider it this way," he appeased Clay. "He makes you look good."

The poor jest did nothing to lighten the atmosphere. Clay continued to glare at him.

The bowl of fruit came, along with the rum, and Socrates started eating noisily as Adrian poured a very large portion of liquor for himself.

"Bad day?" The question came from Clay.

"You can say that. And you?"

"You could say that."

They both glowered some more, and then said, almost together, "About that bet . . ." and "I concede."

Adrian's lips twisted into a slight smile. "So soon."

Clay regarded him solemnly, even a bit drunkenly. "I hate to admit it, my friend, but I fear her eyes are for you. Now I would like to know your in-thentions." His voice was slurred.

"Intentions?" Adrian furrowed his eyebrows.

Clay straightened up and glared at him. "I like Miss Lauren. Don't ever hurt her," he added as he lifted his glass and emptied it in one long swallow.

"Gallantry?" Adrian's question was part taunting, part curious. Clay was notorious with the ladies.

Clay regarded him with narrowed eyes. "You're like ice, Adrian."

"I don't feel like ice at the moment."

Clay looked at him closely. Adrian looked tired, in ways that came from more than fatigue. "What happened?"

Adrian shrugged. "I suppose you heard. I took a shot coming out of Charleston. One man died. The other . . . his leg was amputated this afternoon. I don't know if he'll live."

Clay's hands tightened around his own glass. He'd not lost a man yet, but he knew he had been uncommonly lucky. "I'm damned sorry, Adrian."

"The bloody net is tightening," Adrian said.

"If only England . . ."

"But England won't," Adrian said. "Too many people there hate slavery."

"This isn't about slavery."

"Isn't it?" Adrian challenged.

"I don't have slaves. My family doesn't," Clay said heatedly. It was a defense he made often, and he didn't like making it to Adrian.

Adrian's look was wry. "I know why I'm taking chances, Clay. There's something I want very badly. What about you?"

Clay stared at Adrian. They had never talked about their motives before. "Hell," he said, "I don't know."

Adrian knew that Clay did know but didn't want to talk about it. He shrugged, and without further comment they turned their complete attention to rum.

CHAPTER 8

Larry beckoned to her through the fog, his shape forming and dissolving every time she tried to reach out.

He stood on the bow of a ship, his blue uniform covered with blood.

She was on another ship, and she begged to go to him; but the ghostlike images with her paid no attention. "Button," she heard Larry call. "Button." But the voice was dronelike, not real.

The image started disappearing, and she cried out to him. As on the night he died, his pain was her pain. She felt it deep inside her, like a burning sword.

"Larry. Larry." Louder and louder. She could hear the panic in her voice . . .

"Lauren." She felt herself being shaken, but she didn't want to wake. She wanted to hold out her hand to Larry, to bring him back.

"Lauren." Another voice, low and commanding, and the last whisper of her twin disappeared.

Lauren opened her eyes, feeling the wetness as she did. Both Corinne and Jeremy stood there, he holding a candle, she perched on the side of Lauren's bed, her hand touching Lauren's face.

"You've had a bad dream," Corinne said softly. "Poor love."

Lauren looked up at Jeremy. His wrinkled face was even more creased, his eyes tired.

"I'm sorry," she whispered. "I'm sorry I woke you."

"Hush dear," Corinne said, her hand holding tightly to one of Lauren's. "Can you tell us about it?"

Lauren shook her head and sighed. She knew she would sleep no more that night, fearing to dream again.

Socrates woke Adrian early next morning. Payment, Adrian supposed bitterly, for leaving him alone so much in the past few days.

His head felt like the cotton he transported, and his mouth was as dry as the Arabian desert, but he struggled up, slowly and carefully, as if not to jar some very fragile parts of himself.

Adrian always kept a supply of fruit and sea biscuits in the room for Socrates, and now he pacified the monkey with some while he shaved and dressed. There was a great deal to do today, and he needed a clear head to do it.

A clear head?

It felt like a bagful of rotten apples. Groaning, he pledged he would never repeat last night's performance.

He took one last look at his still-red eyes, swore again, and then strode from the room, down the wide stairs to the grand reception area of the hotel. Socrates stayed at his side, as Adrian knew he would. Although the monkey sometimes scampered ahead or inspected someone or something along the way, he never allowed Adrian too far away. Adrian had never needed a leash for Socrates—not for that reason, anyway. His coin usually satisfied other problems: a purloined apple, or an overturned cart, or, once, a watch grabbed from a pocket.

Usually Socrates's misadventures amused him, but now Adrian thought only of getting through the day.

He stopped at the hospital, reassuring himself that Terrence was doing as well as could be expected. The man's lips were clenched tight against the pain, and his eyes often wandered down to the empty place where his leg had been; but he managed a joke and Adrian knew he would be all right.

Adrian then went to the Confederate agent—it was a visit he should have made yesterday.

"I understand I'm to carry a special cargo," he told the agent, a man named Jones.

Jones nodded. He'd received word two days earlier. While Adrian had waited in Charleston, the message had traveled by telegraph from Charleston to Richmond, and then went north by a courier who booked passage on the first ship to Nassau. The cannon was to be readied for the *Specter*.

"Has it arrived?"

"Yesterday," Jones said. "Your timing couldn't be better."

"How much space will the cargo take?"

"Nearly one fourth of your hold. I was . . . we were hoping you could also take in some medicines."

Adrian nodded, only briefly considering the irony of the split cargo. He wished his head were clearer as he gave the agent a capacity, and the man nodded his thanks.

Adrian would still have more than half of his cargo space empty. He spent the morning on the docks inspecting incoming goods, choosing items that would bring the highest prices. The result was a combination of the fanciful and practical: champagne, French brandy, and silks; nails for coffins; needles; corsets; and salt, which was purchased from a New England merchant.

Much of the day had passed when he completed his bargaining. Most of the cotton he'd carried from Charleston had been unloaded. The new cargo would soon be loaded, and the *Specter* would leave the wharf and anchor out in the harbor, waiting out the bright moon with the other blockade runners.

Four days with little to do.

As if driven by a force stronger than himself, he found himself walking quickly toward Jeremy Case's store.

She was not there, but Jeremy was.

"Lauren?"

Jeremy hesitated. "She's resting."

Adrian's still-aching head absorbed the words, the tightness in his stomach becoming increasingly painful. "Is anything wrong?"

Jeremy regarded him gravely for several seconds. "I think she misses home, her family. She had a nightmare last night."

"Perhaps I should leave then." The words were part question. He didn't want to go. He thought of Lauren's smile, her eyes with all their questions, and he ached for her. It was an unfamiliar feeling, this strong affinity with someone else. He had worked hard to divorce himself from strong personal ties, and he'd succeeded admirably. Never having known love within his own family, he didn't really understand Lauren's grief. But he'd seen pain in her eyes when she had spoken of her father and brother, and now he knew a compelling need to make her smile, to chase away the unhappy memories.

"I'll ask her," Jeremy said.

His lips smiled, although Adrian noticed the smile didn't quite reach his eyes. Funny, he'd never noticed that before. Adrian was usually quite good at reading people, but now he felt something odd, something hesitant, in the storekeeper, as if . . .

But then he was gone, and Adrian dismissed the thought as only imagination, the result of a thoroughly mistreated body. Socrates was prowling around the store, finding a licorice stick and helping himself, smacking his lips loudly until, almost unwillingly, Adrian smiled. Licorice was a weakness of Socrates's, and he always ended up with black stickiness all over himself, but the animal grinned with so much pleasure that Adrian felt some of his tension draining away. He picked up several more sticks for later, and placed a coin on the counter to pay for them.

Footsteps sounded on the steps, and he turned around, but his reactions were slower than Socrates's. The monkey ran toward the stairs and threw himself into Lauren's arms. Adrian heard her soft laughter, then her greeting to Socrates, and winced as he knew what would happen next.

There was a smacking sound, and Adrian looked up to see Lauren's cheek covered with a sticky black substance. Her hands were likewise covered, and Adrian expected horror at the very least.

"Socrates!" he roared, and received an indignant glare from the monkey. Adrian closed his eyes in despair for a moment, then heard Lauren's giggles, which erupted into laughter. He thought he'd never heard anything quite as engaging.

"Don't scold him," Lauren said. "I like licorice too."

Socrates grinned happily at Adrian as he scampered down, but one of his hands continued to hold Lauren's.

Adrian took out his handkerchief. "You look like a chimney sweep," he observed solemnly. "And you really shouldn't forgive him."

Lauren looked up into his face, her own eyes dancing. "I never had a pet," she said. "I always wanted one, but Father said there shouldn't be animals around the house where he treated patients. He . . ."

Her eyes suddenly clouded as she remembered how she and Larry had begged, and finally worked out an arrangement to share a pony with one of Larry's friends. Larry had liked animals too . . .

Socrates pulled on her hand, as if sensing her change of mood, and Lauren had to smile.

"He's wonderful," she said.

"You're a crowd of one who thinks so," Adrian said, his headache beginning to dissipate.

"Don't you?"

Wryly, his eyes traveled from the licorice-covered paws to Socrates's beady eyes, which were now fixed adoringly on Lauren. "Well, he has good taste," he said, avoiding the question.

Lauren laughed again, and some of the sadness left her eyes. "In licorice, you mean."

"And in friends."

Lauren blushed, that almost shy, becoming blush that he was now expecting.

In the sudden silence, Adrian asked what he knew he'd come for, though he had not admitted it until this very moment. "I was hoping you could join me this evening for supper." He saw denial in her face, and he hurriedly added, "Myself and Socrates, of course."

"He joins you at all meals?"

"Often. And much to the dismay of other diners." Adrian grinned. "His table manners sometimes leave a bit to be desired. But innkeepers like him. He pays well."

"And you?"

"Well known for my miserly ways."

She couldn't help but smile at him; he was so completely captivating with that wicked expression. Her heart bounced in the most uncontrolled way as her gaze met his very, very blue eyes.

Shaken by the intensity that flared in them, she sought to defuse the heightened awareness between them, to relieve the pressure that was climbing so rapidly. "So Socrates is the welcomed one."

"Sadly," Adrian admitted with a feigned wistful expression.

"I've been warned against charming profligate monkeys."

"Obviously it did little good," he countered, as he regarded her smudged face with wry humor. His hand, still holding the handkerchief, went to her face, and very gently, carefully, wiped some of the black from her face. His fingers touched her skin and hovered there, neither Lauren nor Adrian moving, their gazes locked.

Lightning flashed between them. His fingers burned from the touch, yet he couldn't move them, couldn't turn his eyes from her flashing ones, couldn't control the violent storm that was encompassing both of them. And most frightening of all, he didn't want to.

For the first time in years, he didn't want to rule, or control, or command. He wanted merely to ride out the storm, to feel its fury. And glory. He felt his fingers tremble as something clouded her eyes, filling them with fear and something else, something almost . . . guilty.

He didn't want her to move. He wanted this singular moment to last, but it was Lauren who shattered it, her slender body stiffening, her eyes growing wary, her mouth trembling as she tried to shape words.

His hand fell reluctantly from her face.

Her own hand replaced it, as if soothing a burned place, and making the black licorice smudge even worse. "I'll be back in a moment," she said shakily. "Your handkerchief, I think, could be best used elsewhere." Her eyes went meaningfully down to Socrates, who had released her hand and was now peering curiously at a bolt of cloth. Adrian reached him before the animal could touch anything, and found his own hands suddenly patterned with black.

"I'll bring you some water," Lauren said lightly; but her eyes had clouded. Adrian knew she had distanced herself from him, as she had several previous times. He wondered about that sudden reserve, as she whirled around and disappeared up the stairs.

While he waited, Adrian looked around the store. Jeremy had a little of everything—except, he noticed, guns or ammunition. There were music boxes, fine wool shawls, exquisite lace, imported candies, and miniatures that, Adrian thought, probably did well among seamen heading home. There were cigars and fine brandies, both items popular with the blockade runners, and he knew that many stopped in here frequently.

Lauren was back with a bowl of water and soap, and Adrian awkwardly tried to clean his wayward pet while Lauren watched. Some of the smile returned to her lips as more water went on Adrian than Socrates.

Adrian's lips finally cracked too, and Lauren took over.

Socrates stayed still for her when he didn't for Adrian, and Adrian wondered what magic she held in her hands.

"You never answered," he said.

Lauren looked at him gravely, a question in her eyes.

"Whether you'll have supper with me? Will you?" he asked, holding his breath like a schoolboy as he realized how much he wanted her to say yes. After two days with Terrence, he needed her company, the pleasure he found in her presence. The pleasure, and the laughter.

And even the lightning. Perhaps that most of all.

"No," she said, a slight quiver in her voice. "I can't today, but perhaps . . ."

"Tomorrow? I can rent a carriage. There's a fine beach not far away."

She took one last swipe at Socrates's licorice-mustached mouth, and stood straight again. There was something hesitant, even secretive, in her eyes as she regarded him carefully. "I don't know . . . Jeremy might need me." They were both aware then that Jeremy had not returned after sending Lauren down.

The same errant frustration that had struck him the night of the dance returned. "I think we can persuade him," he said. He wanted to spend time alone with her, to explore the explosive feelings so new to him.

Lauren knew that he could. It would help Jeremy's plans. She wondered whether they were any longer *her* plans. She was terribly afraid that they would be even less her plans if she spent any more time alone with Adrian. She finally nodded her assent. "If he agrees," she said.

Jeremy was indeed upstairs, and he readily agreed to the picnic.

"I'm not . . . sure," Lauren told him.

"I heard something yesterday," he said softly. "Our captain is carrying cannon on the next trip. There's a battle brewing, a big one, and we can't allow those guns to reach the Confederacy."

Lauren felt her heart drop.

"It could mean hundreds of lives, Lauren." He looked at her.

"All right," she managed. "I'll go."

Adrian left minutes later, saying he would call for her the next day at midmorning. He turned just once to look back, and he wondered whether he imagined the mist he thought he saw in her eyes.

Adrian ran into Clay again that evening at the Royal Victoria.

Adrian grinned.

"Your mood has improved considerably," Clay observed with envy. *His* head still hurt like hell.

"Believe it or not, I'm going on a picnic tomorrow."

"A picnic, for God's sake!"

Adrian shrugged. "Courting's bloody hell."

"That's what you're doing?"

Adrian grimaced. "Damned if I know what I'm doing. And it isn't as if there's much else to do. Three more days before we can leave."

Clay suddenly tensed. "I heard about that cannon you're carrying."

Adrian closed his eyes in frustration. But he should have known. Nothing on this bloody island was secret. And he knew well there were Union spies in Nassau, some obvious and some not so obvious.

"The Yankee authorities are raising hell about it," Clay continued. "Don't be surprised to receive a summons from the governor."

"A good reason to get out of sight, then," replied Adrian.

Clay sighed. He tried to remember parts of their conversation last night. He thought he had asked Adrian's intentions. Had Adrian replied?

"Adrian, are you sure you know what you're doing?"

His grin returned. "Do any of us?" he asked lightly as he left the room.

The picnic was postponed. A crewman from the *Specter* dropped by the store with a note and apology. One of

Adrian's crewmen had been injured days ago, and his condition had worsened. Adrian had to stay with him.

Lauren sat in her room and tried to read. But all she could understand, or think about, was a quote about being hoisted on one's own sword or some such thing.

Although she had been hesitant about accepting Adrian's offer, she had, once her decision was made, looked forward to it. Not only looked forward, but more. Expectation and optimism had bubbled inside her all night at the prospect of being with Adrian.

And then the message had come, and she had felt a crippling disappointment for herself, and a deep sadness for Adrian's own pain.

Throughout the day, she could think of nothing but Adrian. Adrian, who cared enough about his men to put them before anything else. Again, the image didn't fit the portrait Mr. Phillips had painted.

However, nothing about Adrian Cabot was simple, she'd learned.

A man who trafficked in death, yet who spent days sitting with an injured man.

A lord of England who apparently preferred the companionship of a monkey to that of his fellow man.

A noted rake, according to gossip, who had saved her from rape or worse and then treated her with the utmost courtesy.

A murderer who took joy in the smallest of sea creatures.

And a man who seemed open and easy, but who, Lauren had slowly discovered, was just the opposite. He kept a great deal to himself, including his deepest feelings.

Or was it only because *she* was hiding so much that she imagined others capable of such deceit?

She looked out over the Caribbean sea, to the pure blues that contrasted to the now-murky darkness of her life. She didn't like the comparison.

I won't do it, she thought suddenly. I'll tell Jeremy tonight that I won't do it. And I'll go home where I belong. Adrian will never know.

But Lauren knew *she* would know. That she would live with his smile the rest of her life.

Dear Lord, how much she wanted him! It was an ache in her body, in her very soul, that she somehow knew would never go away. She remembered his comment several days ago, when they were on the beach. He'd said she was an honest woman, and she'd asked whether that was so important. "Yes," he'd answered so directly.

Honest. What would he think when he discovered she had lied to him from the very beginning, that she had lied to deliberately trap him?

"Forgive me, Larry," she whispered in the soft sea breeze. "But I can't. I just can't."

Terrence died the day after the canceled picnic. Except for some business he could not delegate, Adrian stayed with him. He ignored several urgent summonses from the governor.

The infection had spread, rapidly and virulently, running its course in even faster time than usual. The doctor could merely stand by and shake his head.

Much to the doctor's distress, Adrian brought Socrates several times, but Terrence was one of the few crewmen who had truly liked the monkey. It was, Adrian commented, because Irishmen and Socrates had a lot in common, bad tempers not the least of it.

Terrence had forced a smile. "Treacherous Englishmen," he claimed, "have caused such to be true."

They talked about England and Ireland, trading joking insults, as the lines in Terrence's face grew deeper, as the struggle to keep from crying out became more difficult. But still they pretended that nothing was wrong, that nothing was going to change—until Terrence lapsed into bouts of unconsciousness. And then Adrian was just there, not wanting Terrence to die alone. Just before the end, Terrence opened his eyes, and there was a clarity in his eyes that hadn't been there the past few hours. "My family?"

"I'll take care of them," Adrian whispered. "I swear."

"An Irish oath?" There was a grimace meant to be a smile.

"Aye," Adrian said, his hand holding Terrence's, feeling his pain through the bone-crunching grip of the Irishman's fingers. And then the fingers relaxed, and the man's eyes closed.

Fighting an aching despair, Adrian made arrangements for Terrence's burial, and then found himself walking along the docks toward the back of Jeremy's store.

The sun was setting, an incandescent ball of fire falling into the sea, sending waves of blood-red color reflecting in the sea. The moon was already visible, looking so luminous he thought he could reach up and poke a finger through it. Any other time, he would have appreciated the contrast: the fiery departure of the sun and the cool perfection of the early evening moon.

But not now. He just saw the fire and blood.

And he needed something more. He needed peace. He needed something to touch, something real. Suddenly, it seemed everything in his life was elusive, mere wisps that he would grab and find slipping from his fingers.

He saw her then, in her uncle's garden, standing under an old cotton tree, surrounded by bright blooms that gave her own subdued coloring a serenity he craved. Adrian had never understood his attraction to Lauren until now.

She was real. Not merely a figment of young hot desires as Sylvia had been, but a flesh-and-blood woman who made him laugh and feel pleasure, who warmed a place that had been empty for a long time. As she did now, making some of the cold, hurting pain of Terrence's death soften and become bearable.

He walked slowly toward the gate, wondering only slightly that she was there, as if waiting for him, as if knowing he needed someone, needed her.

Her face, the lovely composed face that was so expressive, that so easily reflected pleasure at Socrates's antics, or anger the night she was attacked, or passion as she had those few electrifying moments in the store, now had a wistful look, the sad, grieving look that touched the core of his heart. For a moment, there was something else in her face and he was afraid she would flee, but then she moved toward him, and they met at the gate.

Almost unconsciously he opened the waist-high gate and entered, saying nothing, but holding out his arms in anguished need, and she, sensing it, walked into them.

Adrian held her tight, letting her soft, flowery scent wash away the stench of the hospital, the odor of death and decay, letting her touch soothe and heal in a way no one else's ever had, not when he was a child, not when he was a man.

"He died, Lauren," Adrian found himself saying. "Terrence died."

He didn't have to say anything else. He'd known he wouldn't. Instead, he felt her arms tighten around him, felt the comfort and understanding in her embrace, and he lowered his head, his lips touching the soft skin of her face, moving, moving until they found her mouth, and felt the yielding of her lips.

There was desperation in the kiss, a mutual desperation that was explosive. Lips were almost frantic with the need to touch and feel and taste, to comfort and be comforted, to explore and be explored.

The need was burning straight through Adrian, like nothing else in his life. Not Ridgely. Not the pain of constant rejection. Nothing mattered but Lauren Bradley and the way she made him feel.

Her body melded to his as if made to do so, and her lips opened, allowing his tongue entrance as her hands went up around his neck, soothing, caressing, demanding things he suspected she wasn't consciously aware of. He closed his eyes for a moment, allowing himself to be swept away as if in the eye of a hurricane. Electric tension vibrated all around them, the now-familiar lightning vibrant in the air, glorious and brilliant and splendid.

Adrian didn't want to let go. He never wanted to let go. His hands moved along her back, feeling the slender curves of her body through the curve of the dress, and a lock of honey-colored hair rubbed against his face like silken threads. He'd kissed a hundred girls or more, and bedded a number of them, and yet none had ever touched him as she did. Lauren had reached him and touched the deep private part of him he'd always kept locked tight against intrusion; now the fabric of that protection was ripped away, and he felt raw and naked.

But he didn't care. For some reason, he trusted her as he hadn't trusted before. His lips turned greedy as they plundered her mouth, as his tongue tentatively, and then more surely, probed and tickled and explored. And she responded each time, her own body a natural adjunct to his, bending and yielding; her hands explored his back much as he had hers.

Lauren felt mindless . . . like a puppet guided by feelings she couldn't control. Of all the things she had done in her life, this was the most foolish, the most dangerous.

But she couldn't move, couldn't act independently of all the emotions she felt. Nothing in the world could have affected her as much as Adrian's face when he'd entered the garden, the deep grief in it, the crooked smile that was no smile at all but only a futile attempt at one.

And he had come to her!

His hands were first rough with need, but then gentled just as she discovered that she wanted the roughness, wanted the implied need in it. Because she understood it. She wanted to clutch him with all her might, to keep him close and feel his warmth, ease his wounds.

An honest woman. Lauren knew that was what Adrian thought she was.

She suddenly jerked away, the taste of his mouth, of his tongue, now a part of her. She jerked away, the sweetness turning to bitter fruit, to the acid taste of betrayal.

"Lauren," Adrian said in a low, confused voice.

She looked at him like a wounded fawn, her misted eyes like the green-gray of a storm-tossed ocean.

And then she gathered her skirts and ran inside before he could see the tears that were starting to run down her cheeks.

CHAPTER 9

She'd run away again.

Lauren sat on her bed and allowed the tears to flow. It was the first time she'd cried since she'd heard of Larry's death.

Once again, she felt a terrible loss, made especially painful by the sense that this one was partly of her own making, caused by her own stubborn, headstrong actions. When she had taken on this task, she had not considered the human beings involved. Moreover, by being true to one part of herself, she was betraying another.

And she didn't know how to make things right. So she'd run again, something she'd never done before meeting Adrian Cabot.

Lauren didn't know how long she sat there before a soft knock came at the door, summoning her to supper. Again she felt like a traitor. This time to Jeremy Case, because some time tonight she must tell him she could no longer do what she'd promised.

Supper turned out to be a somber affair despite Corinne's attempt to make it otherwise. Lauren felt Jeremy's eyes on her; his scrutiny was knowing, not condemning but sad.

Lauren told the Cases that she'd seen Captain Cabot, that one of his crew had died and that was why he had not accompanied her on the picnic earlier.

Corinne looked at Lauren with compassion. "This war . . . I'll be so glad when it ends."

"Amen," Jeremy said softly.

Lauren wanted to add her own plea, but how could she? She was failing them all. Suddenly she pushed back her chair and, her voice choked, asked to be excused.

She bolted for the door, for the garden, for air.

Lauren reached the cotton tree, where she had kissed Adrian, and stopped, hearing Jeremy's voice behind her, calling softly. She turned around, and her eyes met his. "I can't, Jeremy. I can't go through with my part."

His hand reached out to touch her arm. "You must, Lauren. We can't let that cannon get through. Hundreds of Union lives lie in the balance."

"No. I won't. You should have seen him tonight. He was hurting."

"We all hurt, Lauren. But I suspect your captain less than most."

Lauren stiffened. "Jeremy," she began to explain. "I thought . . . Mr. Phillips said . . . but he's not like that. He saved my life, and . . . well, he cares about people."

Jeremy hesitated, hating himself for what he was about to do. "Your brother?"

Lauren looked at him miserably, then looked away, guilt weighing on her again, guilt at betraying Larry . . . at betraying Adrian. She would have to betray one or the other.

But Adrian was alive, and Larry wasn't.

"There's something else," Jeremy said quietly.

There was an edge in his voice, an inflection that made her stiffen. "What do you mean?"

"I didn't want to tell you this, Lauren, but he's not the man you apparently think he is."

Her hazel eyes met his clouded blue ones in question.

"I heard about it yesterday." Jeremy hesitated. "I didn't want to tell you, but your Captain Cabot and Clay Harding . . . they have a bet . . . on which one could . . ."

Lauren felt herself go icy cold, as if she had stepped out of herself and was looking at a statue. "Which one could . . . what?"

Jeremy looked at her steadily. "Bed you. The prize was dinner for their crews, loser to pay."

"Crews?" she echoed in a hollow voice. A bet. A contest. Common knowledge. "No," she whispered, as she remembered the past few days. Clay's attention, Adrian's annoyance at finding her with Clay. It fit. Everything fit, even the fact that she had never been courted this way before.

It wasn't because she was suddenly a swan. She was the stakes in a wager. A wager between two arrogant men who were playing a game, just as they threw coins out windows for amusement. Just as carelessly, just as mindlessly, just as heartlessly.

Dear God, what a fool she had been.

Lauren closed her eyes, thinking of Adrian's dark blue eyes that had seemed so full of grief hours ago. A trick. A bid for sympathy. Was that all it was? Hadn't Phillips warned her?

She felt herself shiver in the warm air. But the coldness was in her brain, in her heart. A numbness that blotted out the pain she knew was there, that she knew she would soon feel in all its intensity.

And she had been worried about betraying *him*.

Still, a part of her didn't want to believe it. Jeremy wanted something too, needed something. Perhaps he was lying. He, too, wanted something from her.

But when his eyes met hers, and she saw his own guilt and compassion, she knew he was telling the truth.

She sank down on the bench in the garden, her gaze falling to the ground. She meant nothing to Adrian Cabot.

She had no need to worry about betraying him. None at all. And she'd almost betrayed herself, and everything she believed in, for a mirage.

She felt the icy numbness lift, felt the pain and disillusionment and grief. She looked up at Jeremy.

"What do you want me to do?"

"Get aboard the *Specter*. Disable it." Jeremy's voice was flat as he said words he didn't want to say.

Lauren closed her eyes. She remembered the sessions she'd had with Mr. Phillips, and then with some ship engineers. She had been told to try to get passage on Adrian's ship, but at that time the intent was mostly to discover where he hid along the coast. Yet she was also shown how to disable a ship with little more than a handful of sand. She'd never thought she would have to do it.

Cannon. Adrian. Larry. The images all moved in a macabre dance in her mind. "Adrian . . ." The name came to her lips with difficulty. She had loved the sound. Now she thought back to her Latin lessons. Adrian—"the dark one." She had thought him sunlight, but the name had been rightly given. "How? He said he doesn't take passengers."

Jeremy turned away from her. Dear God, how he hated this. "If you threatened to go with Captain Harding . . . ?"

"He'll know," Lauren whispered. "Captain Cabot will know something's changed with me." She couldn't bear to say Adrian.

"Lauren, I wish I could help you. I wish you could just go home. But we need you now."

Lauren turned on Jeremy. She felt used by everyone, even if she had asked to help. In Washington, she'd felt noble. Here, she just felt . . . dirty. "Why do you care so much?"

Jeremy hesitated. But he owed it to her; he was asking a great deal, and he knew it.

"I'm from Virginia, Lauren. My father was an overseer on a plantation. I grew up with the slave children. One boy was a particular friend. Before he was sent to the fields, we went fishing and hunting together, though he was never allowed to hold a gun. When he was ten, he was sent to the fields, while I was allowed to attend classes with the plantation owner's children. Late at night, in secret, I used to teach him what I had learned. It was against the law to 'educate' slaves. My father would have beaten me if he'd known."

Jeremy's voice drifted off, and the usual brightness of the blue eyes dimmed. "I was trained as an overseer, while Cato worked the fields—though he was the smarter of the two of us. He grasped my lessons far faster than I did. But teaching him was the worst thing I could have done. It only fired his hunger to learn more—and to learn more, he had to escape."

Lauren listened, mesmerized. So Jeremy, too, had a buried pain.

"He fell in love with another slave, who was sold away. Cato escaped and went after her, intending to take her North with him. I helped. I thought I was helping. But"—he shrugged hopelessly before he continued in the same tight voice—"someone followed me—my brother . . ."

The pain had turned into agony, and his voice was barely audible. "The three of us were taken by slave-catchers. They hanged Cato. I was sent to prison for five years."

"And the woman . . ."

"I don't know," Jeremy said hopelessly. "After I was released from prison, there was no place to go. My family had disowned me, and God knows I could never face my brother again without . . . trying to kill him. I couldn't stay in a country that tolerated slavery, that condoned what had happened. I found a berth on a ship headed for Nassau, and just stayed here. I got a job with a merchant, married his daughter, and eventually became his partner."

"Corinne . . ."

He nodded. "She doesn't know anything about my time in prison. I could never tell her."

Lauren was silent, thinking how much Jeremy Case had suffered for doing what he thought was right, for following his convictions. He was still doing that. He could lose his business, even his life, to some hothead, if his sympathies and role were known.

Lauren had always been opposed to slavery, but in a distant sort of a way. It had never actually seemed real to her, but now it became very real as she thought about a man and woman in love, one sold away and the other dying because he wanted to be with her. No matter how she felt about Adrian Cabot, how could she not do everything she could to end that evil, to help halt the terrible bloodshed now going on? She *could* act. She *could* pretend. She *could* do whatever was necessary.

She straightened her back and put her hand on Jeremy's. "I'll do it," she said.

His eyes looked at her sadly. "I wish it wasn't necessary."

Without any more words, they rose from the bench and, each lost in private thoughts, went inside.

The very ease with which Jeremy's plan worked deepened Lauren's guilt.

When Adrian appeared the next day, she met his eyes and told him she was ready to go back home to the South and do her part. "Will you take me?"

He seemed stunned. "But I thought you planned to stay here a while."

"I did," she said, "but I've been thinking how selfish that is. My father was a doctor. I know nursing. And the South needs those skills. I just can't sit here and wait the war out."

"I don't take passengers," he reminded her evenly, and Lauren knew he believed her and accepted her reasoning. She tried to dismiss the ugly snake of shame beginning to writhe inside.

Think of the wager, she told herself, as she met his worried blue eyes, as her gaze raked over his grim mouth. Both of them ignored Socrates, who looked from one to another as if understanding that a battle of wills was transpiring.

"Then I'll go with Clay," she said, just as evenly. "I'd

rather go to Charleston . . . I have friends there, but . . ."

"Damn it, Lauren. The South's no place for you now. Neither are those charnel houses they call hospitals."

"*You* take chances," she countered.

"That's different."

"Because you do it for money?" Lauren hadn't meant to say that, but the anger that had been seeding inside her was now begging to be harvested.

They had gone into the garden after meeting in the store, and now Adrian stepped backward and leaned against the cotton tree, his face blank, although she saw a muscle working in his cheek.

"Yes," he said flatly. "I do it for money. Does that offend you?"

Lauren knew she had said too much. Though he looked relaxed, there was a restless violence radiating from him, and she wondered whether it was from her question or from the natural beginning of nerves preceding a run. Jeremy had warned her not to go far by herself these days. All of the runners would be leaving soon, and their crews were volatile with a kind of excited anxiety. The waiting, she had been told over and over again, was the worst part of blockade running, and by the time the wait was over, emotions were at a high pitch. But she hadn't expected Adrian to experience such human feelings. Except for the surface appearance of grief yesterday, he always appeared so sure of himself, so much in control, so much the gamemaster.

"Does it?" He repeated the words again.

Lauren saw the quiet anger in his eyes, and she couldn't answer. She'd already said too much.

"I thought women liked money, no matter where it came from," he said, and Lauren heard the sudden bitterness in his voice. It startled her even more than the suggestion of anger. She didn't understand either.

"You're angry," she observed.

"I don't like being judged," Adrian replied. Especially by you, he wanted to add, but he couldn't. He had been judged all his life, mostly to his detriment, especially by his father. He hadn't expected it from Lauren, not after yesterday. But something was different about her today, although she was trying to hide it.

"I'm sorry," Lauren said. "I wasn't aware I was doing that. But aren't you judging all women?"

Adrian flashed her that dazzling smile of his. There was chagrin in it, and a bit of mischief. "Aye," he admitted. "I suppose I was."

For a moment, Lauren had doubted Jeremy, doubted his information that there had been a wager, but Adrian's barb about women had vanquished that slight doubt.

"Will you take me?" she asked again.

Lauren felt his touch, so light, so very light, as his fingers made a trail down her face to her chin, lifting it until her gaze met his directly.

"You are so determined?"

Lauren felt her skin burn, her heart quicken like a roll of drums, her breath catch in her throat. She was winning.

And she didn't want to win.

"Yes," she managed to say.

"I'll take you, then," he said softly. "I think you'll be safer with me, in a civilian ship."

The snake of guilt crept around her heart, squeezing it even tighter than it already was.

"Thank you."

"I'm not sure you should be doing this."

Lauren wasn't either, but she was committed now. Wholly and irretrievably.

"Lauren . . ."

The sound of her name on his lips was so soft. She looked up at him. His face was somber, even a bit puzzled. "I'm sorry if I . . . upset you yesterday. I shouldn't have come here then."

He shouldn't have come when he'd needed someone. That was what he was saying. But could she believe him? Could she ever believe him again? And if she did? It wouldn't change anything. So she chose not to believe him.

Mr. Phillips had said he wouldn't be hurt, only detained a few weeks. He would lose his ship, and cargo, but that was part of the risk he took for such large profits. Part of the gamble.

And he liked gambling.

"When will we leave?" Her tone was so much steadier than her heart was. Her hands were buried in the folds of her dress so he couldn't see the way they clenched and unclenched.

"I'll come for you tomorrow evening," he said, his eyes searching, puzzled.

"Will you sail then?"

He shrugged, giving her neither a yes or no.

She was saved from any other conversation by Socrates, who had climbed the cotton tree and now leaped down next to her, holding out his arms to be picked up.

Adrian shook his head. "I've never seen him take to anyone as he has you. He'll be glad to have you along."

Lauren couldn't resist her next words. She wanted to hear them even though she knew how unwise it was. "And his master?"

"No," he said frankly. "It's dangerous, Lauren. And you're going to have to do everything I tell you, when I tell you. I want your promise on that."

She swallowed. So many promises. All of them conflicting. "Yes," she finally said.

Adrian was suddenly all business. "I have to go, some business with the governor. I'll be here tomorrow night at eight . . . if you still want to go. Think about it carefully, Lauren."

She nodded. He had no idea how carefully she would think about it.

He leaned down, his lips brushing hers. Lightly, this time. And with control.

"Good day, Lauren."

Adrian could no longer ignore the messages from the governor, and went to see him.

"I have a disturbing report, Captain Cabot," the governor said.

Adrian furrowed his eyebrows together. "How does that concern me?" He was already prepared; the bill of lading and description of cargo papers were in his hand.

"The U.S. Government claims you're shipping cannon. You realize, of course, war goods are strictly prohibited by the Neutrality Act."

"Of course, Governor. But someone's mistaken. I have a list of my entire cargo here. Furniture, dress goods, women's needles. Corsets. Brandy. Surely you don't consider those military articles."

The governor gave him a dry look. "You'll swear to this?"

"Aye," Adrian said. "I checked the crates myself; they're all properly labeled, sealed since their inspection by British authorities in London."

Which meant, they both knew, nothing. Bribes were commonplace in inspections. But it gave the governor the out he needed.

"You will be sailing soon?" The suggestion was quite obvious.

"Very soon."

"I'll have to make a written report of our conversation to the U.S. Government. But I'm very busy today and tomorrow. I may not get to it until Wednesday."

Adrian grinned. "I understand about your heavy work load, Governor."

"Have a safe trip, Captain."

"Thank you, sir."

Adrian left Government House and went to the Royal Victoria, where he'd left Socrates. He sauntered through the gardens, stopping by a giant cotton tree, which dwarfed the one in Jeremy's garden. But it reminded him of Lauren. Something had happened in the brief span of time between last evening when he'd left her and today. There had always been an air of reserve about her, but never as strong as it had been this morning. And some of the brightness had faded from her eyes. Was it the decision to return to the South? Or was it he? Did it have something to do with the kiss yesterday, the kiss that had rocked his very soul?

He knew now how eager he had been to see her, though he hadn't admitted it to himself, and how frustrated he'd felt when she had been so cool, even hostile. He recalled that she had also displayed some hostility when he'd first encountered her, but then she'd had reason. Socrates, after all, had nearly plunged her into the ocean. But now . . .

She was like a multifaceted gem. Every time he looked at her, he saw something new: a different shading, a deeper mystery, a new light or brightness or shadowing. Lauren challenged him, delighted him, interested him as no other woman had, evoking a tenderness he hadn't known he had.

And now it was as if she closed the door on him. And he didn't know why.

He would have three days to find out. And he intended to do exactly that.

Adrian decided to stay on the *Specter* that night. He wanted to check the loading of cargo himself, to make sure the weight was evenly distributed. He wanted nothing to go wrong this trip.

He had told Wade that they would have a passenger who would occupy Adrian's cabin, and that he would move in with his first mate. Wade had merely lifted his eyebrows in surprise.

"A passenger, Captain?"

"Yes," Adrian said shortly, cutting off any other questions.

Wade tugged at his hat. "We've had an invitation tonight, Captain."

"An invitation?"

"Captain Harding, sir. Something about the crew invited for dinner. A bet?"

Adrian swore to himself. He'd forgotten about the damned bet once Clay had admitted defeat. "Bloody hell," he muttered. "You go. I have work to do."

Wade grinned. "You sure, Captain?"

"I'm sure," Adrian growled. The last thing he wanted to be reminded of was that damnable bet. But the invitation had already been given his crew members, and he didn't want to disappoint them. Not now. Not before a run.

After most of them had left, leaving only a skeleton crew aboard, Adrian went up on deck.

The lights in Nassau were bright, twinkling like so many stars. He found the ones belonging to the Case home and wondered which shone from Lauren's room. He thought about her too much, he chided himself, when he should be thinking of nothing but the run ahead. The Yanks would be in full force along the southeastern coast, their patrol boats circling the harbors and their fast cruisers patrolling the sea between the Bahamas and the Carolinas.

He wished he had guns, that the ship was not so vulnerable. There was only a handgun in the cabin, and he was well aware of the price of using even that against the Yanks. Not only his ship, but his life was at stake. And right now, his life seemed very precious to him.

How many more runs before he could purchase Ridgely? Would the man who now owned the estate even sell? And how would Lauren Bradley like Ridgely, the rolling green hills, the dense private forests, and the gracious manor house? He wanted her to see it, to understand his love for it.

Exactly when had she crawled into his heart? From the moment she had curtsied to Socrates, or when she'd laughed when she removed her shoes at the beach, wriggling her toes in the sand, or when she'd danced with him at the Governor's Ball, or when she'd held him tight against his grief yesterday? He didn't know. He only knew she had become vitally important to him.

He was taking her to Charleston, because he realized she was going to go, one way or another. And he'd rather have her under his protection than Clay's. He would know where she was, where she was going, would know how to reach her.

One of the lights in the Case home flickered off.

Lauren's? He pictured her lying on a bed, her honey-colored hair fanning over a pillow . . .

And he felt his belly tighten, his manhood swell against the tight trousers he wore, his blood race. "Lauren," he said softly into the sea breeze.

CHAPTER 10

Lauren stood on the deck of the *Specter* as it moved slowly away from the wharf. Lights still shone from its interior and from the oil lamps on deck, but she knew they would soon be quenched, and the *Specter* would become true to its name.

She felt the barely suppressed excitement of the men scurrying around her, and that feeling communicated itself to her, became part of her. Now she had some understanding of what Adrian had said. Every nerve in her body tingled with a mixture of fear and excitement, and all her senses were alive and humming and expectant.

Lauren looked upward to the dark night, where only the slightest slice of moon broke the field of stars. Wisps of clouds moved lazily against the sky, like pieces of lace.

She listened to the hum of the engines under her, the slap of waves against the bow of the ship, and she watched as other sets of lights moved out to sea with them. She counted nearly sixteen clumps of lights moving, and even more still behind in the harbor. Many of those would be gone too, by first light.

It was a sight she knew she would never forget, the silent, wraithlike silhouettes moving into harm's way, like an army of ghosts.

Soon, she knew, the ships would move away from one another, their captains each plotting different courses so a lucky Yankee patrol boat wouldn't find more than one at any time. In this business of hare and hounds, there was no safety in numbers.

She shivered as she thought of the dangerous game ahead, the now-familiar sickness in the pit of her stomach stronger than ever. She had met many of these captains now, met them and liked them. They were no longer the Evil Enemy, but men who laughed and teased and loved.

How could she have such a divided heart?

Lauren looked toward the front of the ship, toward the wheel where Adrian stood with the young man he'd introduced as Johnny, the pilot. The pilot was nothing more than a lad, a boy with a devil-may-care smile and tousled hair, and a wide grin. He was the only Southerner among the crew, and Lauren was only too aware that he would be subject to imprisonment, unlike the others.

But then he, too, was getting rich for the risks he took. Jeremy had said the pilots received three to five thousand dollars per run, a fortune. But still . . .

Lauren turned her gaze to the sea. It was gentle here, and still as clear as a piece of glass. She heard a nearby ripple and knew it must be a fish. She wished for a moment that she were that creature; free of conscience, of living with the consequences of one's actions.

She was aware of Adrian's presence almost immediately, although he stepped so lightly. It wasn't sound that made her aware; rather, it was the heightened tingling of her senses, a sudden tension in the air.

"Peaceful, isn't it?" he said.

"For how long?"

"If we're lucky, two and a half days."

"And then?"

"Then we wait for a fog to take us into Charleston and hope we don't blunder into a Union ship."

"Thank you for your cabin."

His hand settled lightly on her shoulder, and she felt its warmth roll through her like hot syrup. Compelled by a need she tried unsuccessfully to fight, she felt her body move back, touching his hard one. But the night was magical, the sea air tangy and exhilarating, his touch irresistible. She had tried to avoid him until that moment he had fetched her from Jeremy's and again had maintained a reserve as he had taken her aboard and showed her the small cabin . . .

She had immediately noted its austerity, the maps, the books. "This is yours?"

He nodded. "I'll move in with Wade, my first officer."

"I . . . can't take your cabin."

He gave her a devilish grin. "We . . . could share it," he replied suggestively.

Lauren knew she was blushing again, especially as she felt a strange yearning in the depth of her. She turned away.

Adrian's tone immediately changed, became apologetic. "I'm sorry, Lauren, but we don't usually take passengers. This is all we have. I can take you back to Jeremy's."

Lauren bit her lips. The cabin was not nearly as grand as she'd expected he would have. There were no windows, no comforts, only a narrow bed set into the wall, a small desk anchored to the floor. A bookcase was built onto one of the walls, and it was filled. There was a small seaman's chest and some hooks for clothes, and two more for oil lamps. That was all.

But it smelled of him, of soap and leather and musk. And even the austerity of the small, almost cell-like room was compelling because it was his.

"It's fine," she said in a soft voice, trying to close her mind to the need inside her. How could he still affect her this way when she knew that she meant nothing to him, nothing more than a grogshop wager?

Socrates scampered into the room to a small box with a bundle of rags in it.

"I suppose you don't mind sharing with Socrates," Adrian said with that slight self-mocking smile that was always like a blow to her stomach.

"It's more respectable," she retorted.

"There's nothing respectable about your being here alone on a runner," he said dryly. "I still wish you would reconsider."

Lauren had shaken her head. She wanted to reconsider. Oh how much she wanted to reconsider! She thought of the small cloth bag of sand in her portmanteau.

"I have to go above," Adrian said. "Make yourself comfortable."

"When will we leave?"

"In a few hours. You might like to come up and watch. A number of ships are leaving tonight . . . it's an interesting sight."

"What about Union patrol boats?"

"They can't do anything in the Bahamian waters, and that takes in a very large area. They can try to follow us out, but with a dark night and our lights out, the Union ships are easy to elude."

Lauren had spent only a few minutes in the cabin before feeling unaccountably confined. She could barely stand the closeness of the walls. But she hesitated to go up on deck. Adrian would be there, and she didn't know whether she could bear being close to him, for her body was sure to betray her the way it always did when Adrian Cabot was around.

But neither could she stand her own thoughts, nor staring at Adrian's possessions, nor the lingering scent that remained in the room.

In three or four days, if all went well, this cabin would no longer belong to him.

If everything went well . . .

*   *   *

"Lauren." Adrian's voice was soft in her ear, and she returned to the moment, to the seductive night, and the danger. His danger. Her own danger when she was with him. Dear God, how could she survive this?

Hate him, she urged herself. Hate him for what he is, for what he's doing, for what he wagered.

But that was like hating the warm, bright sun, hating the brightness while the body drank up the warmth.

"Frightened?" he said, his hand on her shoulder tightening ever so slightly.

Lauren kept her gaze away from him. She couldn't look at him now, at the eyes so deep a blue she could never find its source, or identify the currents that ran in them. She didn't understand him, or the many contradictions she saw in him.

"Yes," she said. But not for the reason he believed.

"The run is really fairly safe," he said, leaning over, his words a soft whisper in the night as his breath touched her ear, and she shivered in the warm Caribbean night. Or was it morning?

His hand dropped from her shoulder, and both of his arms went around her waist. She found herself leaning back against him. It was so natural, as if it was meant to be, this fusing of bodies.

The lamps on the ship were quenched, one by one, and she turned, looking askance at him in a night lit now only by a host of stars that were bright in the sky but flashed precious little light to the earth.

"It's time," he whispered, "to get lost in the night."

Lauren watched as distant lights also disappeared, one by one, and she and Adrian seemed alone in the total blackness of night. Even the loud voices of the crew had quieted to whispers, and only the sound of water against the hull made music in the vast emptiness.

The sudden void matched the hollowness inside her. Adrian's arms were still around her, and something deep inside her relished the comfort of his embrace. But it was all false, she reminded herself. He doesn't mean it, any more than she did.

She forced some words out. "Isn't it dangerous . . . without lights?"

"Johnny's the best pilot in the business. He can sense— see—every reef, every jut of land in the blackest of nights. Damned if I know how. Part owl, I suppose."

Keep talking. Keep talking so you won't feel. Lauren shifted slightly, and Adrian's arms moved with her. The friction of skin against skin, body against body, sent waves of painful pleasure washing over her. She wanted his hands to move again, to reexperience those wonderful sensations that made her feel so alive.

There was a tug on her skirt, and she looked down, barely able to see Socrates in the darkness. Then she tipped her head upward. The shadow of Adrian's head, the outline of those hard, clean features so close, came even closer as she felt his lips touch her cheek and his hands turn her ever so slightly so she was at his side rather than in front of him.

Her heart thumped so loudly she thought he must hear. Her hand trembled where it lay on the railing. His lips moved to touch her lips, softly, searchingly.

Lauren knew they were lost in the shadow, in the inky darkness, so the members of the crew could not see. It was as if they were alone in an infinite empty vault, nothing real except each other. She felt his lips press tighter against her mouth, and she realized she was responding, her mouth opening to his gentle probing.

Emotions flooded her. Wild, runaway emotions. Pleasure. Need. Anticipation. The danger, the tension, made everything so much more intense, magnified her sensations until she didn't know how she could bear them, to hold them inside without exploding. She was learning quickly what Adrian had meant about danger.

Or was it the danger?

She stepped back frantically. "No," she whispered, and his arms loosened from around her. His lips whispered against her cheek, and then his hand caught her chin, making her look up at him. She couldn't see his features well, but in her mind she saw his slight smile, the question in his eyes.

"You're like quicksilver, Miss Bradley," he said softly. "You keep running away from me. Why?"

Because I hate you. And I'm so afraid I also love you.

"I'm tired," she said aloud, her voice unsteady.

Adrian sighed. His head started to lower again, and Lauren knew he meant to kiss her, to kiss away her rejection, but she spun away, afraid that he would do just that.

"Please, Adrian."

"We'll talk tomorrow," he said, his voice suddenly hard and uncompromising, and she knew she was going to need to give some explanations the next day. She knew he must be totally confused, the way she yielded one moment and ran the next. The good Lord knew she was confused!

"I'll walk you to the cabin," he said, his hands leaving her as he stooped down and swept up Socrates. Adrian's right hand took her arm firmly, guiding her through the dark night air to the steps that led down to the cabin. The interior was even darker than the deck, and she wondered how he stepped so surely. She felt totally blind, completely at his mercy.

The engines hummed as Adrian's hand steadied her uncertain steps, his warmth and scent intoxicating in the cocoon of the ship, of the night. She stumbled, and his arm went around her again, keeping her from falling. Lauren felt as if he were an integral part of her, and she knew she would never be whole again when he was gone.

When he was gone!

And then they were at the cabin, and he'd opened the door. He released her, and she heard the sound of a match striking, and the flare of a lantern. "It's safe to use a light in here," he said. "There are no windows."

The lantern, really a strange-looking oil lamp designed specifically for ships, was hung from a hook, its flickering flame sending darts of light around the cabin, illuminating his face. There were so many questions in his expression— questions she could never answer.

Socrates jumped to the floor and went over to his bed.

"I'll take him with me," Adrian said.

"Why don't you leave him here?"

"Are you quite sure about that?" Adrian's voice was now tinged with amusement. "Sometimes he decides he prefers the bed. You might wake up with a bony paw clutching at you."

"At least he'll be company."

His eyes sparked, the deep blue of them catching fire from the flame. "I find myself jealous. And of a monkey. I'll have no pride left, Miss Bradley," he teased.

"I think that unlikely," she retorted.

"You do unprecedented damage to it."

"I believe you will recover."

"Doubtful." An endearingly wistful smile played over his face.

Another ploy? "Good night, Captain."

"Adrian," he insisted.

"Lord Adrian," she said, trying to keep a certain distance.

"Lord Ridgely, to be correct," he said dryly. "You sound as if you dislike lords?"

"I've heard they play games," she charged unwisely.

"What kind of games?"

"With hearts." *With my heart.*

He was silent, his eyes dark and secretive, a muscle twitching in his cheek. She wished she knew why.

"Don't they?"

"Not all of them. Do all women play games?" There was a sudden harsh edge to his voice.

Drat the man. He had a way of putting her on the defensive. Of turning her words against her. And he had wagered on her! Her anger rose again, protecting her from her own weakness. But she knew she had to guard against that too. She had already said too much. But the skin where he'd touched her still tingled, still burned, and she knew if he kissed her, she would be lost again.

She prayed briefly, and her prayers were answered. His low voice, rumbling through her consciousness, made her reply unnecessary.

"I have to get up on deck. These waters are still danger-ous. Good night . . . Lauren."

There was an unusual curtness to his words, and she felt a now-familiar pain stab through her. If his censure hurt now, dear God, how much was it going to hurt when he learned the truth?

"Captain," she acknowledged, and turned to watch him duck his tall shoulders to go through the door. And then he was gone.

Adrian spent the night at the wheel, Johnny next to him until they were safe from the reefs. Then Johnny went to bed while Adrian, wanting the solitude, stayed at the wheel.

He needed the time to sort out his thoughts about Lauren Bradley.

He had thought he had found something different, something fine, with her. He had never talked to a woman like he had to her on the beach, nor had any woman aroused the kind of gentleness she did. Being with her, he'd discovered to his surprise, had filled some of the empty places within. It was like finding a part of himself.

Or, at least, so he'd thought for a while. Those hazel eyes had a way of regarding him with such vulnerability and determination that he wanted to hold her and protect her.

And make love to her.

But in the past few days, some of her acceptance of him, their ease with each other, had vanished, and he didn't understand why. He had been the perfect gentleman, al-though it had not been easy. He was used to quick suc-cesses, but then he had not earnestly courted since the disaster with Sylvia. He'd indulged himself with light skirts, women who asked little other than an afternoon's enjoyment.

He wanted more from Lauren Bradley. He was not sure how much more at this moment. But a need was there, a strong need that was both new and compelling. And she had seemed willing enough for a while to explore whatever it was that ran between them with such elemental force. But she'd suddenly turned skittish, like an untutored filly before a race, sensing something, getting caught in the excitement, but not quite sure what was expected of her.

He chuckled at his own whimsy. He was probably making far more of this than he should. Still, the need in his groin was strong, and the depth of the longing someplace else was more terrifying than any Yank cruiser. He had been so damned alone for so long. All his life. And for a few fleeting hours . . . he'd felt as if he really belonged somewhere.

He cursed, the sound ragged and frustrated.

There were few places to hide on the ship. In fact, there were none, Lauren discovered the next day.

As they had last night, the walls of the cabin closed in around her, and she wondered how Adrian tolerated it. Lauren had always loved the out-of-doors, had always kept her window opened at least a little, even in the worst of wintertime. She had rejoiced in long walks, and in watching the sun and the moon as they traded places in their endless cycles. And she relished the breath of air against her skin.

But this small cabin was airless, and she felt entombed. Yet she knew Adrian would be wherever she went.

Socrates was still sleeping when she rose, and Lauren was not sure of the time. She lit the oil lamp and watched him for several seconds. He looked a little like a sleeping child, his features relaxed, his legs and arms sprawled in four directions.

There was a knock on the door, and she hurried to answer it, her heart speeding, but it was not Adrian. A sailor she'd seen when she boarded stood there with two steaming pails of water in hand.

"Captain's compliments," he said stiffly, as if he'd been told carefully what to say. "I'll fetch yer breakfast d'rectly."

"The captain?"

"Sleeping, miss. He bedded down at daylight, but he said to ask whether you would sup with him tonight."

The sailor was young, no more than twenty, with a pronounced English accent she guessed was Cockney.

A reprieve, Lauren thought. A brief one. She opened the door wider to allow the sailor in. He went to a cabinet Lauren hadn't even realized was built into the wall and took out a bowl, carefully pouring the contents of one bucket into it. " 'Ere's more if you need it," he said of the other bucket. He started to back out. "What should I tell the capt'n 'bout supper?"

"That I would be pleased," she said, "and thank you for the water."

The sailor blushed.

"Do you think it would be . . . all right to look around the ship?"

"Aye, ma'am. Be pleased to show you meself. Capt'n said I'm at your . . . service." He said the last uncomfortably, as if the words were new.

"After breakfast then," she said.

"Aye, miss." His face crinkled into a full grin. "It be a fine ship." Pride was evident in his voice.

After he left, Lauren quickly washed and dressed, finishing just before a knock came again, and the same sailor appeared, a tray in hand, smells wafting up that would have been appealing if she had an appetite. The very thought of food, however, made Lauren wince. For a moment, she hoped it was seasickness, but she knew it wasn't.

It was an altogether different type of sickness, one she was afraid would haunt her forever. But after the sailor left, she forced herself to eat. Then she checked the small trunk she had brought with her, and found the bag of sand she'd collected earlier yesterday. She played with the sack with her hand, wondering if so small a thing could really disable a ship. She had been assured it could.

"There *is* something you can do, Miss Bradley," she heard Mr. Phillips say again in her mind. "Sixty percent of the South's arms come in through the blockade runners, nearly all its paper for cartridges, and three fourths of its powder."

Then Jeremy: "We can't let the cannon get through."

And Larry: "I've got to go, Lauren. I must. The Union must stay together . . . we all have to do what we can."

Lauren pressed her hands against her ears to stop the voices. But now there was Adrian's, deep and sincere. "I don't want to see you hurt."

And Jeremy again. "There was a wager . . ."

"Go away," Lauren screamed to them all. But it was a silent scream, and useless. The voices remained.

Even as she wandered over the ship with her guide, who gave his name as Dicken, she looked for the tall, rangy form of Adrian.

Dicken was right. Even to Lauren's unpracticed eyes, the ship was a sleek, lean beauty. Perhaps, she thought, it was Adrian's British Navy background, but the *Specter* fairly shone, even with its decks piled with cargo. Every piece of wood was polished to a sheen. The crew was just as sterling, each member wearing a clean uniform and doffing his hat when she approached. There was pride in both, the crew and the ship.

When they'd finished the round, Socrates dashing ahead and looking around as if for his master, Lauren asked to see the engine room.

Dicken looked startled. "The engine room, miss?"

Lauren eyed him steadily. "I've never been on a steamship before."

The sailor looked doubtful. "It's awful 'ot down there, miss."

"Please," Lauren cajoled.

"I don't know if the capt'n would like it."

Lauren gave him her sweetest smile. "I don't think he would mind."

Dicken finally shrugged his assent, remembering his orders, to make sure Miss Bradley was comfortable and happy. "Well . . . if you say . . ."

The door to the cabins and sleeping quarters was near the bow, but the engine room was located down the steps from the stern. She had expected the room to be dirty as well as hot, but like the rest of the ship, it was unexpectedly clean, except where the coal was stored. "Newcastle coal," Dicken said proudly. "The captain gets only the best."

There were four men inside, each working in steady motion, shoveling coal into the boilers. Three of them were shirtless, and the fourth man, wearing a shirt open to his waist and an officer's hat, came over. "Miss?"

Dicken turned all shades of red before he stuttered, "Miss Bradley, this is Mick . . . our engineer."

"So this be the pretty passenger I've been hearing about," Mick said with a wide grin. "Didn't expect to see you down here."

"I've never been on a steamship before," she said. "Can you explain it to me?"

Mick beamed at the attention, and especially at showing off his pride and joy. "Sure as sin," he said, then he reddened slightly. "Sorry, miss. We're not used to passengers on the *Specter*, especially fine ladies."

Lauren spent the next half hour listening, never having to interject a comment. He showed Lauren the brightly painted red machinery, the shafts working the paddle wheels, patiently explaining the function of each. Mick was much easier to follow than the men in Washington, but the principle was the same, Lauren soon discovered. Everything was exactly as described. She felt her heart pound. She'd been half-hoping her task would be rendered impossible . . .

But Mick not only explained, he invited her to return. "Any time you get restless . . ."

And Lauren could mutter only a weak "Thank you."

Fresh air greeted Lauren as she and Dicken left the ship's interior for the deck. Her dress was sticky with the heat from the engine room, and her mind was whirling with the implications of what she'd just seen. She leaned against the smokestack, breathing in the fresh, clean air, trying to clear the webs from her mind.

The sun was bright, and pounding down on the ship, and the sea was like glass, glittering with gold reflections, as the ship cut through the water at what was to Lauren a miraculous speed. She felt herself shiver in the heat. Socrates, as if understanding, crouched down next to her, his beady eyes gleaming.

She looked up and around. There was no flag flying now, and she knew the ship must be barely visible between the sea and the sky. Just as she tried to relax, to allow the brisk sea breeze to cool and soothe her, she heard a shout.

"Sail on starboard!"

CHAPTER 11

Fear and exhilaration mixed in the pit of Lauren's stomach as, almost immediately, she saw Adrian stride quickly on deck.

Although she knew he'd probably had no more than four hours' sleep, he looked alert and wide awake despite the hint of stubble on his cheeks. He was wearing a white shirt he was now pushing into a black pair of trousers, and he had nothing on his feet.

Lauren didn't know whether he saw her or not. He went directly to the wheel, and almost instantly there were two other men with him, one she recognized as the first officer and the other the pilot.

Dicken also appeared, sidling up to her protectively.

Lauren looked with amazement at the calm faces of the crew, although their steps were quick. She turned to Dicken. "You said the *Specter* could outrun anything."

Then she heard a noise, like a muffled explosion, from a

distance. She could barely make out smoke, much less the outline of a ship, and she marveled that the men on board had detected the ship so quickly.

"We can outrun the best of 'em," Dicken said, "but they're signaling, meaning there's more of 'em out there. They'll try to run us into a trap."

Another boom sounded, and Lauren felt her skin tingle. There was another, then silence except for Adrian's commands.

"Raise the flag," she heard him say, and she watched as two men attached a flag to a pole that ran alongside the smokestack. "British," she observed aloud.

"Won't fool no one," Dicken said. "They stop every ship."

"Ship ahead," came another call.

"Mr. Green." It was Adrian's voice, different from when she'd heard it before. Now it was authoritative, commanding.

Dicken hurried from her side and went to Adrian, talked to him for a moment, and then nearly ran back. "Capt'n says for you to go to the cabin."

She shook her head.

"Capt'n said you wouldn't want to. He said to tell you to take Socrates. Not that I would mind if something 'appened to 'im. Foul beast, he is."

Lauren looked toward Adrian, and he grinned, his white teeth flashing in his tanned face, his chestnut hair blowing in the breeze. As usual when she saw him, her heart accelerated, but now it was racing double-time. Adrian Cabot looked so free, so totally in command. Nothing could happen as long as he was at the wheel. She knew that as well as she knew dusk would fall tonight.

And she didn't want to go. She heard the orders being passed, felt the movement of the ship as it changed course, the thunder of faraway cannon, and she wanted to see it all, not cower in a dark room.

Socrates, however, was another matter. He was jumping up and down next to her, obviously frightened. She nodded, intending to leave the monkey in the cabin and return. Lauren leaned down and picked him up, feeling the coarse fur as he hugged close to her, his paws tightening round her neck.

She looked around. There was a dense cloud of smoke in another direction, and she looked again at Dicken, who shrugged. "They're signaling with their guns, but the capt'n will outwit 'em. 'E always does."

"Another sail, Capt'n." Lauren heard the disembodied voice. She knew she should be pleased at a possible Union trap, but she looked at Adrian and knew again that terrible pull of loyalties.

Socrates chattered unhappily, and she made her way to the cabin. It was dark; she had already been told never to use the oil lamp when under attack. She wondered what cargo was in the hold, other than the cannon. Ammunition? Oil?

She heard another peal of what sounded like thunder, and it seemed louder, even where she was deep within the ship. Socrates had fled to his bed, where he sat like a little wizened old man, scolding angrily. Lauren felt a little like doing that herself, yet something stronger compelled her to leave, to go on deck. She couldn't bear staying here, imagining the worst, locked in the airless, tight gloom of the cabin.

She opened the door. The short, narrow corridor was clear. She quickly moved to the stairs leading up to the deck and opened the hatch door, moving to where one of the paddle wheels churned the water, and she tried to lose herself in its shadow.

It seemed to Lauren that each time the *Specter* darted in a new direction, a new call sounded, announcing the presence of yet another gunship. From the billows of smoke, she counted four, and the *Specter* was racing toward two of them now, the speed of the ship amazing to her after the schooners she had taken from Maryland to England, and then England to Nassau. Mick, the engineer, had told her the *Specter* could reach eighteen knots and better, but she'd not really believed him till now.

The noise of laboring engines overwhelmed even the

sound of the paddle wheels pushing against water. Wind caught the hair from the twist on the back of her head, and it whipped around her, as she tasted the salt of the sea spray. Never had she felt so alive.

As they approached the two Union ships, she realized suddenly what Adrian was planning. He was counting on the speed of the *Specter* to throw off the gunners until he ran between them, and then they couldn't fire or they'd risk hitting each other. A technique he had used before, she thought bitterly.

She felt her fingers clutching her dress, remembering Phillips's explanation of how Larry had died. And with it, she remembered the night she'd had the dream. A dream of fire and pain.

A cannon boomed, and water whirled up in a cloud in front of them. The ship moved suddenly to starboard but kept its speed, racing toward its tormenters. Another shot hit the water to the left of them, and then another behind. The ship zigzagged, the engines pounding.

Lauren felt the splash of cold water as a shot hit the water near her. She heard a loud curse. She looked toward Adrian, who glared at her before his attention went back to the ships ahead.

Soaked, she moved away from the railing of the ship, closer to the wheel, to him. She watched as his hands moved so easily on the giant wheel, twisting and turning. Both ships ahead were now firing, and shots splashed around them, but none found its mark, and then they were between the two ships, so close she could see the faces of the men. Enemies now. Enemies firing at her.

The *Specter* passed the Union ships, and Adrian made another sudden turn, moving to the left and behind one of the ships where there were no cannon. The other ship could not fire for fear of hitting his companion vessel.

Lauren saw the closest ship turn, but it was a sailing vessel, and the wind was still. By the time it was in a position to fire, the *Specter* had moved away, the splashes from cannon shot falling farther and farther behind. There was a shout from the *Specter*'s deck, one of victory and mockery. Damning curses from the pursuing ships could be heard on the *Specter*.

Trembling with the aftermath, Lauren felt like joining the triumphant chorus. Even with her limited knowledge, she knew she had witnessed a brilliant display of seamanship.

She looked up toward the sky. It was already late afternoon. The chase had taken hours, although it seemed like minutes. The silhouettes of the Union ships grew fainter and fainter, as the *Specter* plunged on through the sea.

Lauren felt her wet hair plaster itself against her cheek. Her soaked dress clung to her body, and yet she felt no discomfort, only the lingering of tingling nerves, a giddiness. She looked at Adrian, at the victorious smile on his face, at his lean form braced against the wind and the rich chestnut hair falling over his forehead as one hand left the wheel and pushed it back. His white shirt was billowing in the wind, the dark trousers molding those strong muscled legs, and his bare feet set solidly on the wood deck. Her emotions swelled with the magnificence of him, the pure power and freedom, the pride that radiated from the set of his body.

He had won, and he was enjoying every second of the victory.

Lauren's own elation slowly faded. How much simpler if they had been stopped now! She dropped her gaze to the sea, now so deeply blue it was unfathomable. Like his eyes. Like everything about him.

She watched as Adrian turned over the wheel to his first officer and stalked toward her, his expression stern.

He stopped and glared at her. "If you were one of my men, I would throw you in irons."

Despite herself, Lauren was intimidated. His eyes were dark, showing little but a frown that matched the expression on his lips.

"I couldn't stay down there," she defended herself.

"I had a man die a week ago because he was on deck, Lauren. I didn't want to bring you, but when I did, I expected you to obey my orders, just as my men do. You agreed."

Lauren wanted to feel anger at his sudden arbitrary harshness, but she could only think of the grief in his voice that afternoon in the garden, when he spoke of losing a man. His anger, she realized, was fear. Fear for her.

The same kind she'd felt for him those nights he was gone, and again minutes ago.

"I'm sorry," she said, her eyes meeting his.

His hand went to her shoulder, and she felt the tension in his fingers. "I shouldn't have . . . brought you. If anything happens to you . . ."

You could have surrendered, something whispered inside her mind. But then she remembered how he had looked at the wheel. Surrender wasn't possible for him. It would never be possible for him. Not even for her. Not for anything. Not if he thought he had the slightest chance.

And if he didn't have even that chance?

Would he still defy the odds?

But her gloomy thoughts scattered like seed to the wind when his hand touched her wet hair. "You're soaked, Miss Bradley." His smile was wry as he looked down at his own clothes. "And I need some dry clothes, not to mention a few more of them."

Adrian looked to the sun dipping toward the flat blue horizon. "And I'm as hungry as a whale." He grinned suddenly, his face lighting up with that blinding smile. "Why don't we both go below, and I'll order some dinner for your cabin?"

She nodded, mesmerized as always by his smile. She couldn't have demurred if she'd wanted. And she didn't want to. God help her, she didn't.

Adrian was apologetic about the sparseness of the meal, but he treated her as if she were a queen about to sit down to a banquet.

"We don't have a cook as such," he explained dryly as he uncovered a dish of stew, some biscuits that looked as flat as stones, and a bowl of fruit. "But," he added with relish, "we do have fine wine."

He poured them each a glass and then placed a plate of fruit on the floor for Socrates. He had fetched Socrates right after the confrontation with the Union ships and taken him to his cabin. Both had appeared wearing a clean set of britches.

Socrates started to reach for a banana, and Adrian, with an engaging smile, stopped him with a word. "Say grace, Socrates." Adrian's eyes turned expectantly to Lauren as Socrates clapped his hands together and bent his head.

Lauren couldn't stop the delight flooding her. Socrates peeked up from his hands as if asking whether his prayer had been long enough, like a small boy in church.

"Does he know other tricks?"

"He can play dead," Adrian said, as Socrates quickly gobbled down his banana. "Sometimes he cooperates, and sometimes he doesn't."

"And when he plays dead?"

"He's absolutely still," Adrian said. "Then you can touch him on the arm, and he'll slowly start to move. But . . . then, sometimes he decides he doesn't want any part of it and pays no attention at all."

"Did you teach him?"

Adrian shook his head. "He already knew a lot. I discovered his tricks one by one. Somehow the word 'dead' came up in a conversation, and he just flopped over. I started experimenting after that, testing words and watching him. I'm sure he has tricks I don't know about."

"How did you find him?" Lauren was fascinated, both with Socrates and with the way Adrian's face opened up when he talked about him.

"His owner was beating him. I don't think he was the original owner because I doubt whether Socrates would have learned any tricks with someone cruel to him. He can be . . . stubborn at times, especially when he feels mistreated."

"And the name?"

"Mine," Adrian admitted wryly. "When I first brought

him to the ship, he sat in the chair where you're sitting, looking like a wise, sad old man. My crew has a few other names for him."

Lauren tipped her head. "Why? He always seems well behaved."

Adrian laughed, a full deep-throated laugh that filled the room. "He likes you. And for some odd reason, he seems to behave when you're around. But the day I met you, he'd just about destroyed this cabin, and he has bitten nearly every member of the crew. He's damned independent, and a bit of a rogue. Perhaps that's why we get along."

"Are you a rogue, Captain?"

His eyes met hers. "I'm told so."

A familiar tingling started in the small of Lauren's back, working its way upward. She wanted to lean over and touch him, to feel his touch again. Was it *because* he was a rogue? Had she some terrible weakness she'd never realized until now? But though he sometimes looked the part, she'd never really seen him do anything ungentlemanly. He'd never acted the rogue with her, and she had the strangest need for him to do so.

The excitement she'd felt up on deck during the duel of ships returned, stimulating all her senses, bringing alive all the sensations she'd never known were possible. The scent of him was sharper, the nearness more intoxicating, the exchange of words more suggestive.

Nothing was real at the moment except Adrian Cabot —the bright, searching look in his eyes, the teasing around the sensual lips, the bright heat of his presence.

Lauren struggled against the almost drugged feeling she had. And she had only one weapon to shield herself.

"How did you become a blockade runner?"

"I was drummed out of the British Navy," Adrian said, his lips quirking up at one side.

Lauren looked at him in disbelief.

"At least informed I should probably leave," he amended.

"Why?"

"You are the most inquisitive woman I've ever met," he said, changing the subject. He realized at the same time that her curiosity was one of the reasons he was so attracted to her. He usually became quickly bored with the women he met, but Lauren was interested in everything, her mind bright and eager. And despite his anger at her disobedience this afternoon, he'd somehow known she would be there on deck, and in some strange way he would have been disappointed if she hadn't been. Bloody hell of a contradiction, he told himself, but she'd mixed him up like that ever since he met her.

"You're changing the subject."

"So I am," he said complacently. "I would rather talk about you."

"I'm not at all interesting."

"I don't think I believe that, Miss Bradley."

Lauren felt that tingle grow into full-scale buzzing. He had a way of saying "Miss Bradley" that curled her toes. His lips fondled and teased the name, his voice drawing it out with extraordinary sensuousness.

He poured her another glass of wine, and Lauren sipped it nervously. Her appetite had died in the intensity of the feeling between them, and her body seemed to be straining forward, as if to get closer to his.

Lauren's glance went down to his hands, which were holding a glass of wine. The hands were strong and capable, the fingers curled around the stem of the glass with restrained strength.

Like everything about him. Despite his outward ease, Lauren had already felt the restlessness, the power, the unpredictability that dwelled within him. As he said, he was at least part rogue. And that part was irresistibly attractive to her. She'd heard of women who were attracted to that kind of man, to danger and to dangerous men.

She'd never thought she was one of them. But then she was learning a great deal about herself, some of which she wasn't sure she liked.

She'd once thought a long walk in the woods was life's supreme pleasure. But after this afternoon, after feeling the spray of water from cannon shot, the elation of watching Adrian elude his pursuers, of seeing the brilliant smile of victory, she knew nothing would ever compare with those hours aboard the *Specter*.

"Lauren?" She looked up and met his intense gaze. "Where did you go?"

"Go?"

"In your thoughts just then?"

"Home."

"Maryland?"

No, Delaware. To a house on the edge of a lovely wood, to peace and safety. To a peace forever gone.

She nodded.

"Tell me about your brother and father," he said softly, the teasing gone.

Lauren swallowed. Perhaps it would help to talk about Laurence. Perhaps it would strengthen her resolve, fortify her against his appeal.

"Larry was my twin," she said, hating the trembling in her voice. "Both he and my father were doctors."

"Twins," he said. "There's a strong bond."

"I knew . . . when he died. I felt it," she said. "He was hundreds of miles away, but I knew."

His hand released the glass of wine and reached for her hand, his fingers grazing over hers, the contact light, meant to be comforting.

But he didn't say anything, and Lauren was grateful. She didn't think she could bear to hear sympathy or platitudes from the man responsible for Larry's death. And he was responsible. She had to keep reminding herself of that.

Still, she did feel comforted in a strange way.

"Your father?"

"A fever. Several months before . . . Laurence."

"Laurence," he repeated. Lauren and Laurence. So closely named. So obviously close in mind. He knew, from the wistful expression on her face that her brother's death had been a terrible blow. His own brother's death had been painful, even though they had not been close, even though

Adrian had felt betrayed in so many ways. But John had been his only family, and he'd felt the loss acutely.

Still, his own bereavement had obviously been far less than the grief Lauren had experienced. For one of the few times in his life, he felt protective. And he hurt for her, for the sorrow in her eyes, for the loneliness he knew she must have felt, still felt. Adrian wondered whether she seemed so elusive because she darted in and out of grief. An obviously recent grief.

He rose and went around to her, resting his hands on her shoulders, feeling the tenseness in them, the sadness she was so obviously holding inside. He missed the laughter, the challenge, yet he liked this side too. This caring, sorrowing aspect showed him another dimension of her. She looked up, her eyes wide and confused and full of something that made his heart tear inside.

Adrian leaned down and kissed her. He felt her mouth respond, slowly at first, and then with a sudden reckless craving.

He pulled her up, and his arms went around her. He wouldn't let her run. Not this time.

His lips encountered something wet and salty, and one of his fingers went to her face, tracing a narrow path. A tear or two, no more, had wandered down her face. He kissed the moisture away, and then his mouth moved slowly along the soft skin of her face, and he felt her breath, a warm breeze whispering against already fevered flesh. A blaze flared in his lower regions, wild and hungry. She was like a tempest: sudden, intense, beautiful; her moods were as changeable and swift as the most unpredictable storm.

He ached as he had never ached before. There was a growing pressure inside, so strong he could barely contain it, yet she'd been so skittish. She was a lady, entirely a lady, and she would rightfully expect marriage. Yet even now he was not sure of his future, or whether he could recover Ridgely. For so many years, that and that only had been the focus of his life. And during those years, he'd held himself apart from women, giving them his physical self but no more. He knew Lauren Bradley would never be satisfied with that.

He knew now that neither would he.

But first he had to regain Ridgely. He would never be whole again without it.

Even Ridgely, however, faded for the moment as passion spurred passion, and need goaded need.

His lips moved down to hers, and her mouth opened. Swirling eddies of desire enveloped them both, tumbling them along in a vortex that eclipsed everyone and everything except each other.

A whisper in the back of Lauren's mind warned and berated, but it was chaff in the wind, unsubstantial compared to the power of her other feelings. She wanted to touch and press and explore. She wanted to feel him close to her. She wanted to prolong the dizzying, warm, exciting feelings she knew she shared with him, for he, too, was shaking slightly, and part of her savored her ability to do that to him. He had often seemed so aloof, as if nothing really touched him.

But she was touched too. And she was afraid nothing again would ever be the same in her life. Yet she could no more resist the magic of the mood, of the moment, than she could stop breathing.

She was responding to his every movement in a way she'd never thought possible. She had always been passionate in her beliefs, in her love of nature, in her fierce loyalty, but she'd never believed she had a woman's passion. Now she did. And she didn't know what to expect, or what to do, or what would happen. She only knew her body was reacting completely on its own, in ways she considered wanton and loose.

And yet that knowledge meant nothing compared to the warm, irresistible feelings flowing through her body like a tide. Swelling and ebbing, and then swelling again with renewed energy. Feelings and sensations so new as to disable and disarm.

Lauren found her tongue every bit as aggressive as his as she followed his lead, exploring and teasing and adventuring. She savored each new jolt of sensation, of dizzying gratification. Her gaze found his eyes, and they were no longer that cool deep blue, but more like blazing blue fires. She felt the tension in his body, the barely restrained passion in his hands, which moved seductively at the small of her back. Their touch, even through her clothes, made her shiver.

The kiss deepened, his lips hard and demanding against her now tremulous ones. And suddenly fear overwhelmed her. Everything was happening so fast. So much want. So much need. So much feeling. Her hands, which had been around his neck, stopped their movement, the slight whisper-soft tickling of his skin. She leaned back in his arms, seeking a respite from the emotions overtaking her, emotions that were overruling every sensible, reasonable, responsible part of her. She felt a bewildering pain in the deepest part of her, a longing for something she didn't understand, and the strength of that need terrified her.

Adrian felt the slight stiffening, and reality jarred his senses. She was not a "light o' love," not one of the experienced courtesans he'd known in London. Her eyes now were wide with a mixture of wonder and dismay. And she was more enchanting than any woman he'd ever met.

There was so much unexpected passion in her, passion made more fascinating by her innocence, by the sense of discovery he saw in her eyes and face. He knew he was the first to awaken it, and he yearned to bring that discovery to the ultimate fulfillment, to see those eyes brighten and shine as he knew was possible.

But not now. She was an innocent, and he was in a dangerous profession. Moreover, he had a goal to accomplish before he could offer a woman security and an honorable name. He could not risk leaving her with a babe, not now. No matter how much he wanted, needed, her.

His hand wrapped around a tendril of hair the texture of finest silk, and he knew a fierce throbbing ache in his groin. It would be so easy to take her back in his arms, but for once his own needs were less important than someone else's. His hand went to her cheek.

"You feel so soft," he said in a low voice, wanting to say something else. But everything had been too quick, and the future was still too unsure. They needed time to explore their feelings. He would be in Charleston often.

"Adrian . . ."

His name on her lips was husky. It had an inflection unlike any he'd ever heard before. Gentle. Hesitant. He liked the sound.

"I'd better go," he said, his fingers rubbing her chin, the tip of one finger tracing the line of her lips, "before I do something you might regret. I don't want that to happen."

Lauren didn't want him to leave. She didn't want to be here alone with her thoughts. But she also knew if he stayed much longer, she would be lost.

Her body trembling with need and regret, she nodded slowly. Still her hand rested on his waist, reluctant to relinquish the contact.

She didn't want to face the shadows of night, the need to think again about what had to be done, to realize that in two days she would never see him again, that, if she did, the emotion in his eyes would be harsh and condemning, not fiery and soft at the same time.

Lauren forced herself to turn away, her feelings desolate and empty as she did so.

"Lauren . . ." She heard the rumble of his voice behind her, "When we get to Charleston . . ."

But she never heard the end of the sentence, for there was a knock on the door.

"Capt'n, we've sighted another sail."

Lauren turned back, saw his face tense, the soft voice suddenly hard. "Stay here this time," he said. "Your promise, or I'll send a man down to stand at the door."

She nodded. At the moment, she wanted nothing so much as to hide. Not from a Union ship, but from the weakness he created in her. As the door closed behind him, she whispered, "Be safe."

CHAPTER 12

Socrates was gone when Lauren woke the next morning. She had lain awake late as she felt the ship's direction and speed change, and then she relaxed as the engines resumed a normal pattern. Evidently Adrian Cabot had eluded his pursuers once again.

Somehow, she had finally dozed off, haunted by images: Larry and Adrian, her father, Mr. Phillips, Jeremy. All were standing over her, arguing, the faces twisted with their own passion.

The bed, when she woke, was a mess, the sheets twisted as if a battle had been fought there. She looked for Socrates, but he was gone, and she knew Adrian must have been here last night. None of the doors had locks on them.

Had she said anything in her sleep?

It was disconcerting to think of him in here when she was unaware. The little curl of warmth that was so confusing was back in the pit of her stomach. She could picture him in that white flowing shirt and tight britches, chestnut hair falling over his forehead. She could envision his looking down at her. Had she been tossing then? Did he wonder why?

I should be angry. But she wasn't. There was a feeling of comfort, instead, of being looked after. A feeling she needed to toss to the winds.

She dressed hurriedly, not waiting for the water she expected would soon come. Lauren wanted to go on deck, to discover what had happened last night.

To see him!

Sometime during the night, her resolve had stiffened. She had to do what she was sent to do, even if she paid for it the rest of her life. That she would indeed pay, she was sure. But Larry had done his duty, and more. So had Jeremy. And so did many thousands of young men. She could do no less. But in the meantime, she would store images and memories in her heart and mind.

She knew he'd never forgive her. The ship meant much to him. And betrayal was, in his view, the unpardonable sin. There had been deep bitterness in his voice when he'd talked about honesty.

But then, hadn't he wagered on her? Wasn't that dishonesty?

She sighed, wishing the battle within to end, though she suspected it wouldn't, not until this whole sorry affair was over.

At least Adrian wouldn't be physically hurt. Without guns, he couldn't fight, not if the ship were disabled. He would have no choice but to surrender before anyone was hurt. And if the ship were seized, Adrian would no longer run the blockade. He would be safe for a while. And he would be held no more than a few weeks, Mr. Phillips had said.

Lauren suspected even a few weeks would be hell for Adrian.

But the number of lives saved . . .

The day was glorious, the sun a huge golden ball that touched the dark blue of the water, showering the swells with golden mist. There was a peace this morning on the ship. Sailors leaned indolently into a brisk breeze as they scanned the horizon. The sea appeared empty of any invaders except themselves, and the ship cut through the sea with a cocksureness that reminded Lauren of her master. She often looked at the boxes piled on deck and wondered what they contained. Rifles, ammunition, or more benign goods? She suspected the cannon was below, safely tucked away in some dark hold, ready to explode in destruction and death.

But that seemed so remote on this tranquil morning.

She felt a presence near her, and she knew with the instinct that was still so surprising to her that it was not Adrian.

"Peaceful-looking, isn't it, miss?"

Lauren turned. Johnny. That was his name. The pilot. Adrian had told her he was the best in the business, but he looked impossibly young with his cocky grin and cowlick, and freckles across his nose.

Lauren nodded.

"Shouldn't have any more trouble until we near the coast," he said. "The Union patrollers stay just outside the Bahamian waters and along the Carolina coast."

"What happened last night?"

The pilot shrugged. "Saw some lights and headed in the other direction. I don't think they even saw us."

"Is every run like yesterday?"

"Oh no, miss. There's been times we've sneaked through without being sighted at all."

"Captain Cabot said you lost a man a few days ago."

Johnny's face sobered. "Aye, it hurt the captain mighty bad. But he'll take care of Terrence's family."

"Are the risks worth it?" Lauren asked.

Johnny shrugged. "They are to me. If I wasn't here," Johnny said, "I'd most likely be on a battlefield. Gi' me the sea anytime. Don't you worry, miss. The captain's the best."

Johnny left then, leaving her alone, leaving her wishing that her own safety was her only worry.

*   *   *

The morning seemed to crawl along. Wade Tyler, the first officer, told her that Adrian had not gone to bed until dawn and probably would not stir until late morning.

Lauren returned to her cabin and washed, then nibbled at some biscuits and eggs Dicken brought her. When she returned to the deck, even the brilliance of the day seemed muted by her mood. She sat on a box watching the crew for a while; then, restless, she walked around the ship, stopping to peer down at some playful dolphins chasing behind the *Specter*. But their antics only made her think of Socrates. What would happen to Socrates if Adrian were arrested?

As if he were summoned by thought, she heard the patter of small feet against the deck, and bright chatter. A hairy, bony arm reached out and disappeared into her skirt. She leaned down, offering her hand to Socrates, and he used it to propel himself up into her arms. The mouth reached for her cheek and gave her a loud, bussing kiss.

"I fear Socrates is in love," Adrian chuckled. "I've never seen him do that before."

Lauren turned slowly. "He was gone this morning." It was part statement, part question.

Adrian's expression turned devilish, the sandy-colored eyebrows arching with mischief. "When I came down this morning, I heard a noise from your cabin. I was afraid the little imp here might be keeping you awake. I did knock, lightly, but when you didn't answer, I thought I would fetch him. You look lovely when you're asleep, except the bed looked as though it had been through a battle."

Lauren turned away. She was dreadfully afraid she was blushing again. "I . . . had a nightmare."

"Then I wish I'd come earlier, and chased it away."

Lauren said nothing, just stared out at the sea.

"How would you like to take the wheel?" he asked abruptly.

She looked back at him. He was wearing a different shirt today, but it was of the same style as yesterday, with a wide slit at the neck, displaying curly sandy hair on his chest. It was tucked into a pair of snug blue trousers, and now he was wearing black boots that came almost to his knees. He looked like a freebooter, which was exactly what he was, Lauren thought. She wished she hadn't discovered that her taste apparently ran in that direction. But perhaps steering the ship would distract her from wayward thoughts.

His hand went to her elbow with a light but firm touch, and even without agreeing, Lauren found herself being guided to the huge wheel. Wade grinned at her as he relinquished it, and Adrian fitted her neatly between himself and the wheel.

Adrian guided her hands to it, and then one of his own took the giant wheel as the other clasped the back of her right hand, and together the hands, his and hers in concert, moved along the rich polished wood as he gave her a feel for its movement. Then Adrian released the wheel and moved his hands to her arms, giving her complete control of the ship.

Under Adrian's hands, the wheel had seemed light, easy to move, but now she discovered the strength it took, and she understood the muscles in his arms and chest. The wheel wanted to go one way while Adrian told her to turn in another, and she fought the current, feeling a thrill of pleasure ripple up her spine as she succeeded. She felt the power of the ship, and the power in her, as she made the heavy vessel accede to her commands. She savored the aroma of saltwater and soap from Adrian's nearness, treasured the warmth of his hands and body. Basking in the hot sun overhead and the cool breeze, she relished the freedom she knew in this one instant of time, this one unforgettable moment of perfect harmony.

Spontaneously, she turned around and looked at Adrian, full of delight and discovery. "This is wonderful!"

He smiled slowly. "I thought you would like it."

"I've never felt anything like it."

"There's only one place better," he said.

She was staring back at the sea ahead. She couldn't imagine a better place. "Where?"

"A place in England. The greenest fields you've ever seen. Riding over them at daybreak is as close to paradise as you can get."

He had seldom talked about England, and his life there, and now Lauren heard the longing in his voice.

The ship kicked up as it hit a particularly large wave, and spray flew up, raining them both with moisture. Lauren laughed. "It must be wonderful indeed to surpass this. Is it your home?"

"It was." The reply was short. She thought she heard something else, but it was lost in the wind.

And then he changed the subject, explaining to her the speed of the ship, the capabilities, just as the engineer had yesterday. There was pride in his voice as he told her he helped design it.

She tried to steer the conversation back to England. "You sounded like you love the land. Are you a farmer in a sailor's disguise?"

His hands fell from her arms to her waist, tightening there. "I'm a sailor by circumstance," he said. "And by my father's design. But, believe it or not, I'm a farmer by nature."

Lauren couldn't still the surprise that galloped through her. Rake, pirate, brigand—none of those labels would surprise her, but the soft yearning in his voice when he'd made the last statement did. She realized how little she knew about him, how much he kept to himself.

But then, he didn't know her either.

So why was the attraction so strong between them, the magic so real?

At least it was for her. Inexperience, perhaps. Did he do this to every woman?

Each smile, each touch, seemed hers alone. She would think so, anyway. For this time. For these moments. For these hours.

What would she do back in Delaware, in her cottage? In a world inhabited by those who told her what she could not do, rather than one who urged her to explore, who took her sailing to a deserted island, who placed a ship in her hands, and who had a monkey . . .

Suddenly her hands faltered on the wheel, and Adrian caught them, pressing his sun-warmed ones against hers with strength and confidence. Lauren and Adrian were one again as they stood in the sun, on the deck of a ship surging forward on a vast ocean. One as her soft body melded into his strong, hard one, one as his breath whispered along her cheek, one as their hands mingled and tightened against each other.

One. And Lauren knew at that second that she would never be whole again, that part of her would always belong to Adrian Cabot.

The day faded into a brilliant climax. Clouds had suddenly appeared, and the rays of a dying sun bounced off them, distorted them with vivid scarlets and veins of radiant gold. Streaks of blood seemed to dart through the sky. Lauren shivered.

Adrian was back at the wheel, his profile to her. Had she not had an obstacle the size of a boulder rolling around inside her stomach, the day would have been perfect. Adrian had been a wonderful companion throughout the afternoon: amusing, thoughtful. Yet he had said little of real importance to her, and she had not asked. She no longer wanted to know. The more she knew, the more she would care. And she already cared much too much, so much that every time she looked at him, her stomach flip-flopped and her legs grew weak.

Tomorrow they would reach the Carolina coast. Tomorrow she would spill her sand into the shafts of the paddle wheels. Tomorrow she would betray him and his crew.

Tomorrow . . . all her tomorrows would be locked in the past.

The fiery seascape softened, the volcanic shades fading as dusk caught and tamed the sun. The evening breeze quickened, and gusts of wind whipped her hair, and her dress against her legs, as she turned again to watch Adrian.

His own hair tumbled in the wind, his shirt blown against his chest, outlining every muscle. He turned around and gave her a grin of unbridled pleasure in the evening, in the forces of nature, in the sharing of something so inherently sensuous that Lauren felt her body consumed by it. "No," she whispered, a sound completely lost in the drafts around her.

She hurried once more for her cabin.

For her life.

Adrian watched her go. There had been something like panic on her face.

In a way, he understood, for he felt a bit of panic himself. He didn't understand why or how it had happened, but Lauren Bradley was becoming as indispensable to him as Ridgely. He'd never before felt the kind of elation he'd felt when she looked up at him at the wheel, her face so full of exhilaration, as if she understood and shared his own.

He wished he knew more about her, about the way she felt. There were moments of openness, but they were gone almost immediately. Something was gnawing at her, something deep and painful, and she kept it sealed as tightly as an aged bottle of brandy.

And since he was practiced at guarding his own thoughts and hurts, he was hesitant to pry.

He had been surprised 'from the beginning at how at ease he was with her, and he'd found himself saying things he'd never said to another woman: about England, his grief over Terrence, his brother. Pleasure was one thing; giving away part of your soul was another entirely. But he had been giving away part of that soul, piece by piece, first on the beach, and then after Terrence died, and again today at the wheel. And now Lauren had a substantial piece of him, and he had no idea how she would treat it.

Darkness fell; the clouds overhead blocked out even the brightest of stars. He felt the sea gathering its strength, and he knew a storm was not far away. In this instance, he welcomed it. A storm would benefit him, make his ship even more invisible to Yankee eyes. There was a danger, of course, of collision, but that was minor compared to the threat of cannon fire. His luck was holding.

A few more runs and he could return to England to make an offer for Ridgely. Perhaps Lauren would go with him. She apparently had no family left, no ties, and he knew she would like England. She had a sense of adventure that he'd never seen in a woman before, a sense of curiosity and discovery that matched his own.

Rain started falling, and he thought about fetching his slicker from his cabin. But he was afraid he might dally there, as he had last night, and he needed to be at the wheel, now that the storm was whipping up.

He enjoyed the splash of refreshing rain on his body. Bloody hell, but he felt good. Alive. So damnably alive after being with Lauren. And finally free of at least part of the past.

Gloriously free!

Although the engines kept the *Specter* from tossing on the seas as wildly as a sailing ship might, the steamship still rolled and crashed into high waves. Lauren, who'd never been seasick, started feeling ill.

Miserable, she clung to her bed, Socrates sitting and scolding unhappily next to her as the ship plunged up and down. Knowing he would be on deck, she thought of Adrian standing amid the raging storm like a Viking of old, probably laughing at the elements that sought to tame him.

The ship plunged down again, and Lauren thought all her problems might be solved quite a different way, after all. Her glance went over to the trunk she had brought aboard, the trunk with the sand. If the weather continued like this, she'd probably have no chance to get in the engine room, anyway.

Lauren started praying. Praying that the storm would continue.

But by noon the next day, the skies were blue again.

Lauren realized that early, when Dicken brought her water for washing, and some breakfast she couldn't eat.

He'd also told her the storm was over, that the *Specter* had made even better time than they'd expected, and that they would be approaching the Carolina coast by noon.

Lauren's stomach started feeling even worse, and it wasn't entirely due to seasickness.

Never a coward before, she hid in her cabin, telling Dicken that she was feeling ill. He took Socrates out with him, to get him some supper as ordered by Captain Cabot, he'd said, his mouth twisting into a frown as he reached down for the monkey.

How was the captain? Lauren hadn't wanted to ask, but the words came out anyway.

Dicken shrugged. "You can never tell with the captain. He was up all night with the storm, and he'll stay awake now until we're safe in Charleston."

"You said we were near the Carolina coast. Aren't there patrol boats?"

"Aye, but we usually see them first and run. The captain can outsail anything," he said in an increasingly familiar refrain. "Before long, we'll duck into a riverway until dark."

Lauren shivered despite herself. She didn't have much more time.

Dicken noticed, and attributed the tremor to seasickness. He'd had it a few times himself and sympathized, knowing that the best thing was to leave the victim alone. "I'll tell the captain you aren't feeling well."

That was the last thing Lauren wanted, for she knew it would bring him to her. And the last thing she wanted now was the captain's presence in her cabin, to be alone with him.

She shook her head. "Some fresh air will feel good. I'll be up as soon as I dress."

He nodded, and Lauren sighed in relief as the door closed behind him. Hours now. Only hours left before the ship would make its run into Charleston.

She tried to remember her lessons, anything to keep from thinking about Adrian. The bearded engineer in Washington had been skeptical and impatient. He had told her exactly where to put the sand, how long it would take for it to foul the shafts and stop the paddles. He had not expected her to do it, had expected it all to be a waste of his time. He'd made that quite obvious. But Mr. Phillips had insisted that they study the plan over and over again until Lauren believed she could follow the instructions in her sleep.

And that was what she would do. Not in her sleep of course, but automatically. Unfeelingly. As if someone else were destroying Adrian's ship.

Nothing will happen to him. Nothing will happen to his crew. How many times had Mr. Phillips assured her? If his ship were disabled, he'd have no choice but to surrender. And then a few weeks of detention. Nothing more. It would take him months to get a new ship, perhaps longer. And a thousand fewer guns would be delivered, not to mention the cannon below.

Nothing will happen to him. She had to believe that.

She chose her most unflattering dress. It seemed to fit the day. It was one of those from her mourning period, a dull gray pattern with a high neck and long sleeves. Then she twisted her hair in a knot at the back of her head. Perhaps her choices would put Adrian off, would reestablish the barrier between them.

The sun was high and bright when she finally reached the main deck. The storm had washed the sky, and made it so pure a blue that it hurt.

The first officer was at the wheel with the pilot. Adrian was nearby, scanning the seas with a glass. Socrates was huddled next to him, his hand over his eyes, as if he, too, were looking for danger. She had to grin at the way the monkey sometimes imitated Adrian.

Lauren followed their gaze. She saw nothing except the deep blue of the Atlantic and the creatures who, unlike them, belonged in it. There were no other ships, but she did see some dolphins swimming alongside, playing tag with the *Specter*.

Again she looked out to the horizon, squinting against the sun to see better. Finally she saw some birds soaring in the sky. Seabirds! They were nearing landfall. That's what so interested Adrian, not another Union ship.

Her gaze invariably returned to Adrian. He was in the same clothes he'd worn last night, and they were wrinkled, having apparently been soaked and dried on his body. A light beard covered his cheeks. But she would have known the silhouette anywhere. Perhaps it was the mark of English nobility; he seemed the picture of pride and arrogance despite the unkempt clothes.

As usual, her bones seemed to liquefy as she watched him. As if he sensed her presence, he turned, taking the glass from his eye. His gaze raked her, slowly moving from her hair down to the bottom of her skirt and then up again.

The look was so intense, so personal, that she had the sensation of his touching her, just as he had in the cabin before, and she felt as weak and helpless against the gentle assault now as she did then.

His eyes crinkled with amusement as they studied her costume, his head tipping slightly with question.

And then he winked, and Lauren knew all her precautions were for naught. In some ways, he could see right through her. Why, then, couldn't he in more important ways?

Lauren suddenly realized she wanted him to, wanted him to stop her.

Adrian looked down a moment at his own clothes, smiled wryly, and gave her that heart-stopping grin. He handed the spyglass to Johnny and made his way toward her.

"It's been a busy morning. We've been ducking patrol boats," he said, as if explaining his appearance.

"Are there more than usual?"

He shrugged. "Not really. It's mostly a matter of seeing them first and running."

"And you can outrun anything afloat," she recited the litany.

He grinned even wider. "Aye."

Lauren was always captivated by him, but now he was even more irresistible—if that were possible. There was an elation about him, a small boy's joy, that made him vulnerable as he hadn't been before. He'd always appeared so in charge, so contained, even when he told her about the man he'd lost. There had been grief then, and he'd shared it with her for a few precious moments, but still there had been a strength in him that kept reminding her who and what he was.

Now, as she looked at the wind-burned face with the eyes that twinkled and teased and took full pleasure in life, he seemed unguarded and accessible and . . . exposed.

"You're feeling better?" The gruffness in his voice said so much more than a simple question.

She nodded, her heart beating so rapidly she couldn't speak.

"Dicken said you were seasick. I thought about coming to see how you were, but I couldn't leave the wheel."

Lauren didn't say anything. She didn't want to look at him, at the concern in his eyes for her, at the face which should be lined with weariness, but wasn't. How did he keep going like this? Excitement? Adventure? Pure determination? Why did he always seem so much bigger than life?

She forced herself to speak, to break that spell that always wrapped itself around them, binding them together like the thin but nearly indestructible fibers of a spider's web. "Dicken said we'll wait in a river until dark."

Adrian looked toward the birds, now growing closer. "Two hours, perhaps less, and we will be entering the river."

"Which river?"

Adrian shrugged. "We keep all the rivers nameless. I think only Johnny knows them, and he never mentions the names. There's a lot of loose mouths in Nassau . . . and listening ears."

"*You* don't even know?"

"I don't want to know. That's Johnny's job."

"He's . . . from the South, isn't he?"

Adrian nodded.

"If . . . if anything happened to the ship, I know . . . I understand that you'll be released. What about him?"

Lauren saw some of the pleasure fade from Adrian's face. "I have British papers for him, and we've taught him some good British oaths."

Lauren felt the tiniest bit of relief. "What's a good British oath?"

Adrian feigned horror. "What a question for a well-brought-up young lady."

"For English well-brought-up young ladies," she corrected, trying to separate herself from the ladies he'd known before.

"For any well-brought-up young lady," he insisted with a grin, one of his hands going to touch a curl that had escaped the prim bun she had so carefully designed.

Even the air vibrated with the energy, the excitement, sparked by his touch. His fingers brushed the skin of her neck, and already the fire was starting there and moving like a field blaze to the core of her. She shivered, again experiencing the confusion she always felt with him.

"Captain!"

He turned. Johnny was gesturing to him. "Land ahead."

Adrian put his hand around her waist and guided her toward the wheel.

"The river?"

Johnny gave Adrian the glass, and Lauren watched as he put it to his eye, his mouth forming a satisfied smile. "You're a wonder, Johnny," Adrian said, handing the glass to Lauren and guiding her direction. Through the glass, she could see land, the flat sand dunes and, beyond that, trees. She didn't see a river.

She looked at him questioningly, and Adrian's smile broadened. "You'll see as we get closer."

"And then?" she questioned.

"We'll lie at anchor until dark."

"How far are we from Charleston?"

"A few hours."

Lauren felt a knot of frustration. She could visit the

engine room by day. How would she explain a nighttime visit?

"Will you get some rest?"

Adrian shook his head. "I'd rather enjoy the company of a pretty young lady."

"I think this lady needs some rest after last night."

Adrian looked immediately apologetic. "Of course. We'll have time in Charleston. I intend to spend a lot of time with you, Lauren Bradley."

Time in Charleston! Lauren felt her fingers shake slightly. There would be no time in Charleston. No time ever.

Lauren never knew how she managed to reply, how she managed to get to her cabin. She didn't know anything but a hurt so strong that it seemed to swallow her.

CHAPTER 13

It's all a game to him. Nothing more than a bet.

Lauren tried futilely to comfort herself.

Time crawled by, and yet it went much too fast.

She heard, felt, the engines slow, and then stop. Next was the heavy grating sound of the anchor being lowered.

Lauren tried to sleep. The good Lord knew she'd had precious little the night before, but drowsiness wouldn't come. And the tiny cabin grew hotter and hotter in the humid stillness of a Southern river.

She opened the trunk and looked at the sackful of sand for a long time. Slowly she poured its contents into the reticule she had made a point of carrying whenever she went on deck. Each grain of sand seemed to weigh a ton.

When she finished, she looked over Adrian's collection of books in the built-in shelves, and chose one at random. Anything to divert her thoughts from the upcoming act of betrayal.

Would he realize who was responsible? Would the plot even work? How could a few handfuls of sand disable a powerful ship such as this?

And where would she go? Back home? To what?

Her eyes went desperately to the title page of her book: *The Scarlet Letter*. She remembered the novel from school, a study of good and evil. How apt, she thought bitterly. It seemed a strange choice for an English sea captain and lord. She went back and studied the others. There were several books on shipbuilding and seamanship; a collection of Shakespeare; several English novels and even more American ones, including two books by Herman Melville and a second Hawthorne. All looked well read.

Another side of Captain Adrian Cabot. Her hand caressed the book, as if it were caressing him. She knew so little about him. She wanted to know so much more. And she would never have the chance now.

When she heard a knock at the door, she knew immediately it was Adrian. There was an authoritative quality that belonged to him alone.

The door opened before she could say anything, and he was suddenly inside, dominating the room as he did everything. He was carrying a tray with a bowl on it, and a pewter mug.

"Some soup and sherry," he said. "Best thing for a touch of the sea."

He had shaved and changed clothes. His shirt was white linen, which, even in the lantern light, contrasted with the rich deep gold of his skin. His legs were encased in gray trousers, which hugged the long muscled legs. As always, he exuded masculinity. Masculinity and raw energy. The latter radiated from him in waves as he sat the tray down on the table, pulled out a chair for her, and sprawled his long body over another chair.

Lauren knew she did not look her best. Much of her hair had worked its way out of the ridiculous bun, and her heavy dress was wilted and damp from the heat. She was miserable from the closeness of the cabin, and from nervousness, and doubt.

But Adrian, who had been awake for at least twenty-four hours, looked fresh and infuriatingly handsome. Lauren didn't realize she was scowling at him until he leaned his head slightly to one side. "That bad?"

"Worse," she replied.

"Would it help to know I made the soup myself?"

She looked at him with disbelief.

"My own hands," he added with a lopsided grin. "We don't have a regular cook, and we all learned long ago to take care of ourselves."

"An English lord?" she said dubiously.

"A hungry English lord," he retorted. He stretched out even farther until he seemed to take up the whole room.

Curious, Lauren took up a spoon and asked, "Where's Socrates?"

He flashed a grin at her. "I bribed him to stay in my cabin. A few bananas and a piece of bark."

"Bark?"

"That's how he keeps his teeth sharp."

Lauren looked suggestively to where he'd showed her one of Socrates's bites. "I would think that was the last thing you would want to do."

"The last thing my crew wants me to do," he corrected, and glanced down at the untouched soup. "And you are delaying."

Lauren took a sip of the sherry, feeling the liquid slide easily down her throat. She eyed the soup hesitantly, her fingers still clutching the spoon. She wasn't sure she wanted to eat soup made by him . . . just for her. Guilt was already piling upon guilt. She wished he weren't so kind, weren't looking like an anxious child awaiting approval.

"The adventurous Miss Bradley trembling at a bowl of soup?"

She looked up at the mischief in his eyes. "Not just any bowl of soup," she challenged straight back.

"Would you like a taster?"

"Like the Roman emperors?"

"Or empresses."

Lauren took another sip of sherry. Liquid courage. Liquid foolishness, but her senses were singing now, and once again nothing was real but the man across from her with the enigmatic eyes. He was a study in contradictions. A sea captain and cook. An English noble and gunrunner. A man of tenderness who nonetheless bet on a woman's virtue. A man who revealed little but who could charm the world into doing his bidding.

"Shouldn't you get some rest?"

"Not tonight," he said. "None of us will."

"What if a Union patrol boat finds this river?"

"Few of their ships can enter these rivers," Adrian said lazily. "We have a very shallow draft and can go places most of the Union ships can't . . . and then, remember, you couldn't see the opening of this river. It's only a slit, looks more like a creek. We're safe enough here for a few hours."

"Then why don't you get some sleep?"

He shrugged, and his fingers tapped on the table, not with nervousness but confined energy. "Anticipation, I suppose . . . it's difficult to sleep this close to the coast. But tomorrow in Charleston, I'll sleep away most of the day, and tomorrow night I'll show you the city."

"Adrian. What if . . . if the *Specter* is captured? What would you do?"

"You're not eating the soup," he observed.

Lauren had never been less hungry in her life, despite her lack of food during the day. "Now you're changing the subject."

"We're not going to be captured, Lauren. You're safe on the *Specter*, or I would never have agreed to bring you." There was an arrogance in the words that would have been unattractive from most men. From Adrian Cabot, they were merely a statement of fact. "Now try the soup," he urged.

His eyes commanded her, overwhelmed her, and to break their hold, she did as she was told. The soup was now lukewarm, although it had been steaming when Adrian set it down. And it was surprisingly good. She took another bite, and then another, finally looking up to see a grin of satisfaction on his face. She wanted to put her hand to where his mouth was, to touch it one last time, to feel his lips on hers.

Instead, her hand went up to push a wayward ringlet of hair from her face. He couldn't want her now, not the way she knew she looked. He couldn't. She bit her lips nervously as she stole a glance at his eyes.

Adrian watched her. There was something so completely appealing about her. Perhaps it was her large hazel eyes, always full of emotion, although he could never quite interpret the feelings there. Some of them, yes. There was a haunted quality, and a kind of fear lurked there, a fear he didn't understand—he only knew she didn't fear him. Not the way her body leaned against his with such trust . . . when she permitted it. But she usually projected a control that was unusual in a woman, and now it was gone, and she looked wistful and sad. Her honey-colored hair had escaped the severe bun and fell in waves around her face, and her dress clung to her figure in a way that showed every soft curve. She made him feel protective, even though there was fine steel in her. He had seen it that night she was attacked. There was nothing weak or missish about Lauren Bradley, but he longed to reach into her and extract that sadness from her eyes.

And there was loneliness, a loneliness that struck a chord within him. How many years had he been alone? All thirty-six. He was still alone. He'd had only Ridgely to dream upon.

His hand reached across the table and took hers.

Lauren felt the oddest mixture of intense heat and freezing cold, of wanting to respond, wanting to pull away, but she couldn't move, not any part of herself. Her eyes were fixed by his, like a butterfly on a pin, her own wings fluttering frantically inside.

"We will have time together in Charleston," he said. "There is something . . . compelling between us, something I think we need to explore."

"You must have had . . . something compelling before?"

His hand left hers, and he leaned back in his chair, studying her carefully. "I thought so . . . once," he replied slowly.

"And . . . ?"

"She didn't feel the same way."

Lauren heard a touch of remembered bitterness in his voice, and she recalled the conversation about trust. She wondered if that woman had inspired it; then her thoughts turned back to herself. What would he think about *her* in the next few days?

She realized that deep down she was seeking a reason, any reason, not to do what she planned to do. Shivers darted up and down her spine.

"Why do you continue to risk your life, and your crew and your ship?"

His grin was lazy and wicked, all seriousness gone now as though he'd given away enough today. "I told you. And you saw for yourself. Don't tell me you didn't feel the excitement when we evaded those Yankee ships. I saw your face."

And she couldn't. Yet that wasn't reason enough. *Give me a reason. Please give me a reason.*

"A game?"

Adrian wished again he could decipher the emotions in her eyes, but he couldn't. And he couldn't tell her about Ridgely, not yet, not until he knew he could get it back. Perhaps it was superstition; to mention a dream invited failure. Or maybe he didn't want her to know his family's failures, that he was landless, that he had been penniless until the war came, that he inherited naught but an empty, scandal-ridden title.

"A game," he confirmed. "An exciting, profitable game."

He moved back in his chair, grinding it against the floor. "And I'd better return to my duties to make sure it remains that way."

Adrian moved with the restless grace that always fascinated her. He hesitated as he reached her, then bent down, his hand bringing her face to look up at his. "I may not have another chance tonight to do this."

His lips met hers, and they fused in sudden, fierce desperation.

Lauren was saying good-bye. Try to understand, she suddenly, silently, frantically demanded of him.

And then she was standing up, propelled by his hands, until she merged into his body. His hands caressed the nape of her neck, and his tongue played along her teeth until she opened her mouth, and it darted in, moving, sweeping, teasing, seducing until she was a quivering mass of jelly. The fierce heat she'd felt earlier simmered into a soft boil, like candy she used to cook for her brother.

Pain washed over her. Pure, undiluted pain so agonizing that she didn't know where it started or ended, or its cause. Her brother? Adrian? She had lost the former, and in avenging him she would lose the latter.

The kiss deepened, filling her mind and senses, as their bodies pressed against each other. She could feel his hard muscles tense and move, and it aroused a hunger so strong she thought she would explode from it.

Sweetness and violence. They were both there. The sweetness was in the touch of his hands, the tender kneading, the gentle exploration, and the violence was in the voraciousness of his kiss. There was a promise in the kiss.

A promise . . .

She twisted away suddenly, her mouth stinging from the heat of his lips as she gasped for air, and sanity. Lauren looked up at his blue eyes, brilliant with passion and elation.

As they had been when he'd escaped through the Union net.

A game. It's all a game to him. But why then did she see something else? Because she wanted to. But that was folly.

Her body shook in reaction, and she felt his hand steady her. She didn't want to continue looking at him. But she couldn't help it. There was a wry, puzzled look on his face. His free hand came up and traced the contours of her face.

"You're a mystery, Miss Bradley." His voice was soft. "You always run away, and yet . . ."

Lauren tried to gather her wits about her, but they lay in a puddle at her feet. "You go too fast, Captain."

"Do I?" His voice was quizzical. "As I said, we'll have time in Charleston."

"But you'll be dashing in and out."

His eyes, however, vowed otherwise. "I'll make time. And now I'd better leave while your virtue is still intact. You're dangerous, Lauren Bradley, in more ways than one."

He gave her one last, lingering look, leaving Lauren to slump like a rag doll in the chair as the door closed behind him.

As dreams closed behind him.

The engines of the *Specter* seemed magnified in the still night. A whisper of smoke followed the ship in a lazy curl upward into a dark, moonless night as Lauren went up on deck, her reticule fastened firmly around her wrist.

She had brushed her hair, letting it fall free, and changed into a clean dress. Like most of her clothes, it was a modestly cut gown with a high neck and puff sleeves, but the rich violet color contrasted with the honey of her hair.

Her face was pale. She bit her lips to put some color in them and pinched her cheeks. And as she studied herself in the mirror, she told herself again that Adrian was merely flirting in his careless way, that a man of his background and experience could not possibly be serious about her.

The night air was like a tonic, mixing with the sherry she'd had in her cabin. Adrian had left the bottle when he departed the cabin, and she had sipped another glass to bolster her courage, to dull her conscience. Or perhaps enhance it. She *was* doing the right thing, the honorable thing. She had to believe that.

She could not see land, only the open sea. They had been under way now for nearly an hour. How much longer? The reticule on her wrist grew heavier and heavier. And yet she knew that timing was important. If the ship lost power far from the patrolling Union gunboats, it might well be rescued by a Confederate ship or another blockade runner. The disabling must be done near Charleston, near the heavy cordon of Union patrol boats.

Lauren allowed herself to think of nothing but her mission. She shoved aside every other thought, need, reservation.

Taking several deep breaths of air, she looked around the deck of the ship. There were only shadows in the dark of the night but she knew every available sailor was on lookout. Adrian, distinctive by his height and stance, was at the wheel with the pilot. There was no noise among the crew members. Words were spoken at a whisper, as though the wind might carry voices to the enemy awaiting them.

The ship was moving slowly, and Lauren was aware the *Specter* was at half-speed as the crew waited for high tide to make its dash into Charleston. When she felt the engines increasing speed, she would visit the furnace room. Just a few hours now.

Lauren didn't know how long she stood there clutching the railing before the movement of the ship accelerated. The throb of her heart did the same. They were beginning the run into Charleston. She looked around to see whether any eyes were on her. Surely someone would suspect, should suspect, but all eyes were focused seaward.

Her heart in her throat, she moved woodenly toward the hatch leading down, pausing at its door for a miracle, a reprieve. But there was only the dark night, the pounding of engines, the rhythm of the paddles.

Lauren climbed down and made her way down the corridor until she reached the engine room. Four men were shoveling coal while two stood by, apparently taking a few moments' respite. Their clothing and faces were almost completely covered by coal dust, and sweat was running in streaks down their necks.

The room was miserably hot, and she wondered how they stood it. She looked at the shafts that drove the paddles. Just one disabled shaft would be enough to cripple the *Specter*.

Will turned and winked, acknowledging her presence.

She half-expected to be ordered out. She hoped she would be. But he merely yelled over to her, "Want to see her go at a run?"

She nodded.

One of the other men grinned as she moved toward one of the paddle-wheel shafts and leaned against it.

The men all turned back to their individual jobs. Mouthing a fervent prayer she was doing the right thing, she loosened the drawstring around the reticule and turned slightly, using her body to shield her hands from eyes that might move back to her. The machinery was unprotected, the sand flowing easily from her small bag into the shaft.

Lauren felt the heat now, heat so intense that she almost fainted. Heat that came from more than one source. She knew her face was shiny red, and she straightened, almost falling in the effort. One of the men saw her uncertain movements and quickly came to her, his hand steadying her.

This must be what hell is like, she thought suddenly. She felt herself being moved, almost like a puppet, toward the hatch. Once outside, her lungs grabbed for air, fighting to breathe, fighting the constriction in her throat.

"Miss . . . ?"

She looked up at the man. Her own dress now was coated with black from his hands. She felt as if she were wearing a scarlet letter like in the book she'd tried to read all afternoon. Would it ever come off?

Lauren leaned against the wall. "I'm fine now," she whispered. "I just got a little warm. I'm sorry."

"That's all right, miss. Can I 'elp you back to the cabin . . . or above for some air? Cabin's most fitting place for you, though. We're getting close to Charleston."

She nodded. "I'm fine now. You go back."

He looked at her dubiously. "You sure, miss? The captain would have my berth if aught were to 'appen to you."

She managed a weak smile. "Yes, I'm sure." To prove it, she took several steps, feeling stronger with each one. When she looked back, he grinned and turned, disappearing into the engine room.

Lauren hesitated at the cabin that she knew Adrian had been sharing with Wade. Was Socrates there? She needed someone, a companion to talk to. Even a monkey. Perhaps best a monkey.

She knocked first, even knowing both the first officer and Adrian were topside, then opened the door. Socrates looked up from a mess of clothing on the floor. He was, apparently, making a nest of some kind. But on seeing her, he sped over to Lauren, holding out his arms as he had done before, cackling gleefully.

"Why don't you come with me, Socrates?"

He nodded, as if understanding perfectly, and they left the tiny cabin and went to Adrian's slightly larger one. Lauren slumped down on the bed, exhausted and hot and consumed by raw anguish.

Socrates huddled next to her, as if trying to fathom a pain he sensed but didn't understand.

And she waited for the inevitable, her heart cracking a little wider at each groan of the ship.

CHAPTER 14

Adrian heard the low call, "Sail ho," just as he glimpsed the white sail.

The Union Navy had steamers, but most of the blockade fleet was still composed of sailing ships: easy to see, easy to outrun. The Union obviously depended on numbers to do its work.

He still had the wheel and would continue to have it until just before they reached Charleston.

Adrian prayed that the enemy hadn't yet seen them. The hunter had white sails silhouetted against a black night, whereas the *Specter*'s graceful gray hull showed only about eight feet above the waterline. Only anthracite coal was burned, leaving a mere wisp of smoke, and steam was blown off under water to stifle the noise. The engine room hatchways were now screened with tarpaulin; even the binnacle was covered and, in order to see the dimly lit compass, Adrian had to peer through a conical aperture.

He changed direction away from the sails. He had some time before they should start the run into Charleston. He would circle around and then set course to spurt between forts Moultrie and Sumter. Those were the trickiest moments. And although he had a dark night, he prayed for night fog, which would further cloak the *Specter*'s movements.

As the enemy sails disappeared out of sight, Adrian momentarily allowed his thoughts to return to Lauren. She'd been tense earlier as she stood on the deck. He didn't think it was the prospect of entering Charleston, for he had seen her exhilaration before when she'd watched the *Specter* outrun the Union patrol boats. He had suspected then that he loved her. She touched the core of him as no one else ever had, that moment when her hair flew free with the wind and water splashed against her, plastering her dress against the shapely figure. She'd smiled, a smile full of wonder and excitement, and he'd had to catch his breath. She was a woman who would always take chances, who wasn't bound by convention and rules, although she was still finding her way.

He grinned as he remembered her first reaction to Socrates, the whimsical curtsy when most women would shy away with fear, and the day on the beach when she'd dug her toes in the sand like a child given her first piece of candy.

And then the smile faded as he recalled the expression on her face in the cabin earlier. He had the most disconcerting feeling that there was something he should know, should understand . . .

"Captain?"

He turned.

"Another sail, sir."

He turned all his attention to the sea. They could expect continual sightings until they reached the quay in Charleston. This was no time for romantic musings.

They were all looking now for dim lights around the coast, lights manned by the Confederate States Signal Corps to guide them in. The lights were dim, so they wouldn't assist the Union Navy and expose the runners, but still visible enough to penetrate the utter darkness of the coast.

Johnny was the first to sight the lights, and from now on he would direct the *Specter*'s run. Adrian gestured for a man to approach. "Tell Dicken to go down and look after our passenger. She's not to come up." Adrian remembered only too well the last hours of the man who'd been wounded on deck.

The seaman nodded and disappeared.

They were now scarcely ten miles from the entrance into Charleston. There was no fog, and Adrian had to decide whether to go ahead and begin the run or wait. Both courses presented dangers. The longer they stayed in these waters, the more likely they would be sighted, but the fog would greatly diminish the threat on the actual run.

But they had speed, speed that few of the Union ships had, and most of the Union gunners had yet to master their skill in hitting the fast blockade runners. "We go," Adrian said, and whispered into a tube that went down into the engine room, "Three-quarters speed."

The tempo of the engines increased.

"Ship starboard," a man reported, and Adrian looked at Johnny who nodded. "Hard aport."

They seemed to slip by unnoticed, but then there was another ship ahead. At that moment, Adrian felt a change in the sound of the engines, a hesitation. "Will?" The word was whispered down the tube.

"Something's wrong with the starboard paddle wheel, sir."

Adrian cursed to himself. The loss of one of the paddle wheels would send the ship in circles, and the timing couldn't be worse. They were in the middle of the blockading fleet now, and he was carrying some of the most important cargo of the war. And then there was Lauren.

"Cut engines," he said, hoping the dark night would render them invisible until repairs could be made; they had to be made before morning.

Adrian tensed and felt the apprehension of the others

around him. There was always a danger of steam blowing when engines were unexpectedly stopped, but silence followed. Complete silence.

He gave orders to Wade, and then ducked behind the tarpaulins covering the hatchways down to the engine room. Will was sweating profusely as he checked the gauges.

"Something's fouled the wheel," he said. "Don't know what in the blazes it could be."

"Can you fix it?"

"We'll have to take the bloody thing apart."

"Do it," Adrian said tersely, and left to go back above. His fabled luck was certainly failing him now. He thought of his pistol in the footlocker in his cabin; it was the only weapon they had. And he thought of Lauren. "Bloody hell," he swore. He had to tell her of the danger they faced now.

Quick steps took him to the cabin, and he knocked impatiently before opening the door. Dicken was inside, looking uncomfortable in the chair at the table. Lauren was sitting with Socrates at her side, but she started to rise when she saw him. He shook his head, his hand resting briefly on her shoulder. "I can't stay. I wanted you to know we're having some engine trouble . . . to assure you I won't . . . allow you to be hurt."

Her face didn't change expression. It was set and still, like the face of a statue. The hazel eyes were larger than he'd noticed before, and their depths were whirling with emotion, like swarming clouds in a stormy sky. Once more he wasn't able to fathom them. He leaned down, his lips touching her cold ones, and he felt her shiver. "It'll be all right, Lauren," he said. "I swear." He went to his footlocker, opened it, and took out the pistol.

"You can't," he heard her whisper. "You said . . ."

"I won't use it," he tried to reassure her. But it gave him some sense of control. He wouldn't, couldn't, allow anything to happen to her. He tucked the gun in his trousers and took a jacket from the locker, pulling it on and buttoning it to cover the pistol. "Dicken, stay here with her."

Dicken nodded.

Adrian hesitated, taking one last look at her white face. "Take care of Socrates."

Lauren moved as if to rise. "Can't I go with you?"

He grinned suddenly. "I'm afraid I don't need any distractions now, and I don't want to worry about the imp here. Or you. Please?"

Her face seemed to break then, and he wanted to touch her. But he couldn't. He was needed at the wheel. Still, all the way back, the look on her face haunted him, the grief he saw in her eyes. For him? He shook his head, concentrating all his attention on the problem at hand.

The crew on deck was so still that Adrian could hear their breathing. They stood rigidly, staring out at the blackness around them, listening for voices, for paddle wheels of other ships, for the flap of sails. Apprehension and fear had an odor, and it was evident now. Adrian knew it wasn't for lack of courage, but born of helplessness, of sitting like a wounded duck with no weapons. What in bloody hell had happened? Will kept the machinery in immaculate condition. What could possibly have fouled the machinery? A seed of suspicion started forming in his mind, but he wiped it away quickly. Impossible!

The sound of engines came to him then, and the pace of his heartbeat increased. A flare went up, and then another, and he saw a ship just in front, and then another to the starboard. Every man on deck was outlined in the garish light. He heard shouts, voices, an order to prepare to fire, and then the roar of cannon as shot went hurling over the bow of the ship.

Adrian turned to Johnny. "Can you swim from here?"

Johnny looked toward the shore and mentally judged the distance. Adrian had had British papers forged for him, and Johnny had practiced an English accent, but too many people knew about him in Nassau, and he could too easily slip into his Carolina twang. If identified, he would spend the rest of the war in prison. "Aye, Captain. Used to swim all the time as a kid."

Others had heard the conversation, and a rope was lowered over a darkened part of the ship.

Adrian held out his hand. "Good luck, Johnny."

Johnny grinned as he grasped it. "See you in Nassau soon, Captain." He gave a brief salute just before slipping down the rope into the water.

Another flare lit the sky again, then a third. Adrian whispered down into the tube to the engine room, "Will?"

"Nothing, Captain." The reply was despairing.

It was too late in any event, and Adrian knew it. Even if they could start the engines, they were completely boxed in. He felt an iciness seep into his bones. He had never surrendered, and he hated the bloody thought.

Another shot went over the bow, falling just beyond the deck. If Lauren were not aboard, he might have tried something, anything, but now he couldn't risk it. He turned to Wade, who was next to him. "Go to my cabin and burn the logs and manifest."

Wade nodded, and grimly turned on his heel and disappeared.

Adrian turned to two other men. "Thomas, light the lamps, and you, sailor, hoist a white flag."

The *Specter* was bathed in flares now. Adrian heard a booming noise from a distance. Another runner, he thought detachedly. Some other runners would probably get through now, since so much attention was being centered on him. Adrian wanted to think of anything but the next few moments. His hand ran over the mahogany wood of the wheel. It had been a good ship. His home for a year. More than that, he had put his heart into its design and construction. His heart and his hopes.

He flinched as the white flag fluttered upward. His ship was now bright with lights, and he watched the nearest Union cruiser lower a boat with a group of men aboard.

"Lower a ladder," he told one of his own men, "and prepare for a boarding party."

Wade appeared next to him. "Papers are burned, sir."

Adrian took his hand from the wheel. He'd said his

farewell. "If we're separated, you and the rest of the crew go to Nassau and wait for me there."

His face still grim, Wade nodded.

"It shouldn't be more than a few weeks at most," Adrian said confidently. "We'll get a new ship."

They heard the slap of the boarding boat against the side of the *Specter*, and then six men boarded. They were led by a young, flushed-faced lieutenant, his hand on a sidearm strapped to his waist.

"I'm Lieutenant Edmond Porter. Captain . . ."

"Adrian Cabot."

"So you're Cabot," the officer said. "I'd expected a better chase," he added with arrogant contempt.

Adrian's fist knotted. There was hardly concealed glee on the Union officer's face, and Adrian understood why. The Union crew credited with the capture of a blockade runner received portions of the prize, and Adrian was well aware there was an extra bounty on the *Specter*. But still, the young officer's attitude galled him, and Adrian's fists flexed with his own impotence at the moment.

"Assemble your crew to the bow," the officer ordered pompously, and Adrian, having no choice, did so. "Including those in the engine room," the Yank added.

Adrian walked slowly to the tube near the wheel. "Will, bring your men topside." He then turned back to the officer, feeling the pinch of the pistol in his belt. He was surprised the officer hadn't asked for weapons, but then the man was young and arrogant and enjoying every moment of this, enough to be careless.

"You will accompany me below," Porter commanded. "I want the crew roster, the manifest, and logs."

Another boat was now below and more men were swarming up on deck. Blue uniforms were everywhere.

"I have a passenger, a young lady."

"Anyone else?"

Adrian shook his head.

The man grinned knowingly. "Alone?"

Rage slowly filled Adrian, a deep burning rage. The indignity of surrender was being compounded by this puppy's insolence. The ship was gone. The cargo. Possibly Ridgely. He didn't want to think about Lauren. She could be lost to him now. It would be months, perhaps even a year, before he could get back to Charleston. Somehow, her loss seem to minimize the others.

"A lady," Adrian emphasized, his anger now spilling over, "who deserves courtesy."

"A Southerner? A slave-owner?" the man said contemptuously.

A muscle strained against skin in Adrian's cheek. He had never wanted violence as much as he did this moment. But there were two other Union sailors behind him, and he'd surrendered.

Surrendered. He still couldn't believe it, couldn't believe anything that was happening. He would go to prison now, for weeks certainly, perhaps for months. The Yanks, he knew, would try to hold on to him as long as possible.

They had reached Adrian's cabin. He stopped at the door and started to knock, but the lieutenant pushed him aside and jerked the door open. Dicken was still in the cabin, and he stared at the newcomer. Lauren was standing, closely holding Socrates.

The Union officer glared at Dicken. "All crew members are supposed to be at the bow." He took several steps toward Dicken, but apparently Socrates thought he meant to attack Lauren, because the monkey suddenly launched himself at the lieutenant, his teeth going through the uniform jacket.

The lieutenant shouted and tried to dislodge the animal, as the other two Yankee sailors grabbed Adrian, who'd made a step forward. He threw them off just as the lieutenant pulled his pistol from his holster and aimed at Socrates.

Both Adrian and Lauren reacted at the same time. She threw herself at the lieutenant just as Adrian grabbed the gun tucked in his trousers and fired. He'd meant to fire at the gun in the Yank's hand, but Lauren's movement had propelled the lieutenant forward, and the bullet caught the lieutenant in the shoulder. At that moment, Adrian felt his arms being seized again, and this time he didn't resist.

He knew he'd just violated surrender. Not only that, he'd shot a Union officer. He'd lost his neutrality.

Dicken stepped in front of Lauren to protect her while Socrates retreated to a corner, looking with interest at the confusion he'd created.

The lieutenant had fallen to his knees, one hand clutching at his shoulder, and the doorway was filled with other blue-clad sailors who'd been summoned by the shot. Lieutenant Porter looked at Adrian with eyes filled with hate. "I want him in irons." The lieutenant looked at Dicken. "Where do you keep them?"

Dicken just looked at Adrian, whose eyes flicked over Porter with grim humor. "We don't carry them."

"Then tie him. Securely." He turned to Lauren. "And watch her."

One of the newly arrived Union seamen went over to the bed and ripped a sheet into long strips, and Adrian's arms were twisted behind him, the wrists bound tightly. Adrian stood still, his features controlled, his eyes blank as he felt a helplessness he hadn't felt in years, not since . . .

A last jerk on the knot made him square his shoulders. He felt a overwhelming sense of failure, of frustration, even of humiliation that Lauren was watching his capitulation. A cheek muscle strained against his skin as he tried to disguise his anger.

"And shoot the damned monkey," the lieutenant directed one of his men.

Adrian strained against the bonds and the hands holding his arms, but now the grasp on him was firm. As he struggled, Lauren grabbed Socrates, holding him tightly. "If you shoot him, you'll have to shoot me too."

"Lieutenant," one of his men said, "the captain won't like it if a civilian woman is hurt." He was an older man, a boatswain by insignia, and his voice was soft and respectful, but nonetheless carried a warning.

Porter's face was scarlet with pain and anger. "Get him out of here," he said, pointing to Adrian, and Adrian was pushed out into the corridor.

Adrian turned around, watching as two other men

leaned down to help the lieutenant up. He heard the man groan, and he didn't feel regret for his actions, though he did feel for the consequences. But he knew now Lauren would take care of Socrates . . . and that the Union boatswain would protect them both.

When he was finally pushed up on open deck, another Union officer, an older lieutenant, had arrived.

"What in the hell is going on here?"

Adrian stiffened.

Just then, Lieutenant Porter, holding his shoulder, emerged from the hatchway. "He shot me, sir. I want him placed in irons."

"That young idiot was going to shoot my pet," Adrian retorted through his teeth.

"Lieutenant?" Inquiry was in the older man's voice.

"The damned beast attacked me, sir."

A faraway thunder told of another battle elsewhere. The older officer listened a moment, then shook his head and motioned to the two men assisting Porter. "Get him over to the doctor on the *Allegheny.*"

After the lieutenant was helped into the boarding vessel, the other man took a long, steady look at Adrian. "I'm Greenway, first officer of the *Allegheny.* You're Cabot?"

Adrian nodded.

"What happened to your ship? Why did you stop?"

Adrian shrugged. "One of the paddle wheels."

"And down there?" He motioned to the hatchway from which the lieutenant had emerged.

"Your lieutenant is a fool."

The man didn't disagree. "Can the engine be fixed, or will we need to tow it?"

Adrian shrugged. It was no longer his problem.

"Your logs?"

"Destroyed."

"Manifest?"

Adrian nodded again.

"Is all your crew British?"

"Yes."

"The pilot?"

Adrian remained silent.

"You are in a very precarious position, Captain. Regardless of provocation, you shot a Union officer. Your cooperation would help."

Adrian laughed bitterly. "Would it?"

They both turned as they heard an angry chattering. Lauren, firmly holding Socrates, approached. Socrates, sensing something wrong, fought his way down and ran to Adrian, pulling on his coat.

Greenway arched one of his eyebrows. "That's your pet?"

Lauren approached Adrian, reaching down and taking the monkey again. "He thought that officer was attacking me."

"Captain Cabot?"

"No, Socrates."

"Who in the hell is Socrates?"

"The monkey," Lauren explained patiently, but her eyes hadn't left Adrian's face, as if she were memorizing it.

Adrian remembered the frustration he'd felt when he discovered his brother had gambled away everything. He knew the same fierce sense of helplessness now. His wrists remained tied behind him and, despite the conversation, Lauren's face was taut and strained, her voice tightly controlled. Under any other circumstances the exchange would have been humorous, but there was no humor in it for any of them now.

Especially not for Adrian. There was something about Lauren that turned him cold inside. He was grateful for her protection of Socrates, but there was something in her face, something that begged his understanding. And there was a stiff reserve, as if she had to stay away from him.

"And the young lady?" The question came from the Union officer.

"Miss Lauren Bradley. She's a civilian taking passage."

Lieutenant Greenway bowed slightly to Lauren. "Both you and the . . . Socrates . . . will be given every consideration. I regret Porter's . . . actions."

He motioned to the boatswain. "Please take the lady

and the . . . animal to the *Allegheny* and tell the captain we need a towline. Also some irons. We'll keep the *Specter*'s crew here."

Lauren, who had started moving away, turned back at his words. "Irons?"

"Yes, miss. The captain violated his surrender."

"But . . ."

"It's no longer your concern, miss." He turned, leaving Lauren no choice but to accept the lead of her escort.

Greenway then turned to one of his own men. "Check the engines and have a crew ready to help with a towline. I want to get under way. Captain Cabot, you will join your crew at the bow."

As an insistent hand tugged at Lauren's arm, she hesitated, then turned back to where Adrian was watching her with hooded eyes, visible in the light of lamps now lit throughout the ship. "I'll take good care of him," she told Adrian. "I'll find a way to get him back to you." There was desperation in her voice, even a plea.

But he was being pushed toward the bow, and when he was finally able to look around, she had disappeared over the side of the ship.

Lauren sat on the bow of the Union steamer, the *Allegheny*, and stared at the *Specter* still being towed behind. She had, apparently, done an excellent job. Union engineers had worked on the *Specter* all day to no avail.

Adrian was still on his ship. No, she thought, the *Specter* was not his ship anymore. It would never be used again to transport war goods to the Confederacy. Its cargo of cannon would go, instead, to Union forces.

Emptiness had settled inside her. Emptiness and loss and grief. They had seeped into the core of her bones, and she hurt for Adrian, for herself. She had committed an unforgivable offense against him, no matter how worthy her motive. And nothing ever could repair the damage. Especially not now . . . not after Adrian had shot the lieutenant. And even that was her fault. If she hadn't moved forward as she had . . .

What would happen to Adrian? She knew he could even be charged with piracy now, though she doubted that would happen. But he had assaulted and shot an officer. He had violated the neutrality laws. And she knew how much Phillips, and the American Government, wanted him. They had the excuse they needed now to hold him for the duration of the war.

She kept seeing Adrian's face as his hands had been tied. Even then he'd dominated the room, permitting no emotion to show except the strain of a muscle in his cheek.

Oh, Adrian. What have I done?

The sea was calm, its color a deep, dark blue, like Adrian's eyes. It had been a day and a half since the capture of the *Specter*, and the captain of the *Allegheny* said they would arrive in Baltimore later today. She had not mentioned her part in the crippling of the *Specter* to him; she couldn't bear to mention it to anyone. She would have, though, if they had tried to take Socrates from her. But the Union captain had been the soul of courtesy, even tolerating Socrates's snapping.

Where was Adrian now? The boarding officer had asked for irons, but surely . . .

She couldn't bear to think of proud, restless Adrian in irons.

She felt a tug on the leash. She was keeping Socrates on one now, because she was afraid not to. He had already bitten two sailors, not to mention the wounded second lieutenant, his arm now in a sling, who glowered at them both whenever he saw them.

Socrates obviously missed his master. He searched every passing face, his expressive face anxious, and Lauren even imagined that he eyed her with accusation. The monkey ate little, and played even less. His only activity now was watching. As Lauren watched.

Adrian lay on the bed in the first officer's cabin of the *Specter*, his wrists encased with heavy iron bands. He would have been lodged in the hold, he knew, if every inch of space hadn't been filled with cargo. So he was locked in here, a guard outside.

The ship seemed eerily quiet without the noise of the engines, and the tow kept the ship rocking without engines or sail to stabilize her.

He'd had only a few moments to speak with his crew members, with Will, and that conversation haunted him. Will still didn't understand how the shaft had been disabled. Adrian was afraid, however, that he did. Especially after Will told him Lauren had been in the engine room.

He hadn't wanted to believe it. But the evidence was there.

He moved from the bed and stood, leg irons clanking on the floor, then paced restlessly in short, hobbled movements. The irons had already chafed his skin, and walking made the pain excruciating, but he had to do something or go mad.

Greenway, who had taken charge of the prize, had been almost apologetic as he ordered the irons, but he was taking no chances. The crew of a runner captured months earlier had retaken the ship from the prize crew, much to the embarrassment of the capturing ship and the United States Navy. The fact that Adrian had concealed a gun, and used it, had sealed the man's decision.

Pain aside, the irons were galling and humiliating. A visible sign of defeat and surrender.

And betrayal. Another betrayal.

The pain from this one was even worse than the first. His heart, he knew now, had been more involved, much more involved. He hadn't realized how much until now. Adrian suspected he would always have a raw, festering wound deep inside.

He'd had time to reason it all out. At first, he'd been puzzled. Lauren had not sought him out in Nassau. He'd done all the pursuing, and she'd done all the running. And then he'd realized it had been the running that so fascinated him.

A very clever girl, Lauren Bradley.

Adrian turned again, facing another blank wall. The

cabin had been thoroughly searched before he was placed
here, the mirror removed as well as any object that could
possibly be used as a weapon. Greenway, unlike the
younger officer, was thorough.

Lauren. He could think of little else. His mind recalled
all their conversations, all their meetings, trying to find
something that should have warned him. But there was
little, except that elusive quality about her.

And why? She was definitely not a typical spy, if there
was such a thing. He would still swear she was a virgin; no
one was that good an actress. Her tentative responses, the
wonder in her face as he kissed her, the shyness. Nor did he
think she faked her attraction to him, the attraction that
ignited between the two of them like a Roman candle.

Neither, he thought, could she pretend her affection for
Socrates. The little monkey, Adrian had discovered, was
rather a shrewd judge of character, and did not take easily
to human beings.

Tired of the clank of chain against the bare wood floor,
Adrian sat back down, his upper body against the wall of
the cabin, and stared at the links binding his wrists. He
wanted to hate her for this, but he couldn't. He knew she
must have had powerful reasons. But he wouldn't trust her
again. Not ever. Except with Socrates. He knew, in some
unfathomable way, that the monkey was safe. It was odd—
he trusted her in this one way but would never again trust
her in any other thing.

Why, bloody blazes, why? A sense of duty? Patriotism?
He suspected something more. She had spoken wistfully of
a brother and father. Had they anything to do with this?

He brushed back his hair, glaring at the short length of
chain between his wrists. He might as well get used to it.
Bloody Christ. He would never get used to it. He closed his
eyes against the thought of prison. This war had years left
to run.

Why, damn it, Lauren, why?

But it was fruitless to speculate. It had been a mistake to
trust again—a very costly mistake.

CHAPTER 15

With Socrates at her side on his leash, Lauren watched from the deck of the *Allegheny* as the prisoners were taken from the *Specter*.

She knew she shouldn't watch, and yet she felt drawn to the spectacle. She had read someplace that a criminal returns to the scene of his crime, and now she understood the compulsion.

Her hands dug into the railing of the ship as first the crew was marched away under heavy guard, and then Adrian. He was wearing the formal attire of a sea captain: a finely tailored gray uniform coat and blue trousers, a captain's hat perched jauntily on brushed chestnut hair. But his wrists were shackled, and four men surrounded him.

Her heart stopped beating, a lump catching deep in her throat. The emotions of the past few days, so fierce and turbulent, all came back with a vengeance, and she held on to the railing for dear life.

Socrates, too, saw Adrian, and screeched, leaping against the leash. Lauren reached down and picked him up, holding him tight as the monkey fought to climb down, his chattering now a mixture of anger and anxiety.

As if in response to the frantic sounds, Adrian, who was stepping off the gangplank onto the wharf, looked up. His gaze went to the *Allegheny*, searching its deck until it found her. He stopped, surprising his guards, one of whom stumbled against him and said something. Lauren saw his expression harden for an instant, then he turned back to her, his mouth bending into a wry smile.

And then he winked. Lazily. Arrogantly. As if he owned the world.

Did he not know? Did he not realize her part in this? Lauren desperately didn't want him to know she'd betrayed him. Better for him that he believe it bad luck. And yet, she felt even worse than before. Perhaps some of her guilt would be lessened by his knowledge, by his hatred.

As he turned away from her, she knew she would never forget that last flash of acknowledgment.

She heard footsteps behind her. It was the captain of the *Allegheny*, who also watched as Adrian and his guards disappeared into the crowd.

"Where will they take him?" Lauren's voice was strained. The captain carefully averted his eyes. As far as he knew, she'd been a passenger on the *Specter*, and therefore a Southern sympathizer.

"The city jail, I suspect, until the government decides what to do with him. His crew will also be held there until the prize court makes a decision."

"Prize court?"

"A court is held whenever a ship is taken, a formality to determine that the ship is liable to seizure."

Lauren met the officer's eyes. "You know, Captain, that the shooting of your lieutenant was an accident. If your . . . officer hadn't attacked a helpless little . . ."

"Helpless?" The captain looked at Socrates with dislike. The monkey had bitten several of his men and disrupted the ship.

"He was just protecting me. And Captain Cabot was trying to protect both of us."

The captain looked uncomfortable. "He should have surrendered his gun."

"But . . ."

"There's nothing I can do, Miss Bradley. The matter is now in the hands of the Naval Department."

Socrates was making small sad clicking noises, and looking at her as if she'd betrayed him as well as Adrian. And she knew she had.

"And you, miss, where will you go? Is there any assistance I can give you?"

Lauren stiffened as she immediately made up her mind. She would go to Washington and see whether she couldn't repair at least some of the damage she'd caused. She would plead with Mr. Phillips.

"You can have my trunk delivered to a hired carriage."

"It would be my pleasure. But if there's anything else, if you need any funds . . . ?"

Lauren looked up at him sharply. Did he know? She still felt as if she were wearing her own scarlet letter. Spy. Betrayer. But there was only kindness and concern in his eyes. She thought of Clay and the Union officer she'd seen at the Royal Victoria. Friends, now enemies. Principle divided them. Principle and geography. But what good was principle if it divided friends, if it resulted in killing?

How insane it all seemed now. Reality was Adrian. Adrian standing at the wheel of his ship. Adrian attacking three ruffians. Adrian, his wrists shackled, winking at her as if the world were still his. Adrian who was gone from her forever now.

"Miss Bradley? Do you need any funds?"

She shook her head. "No, thank you, Captain. You've . . . been very kind. But I'll take the carriage to the train depot. I'm going to Washington."

One of his dark bushy eyebrows lifted. "Washington?"

Lauren felt she didn't owe him any explanations. She had thus far stayed to herself, refusing his invitations to share meals and taking hers alone in the cabin. She had not felt like socializing with the man who had taken Adrian and the *Specter*, although she was well aware of the irony of that feeling. She knew the Union captain had put her reticence down to Southern sympathies.

"I have . . . acquaintances there," she said finally.

He nodded. "Well, then, I'll get one of my men to fetch your trunk and escort you to the train." He hesitated as if he wanted to say something else, then turned abruptly and left.

Lauren stayed on deck, watching the crowds swarm below. News apparently traveled quickly, and curiosity seekers were lining up along the dock to see the *Specter*. The ship, she knew from overheard conversation, would probably be put into service now as a blockade patrol boat. Suddenly that seemed very sad. She thought of the ship, Adrian's ship, chasing Clay and the other blockade runners she had met.

What a poor spy she was!

She stayed there, watching as her trunk was brought up on deck, and then an ensign approached and introduced himself. "James Garver," he said, "at your service. The captain said to see you safely on a train."

Lauren nodded her thanks but shied away from the arm Garver offered. Somehow, it was like associating with the enemy.

Mr. Phillips had taught her how to attract attention, and now she would turn it back on him. She would win Adrian's release. She must. And then what?

It didn't matter. Nothing really mattered beyond securing Adrian's freedom.

She leaned over and picked up Socrates. "I promise," she whispered to him. "I promise to get you back to your master." And then she turned to the ensign. "I'm ready to go," she said in a strong, determined voice.

Phillips was not in Washington when she arrived. She had sat in her room in an inexpensive boardinghouse for a week, making daily visits and always finding him gone. She was waiting in front of his office on the tenth day when she saw him. His face split into a broad smile as he asked her to enter and pulled up a chair for her.

"Miss Bradley, my congratulations. I . . . the country . . . owes you a great debt. I just returned from Baltimore, and we have reason now to hold Captain Cabot the rest of the war." Triumph and satisfaction glittered in his eyes. "And we owe it all to you. It was, I take it, you who disabled the ship?"

Lauren forced back the dismay she felt. Reason, she told herself. "What . . . will happen to him?"

"He'll be sent to Old Capitol Prison as soon as the prize court meets," Phillips said, leaning forward in his chair. "And he'll stay there, despite British protests."

"The Old Capitol Prison?"

Phillips took a cheroot from a box on his desk. "It holds prisoners of state, Confederate military, and political prisoners. Our Captain Cabot is a bit of all of them. And finally, it's the most secure prison we have."

"His crew?"

"They'll be held in Baltimore until the prize court makes a decision, and then they'll be released on a ship bound for England."

"But you said they would all be released," she said.

"That was before Captain Cabot so conveniently changed the circumstances," Phillips said, leaning back in his chair with a broad grin.

"He was protecting me," she said, knowing that the real reason, the defense of a monkey, would probably bring little sympathy. "Wouldn't that make a difference?"

"Not at all," he said, missing the odd pleading in her voice. "Prompting him to use that gun was a stroke of genius, my dear," he said. "I would like to send you back to Nassau."

Lauren knew then that no argument would work. Mr. Phillips was obviously gloating. There was no way he would change his mind or intercede for her. If she protested anymore, it might put him on guard, and in the past few days she had developed an alternate plan, just in case.

Perhaps she was developing a talent for intrigue, after all. It was not a comforting thought, but still . . .

The chill that had invaded her at Phillips's praise turned to steely intent. She had heard stories of terrible conditions in both Northern and Southern prisons. Death rates were high, disease and hunger rampant.

What if Adrian died because of her? Even if he didn't, what would years of imprisonment do to him?

A part of her, the cowardly part, had thought never to see him again. She had hoped she could somehow obtain his release with the others of his crew, and by a third party return Socrates. She knew the guilt would show in her face, and she could tolerate anything but his contempt and hatred. But now she didn't have any choice. She had to help him, and she could do that only by herself.

She would have to see him, and once she had won his freedom, she would tell him what she'd done and why. And then she would leave him, forever.

Lauren didn't flinch when Phillips offered her payment. She would need money. And she didn't feel guilty accepting it from him. She had done as she had agreed: stopped the *Specter* from blockade running. It was Phillips who violated their understanding, her understanding that Adrian would be freed.

She also asked for some official identification that she might need to show to federal authorities. She watched as he wrote something on paper, and then put a seal to it.

Lauren took the paper, scanning it quickly, wondering at her new ability for deception. Addressed "To whom it may concern," the note simply asked that any Federal agent, civilian or military, extend all assistance and courtesy to Miss Lauren Bradley.

"When will you be leaving for Nassau?" Phillips asked.

"In two weeks," Lauren said. "I want to go to Dover first."

He nodded. "We *are* grateful, Miss Bradley."

Lauren nodded and left.

*   *   *

Adrian stared at the tin plate of cold beans the jail keepers called food. They were accompanied by a piece of coarse bread full of weevils.

He shoved the rations aside. Bloody rot. He told himself he'd better get used to it. But he couldn't. His tailored clothes were already loose-fitting. He suspected they would get a lot looser in the future.

He turned his attention to his cell. He already knew every stone that made up the walls, every dark inch of the dirty floor, every dismal corner. The six-foot-wide by eight-foot-long interior was bounded on three sides by stone walls and the fourth by iron latticework. The only light came from a dim lantern hung in the corridor.

He'd had to fight himself to keep sane. He could barely tolerate the closeness and darkness of the cell. He'd woken the first night in a cold sweat. He'd been a child again, a child who'd displeased his father and been locked in a closet. He hadn't understood, just as he'd never understood his father's dislike or the often violent punishments that had sent him seeking refuge in the green fields and woods of the estate. They had represented sanctuary. They still did.

Why hadn't he been loved? Adrian asked himself. First, his father had rejected him. Then his brother. Sylvia. And now Lauren. She'd seemed so different, had looked at him in a way no one else had. He'd felt a sense of belonging he'd never known before, a sense of completeness . . .

Fool.

He had been separated from his crew. They had come together for several hours yesterday to attend the prize court. He'd been kept in irons during the short hearing during which his ship and cargo were confiscated. There was no argument to make. The ship was obviously carrying contraband on a hostile coast. Both the ship and its cargo were given to the U.S. Government.

The crew was ordered released, but his fate had already been decided days earlier by the U.S. Navy Department. Despite British protests, the government had declared Adrian a belligerent. He had already been told he would be sent to the Old Capitol Prison in Washington for the remainder of the war.

How long? He rose from the uncomfortable iron cot and went to the grated side of his cage, resting his fingers on the iron. He had been here two and a half weeks and was already going crazy. What would months and even years do to him?

And Ridgely. He could forget about ever fulfilling his vow now. Blockade running was the only way he could ever accumulate enough money to purchase the estate. While he sat in prison, Ridgely would fade further and further from his grasp. He should have known Socrates would be nothing but trouble. Yet he didn't, couldn't, regret stopping the lieutenant from killing Socrates. He would do the same thing over again.

The thought of Socrates inevitably led to thoughts of Lauren, of seeing her aboard the *Allegheny*. He'd heard Socrates and looked up to see her watching him, her face incredibly sad as she held the monkey close to her. Until then, he'd been quietly furious. The more he had thought about the ship's sudden engine trouble during the long hours in the cabin, the more certain he'd become that she'd had something to do with it. Everything had been just too bloody damned convenient, and all the pieces fit. The machinery was kept meticulously clean by the crew; there had been no trouble until the worst possible moment, and Lauren had been in the engine room just prior to the trouble. Her silences, her aloofness, her reluctance to talk about herself, were all further evidence. He'd been a fool not to suspect anything. He'd damned her over and over again, and then he had seen her, and her misery was so evident, his fury dissipated.

He still didn't know why he winked. Whether it was for her sake or his own. His pride, the deep pride that had been bred into him, couldn't admit defeat to her. Nor could he bear the look on her face.

At least he'd been allowed to shave and change to fresh clothes before he'd been marched away under her eyes. But the shackles had galled him. Bloody hell, but he'd hated her to see him like that, bound like a criminal and led around like a bloody animal.

Would he ever see her again? He doubted it now. Some part of him had hoped she would visit him, or that she would be at the prize court. A letter, a message, would have lightened the bleakness he felt.

Over and over again, he had reviewed their conversations, had looked for a clue. It all came back to her brief mentions of a brother and father. She had said she lost them in the war, and her eyes had glazed with unshed tears.

Was that it? But had they been on the other side? Now he remembered that she'd never really said with which army her brother had served. Adrian had assumed . . .

That was the only thing that made sense. He would swear she hadn't done it for money.

He sat back on the cot, tired of the incessant bumping against walls, of six steps one way, and then six the other. In two days, he'd been told, he would be taken to Washington. Perhaps he could find a way to escape. He doubted it, though. He'd been kept in very close confinement, as if he were a prize prisoner.

A prize prisoner?

A prize fool.

Lauren had rehearsed the scene for hours. She had sat with Socrates and went through it over and over again.

"Play dead," she'd command. And he usually cooperated. But sometimes he didn't.

Adrian had told her about the trick, how the monkey would usually remain still until his arm was touched, and then he would move ever so slightly. But what would Socrates do if he sensed Adrian nearby?

Socrates had to cooperate this time. He just had to.

Just as she had plotted Adrian's downfall, she was now plotting his deliverance. She took a train to Baltimore, taking only a portmanteau and leaving her trunk and most of her new clothes in Washington. She didn't need much.

She did not dismiss the possibility that she too might well be in a prison cell in the next few weeks.

Lauren had learned from Phillips that Adrian would be brought to Washington. She'd heard about the security at the infamous prison. She had even wandered by it, and had quickly been told to leave. Onlookers weren't even allowed to stand across the street from it. And any visitors had to be approved by several sources. She suspected Phillips would be among them.

Lauren knew she had to act before Adrian arrived at the prison. He would, she suspected, be brought by train. If only she knew when. The Washington papers, filled with news of the capture of the famous blockade runner, had said Adrian would be brought to Washington within the week. No definite date was given, and the reason, Lauren suspected, was that some attempt might be made to free him.

Lauren visited two gunsmiths in Washington, purchasing a gun at each, pleading the need to travel in "these terrible times" to see her "poor wounded fiancé." She tucked one weapon into a pocket she'd sewn into her dress and the other, a Deringer, in her portmanteau.

She bought a ticket for the train back to Baltimore. It was full of wounded men headed to hospitals in the North, and she was obviously a topic of conversation, a young lady traveling alone with a monkey. It had not been easy, keeping Socrates with her; she was beginning to understand what Adrian had undergone, and her admiration for him spiraled. Socrates went after two people who came too close, and would have bitten them if Lauren had not been quick. One advantage, however, was that few men bothered her after Socrates spit at them.

She found exactly the town she was seeking at one of the stops not far out of Washington. Some of the wounded were being unloaded, so there must be a hospital here. That meant a stranger would not be suspect. She counted the minutes they were at the station. Forty. Perfect.

Just before the conductor warned that the train was pulling out, she grabbed Socrates and her portmanteau and detrained, standing for a moment on the station platform. She asked a ticket agent about a rooming house and the location of the hospital.

Lauren had to visit three rooming houses, all of them private homes suddenly utilized to serve families of those hospitalized, before she found one who would accept Socrates's presence.

"My poor fiancé's pet," Lauren explained dutifully. "He's a terrible little creature, but Adam just dotes on him and . . . well . . . I was told Adam doesn't have long to live and his dearest wish is to see his little friend again." As the woman's face expressed surprise, Lauren hurried on. "After me, of course." She wasn't completely sure that was true now. It certainly wouldn't be true in a few more days.

"Of course," the woman said sympathetically.

The rest of the day went quickly. She visited the livery stable and then a mercantile where she bought some rough men's clothes and packed them in the portmanteau. She refused to give any thought to failure. By the time she arrived back at the rooming house, she'd spent nearly half of the money Mr. Phillips had given her.

Tomorrow, she would see Adrian. Her mouth grew dry at the prospect. And she couldn't sleep.

Had he guessed yet? Did he know?

She felt an iciness that had nothing to do with the weather. Socrates loped around the room aimlessly. She had found some fruit for him, and thin hard crackers, and after he'd finished eating listlessly, he had come and clung to her with desperation and need. He'd never stopped searching for Adrian, and would look at her with great sad eyes that broke her heart.

"I miss him too," she whispered.

But Socrates would have him back. And she never would.

CHAPTER 16

The key grated in the lock of Adrian's cell door, and he looked up in surprise. He wasn't to go to Washington until tomorrow, and the door was seldom opened; his food was passed through a small opening at the bottom of the cell, as was the limited water he was given.

He had been lying on the iron cot, staring into nowhere, trying to summon images of the sea and sky and sun. He had tried to do the same with Ridgely, but he found that too painful now. Also painful were the recurrent recollections of Lauren and the resultant beads of heat that formed in his groin. There was, too, a surprising perpetual ache in his heart.

He had taken off his shirt, and it lay at the end of the cot with his uniform jacket. It was infernally hot in the underground cells, where no air stirred in the high July temperatures. It was perhaps around noon now, he supposed. He had become rather adept at judging time in a place where the sun didn't shine, reckoning from the hours his food was brought. There were two meals a day, a weak gruel and coffee in the morning, usually beans and bread at night, sometimes supplemented with a rare piece of tainted pork.

As the door opened, Adrian moved lazily to a sitting position. His guards were wary because, he knew, much had been made of him. In the first few days of his imprisonment here, there had been a stream of visitors, including senior naval officers, government officials, and British diplomats. But in the past two weeks, there had been none. Decisions had been made, and his transfer to permanent Federal custody had been delayed only until the prize court met.

Adrian had been cooperative with his jailers because there was no reason not to be and because he had innate courtesy as well as pride. His guards had responded with a gruff fairness of their own. Cautious but respectful.

"Visitor, Cabot," said one of the men, a sergeant who supervised this section of cells, the most tightly controlled area of the jail.

More questions, he thought. More questions about the pilot who was missing, about the rivers and inlets he'd used. He'd said nothing, but his captors had persisted, saying things would go easier with him if he talked. He recognized that for the lie it was; they weren't going to let him slip through their fingers.

But at least questions would get him out of this bloody cage for a few moments. He reached for his shirt at the end of the bed, the once fine lawn shirt that was now gray with prison dirt and dried sweat. He then shrugged on his coat, and ran his fingers over his face, feeling the new bristles. He was allowed to shave, under supervision, every other day.

What the hell. There was no one he particularly cared to impress. He grinned suddenly at the sergeant and shrugged. "Who is it?"

The other guard answered with a leer on his face. "A woman."

Adrian felt the beat of his heart quicken. "A woman?"

"And baby. She says it's yours, and she needs some money."

Adrian bit back any reaction. He was long experienced at hiding his emotions, but his mind raced feverishly, running over various possibilities.

A baby?

Some of the expectancy that had risen at the sergeant's first words died. The woman was obviously not Lauren. Then who? Christ knew he'd been like a monk these past eighteen months, not out of choice but out of lack of opportunity. There had been the widow in Charleston, but she'd been too experienced to get caught that way.

He squared his shoulders as he fell in between the two guards. What the bloody hell. Anything to get out of that cell.

Adrian was led down one corridor, then another, and ascended some steps. Finally they stopped in front of a door. Adrian waited as it was opened to reveal a woman, and he recognized her slender body.

His pulse unexpectedly jumped in jerky patterns, like a drunk frog he'd once wagered on in Nassau. He moved inside, forcing himself to lean indolently against the wall as if he hadn't a care in the world.

Lauren had sat primly in a chair, her eyes calm although emotions roiled in her head like a summer squall as she waited for Adrian's entrance.

A bundle lay in her arms, its contents squirming restlessly against the blankets that hid the features, but not the form, of a small creature.

"Play dead," she whispered, and Socrates was instantly quiet, as if he understood that more than a game was at stake. She tensed as she heard the door open, praying that Adrian would understand what was happening.

Her scheme had worked as planned. So far.

Acting came easier now. Tears had flowed easily as she had explained her situation, how she was a merchant's daughter who fell victim to a rogue seaman and then been left alone with a sick baby, thrown out of her own house. She had read about Adrian Cabot's capture and had come all the way from South Carolina. If only she could talk to him, convince him to help, perhaps even marry her.

She was so distraught that the commandant of the prison found himself calming her, searching only her reticule. She did not have to pretend at nervousness. Her hands were shaking with the prospect of seeing Adrian again, of perhaps hearing his condemnation, of being in the same room with him. Already, she felt the familiar trembling, the heat curling her toes. She heard a noise at the door, and her body tensed, hoping that Socrates would continue to play his part.

The sergeant, whom she'd met moments earlier with the commandant, entered and behind him came Adrian. His eyes flared as he saw her, and his gaze traveled from her face to the bundle in her arms. He then went to a wall and leaned against it, his movements lazy and his eyes guarded.

"My dear, you shouldn't have come here," he said softly as she rose and moved to him. His eyes didn't change, but his arms opened to receive her. Lauren felt the quickening of her blood as his eyes met hers in wary but willing conspiracy. The familiar electricity darted between them, the electricity of attraction and desire, and something more, something reminiscent of the night they'd left Nassau when the gunboats were chasing them. Lauren, despite her fear and apprehension of facing him, suddenly felt the exhilaration of shared danger again. She hadn't felt it the night of their capture. She'd been too miserable then, but now . . .

"Sergeant," she said, feeling movement within the bundle and knowing that Socrates was well aware of Adrian's presence, "could you possibly give us some privacy?" Her eyes clouded with pleading tears again.

Anxiously, she watched the sergeant's gaze around the bare room where there were only a bench, a chair, and a table.

"All right, miss. Thirty minutes, but he'll be searched afterward."

It was a warning, and she knew it. She nodded.

The sergeant gave her a pitying last look and went out the door just as Socrates exploded from the linens that bound him and threw himself at Adrian, scolding furiously and nipping at his master's hand.

Adrian released Lauren and leaned against the door, seemingly unaffected by Socrates's bites as he swung Socrates up on his shoulder.

He was thinner. So much thinner. Blond stubble showed on his cheek, and his usually immaculate clothes were wrinkled and stained. His hand lingered on one of the monkey's paws as if reassuring him, but everything else about him was vigilant as his gaze met hers, as if he were contemplating an unpredictable beast.

He raised an eyebrow. "A baby?"

Lauren swallowed the apprehension in her throat. Did he know? Was that why he was being so . . . controlled? Or was it something else?

"I . . . it was the only way I thought I could get to you."

"And they didn't take a look at Baby Socrates?"

"I told them he was deformed, and I didn't want anyone to see him."

His lips twitched. "Deformed?"

"I thought I could hide . . . this." Determinedly, Lauren pulled a tiny Deringer from the swaddling clothes.

Adrian's twitch grew more pronounced. "A pistol-toting deformed baby. Now why wouldn't I have thought of that?"

Lauren felt her own lips twitching. It *was* ridiculous. "Well, it worked," she said defensively.

"Up to a point," he admitted dryly. "Until they search me."

"Isn't there someplace you could tuck it?"

"And implicate you if they found it? I don't think so. They search rather well. I've had experience."

Lauren found it hard to concentrate. His touch had revived all her internal fires. Despite his gauntness, he was undeniably handsome, the stubble on his cheeks giving him the look of a desperado. His brows were furrowed together in a watchful frown, and the quizzical twist of his mouth made her heart wobble like a broken wheel. Yet despite his wariness, there was no accusation in his eyes or on his lips.

Socrates was huddling against him, his face touching Adrian's with uncharacteristic affection, and Adrian, seemingly absentmindedly, was petting the monkey. "Thank you for taking care of him," he said. His face was sternly set now that he had declined her offer.

At the sincerity in his voice, Lauren felt her heart turn over, swelling with an ache she feared would never leave her. "I have another plan," she offered.

Taking her arm, he moved away from the wall and led her to the bench. He guided her down, and towered above her as he sat on the table, his eyes never leaving hers. A small smile played on his lips. "I can't wait to hear it," he said dryly.

Despite her guilt, she felt momentarily nonplussed, even angry, at his lighthearted response. It was almost as if he were enjoying her immensely. Not her efforts, her. It was disconcerting. She wished with all her heart she could read his thoughts, but he was revealing nothing. Though his mouth moved in amusement, his eyes remained steady and unfathomable.

"I understand they're taking you to Washington."

"So I'm told."

"I've bought a horse in a town outside Washington. The train stops there."

"Bought?" His lips started twitching again. "You don't mind jailbreaking, but you draw the line at horse stealing?"

Lauren bit her lip. "I wanted it to be . . . available."

The smile left his lips. "And . . ." he prompted.

"If you . . . had a gun, could you get off the train then?"

"Perhaps. *If* I had a gun."

"Socrates can get it to you."

"How?"

"I'll walk by . . . just when the train slows for the

stop, and make Socrates believe your guard is threatening me. He'll probably attack then, and you can help pull him off. There will be a Deringer—the one I brought today—in a pocket I'll sew inside his jacket."

"And why won't anyone notice me taking a gun from a monkey?"

"I'll get hysterical."

Adrian stared at her. "I never realized you were so devious, Lauren." The words were said quietly.

Lauren's pulse speeded. His eyes, those beautiful, charismatic eyes, seemed to reach into her soul, seeking answers she dared not let him have.

"Socrates needs you," she replied simply after a moment.

"And you?"

Lauren swallowed.

He leaned down, and Socrates scampered off his shoulder. Adrian's face was very close to hers. "Do you need me, Lauren?"

Lauren felt his breath on her skin and his hand on her arm, stroking it in sensuous slow movements. She was held prisoner herself by the raw need that shot through her, the overwhelming need to be kissed by him, to be held by him.

"Do you, Lauren?" The question came again.

"No," she replied defensively, but even she could hear the lie in the word.

"Why are you here, then? Why risk . . . so much?"

Lauren had no answer she could give him.

"Why, Lauren?" His voice was like a spike being hammered into her.

"Because," she replied finally, "it isn't just. That . . . lieutenant was going to shoot Socrates."

"Do you really think they care about justice? There's been a bounty on me, Lauren. All they needed was an excuse. And many would say that's justice of a certain kind." He shrugged. "It all depends on what side you're on."

"How can you be so reasonable?"

He smiled faintly. "I'm hardly in a position to be otherwise. I knew the risks."

"It's not fair," she said suddenly.

His hand touched her chin, moving it upward until her eyes met his. "Nothing in war is fair, love."

Lauren couldn't move her gaze from his. She trembled inside, her stomach tightening into knots. Did he know? And was he right? Was everything fair? Would he forgive her? And would Larry forgive her this, this rescue of the man responsible for his death?

His voice broke into her thoughts. "You could become a fugitive, go to prison yourself."

"No one will know," she said. "I didn't use my own name . . . The guards don't know about Socrates; they believe I have a baby, not a monkey. There wouldn't be anything to connect us."

"And will you go with me?" His blue eyes were dark, secretive even as they sought her own secrets.

"No."

"Why?"

"There's no time for questions," she said desperately. "They'll be back soon."

Adrian looked at the door then. "Aye," he conceded, as he warred with himself. Christ, how he wanted his freedom back. But could he risk hers?

And why was she really helping him? Just because of her sense of justice? Guilt? Love? All three?

Her hazel eyes were large and expectant.

So infinitely inviting.

He lowered his head so his lips could touch hers. He had thought of her mouth so many times in the past three weeks, yet not the most enticing of dreams compared with the glory now as her lips yielded to his with a greed as naked and desperate as his own.

His suspicion—no, his certainty—about her role in the capture of the *Specter* was still very strong, and he sought to discover the truth as his mouth pressed against hers. But the only truth he found was their hungry need for each other, even more powerful now that he'd experienced her loss, and the emptiness that had come with it.

If she *had* betrayed him, she obviously regretted it, or she wouldn't be here. As for betraying him again, there was no reason now. The government had his ship.

Her mouth opened to his, her tongue meeting thrust with thrust, her body melding to his in a way that was becoming achingly familiar. Bloody hell, but he wanted her. All of her.

A tremor rocked him. Weakness. He had no room for weakness, and yet with her he forgot the past, didn't think of the future. The only reality was her eyes that looked at him as if he were a god, her body that responded as if it were part of him, her lips that promised what words did not.

Her arms crept around his neck, her hands running through hair that was now ragged, her fingers kneading his skin as if she couldn't get enough of him. He had closed his eyes for a moment, and now he opened them and saw her eyes glitter with tears.

He knew she'd betrayed him.

And he knew she loved him.

And he knew that, for the moment anyway, he could accept both realities.

Adrian guided her up, melding her body into his. He felt heat and arousal and tenderness as tears touched his cheek like pieces of wet silver. "You are an amazing woman, Lauren Bradley."

He felt her stiffen in his arms, and he sensed her apprehension. "Coming here to the jail," he explained. "Planning all this."

"You . . . will do it, then?"

He nodded. He wanted to bind her to him. The last several weeks had demonstrated how important she was to him. No matter what she had done, or the reasons why, he still wanted her. He would discover the secrets she hid, but he would wait until she was ready to tell him. In the meantime, he would keep her with him. He would find a way. Because he was very, very sure that nothing else would mean anything until he solved the mystery of Lauren Bradley.

There was a shuffling outside, and Lauren swooped down and scooped up Socrates, who was watching them with great interest. A knock sounded at the door, and Adrian had just enough time to issue the magic words, "Play dead," to Socrates before it opened.

As it did, he kissed Lauren on the lips, slowly and seductively and lazily, ignoring several coughs behind him.

"Of course I'll marry you, my dear," he said, a cocky grin on his face. "If only you'd told me about . . . this little fellow earlier. I'll request permission in Washington."

He turned to the sergeant, who was looking awkward and ill at ease in front of the affectionate display. "I thank you, Sergeant, for making an honest man of me, and I'll accept your congratulations," he said, with a grin that appeared sincerity itself as the jailer mumbled something.

Adrian's hand lingered on Lauren's arm, and he felt her trembling in reaction.

"Just a short time, my love." The farewell echoing in the room, he turned and nodded to the sergeant, stepping quickly away as if he were captor and not the other way around, leaving Lauren feeling dazed and weak and strangely exultant.

CHAPTER 17

After Lauren left the jail, she returned to her Baltimore hotel room, her mind in an uproar.

So apparently was Socrates's. He had a tantrum, breaking a porcelain bowl and pitcher. She knew it was because of Adrian, that he missed Adrian. Later, he crawled into her arms and made whimpering noises, and she quickly forgave him the extra money she would now have to pay for the damage.

When he finally went to sleep, she looked through the small pile of clothes she'd taken from the *Specter* for him. She'd learned Socrates's clothes were not an affectation but a necessity, since the monkey had little modesty about intimate functions. She found what she needed, a small loose jacket and matching trousers. She sewed a pocket on the inside of the jacket and put the small Deringer inside, and fashioned a little tie that would keep it in place but that could be quickly released.

And then she'd brushed her hair, looking at herself in the mirror. She didn't know who she was anymore. Certainly, a different Lauren gazed back at her.

How could she even think about helping the man who was responsible for her brother's death?

How could she not?

The Lauren of a year ago didn't have that gleam of excitement in her eyes. She'd been, as her father once said, "like the gentle twilight of evening." Larry had been the glow of the morning sun, the adventurer. She'd stayed home and minded the fires, prepared the food, sewn the clothes. She had been the responsible one, until on impulse she'd agreed to Mr. Phillips's scheme. Now she was on the crest of a wave she couldn't get off.

And the fearsome thing was that she didn't want to get off. She had found the thrill of challenge, of danger, addictive. Just as she found Adrian Cabot addictive.

"Forgive me, Larry," she whispered into the mirror, and yet in some strange way she knew he would understand.

Yet soon it would all come to an end. She would leave Adrian, and he would never find her. Even if he wished to find her, even if he never discovered the real role she'd played in all this . . .

The train station was teeming with crowds, their voices surprisingly hushed and anxious.

A battle was under way not far distant in Pennsylvania, she heard. A place called Gettysburg. Hundreds of thousands of men were engaged. The telegraph said thousands were killed and wounded.

Lauren heard snippets of rumor. The Confederates were breaking out; Washington was in danger again. The Union was losing; the Confederacy was losing.

There was a sense of panic and urgency everywhere.

Cold desolation filled her as images came to her mind. The cannon, the smoke, the death. Some of the expectation she felt about today's plan faded as the war once more became immediate. She had stopped some of the cannon from reaching the South, but had it then been used against

Southern soldiers? Meeting Clay and some of the other Southerners in Nassau had robbed her of any personal animosity. Northerners or Southerners, they were all young men with hopes and dreams and sweethearts and families.

"Any man's death diminishes me." John Donne had written those words more than two hundred years ago. They had always been beautiful words to her, but now they were poignant and real and devastating, for she had in some way become a part of war. She had made herself a part of it.

The news also provided a needed distraction. No one was paying attention to a plainly dressed woman and baby. And immediate sympathy was given when she said she had to find her wounded husband.

She had hoped Adrian would be on the first train, but he wasn't, and she walked to a small park and sat on the grass until she thought it time to return. Socrates grew heavier and heavier, as did her portmanteau.

She arrived an hour before the second train and watched for him outside the station, not wanting to be seen loitering inside. As if looking for someone, she kept moving, the apparent baby in her arms keeping men at a respectful distance. Finally, a prison wagon appeared, and Adrian descended in handcuffs, sandwiched between two men in naval uniforms. She'd seen neither guard before, and she uttered a prayer of thanks; her one fear had been that his guards might include someone who had seen her at the prison. She hurried inside to get her ticket, finding there was none available until her desperation finally touched an onlooker, who agreed to switch to a later train. Then she turned and watched Adrian, as did almost everyone else in the station.

He was taller than his guards, taller than nearly everyone in the station, and despite his now-soiled uniform and the irons circling his wrists, he was by far the most commanding presence. He was clean-shaven now, and his blue eyes were masked with apparent indifference. Several uniformed men muttered insults, others just stared at him; but he seemed impervious to it all, his expression never changing, not even when he saw Lauren.

His gaze cut to the bundle in her arms, and then up to her face. She nodded her head, almost imperceptibly, and he turned his head to say something to one of his jailers.

Lauren also turned away. She didn't want Socrates to sense his presence as he usually, almost uncannily, did.

Ticket finally in hand, she boarded the train, settling down on one of the hard benches in the same coach with Adrian. Her bench faced toward the rear. Adrian was taken to the rear bench, which backed up to the wall, and faced her. They were, however, ten benches apart and, as the coach filled up, she could see only the top of his head.

Belching smoke filtered through the interior of the coach, and the train lurched forward, its whistle blowing, the wheels grinding against the rails. The passenger coach jerked forward in sudden movements and then gathered speed.

She was committed.

The bundle in her arms started moving. She had kept Socrates as quiet as possible, not wanting the trainmaster to prohibit his boarding. Lauren glanced at her seatmates. She had the space next to the window, and two uniformed men shared the bench with her. Directly across and facing her were a man and woman, and a boy of about twelve.

She never quite anticipated how people would take Socrates. She knew that Adrian hadn't cared, but then Adrian had the self-assurance and confidence to readily meet any situation and the ability to charm anyone. Even now, she could see his head bent as he conversed with the men taking him to prison, and at the Baltimore jail it had been apparent that the jail officials, though cautious, had respected him.

Socrates's head emerged first, the funny, charming little old-man head with its inquisitive expression, and then the bony fingers. He was wearing a pair of sailor pants. The jacket, with the Deringer inside it, was in her portmanteau, and not to be worn until just before needed. She'd put his collar on and leash, her hand holding it securely.

"My husband's pet," she explained to the sudden silence around her. "He was a sea captain before volunteering for the Navy. He's been wounded . . ." It was the same story she'd told before, and it generated the same sympathy and interest.

The boy reached out to touch Socrates, and Lauren held her breath, but Socrates tolerated it, and then he scratched impatiently at Lauren's reticule in search of a treat. He was contentedly munching when the conductor came by for tickets, and though the train official raised an eyebrow, he said nothing.

"Does he know any tricks?" the boy said after the conductor departed.

"He can pray," Lauren admitted, charmed by the boy's eager curiosity.

"Make him."

"I'm afraid you can't make him do anything he doesn't want to do," Lauren said. "But I can ask him."

The boy grinned expectantly, and Lauren looked down at Socrates. "Say grace," she said. As on the night Lauren had dinner with Adrian on the *Specter,* Socrates clasped his hands together and bowed his head. Her seatmates clapped, and others around strained to look.

Not the best way to remain inconspicuous, Lauren thought, but then how could one ever be inconspicuous with a monkey? She just hoped everyone would remember the monkey instead of her.

She gave Socrates another treat, and he settled down happily enough for the moment, pleased with the food and attention. Lauren leaned back on the bench, closing her eyes to prevent further conversation as tension balled in her stomach.

It was late afternoon. Adrian looked out the window at the countryside speeding by, and he tried to concentrate on the heavily wooded hills. Given any luck at all, he would soon be lost in them.

His stomach churned, not for himself but for Lauren. She was risking a great deal. The thought of freedom after the last dismal weeks was exhilarating, but he wondered now at his judgment in allowing this.

His hands rested in his lap, the heavy iron weighing them down. The key to the irons was in Ensign Woods's pocket. Inside, on the right. His gaze had followed every move after two men came into his cell, introduced themselves as his escort, and locked the iron bracelets on his wrists with the quick, efficient movements that spoke of experience.

He had been cooperative, even friendly, and they had answered in kind, although he didn't miss the fact that none of their caution relaxed. They adroitly kept him apart from the crowds, maneuvering him easily where they wanted him to go, and he realized this was not their first transfer of prisoners. The best had been sent to escort him.

The second man was an older enlisted man, but one with lean strength and experienced eyes. Eben, he'd said his name was.

Adrian had asked where they hailed from, had expressed interest in their families, and asked questions about Washington and his destination, the Old Capitol Prison. The latter brought only shrugs, and he deduced it was not a very pleasant place. Then he steered them to the subject of the sea, where they'd been and what kind of ships they'd served. Some of the tension eased as the three talked about ports and women and ships.

He occasionally caught glimpses of Lauren between the heads of others, and he heard the laughter and clapping for Socrates. His keen awareness of Lauren pounded in the core of his body. He had to force himself to keep the conversation light and bantering with his guards.

His fingers occasionally played over the chain linking his wrists. It was short, shorter than the one that confined him aboard the *Specter*. His movements were very limited, and he wondered whether he would be able to retrieve the gun from Socrates without being noticed. If only the chain were just a few inches longer.

But it wasn't. He suddenly held his hands out, stretching his cramped arms, and he noticed that the ensign followed every movement.

"Can I stand for a moment?"

The ensign nodded. "Just don't move quickly."

Adrian balanced himself in the rocking coach and stood slowly, feeling life seep back into his limbs. He kept his hands low, not particularly wanting to bring any more attention to his status as prisoner, but his eyes quickly shifted over the occupants in the coach. He saw Lauren was wearing the gray dress again, the one she'd worn the first time he'd seen her in Nassau, and her hat shadowed her face. Her dress was modest and her hair pinned back primly. She would excite little notice, except for Socrates sleeping contentedly in her lap. He had to smile at the picture and at the way she handled the mischievous little beast. No other woman would be doing this, planning and executing such an ingenious escape. No other woman would . . .

"Captain Cabot." The words were curt, an order to sit. His gaze swept around the rest of the coach, taking in the number of uniforms. Escape would be difficult, but not impossible, not with a pistol. There was a door next to him, leading to a platform, and then to one additional passenger coach. He had noted everything as he was led to the train and then to his seat.

"Cabot!" This time the command was very plain. He sat back down, smiling wryly at the ensign.

Bloody hell, but he was tired of being ordered about, of irons and cells. Please God, he'd be quit of them soon . . .

"I need some air," Lauren said to her seat companion.

Both officers stood as Lauren did, backing politely out into the aisle. She had watched carefully as landmarks came into view and disappeared. They would be slowing within a minute or two, and the coach would rock as it had when they'd left Baltimore.

She'd taken out the neat little sailor jacket and put it on a protesting Socrates, and her hand had felt the Deringer inside. Her heart fluttered like a startled bird taking wing.

Her hand trembled slightly, and then something else took over, the same mysterious quality that had taken over her body before, a cold surety mixed with stimulation.

Her hand reassured Socrates as it loosened the hold on his leash.

She moved slowly down the aisle as if faint from heat, waiting for the moment she needed. Socrates trailed obediently on his leash behind her. Suddenly the train lurched, and she aimed herself for the ensign sitting at Adrian's side. The man's arms reached out instinctively to catch her. Socrates reacted, leaping to protect her, his teeth sinking through the ensign's uniform jacket. And then Socrates saw Adrian and, with a shriek, leaped on him.

Confusion reigned. Lauren screamed and held on to the bench as if she were to faint, and the ensign instinctively moved up to steady her as the other guard's eyes followed their movements. Lauren couldn't see. She could only hope that Adrian had the minute he needed to find the small pistol.

She gave him as much time as she could, swaying against the ensign as the train slowed, grinding against the tracks.

The movement suddenly halted, and she fell against the naval officer, the two of them tumbling back on Adrian. Socrates shrieked again, and the whole coach was now in an uproar.

Lauren allowed herself to be righted, and she grabbed Socrates, who didn't want to leave Adrian. But Adrian pushed him toward Lauren as best he could with his shackles. "Damned beast bit me," he said indignantly.

Lauren grabbed Socrates and eyed Adrian's handcuffs accusingly. "You probably poisoned him, you . . . you criminal." She glared at him.

Socrates added his own wrathful chattering to the chaos.

"Miss," the ensign tried, "you must leave. This is a naval prisoner."

"He tried to kill my monkey."

Adrian turned to the ensign. "Wild animals on a train!

What kind of country is this? No telling what kind of disease an animal like that is carrying."

The ensign looked like a man bedeviled. "For God's sake, Captain, it's just a . . . monkey."

Lauren knew she had to leave. Adrian's lips were twitching, and her own laughter was not far behind. She could tell from his expression that he had found the gun; there was no sense in carrying this any further.

She tightened her grasp around a protesting Socrates. "I hope you hang him," she said righteously and turned back toward her seat, grabbed her portmanteau, and made for the door.

Adrian felt the comforting pressure of the Deringer against his waist, tucked now in his pants. Less than four inches in length, it was easily hidden under his jacket.

Timing was so important now. Lauren had told him exactly where to go from the train station. He wanted to leave just as the train started; it would take time to stop it again, even more time to arrange a search.

He looked down. Socrates, in his anxiety, had bitten him, and blood was running down his hand. Nothing could be better. He blessed his cantankerous little friend.

He heard a change in the sound of the engine, as if it were being fired up to move again.

Adrian lifted his chained left hand. "I'm going to bleed all over the train if you don't do something."

The young officer escorting him looked at Adrian's hand with dismay. His own hand was also hurting from the monkey's bite, but it wasn't bleeding nearly as badly as that of his charge. He turned to his companion. "Go find the conductor and see if you can get some water and some bandages. I'll stay with him."

The older man nodded, squeezing past Adrian and the ensign. As he disappeared up the aisle, Adrian slipped the Deringer from his pocket and pressed it into the ensign's side.

"I also need some air."

The officer stiffened.

"Get up very slowly, Ensign," Adrian said in a low voice, audible only to the man beside him. "I've already shot one man; I have nothing to lose by shooting another."

The officer rose, his face a study of chagrin and anger.

"Out the door and onto the coach platform, side by side with me," Adrian said, moving alongside him, his hand covering the Deringer. They reached the door, and Adrian pushed the small barrel into his escort's side even tighter. "Slide the door open. Very, very carefully."

Then they were outside on the small coach platform in the stifling summer heat. The train started to move slowly as the Union officer turned to face him. "The other way," Adrian said. "Turn the other way. Now!"

His face bleak, the ensign did so, and Adrian, glancing quickly around and seeing no one, lifted the small gun and hit the officer at the back of his head just as the train started gathering speed. Adrian caught the falling man and propped him against the side of the rocking coach, making sure he couldn't fall off. He quickly found the key to his handcuffs, unlocking them as quickly as possible. The train was moving out of the station now, the coach passing several cars on a side track.

Adrian swung off the coach platform, just barely keeping to his feet. He took momentary refuge behind the vacant, silent cars, and then quickly made his way to the back side of the station, straightening as he started to mix with the crowds. His clothing was that of a sea captain, not identifiable as belonging to one army or the other, and he knew he should be safe enough in that regard until his former captors sounded the alarm.

He followed Lauren's directions and hurried down the street of what he supposed was formerly a sleepy crossroads. But now its position between Baltimore and Washington had turned it into a bustling hospital and military center, and it was swarming with people and uniforms.

Adrian heard the distant whistle of the train. It was still moving away from them. How long did he have? Would the engineer stop and return to retrieve one lone prisoner?

He rubbed his sore wrists, realizing they were ringed

with red from the chafing of the irons. But his feet kept moving. This turn? He found the alley Lauren had mentioned and turned into it. It ran along the back of the businesses that faced the street, and he followed it until it ended at the back of a large house. Lauren slipped from the shadows of a large tree as Socrates hurled himself at Adrian.

Holding the animal, Adrian went to Lauren, his hand touching her cheek for a moment to make sure she was real.

Her face was anxious, but her eyes sparkled with an excitement he understood. "Your guards . . . ?"

"One is unconscious . . . I suspect the other is looking after him. I dropped off just as the train was pulling away. It will take some time to stop it."

Lauren bit her lip. She had done it, had made good his escape. And no one knew her name; she had used the name of Elsie Brown everyplace. Once she knew Adrian was safely on his way South, she would return to Delaware, stay a week, and then tell Mr. Phillips she'd decided not to return to Nassau. No one would connect her with the escape. Socrates was the only connection between them, and hopefully no one would ask the officers of the *Allegheny* who took possession of a wayward monkey. If necessary, she could say a friend of Cabot's took the animal. Moreover, since she was responsible for Adrian's arrest, surely no one would suspect her now of aiding his escape.

"You must hurry," she said. She leaned down and opened the portmanteau he had seen her carrying. "Change your clothes, and I'll wrap a bandage around your head. Try to look dazed when we go by the livery stable."

He reached out and caught her hand. "You keep surprising me, Miss Bradley."

Lauren averted her eyes and turned away from him. "Just hurry."

Adrian did just that, making use of every movement, buttoning the cotton shirt over his chafed wrists. The clothes were snug but would do. "Lauren," he said, as he completed buttoning his trousers.

She turned around, holding a white bandage that she rubbed against the blood on his hand. Smearing the blood on the clean surface of the bandage, Lauren then stretched up on her tiptoes to tie it around his head and over his left eye until she was satisfied he looked sufficiently wounded.

Lauren tipped her head, admiring her own handiwork. She then handed him a small, wrapped bundle. He raised an eyebrow. "What do we have here?"

She bit her lip. "A . . . gun and some food."

Adrian shook his head in wonder and looked at the portmanteau. "And that?"

She tucked it behind some bushes. It would be awkward to carry it on horseback. The portmanteau had served its purpose.

"Come with me," she said, "and don't talk. Your English accent is . . . distinctive."

He grinned and gave her an abbreviated bow. "You got me this far. I'm ready to do your every bidding."

His gaze stayed on her for a moment. Her eyes were so large and serious, and her mouth trembled as her teeth bit on her lip. The sudden uncertainty didn't go with the meticulous planning he'd experienced in the last few hours. She'd been a superb actress on the train, sure and competent, and she had continually surprised him . . . from the visit in the jail to the skill with which she bandaged his head. He was being forced to accept the fact that Lauren Bradley had talents he'd never suspected, making him ever surer that she had been involved in the taking of the *Specter*.

But it was not the time to bring up the issue.

She was already moving, and he matched her quick movements, turning the corner into the main street. She took his arm, as if assisting him, and they came to a livery.

Two horses were already saddled, one with a sidesaddle. He knew she must have left the train, ordered the horses saddled, and then met him. Again, he marveled at her competence and efficiency.

But her voice, as she addressed the stable owner, was completely different, full of soft pleading and gratitude.

"Thank you, Mr. Simmons. You are so kind. This is my husband, Lieutenant Brown. You must forgive him, but he's still . . . a bit . . ." Her voice fell off, and a tear slid down her face.

"Of course, Mrs. Brown," the man said, "but are you sure he should ride?"

"The best place to heal, Mr. Brown, is in one's home," she said softly. "It's not far, truly it's not." She took some coins from her reticule and passed them to him, and his face lit even further.

"Allow me to help you mount."

Lauren nodded her thanks. "But could you help the lieutenant first . . . he's still . . . very weak."

Adrian had to fight to withhold a smile and continue to look befuddled. Lauren went over to him and took Socrates as the man cupped his hands and helped Adrian up. Lauren handed the monkey back to Adrian, and then waited prettily for the stable owner to help her into the sidesaddle. From the uncomfortable way Lauren settled on the saddle, Adrian knew she was not the best of riders, and again he had to privately applaud her courage and determination.

He maintained a blank stare as Lauren gently urged her horse forward and he moved alongside her. They were almost out of town when three blue-coated soldiers approached from the other direction. Adrian had been listening for the train whistle, for a sign that the train was returning or that an alarm had been raised. There was none, not yet. But he felt himself stiffen, felt every nerve tingle, as the lead officer pulled up when he reached Lauren.

"Lauren," he said, a smile stretching across his face. "It's good to see a face from home." His gaze wandered to Adrian and regarded him curiously.

"Michael," she acknowledged. "I'm helping at the hospital. Lieutenant . . . Brown is one of the patients."

"And . . . Larry? I haven't been home in months."

Adrian watched Lauren's face go white. "He . . . died."

"Damn, but I'm sorry to hear that. I didn't know."

"A few months ago. Michael . . . I have to go . . . the lieutenant doesn't have long."

"You're at the hospital then? I have a friend there . . . Phil . . . you remember Phil Connors . . . have you seen him?"

She shook her head.

"I'm with a supply unit. We were ambushed south of here by some guerrillas, so you be careful riding out . . . even this close to Washington. We hear Stuart's somewhere nearby."

Lauren nodded.

"I'll try to get by to see you, Lauren. I'm sorry to hear about Larry. I know how close you two were . . ."

"Thank you," Lauren said, her face now averted from Adrian's.

The officer touched the brim of his hat and trotted toward town, the other two men at his side.

Adrian's gaze fastened on Lauren, and she lowered her eyelashes, her hands trembling slightly on the reins. "We . . . we'd better hurry," she said finally.

Adrian kept his churning thoughts to himself. He had a million questions, but now, he knew, was no time to ask them. He leaned over and took her reins. "I think we'll head south," he said. "Off the road."

She nodded, her face white now, and strained.

He tightened his legs around his horse and moved off the road and into the woods, his hands holding tightly the reins of her horse.

CHAPTER 18

Lauren could barely breathe. Her heart had stopped the moment she'd seen Michael Sowers, a longtime neighbor and her brother's friend.

She knew he'd also seen Socrates, who had been perching contentedly on the saddle in front of Adrian.

It wouldn't be long before a search was started for Adrian, and the woman who called herself Elsie Brown. And now there was a link between Mrs. Brown and Lauren.

What did they do to women who helped a prisoner escape? She couldn't return to Dover now. She doubted Michael would protect her in this; he was, after all, an officer in the Union Army.

Neither could she go to Nassau. She had also betrayed Jeremy. She suddenly shivered despite the hot day.

Lauren drew a shallow breath and forced herself to look over at Adrian. But he was riding just far enough ahead of her that she couldn't see his face. His back, though, was stiff, much stiffer than it had been earlier as he'd sat the horse so easily. He would know her role now, even if he hadn't suspected earlier. He would have to, with a Union officer inquiring about her brother.

She had planned to leave him today, to turn toward Delaware and make her way back home once he was safely away. And now that course was no longer open to her. She had made so many turns and twists in her life during the past two months that she felt like a leaf in the wind—a fragile leaf about to be crushed.

But given the choice, she knew, she probably wouldn't have done anything differently. She could not bear to see Adrian in prison because of her. Nor had she been able to forgo the opportunity to avenge Larry's death.

And now where was she?

Misery crowded her mind, her heart. She had hoped to be gone when Adrian discovered she was a spy. Now she would have to face him, and, like a coward, couldn't bear it. Not because she had physical fear of him; if she knew nothing else, she knew he would never hurt her that way. But fear because she couldn't bear to see condemnation or contempt in his eyes. He had said trust was important. And no matter how much she had tried to repair the damage, she knew she could never mend the rent fabric of his trust.

Adrian quickened the pace. Lauren found a distraction of sorts in hanging on to the saddle with all her might. The horse's gait was something less than even, and she had little experience with horses. Yet she'd dared not ask for anything other than a sidesaddle—no lady would—and a buggy would have been too slow. She could have, she supposed, sent Adrian on his way with one horse, but she'd had to see him to safety . . .

And, if she was really honest, she had wanted to feel his arms one last time, to taste again the apple of temptation. Well, she certainly had summoned the serpent of her own lies.

They traveled on through the evening, avoiding roads. But hearing troop movements nearby, Adrian would stop and dismount, holding both horses tightly and willing her to be silent. As the evening shadows turned deep gray and then black, the ache in her heart deepened. She watched Adrian's tall back, the lean grace of the body on his mount, and she knew he was as at ease on horseback as on the deck of a ship.

She wished he would speak, but she knew the danger. And what would Adrian say when he did speak? Could she bear his words?

There was a full moon tonight—a hunter's moon, she'd remembered one of the blockade runners call it—and they rode silently late into the night. She thought it must be past midnight when they finally stopped at a stream.

Still in silence, Adrian dismounted. Socrates scampered down and over to a tree. Adrian walked slowly to Lauren and held a hand out to her. Her body ached so from the long ride, from the demands on long-unused muscles, that she stumbled as her feet touched ground and fell toward him.

His arms went around her, and to her surprise they were as gentle as they had been previously. They hesitated a moment before relaxing slightly. In the moonlight she watched his face, severe and unsmiling, his eyes so dark she couldn't read their expression. But then she'd never been able to do that. Even when he'd smiled and been his most charming, there had always been something private about him, something hidden.

Now it was much more obvious. Or perhaps she was more aware after the long ride and the lack of words between them.

She felt his breath on her as one of his arms continued to hold her, while another reached for a curl that had tumbled out of the knot she'd tried to pin so tightly.

"Ah, Lauren, you smell so sweet after that bloody jail."

His head lowered, and his lips caught hers. She had expected questions, demands, accusations, but instead his lips were gentle, incredibly so. They caressed her mouth, then nuzzled her cheeks before returning to her lips. She felt the suppressed hunger bursting from him, the formerly restrained need, and her body trembled with needs of her own, with a longing to bind the shattered pieces of a heart so divided and wounded she could scarcely bear its anguish. She wanted to give herself up to the magic of his touch, to the yearning she felt in him, but the watchful, cautious part of her knew how dangerous that was.

She accepted his kiss, for she could do nothing else. Whatever will she had, he destroyed with a touch, a look. Her lips melded with his, and her whole body quivered with desire. Her heart thudded, the noise pounding in her ears. She felt his strength, and she relished it. She felt his need and blossomed in it. She felt his passion and responded to it, all the doubts and fears dissolving into a cavern of immense longing.

Her blood was hot, rushing like a storm-swollen river through her body. Her hands tightened on his body, on the rough clothes she'd bought him, the clothes that molded his lean, muscled body as it strained toward her. She felt the dampness of his skin, and wondered whether it came from an inner boiling heat like her own, but then all thoughts disappeared as his kiss deepened, his tongue roaming and stroking and seducing until shudder after shudder rocked her body.

If his arms had not been so tight around her, she would have faltered, stumbled against the pleasurable weakness that flooded her body.

"I need you, Lauren," Adrian whispered, the words like a drug to her. Her hand went to his cheek, tracing the hard lines with wondering fingers, and it was answer enough for him.

Lauren felt his hands go to the back of her dress, his impatient fingers awkward in their haste. At every movement, every touch, she felt herself shudder with new awareness of a body she'd never totally understood. All her upbringing, all her beliefs, were being shunted aside now, discarded in the night, just as her principles had the past three weeks. But she couldn't stop now . . . the demand of her body and heart and soul was too great. And there might never be a tomorrow. She felt a warm tear on her cheek as explosions rocked her, as his hands moved inside her dress and camisole and caressed her breasts, playing against the sensitive flesh that was aching, changing, hardening, under his fingers.

And then she was on her knees with him, and his mouth was kissing her breasts, which, like pieces of clay, seemed to take on a life of their own. In wonder, she looked down and watched them swell and tingle and burn. Her own hands were unbuttoning his shirt and stroking the hard muscles in his chest, teasing the wiry hair that looked golden in the moonlight. She heard him moan, or was it she, as his hands moved down and cupped her hips, moving them toward him until she felt the strength of his manhood and knew a whole new dimension of need.

His head suddenly lifted, his eyes going to the moonlit heavens and the stars that were like silver dust on velvet cloth. She heard his exultant cry, a cry of freedom and passion and elation that exploded into the still night air and infected her with its uncomplicated joy.

Tonight was theirs.

His hands removed the remainder of her clothes, his fingers loving, reassuring, caressingly tender. She felt a night breeze brush skin never before touched that way, and his quiet elation became hers as she was filled with so many new sensations, as every nerve in her body sang with life and expectation. She had felt this way before with him, but never to this degree, never to a point where the merest brush of skin became a match to gunpowder, igniting a cordon of explosions, of exquisite, tormenting fires that strained against the boundaries of her body.

Adrian's hands fed those blazes as they moved over her skin, and he lowered her to the ground. She lay against crisp, old leaves, savoring the smell of pine needles and the coolness of earth. Each sensation was heightened by his presence, his nearness. He left her for a moment, no more, and when he returned, she saw his body outlined in the moonlight, naked and beautiful, each muscled contour a wonder of strength and beauty.

Lauren knew she should be shamed and afraid, but she

knew only a fierce expectation and need as new waves of desire washed up and down her body. Instinctively she arched upward, wanting him so badly, so completely, that everything else in the world stopped. Only this moved on, only this pulsing eagerness for something she didn't understand . . .

His body came down on hers, the warmth of his skin touching and brandishing, setting off even more sparks, as his manhood touched the now agonized triangle of her femininity, each of his slow, deliberate movements making her need greater. But still he teased that part of her until she felt a dampness there, then a raw, naked hunger so strong that she could no longer bear the tantalizing pain of desire. Her body instinctively moved up to him, to force whatever was required to relieve the pressure inside, the terrible, driving craving that consumed her.

His lips came down on hers just as his manhood entered her, stretching against some barrier, and then exploding in pain that drew a gasp from her. But then the pain erupted into something else, something so startling and overwhelming that she felt she was being sucked into the nucleus of the universe, an arena of stunning sensations and colors and sunbursts, of feelings indescribably delicious and satisfying. And yet still her body continued to seek more and more of him. He moved in her, a sensuous dance of slow, hypnotic rhythm that her body caught, and she moved with him. Her hips rotated in circular movements, even as she wondered at her own boldness, her own instinctive knowledge, and she felt him go deeper and deeper inside until he reached the very core of her, and his movements became compulsive, as did hers.

Almost . . . almost . . . and then she felt an explosive ecstasy rock her as warm honey seemed to erupt inside her. Her body shuddered uncontrollably with vivid satisfaction and fulfillment, and she felt his body shake with the same tremors, the warmth of his skin now hot and damp, the fullness inside her pulsing with energy and then trembling as his manhood moved against the tender enclosure, once more revitalizing new and different thunderbolts of physical sensations.

"Lord in heaven," he whispered.

"Adrian," was all she could offer in return, but its almost reverent sound was just as awestruck as his exclamation.

Adrian's body relaxed, but his throbbing manhood remained inside her, and she loved the feel of him there, the gentle abrasion that continued to send sweet tremors through her body. He rolled over on his side, carrying her with him, his arms holding her fiercely against his fevered body. The pounding of two hearts seemed loud in the quiet night, and their breaths mingled as his lips brushed her face in wondering kisses, the very tentativeness of which spoke of emotions too deep to express.

They lay there, ignoring the hardness of the ground, their eyes feasting upon the other, their lips occasionally meeting and then separating so they could so gaze on each other, fixing this moment in time, freezing it for the future.

Lauren's body still hummed and tingled, still sought to wrap itself around that part of him that had so awakened her. He felt so good, so natural a part of her. She squirmed slightly, and even that small movement sent rushes of sensation through her.

She wanted never to move. She looked upward to their blanket of stars, and to him again. She wanted to capture forever his dark eyes, fomenting now with so many emotions, open as they had never been before. His hand went to her face, touching it with such tenderness she wanted to cry.

"Did I hurt you?" His voice was low and she heard doubt in it for the first time since knowing him.

Such a wonderful hurt. Such a wondrous kind of pain. She took his fingers from her face and kissed the tips in an instinctive gesture of love. She wanted to say the words so badly, but she couldn't. Not now. Not until she confessed everything to him. She wasn't worthy now.

"No," she finally whispered, and she heard a long release of breath, as if he had been holding it. But didn't he know? Couldn't he tell what he'd just given her? A new world she'd never suspected existed.

Her eyes found his. "Is it always like this?"

He grinned. "No. I can quite honestly say no."

They heard a happy chattering then, and Lauren suddenly remembered Socrates.

Adrian chuckled, a sound that came from deep in his throat, and she felt his chest, on which her chin rested, move slightly. "He's in monkey heaven at the moment," he said. "Tender leaves, fresh bark, trees to climb."

"He won't . . . get lost?"

"Oh no. He never goes far," Adrian replied ruefully, wondering why he was discussing monkeys at a moment like this. Socrates's presence definitely had disadvantages. But Adrian felt Lauren relax, and he found her concern for his wayward pet a trait he liked very much.

And the rest of her character? He wasn't quite sure. The meeting with the Union officer earlier confirmed his belief that Lauren had indeed secrets to hide. And yet he also knew she had risked everything to help him, and was now herself a fugitive. On the long ride tonight, he had thought of little else than the fear and uncertainty he'd seen in her eyes. He'd also seen the flare of determination there, and he was afraid she'd meant to leave him, so he'd seized the reins. She couldn't go back now, just as he couldn't.

But he wouldn't ask questions. He didn't want to force answers, and he knew he couldn't demand trust. He would wait until she told him herself.

Especially when she looked at him as if he'd just invented the world.

He'd discovered one thing, however. She was a virgin. Spy or not, she'd never before used her body as a means of extracting information. He shifted slightly, sliding from her and holding her tight because he wanted to, because she felt so right there.

Adrian had not really known what he expected tonight, or the next day or the next. He'd willed himself not to think about it; for the past hours, escape had been the important thing, and he'd needed no distractions. But he had been very aware of Lauren, of her tense figure, and set, guarded expression.

And he had not meant for this to happen. Or had he?

Adrian ran his arms along her skin. The weather was warm this night, and the pine needles had provided a relatively soft—if, at times, a bit scratchy—bed. He moved again slightly, positioning himself against a tree and pulling Lauren against his chest so he could fondle her breasts.

"Will you go to England with me?" The question came suddenly, to him as well as to her.

He felt her tense. *Talk to me*, he wanted to tell her. *Trust me*.

"I . . . can't."

"Then where will you go? It's no longer Elsie Brown who helped a Union prisoner. It's Lauren Bradley."

She stilled. He could feel her every muscle grow taut.

"I . . . don't know," she said finally.

"To Nassau?"

No. She had betrayed Jeremy, too, in the end. She had betrayed them all: her brother, Adrian, his crew, Jeremy . . . herself.

She shrugged. "Tell me about your home," she said, desperate to change the subject.

"Ridgely?" His voice softened as he said the word, almost making it a song.

"Is that where you'll go?"

"No."

"Why not?"

He was silent, his hand continuing to play along her skin. It should have been a soothing gesture, but it wasn't. It was fraught with danger.

"My family no longer owns it," he told her finally.

She heard the loss in his voice, the poignant ache of regret.

"I had hoped to buy it back," he said, his voice low.

"What will you do now?" She forced the words to break the silent tension that suddenly flared between them.

"Reach Wilmington and find a ship for England."

"And then . . . ?"

"Buy or build a new runner."

Lauren barely suppressed a gasp. All for naught! Her stint as a Union spy had changed nothing. In a matter of months, he would be transporting guns again. And in danger. She couldn't bear either thought.

"Why?"

His arms tightened around her. "I have to get Ridgely back."

"How . . . long will it take?"

"It would have taken only a few more runs with the *Specter*. Now . . . I don't know. I'll have to invest in a new ship, and I'll lose months."

Lauren wanted to understand why Ridgely was so important.

She shivered. "Tell me about Ridgely."

But instead, his hands took her hands and rubbed them. "I think I'd better get something on you first."

For the first time, Lauren felt awkward about her nakedness. It had seemed so natural with Adrian, but now she recalled how far outside the boundaries of accepted behavior she had ranged.

He helped her up, and she was more conscious of his body than ever. She averted her head even as she wished to stare at him, to memorize his perfection.

She started to pick up her camisole and her other clothes, but he slid the sleeves of his shirt over her arms, buttoning it in front as it fell far beneath her thighs. The rough cloth smelled of him and felt good, because she knew it had been on him. He seemed so sure of himself, so proficient, and a pang ran through her. How many other women had he helped dress? How many had he bedded?

And left?

Why should she care so much? She had known from the beginning there could be no future for them, not for an English nobleman who fought for the South and the doctor's plain daughter whose brother died in defense of the Union . . . and whose brother had been killed by the very man touching her now.

Lauren suddenly jerked away. "I'll do it," she said in a ragged whisper.

"Lauren." He lingered on the last syllable of her name, as if he didn't want to let go of it. The thought twisted her heart.

She turned back to him, putting her hand on his face, touching it as if he would break, or disappear, if she pressed. She wondered how he felt, whether what had happened was as cataclysmic for him as it had been for her. But no. He was an English lord; he could have his choice —probably *had* had his choice—of the most beautiful of women.

"Lauren," he said again, and he put his arms around her, pulling her tight against him as if to reassure her, as if he felt every one of her doubts and fears.

"That shouldn't have happened," he said. "Not now."

Lauren was silent. The soft glow sifted from her body, leaving in its wake an emptiness, a huge bleak place. She moved away from him and went to a tree, leaning against it, barely aware of noise as Socrates dropped from one of its branches and ran to Adrian, as if he had been waiting to have his master all to himself.

Adrian had pulled on his trousers, but his chest was still bare, and she saw now in the moonlight how much leaner he was than he had been three weeks ago. In the moonlight his face appeared paler too, and new lines seemed to crinkle the area around his eyes. Because of Ridgely, she wondered, and the thought of losing it?

But then he grinned, the irresistible, charming grin that had captivated her from their first meeting. "You said there was some food . . . ?" He didn't wait for her to answer, but went over to where the saddles rested on the ground. The bundle she had given him earlier lay beside it, and he untied it, finding jerky and cheese and hardtack.

"It's not very much," she said apologetically.

"After the Yank prison, it's a banquet." As if to prove his words, he took one of the pieces of dried beef and chewed slowly, but with unmistakable hunger.

"Was . . . prison very bad?"

"Not when I thought about you." He looked up from the package, and his gaze met hers. His lips still smiled, but some of the guardedness was back in his eyes.

He slid down beside her, offering her a piece of cheese. She shook her head. There wasn't much—she hadn't planned on sharing it; she had thought she would be on her way back to Delaware.

Watching him eat was painful to her. She didn't want to care this much; she didn't want to ache so badly at seeing how carefully he ate and knowing he must have gone hungry in prison. She didn't want to think about running her fingers through the thick hair, or touching the smooth skin of his back. She didn't want to crave the feel of his lips on hers, or the comfort of his arms around her.

Yet she did all of that, with such longing that she was on fire again.

She didn't want to love him. She couldn't love him. But she did. She knew that as she met his eyes and saw them flare with fire of their own, watched his mouth curve into a smile, watched his hands stretch out for her . . .

CHAPTER 19

The nightmare came back with a ferocity that night. Larry was standing there, watching her, but she couldn't see the expression on his face. And then he faded, and she felt the searing pain again.

She reached out, trying to tell her twin not to go; but as he had the night in Nassau, the figure started to dissolve.

Lauren woke to her own moans, and she felt the momentary comfort of arms around her.

"Lauren," she heard a voice whisper. But the voice no longer gave her reassurance. Had Larry been condemning her, warning her?

She opened her eyes slowly and tried to focus. It was still dark, yet now a thread of gray appeared beyond the trees. Adrian's face was very close, his hands oh so gentle. She remembered how tender they had been last night, how she fell asleep wrapped in his arms.

And now his voice was a soft whisper, meant to be comforting. "It's all right, love," he said.

But it wasn't all right. It would never be all right.

She swallowed, turning her head away from him. She felt Socrates next to her, heard the monkey's worried chattering.

Adrian drew a deep breath. "Talk to me, Lauren. Let me help."

But how could she? "I'm all right," she said. "I just had a nightmare."

"Tell me about it."

Lauren forced a shrug.

"You called a name. Larry. Your Union friend said the name Laurence."

Lauren sighed. "My brother. My twin brother."

Adrian's hands stilled. He knew the next question he should ask, but he couldn't. She had said she was from Maryland, and she had a border-state accent. Laurence Bradley could have fought for either army, but Adrian was sure now which one it had been. *Tell me*, he willed her.

Ask, she almost begged out loud, and if he had, she would have told him the truth. She couldn't do it on her own, couldn't blurt it out that she had worked for the Union, had deprived him of Ridgely, at least for the time being. She hadn't known till last night about the estate but that, she realized, didn't matter. What mattered was the betrayal.

She couldn't bear to lose that look in his eyes as his hands caressed her, as if he were feeling all these things for the first time too. She couldn't bear to see the tenderness turn to contempt.

She wouldn't. Not now. Sometime soon, but not now, she would confess. Lauren brushed away the warning in her head, the remembrance of the poem by Sir Walter Scott about the tangled web of deceit. But then she thought of another British adage: "In for a penny, in for a pound."

Her hand curled around Adrian's. She was in for the pound, the whole pound. She would stay with him until

Wilmington. She would make sure he made it safely aboard a ship and then . . .

Adrian's hands tightened around her, as if pleading with her to talk to him.

She turned and looked at him, her face only inches from his. She tried to think of him as she had in the beginning, as her brother's murderer, but she couldn't, not when she saw the concern and worry in his face. Worry for her.

He was so incredibly handsome. Never in her life had she thought a man like Lord Ridgely would be interested in her, never had she thought her body could react as it had . . . as it did.

Part of her wished he would question her, until finally she told him everything, but he didn't. Instead, his hands caressed her, soothing and relaxing wherever he touched. She felt her tense muscles begin to ease, her eyes grow drowsy. Tomorrow, she told herself. Or the next day.

Or the next . . .

She would tell him everything.

When she woke again, the sky was the light gray-blue of just past dawn. She could see the sun beyond the trees, and her hands reached for the body she'd grown accustomed to throughout the night—and found it gone.

Panic filled her for a moment. Then she forced herself to look carefully. One of the horses was missing; the other was contentedly grazing on a spot of grass between trees. Socrates was nowhere to be seen.

She was still wearing Adrian's shirt. Her dress and undergarments—pantalets, camisole, and petticoat—lay neatly folded near her.

Where had he gone? He wouldn't have left her here alone, even if he had guessed, suspected, wondered, about her. She knew that as surely as she knew the sun would rise each day. She moved slowly, feeling the deep ache in her muscles from the ride yesterday and the new, intriguing soreness between her legs.

She groaned to herself. He would want to ride today.

They would have to ride today! They couldn't stay in this area. But, dear Lord, her legs and backside hurt.

Grimacing, she tore a piece from her petticoat and went down to the stream. She used the cloth to wash her face and hands, and then she put her legs in the stream, letting the water soothe the sore muscles. The day was already muggy and uncomfortable, and it would grow hotter. She loved the loose, free comfort of Adrian's shirt and hated to think of exchanging it for her heavy dress.

Lauren took care of her other needs and then dressed. She felt hunger gnawing at her and realized she'd not eaten since yesterday morning. She checked the inside of her dress, where she'd sewed what funds she had, and felt the wad of bills. Perhaps they could buy some food.

Where was he?

She heard noise then, the rustling of underbrush, the soft clip-clop of hoofs on a forest floor. Almost instinctively she darted behind a large oak, her heart stilling. And then she heard a familiar chattering, and a small form hurtled in front of her.

"Socrates," she greeted him.

"You finally woke up." She looked up, and Adrian was sitting his horse before her. He was wearing a shirt now, a blue one, and he held some strange saddlebags. "Breakfast."

Lauren tensed inside. He was wearing a Yankee shirt and carrying saddlebags with the letters U.S.A. on them.

"Where . . . ?"

"Several very careless Yanks," he said. "But don't worry. They'll have aching heads. That's all. I might even have saved their lives. They won't be that sloppy again."

There was a hard note in Adrian's voice, and Lauren reminded herself not to underestimate him. His charm was so easy, his smile so charismatic, she sometimes forgot he'd served in the British Navy during the Crimean War, that he'd survived years in one of the hardest services in the world, that he'd outwitted the Union Navy for a year. Only occasionally did he allow that iron will to show, and then God help the person who stood in his way. She knew that, had known it ever since the night in Nassau when she'd seen him go after her attackers with ruthless efficiency.

Sometimes she forgot how complex he was, and it frightened her now, for she knew how quickly his gentleness could turn into controlled fury.

He dismounted and handed her some biscuits and cheese. "I have some coffee, but we'll have to wait on that. I don't dare risk a fire. This area is alive with Yanks."

She ate silently, her eyes continually going to his face as he, too, ate rapidly and then saddled her horse with quick, experienced movements. When he took her hand to help her mount, he smiled wryly at her involuntary groan. "I'm sorry, love," he said, "but we can't stay around here. Those Yanks will wake shortly."

He looked deep into her eyes. His lips brushed hers before he very easily lifted her up, his hand lingering mere seconds before turning toward his own horse.

"Socrates," he said in a low voice. The monkey took his hand and allowed himself to be propelled up in the saddle. Adrian followed and then guided his horse over to Lauren's, touching her hand. "Are you all right?"

She nodded.

His eyes fairly blazed with intensity as he studied her tense body. Then he smiled with approval, and she would have ridden through fire with him.

Willing spirit or not, Lauren's body objected bitterly after several hours of riding. Avoiding all roads, they journeyed through the woods. Branches hit her dress, and scratched what skin wasn't covered.

Her body ached. The heat made rivulets of perspiration flow on her neck and back and between her breasts. She had tried to brush her hair without a mirror and braid the long strands into a knot, but she felt them fall in damp clumps around her face. She knew a physical misery she'd never felt before.

Lauren kept her mind, however, on those wondrous hours last night, on the closeness of their bodies and the delicious sensations that had saturated her. Whenever she thought she must cry from pain, she looked to Adrian beside her, to the features now carved in her heart, and knew she couldn't show weakness, couldn't slow him.

Several times they heard hoofbeats not far away, and he would dismount and hold the horses' heads down to keep them from replying to their own kind. And then he would mount again.

The day inched on, Lauren growing more and more miserable. They stopped briefly at streams for water, and ate hardtack and jerky at noontime, relying now on supplies from the stolen saddlebags. Socrates, however, happily munched on tree leaves whenever they stopped, and seemed to need nothing more.

Adrian was tireless. Though he looked at her often with sympathy, he didn't suggest they stop. Lauren knew why. The times they stopped for water, she very nearly couldn't get back in the saddle.

They went deeper and deeper into the woods, the world losing some of the brightness among the heavy foliage of the trees, and she wondered how Adrian knew the right direction. He never hesitated, only occasionally looking skyward to judge the position of the sun. He would sometimes leave her, giving Socrates over to her care and cautioning her to stay put. It always seemed hours before he returned, but she supposed it was much less. As she waited, she dismounted and massaged her aching limbs and muscles.

When he returned, she mounted again, feeling new stabs of agony streak through her body. She knew they were headed west to Virginia, but there were so many detours that she no longer had any sense of direction. The air grew clammy and tense, and the sky around them started to darken. Though it seemed she'd been riding for days, she knew it wasn't yet time for nightfall.

Looking up through heavily laden trees, she watched the sky begin to boil. Dark, pregnant clouds roiled in the sky as a heavy shroud of humidity dropped on the earth. Mosquitoes descended in force, and a hot wind stirred the trees, making their movements ominous and threatening.

Lauren watched Adrian look skyward more and more often, his face growing grim.

"We have to find a place to stay," he said reluctantly, and she knew how anxious he was to find Confederate forces. The Potomac River, and safety, couldn't be far away.

She merely nodded. She knew that much of this area had been forsaken by civilians, caught as it was between two armies and subjected to constant raids and skirmishes.

"There's an abandoned farm not far back. It's partially burned but . . ."

Lauren nodded. The wind, which had been blowing hard, was now still, and the air radiated with electricity, with a latent violence ready to explode, and both horses were acting skittish.

Lauren wondered whether Adrian would have gone back had she not been with him, but she also knew she was not a good enough rider to stay on a frightened horse. Heading for shelter was also dangerous, however. Others would also be looking for refuge.

She could only pray that they would reach safety quickly, for this was going to be no ordinary storm.

She didn't know how long they backtracked before she saw a clearing. There were two small fields, both now overgrown with weeds. A shell of a barn and a small, dilapidated house stood together, part of the house leaning crazily. There were pockmarks everywhere, and Lauren realized that a battle had taken place here, leaving its footprints of violence. Parts of the roofs of both buildings were gone, charred edges showing where fire, or an explosion, once ate at the security a family thought it had. What was left looked utterly lonely and sad.

Adrian dismounted and approached her when the storm exploded, huge hailstones mixing with great fat drops of rain. In seconds, she was soaked. Adrian helped her down, catching her as she started to fall. "Go inside the house," he ordered. "I'll take care of the horses."

Despite the pelting rain, she didn't want to go. Not alone. There was something about the house . . .

"I'll help," she said, seizing the reins of her horse from him. Socrates ran nervously in circles, waiting to see where they were going. He was chattering in his scolding way.

The horses whinnied anxiously, pulling against the restraints, as Adrian yelled at her to follow him. He strained against the now strong wind, which had returned with a fury, and headed toward the remains of the barn. Like the house, part of it was missing, and of two doors, one was gone and the other hung precariously from a hinge. But at least it offered some shelter.

Inside, the roof was leaking and the stalls were missing, the wood probably taken for fuel. Wind and rain blew in through gaps in the roof as the horses stamped nervously. But at least they were out of the storm's open fury. Adrian quickly unsaddled the two horses and tied the reins to a ring in what was once a stall. Then he went to the barn opening and looked out, while Socrates huddled in the driest corner of the building.

Lauren followed. The hail pounded on what was left of the roof, thudded on the interior of the unprotected part of the barn. The trees were blowing wildly and, though it was still midday, the overgrown fields were shrouded in dark as though night had descended. Soil and brush swept by in whirling clumps.

Her clothes were plastered to her body, and she saw that Adrian's blue shirt was also molded to his chest, his trousers against the heavily muscled legs. She shivered, not knowing whether the tremors came from the rain or the sight of him standing in the doorway, every hard curve of his body outlined against the storm.

He turned, and his eyes fastened on her, sliding from her soaked hair down the length of her clinging dress. The blue in his eyes warmed to blue heat, like the hottest part of a flame.

He held out his arms, and she went into them, the storm and the wind heightening every physical sense. The smell of earth mixed with the scent of desire that clung to both of them. Heady and wild and savage . . . like the elements outside. The earth was closing in on them, cloaking them with a ferocity that invited more ferocity, that set every nerve end on edge.

Thunder roared, and lightning reached out in furious bright splendor, shaking the earth as it hit a nearby tree. Lauren felt as though the very essence of that electricity had snaked along the ground and reached her, burning its way up her legs, boiling in the soul of her. Her face lifted and she stared upward at Adrian. The same tumultuous excitement shone in his eyes, and his head leaned down until their lips met in an explosion as bright as the lightning striking earth.

His arms wrapped around her, fusing her body to his, and she felt his manhood reach out to her again, pulsing in need. Her breasts strained against her dress, yearning for his touch. Minutes ago, she had ached so much, and all she'd wanted was to lie down, but now her body was alive again, with sizzling fires dancing up and down her spine.

The clap of thunder roared again. Involuntarily she flinched at its nearness and pressed her head against Adrian's chest. She heard his heartbeat, even through the clashing of the elements—the clamorous sound of the hail, the rustle of the rain, the howl of the wind.

She felt the hot warmth gather inside again, and now her body trembled with expectation, with wanting.

Lauren felt herself being picked up, so very easily, and carried to the driest part of the barn. Impatient but gentle hands stripped her garments from her and ran reverently down the sides of her body as she shivered with each magnetic touch. He leaned down and kissed her. Then his mouth moved to her breasts, his tongue teasing and leaving hot wakes in its path. She found herself shamelessly reaching for his buttons. His shirt first, so she could run her fingers against the fine symmetry of his chest, so her mouth could taste him, could lick the essence of him, could make him tremble as she did.

And then his trousers . . . slowly, her hands moved, and she watched spasms tear through his body as her hand freed his shaft, now full and rigid. He moaned, and the sound intermingled with a new roar of thunder as he rolled over and entered her. Then the storm outside was eclipsed by the one they now rode.

Ride the lightning. Somewhere deep in the back of her consciousness, a place not yet dulled by the sensations rocking her, Lauren remembered Adrian saying that. Now she knew what it meant to ride the lightning.

Dear God, how brilliant it was!

Adrian sat against the wall of the barn and watched Lauren sleep. It was still raining hard outside, but the thunder had passed on. He heard rumbling from far away, and knew they were no longer in the heart of the storm.

A small stream of light now filtered into the barn. He watched as it touched the gold in her hair. Her face looked so open, so vulnerable, so peaceful.

His hand touched a damp curl, and then followed the line of her cheek. He heard her sigh, a contented sigh, like a small child. Innocent.

He heard a sigh of his own, but it wasn't nearly as peaceful.

Lauren Bradley was such a contradiction. He remembered the first time he had seen her, wrapped in a modest gown with those hazel eyes shooting sparks at him. He hadn't understood why then—he still didn't, entirely—but she never ceased to fascinate him, nor the passion buried beneath the very proper exterior.

But there was little that was proper about Lauren, he was learning bit by bit. He'd seen a kindred soul the night they'd escaped the Union patrol boats, had watched her face flush with excitement rather than fear. That same excitement had been there at the prison, and again on the train. He suspected that passionate streak had been restrained until their meeting. When it had flared into life, he was drawn to it like a moth to a flame.

He could no longer imagine a life without Lauren. He didn't want to. She'd colored all the gray parts of his life. But he also knew he couldn't trust her. With an aching awareness, he knew she was still keeping much of herself from him. Despite their uninhibited lovemaking, she remained a mystery in so many other ways.

He found it hard to believe her duplicitous, and yet he had seen it time and time again—in the prison, on the train, on the road.

Like Sylvia.

But not like Sylvia. Whatever her reason for doing what she had, it was not simple greed. Still, he should hate her. He should despise her as he had Sylvia.

But he might as well try to despise the sun that gave warmth, because it seared at midday, or the moon that offered both light and danger, or the storm that alternated fury and glory . . .

CHAPTER 20

Lauren woke to the prodding of a bony paw and a feeling of dampness. Before opening her eyes, she stretched like a cat, satisfied and sated.

She still ached. She suspected she would ache for a long time to come, but other feelings overwhelmed the discomfort: a lovely warm, contented feeling deep in the nub of her that drifted through her whole being.

Lauren heard the pounding of rain against the roof. The fury was gone now. Instead, the rhythm was steady, comforting. The very sound was soporific. She looked up lazily. Socrates was scraping his paw across her, grinning at her quite happily. There was a sly look about him, as if he had arranged everything himself.

She was suddenly conscious of her nakedness. It was strange she felt so comfortable with it. There was a wonderful sensuousness about lying on a floor of old hay, the fresh scent of rain-washed air mixing with the musk of bodies. Her head was cradled in Adrian's arms, and her hand moved to touch his slightly damp chest. She moved her head so she could watch him sleep. Pleasure surged through her at his nearness, and she wondered at the rightness she always felt with him, a rightness in her heart if not her mind.

Suddenly she felt him stir.

"Adrian?"

"Hummmmmm." Contentment seemed to flow from the word.

He turned her over in his arms so he was facing her. "You're beautiful when you sleep," he observed.

"So are you."

He chuckled, that deep, wonderful chuckle that went all the way from chest to throat to mouth. "I think I like that observation."

"Good," Lauren said with satisfaction.

He moved reluctantly. "We're not being very cautious."

Impulsively she nibbled at his shoulder.

He grimaced as his body once more started to react to her touch. "Socrates is teaching you some . . . interesting habits."

"Socrates doesn't have to teach me anything. It seems to come instinctively."

"I like the things that come to you instinctively."

Despite his words, he gently nudged her away from him and rose, giving his hand to her and bringing her up gracefully with him.

She couldn't help but wince at the movement; the aches were coming back, and with a vengeance now that she didn't have the narcotic of his body next to hers.

His arm went around her shoulder, and she looked around. With the exception of a small area where they had been lying, the barn floor was wet, puddles scattered throughout as rain continued to fall through holes and cracks in the roof.

"I think we can make it to the house now," Adrian said. "I don't think it will be quite as wet."

Lauren felt a strange reluctance as Adrian went to

where the saddles lay and took out the shirt she had worn the previous night and drew her arms into it. Then he put on his wet pants and gathered the other wet clothes: her dress and underclothing, the blue shirt he'd taken from the Yanks.

He also took the saddlebags with whatever food remained, and swung Socrates up on his shoulder. He then held out his hand to her, the large, powerful hand that could be so tender.

The rain was coming down steadily, and thunder still echoed from some faraway place. The sky was gray, sullen.

Lauren felt a strange hesitancy about the house. It somehow seemed a very sad, indeed tragic, place, but she scolded herself for being foolish. There was a fireplace; she had seen that, and perhaps they could use it. In this weather no one would be out to see smoke.

They reached the porch and found the door half-open. Adrian steered her to the left, where the roof still protected the interior, and she found herself once again reluctant to enter until Adrian pulled her inside.

The room was in shambles. There were torn cushions on the floor, the furniture they once graced now gone, probably consumed in a fireplace full of ashes. Gunfire, or perhaps bayonets, had ripped holes in the walls, and the floors were covered with dirt and trash. Several filthy blankets lay in one corner, playing cards scattered in front of them, as if some men had been interrupted, or frightened, in the middle of a game.

Lauren's eyes traveled to the fireplace, where a coffeepot sat, its bottom and sides scorched black. There was a small frying pan lying on its side, its contents long ago consumed by animals. Rust-colored stains covered the wood flooring. She shivered. Blood. War. Death. All haunted this room, their presence chilling her.

Lauren stepped back. "I can't stay here," she whispered.

Adrian saw her white face, the way her body swayed back and forth. "The barn then," he agreed.

He released her for a moment and went over to the corner, gathering up the blankets, pan, and the deck of cards in the manner of a born scavenger. Tucking them all under one arm, he guided her back out the room. Even he felt something disconcerting about the house.

The barn seemed a haven when they returned, even with the puddles of water and the wind pressing through the cracks. The temperature was still warm, but it would be hard to dry her clothes with this humidity, Lauren reflected.

Adrian disappeared again in the direction of the house and returned shortly with some boards. He set the saddles nearby and laid Lauren's clothes on them, the undergarments on one and her dress on the other.

Next he dug in the stolen saddlebags and brought out more hardtack, some bacon, and a handful of coffee.

Adrian took the pan outside and let the rain wash it out. He cooked the bacon silently, all the time keeping his gaze on Lauren's white face. He grew even more worried when she merely picked at her food.

Her lack of appetite ruined his own. Only Socrates seemed pleased with the meal.

Adrian finally took her in his arms. "I'm sorry," he said. "I wish I had more for you, but we'd better save the coffee until morning."

Lauren tried to shrug off her sudden desperation. She didn't understand it; she had felt a terrible premonition ever since she saw the house, and it had grown stronger when they had gone inside. There had been terrible loss in that house. It made her think of her own losses, past and future, and in those few minutes they had become so strong she felt as if someone had thrust a sword deep inside.

Adrian moved closer to her, his breath a whisper against her hair. She felt his hands tighten around her waist, but she couldn't accept his comfort right now. She moved away from him, keeping her eyes away from the brilliance of his, which always made her forget everything else.

She sat in the dry corner. She could see the sky from there, both through a hole in the roof and out the broken door. The day was gray, dismal, the rain falling in a steady stream that seemed to indicate it would continue that way for a long time.

"Is it safe to stay?" she finally asked Adrian, who was now leaning against a wall, watching her carefully.

"I think everyone who was caught in that storm has probably found shelter by now," he replied. "I suspect they'll stay put."

"How far is the Potomac?"

He shrugged. "No more than a few miles, but now it will be rain-swollen."

"Adrian?" Her voice was almost a whisper.

"Yes?"

"I'm not usually so fainthearted."

He smiled ruefully. "I discovered that the first night we met . . . when you kicked that poor, unsuspecting villain. If there's one thing I know about you, love, it's that you don't lack courage."

"My father was a doctor," she said, ignoring his words, trying to understand her own reactions. "I used to help him . . . I . . . blood never . . . bothered me . . ."

Adrian straightened, his body tensing. This was one of the few times she had volunteered information, although she had said her brother and father were doctors. She'd mentioned nothing about helping them. Perhaps that explained some of her independence, that competence that had surprised him in the beginning, but no longer.

"I don't know why that room . . . bothered me," she continued.

But he didn't want to let go of those scraps of information she just dropped. "And Larry . . . your brother . . . you said he was a doctor too."

If it were possible, her face went even whiter.

"How did he die, Lauren?"

The question was asked in a soft, compelling voice.

"I don't want to talk about it."

"But you have nightmares about it," Adrian pressed. "Perhaps . . . if you talked about it?"

But her face had shuttered, and he felt a sudden coldness inside. She'd done this before, allowed him to get close and then moved out of reach. He knew he should be wary. But all he wanted was to hold her and chase away whatever devils were plaguing her. No one had ever struck such notes of tenderness in him before, and he was amazed at how powerful they were.

He knew, though, that she wasn't going to say any more, now, about her brother . . . or her past.

And they weren't going anyplace, not for a while. He leaned down and picked up the cards he had found inside the house. "What about a game of chance, Miss Bradley?" he said, and her face lit with relieved interest.

"I would be delighted, Captain Cabot."

She was an apt pupil, Adrian thought dryly as he lost another ten pounds.

Her mind was like quicksilver, quickly absorbing the rules and intricacies of the game. And she had a real knack for remembering which cards had been played and computing the odds. She could be dangerous in a London gambling hell, he thought, if indeed women were permitted to play.

But as it was, he had to keep his attention on the game as her eyes sparkled at learning something new and mastering it.

Her one disadvantage, Adrian thought, was her display of delight when the cards were good. Although he had observed the way her face, and eyes, often hid her emotions, she did not hide them in the game of cards, perhaps because it was not that important to her. But to him it signified that deception did not come naturally to her.

They whiled away a good part of the day at the game, Socrates watching intently, occasionally grabbing a card in a bid for attention and then running away with it, teasing Adrian to run after him. Lauren would giggle as the tall, sophisticated English lord reached for, and missed, the small furry ball of energy. He would finally surrender and return to Lauren, while Socrates, grinning happily, would give back the card with a small bow.

As the rainy afternoon wore on, their glances fell more

to each other than to the cards. Lauren felt wondrously free with only Adrian's shirt covering her, free and wanton and wickedly sensuous, particularly as his gaze touched her as intimately as any hand could. She found her own gaze fixing on his chest, the dark blond hairs that pointed like an arrow down to the waist of his trousers, the corded muscles that moved each time he leaned over to pick up a card, or to deal, or gather up the deck.

The movements of their hands grew lazier, each wanting to do something other than hold cards. Their gazes met and held, and yet neither of them made the first move, Adrian remembering her withdrawal earlier, and Lauren afraid of how much she wanted him, how much he meant to her. She felt she was flinging herself off a cliff into an abyss below, and was as helpless to prevent it as a lemming drowning itself at sea.

And then her eyes found his, and she lost herself in their brilliant blue fire. Her hand went out across the cards. He took it, and suddenly they were lying together, their bodies fitting like pieces of a puzzle. Through a soft mist, she watched every nuance in his face as his fingers teased and loved. He moved into her then, his manhood probing gently at first and then filling her completely as her body reacted with shuddering movements, grasping him, loving him . . .

Adrian moved his mount carefully among the trees. He had to force himself to pay attention.

It was dusk, and he'd stirred himself from Lauren's side just moments ago. He still felt the lassitude, the well-being, of the aftermath of love.

He hadn't wanted to leave her, but something nagged at the back of his mind. They had been careless, and bloody lucky so far. He had been so lost in her, in the cocoon they had woven around themselves, that he'd neglected even the basics of caution.

The rain, now light, awakened senses dulled by the intensity of their recent lovemaking. He raked his wet hair with a hand, pushing it back from where it tumbled on his forehead.

He had to know how far they were from the Potomac, how well the river was guarded. With both armies so recently engaged in Pennsylvania, he and Lauren didn't have to worry about stumbling into main camps. But they did have to worry about guerrillas on both sides, raiders and deserters and predators. There would be small troops of men watching on both banks of the river, and he had to figure a way of crossing it.

And then what?

Bloody hell, he didn't know. Would Lauren run? He had seen the intent in her eyes several times. But now . . .

There could be a baby. If enthusiasm had anything to do with it, they had surely created one. He smiled as he considered the prospect. He'd thought never to marry for love, not after Sylvia. He'd even thought himself incapable of that emotion in the past years, but now he realized how foolish he'd been.

He loved Lauren. He knew it. He also knew he couldn't tell her that. Not as long as secrets hung between them— not until she trusted him. He wouldn't risk himself that way. But he was bloody determined he was not going to let her go. One way or another, she was going to England with him.

Despite his preoccupation and the still-driving rain, something alerted him. Perhaps it was his horse, whose ears suddenly perked up. He heard the whinny of horses, and he moved from the path he was following into the woods.

Adrian quickly dismounted and held his hands over his horse's mouth to keep the animal from responding. The sound of hoofbeats was audible, despite the fact that the rain-soaked ground tended to swallow the sound. That meant there were many riders.

And then he heard voices . . . near.

"Goddamn Englishman."

"Captain must be out of his mind. Can't find anything in this mess."

"Let's go by that old haunted farmhouse."

"You can go, Sergeant, not me."

"It's the only shelter within miles."

"No one's gonna stay there, not for long. Remember those last . . ."

Adrian didn't wait to hear any more. He ran his horse a quarter of a mile or so, then mounted and pushed the horse into a gallop.

Lauren kept looking toward the house. She was both repelled and attracted by it.

Her dress was dry now, and she put it on, trying to smooth the wrinkles, with little success. She also combed her hair as best she could, but she couldn't find the pins to keep it in place, so she twisted it into a long braid.

From the barn door, Lauren looked at the house again. She had been restless since Adrian left to scout. She had walked around the wet barn, the hem of her dress soaking up rain from the puddles, yet she couldn't stay still. And something about the house beckoned even as it frightened her.

She held out her hand to Socrates. "Let's explore."

The house was draped in gray. Rain continued to fall, but with less force than before. The clouds above were still full and pregnant, but the tension had flowed from the air —except, it seemed to Lauren, around the house.

Socrates swung up into her arms, scolding, and she knew he didn't want to go in; nor did he want to stay behind.

Lauren approached slowly but inexorably, as if dragged on an invisible leash. Entering the house, she ignored the room with the bloodstains. Instead, she went down a small hall into a room on the left, again as if drawn.

Like the other room, it had been stripped of nearly everything. Her eyes went to the brick fireplace and stayed there. She felt something strange in the room, a chill, but there was nothing menacing about it. She moved to the hearth, her eyes searching for something, though she didn't know what, and then she found it, and the chill seemed to fade. In the hearth, as though thrown against the side, was a book. Lauren leaned down and picked it up.

Just then she heard the sound of a rider outside, and one arm tightened its hold on Socrates while the other held tightly to the book as she moved quickly toward the front door.

Adrian! Adrian was gesturing toward the barn, and she hurried over to it just as he dismounted. "Yanks coming," he said, and he hurried to saddle her horse while Lauren quickly gathered their possessions. She stuffed as many as she could in the saddlebags and the rest into the one of the blankets Adrian had taken from the house. The book she'd picked up went with the frying pan, playing cards, and Adrian's shirt into the blanket. She tucked the bundle under her arm.

Adrian was finished saddling her horse, and he helped her mount, then took Socrates and swung up on his own mount, leaving the barn at a trot. Lauren followed, her precious bundle now tucked under her skirt to keep it from getting wet.

Just as they reached the trees, she looked back. Through the gray fog of rain, she saw the head of a horse, and then blue uniforms, but then the trees blocked her view, and Adrian and she were moving quickly through the forest.

They seemed to go on forever. The rain continued to fall, and occasionally thunder roared. Streaks of lightning flashed in the distance. Water spilled from the leaves, soaking already sodden clothing.

All of Lauren's aches and pains returned. To try to forget the misery, she thought of the book she had found, and wondered about the strange feelings she had in the house. It was almost as if someone had been trying to tell her something.

Nonsense. It was nothing but an ordinary book, and it had been only the silence of the house that made it so eerie. But it still gave her something to think about, something other than how very miserable she was.

And still they went on and on until it grew too dark to see.

Adrian stopped beneath a huge oak. It wasn't a completely satisfactory shelter, for water dripped from the leaves, but they couldn't go any farther, not in the pitch-black darkness. He helped her down, unsaddled the horses, and used the horse blankets to rig a shelter above them. The damp horse odor was strong, but Lauren was ready to accept any small favor of cover at this time. Thank God, it was summer, and there was no chill to the rain, but still the rivulets of water under her dress made her feel clammy and uncomfortable.

Nothing seemed to bother Adrian, however. He moved as decisively as ever and, if anything, looked more dashing with wet clumps of curling chestnut hair falling on his forehead. He bent over her, kissing her forehead and taking her damp form in his arms. "I'm sorry," he said.

And suddenly everything was all right, as it always was when she was in such close proximity to him. But Socrates evidently didn't feel the same. He howled in abject misery and tried to get under Lauren's petticoat, finally succeeding as her skirts took on a life of their own.

Adrian chuckled even as he kissed her. "I'll make this up to you someday," he said.

But he didn't have to. They were here . . . now . . . because of what she had done. He should be back at sea, or in Nassau. Instead, they were in the middle of nowhere in the midst of a seemingly unending storm with few clothes and even less food.

She started to giggle, partially from hysteria. She heard his answering laugh, and it seemed neither of them could stop. And so they sat in the rain under a dripping oak tree in the middle of a war, and they laughed and laughed and laughed.

CHAPTER 21

Lauren and Adrian huddled under the tree until dawn.

They were able to snatch an occasional few moments of sleep until water collected on the blanket and tumbled on them like a waterfall.

Sometimes they just held each other to forget the physical misery, the hunger that revealed itself in occasional rumbles in their stomachs.

The laughter was gone. There were only the two of them—no, the three of them—trying to endure what usually would be unendurable.

But as Lauren felt Adrian's arms around her, she knew she would rather be here with him than alone in a palace.

It made her think of his home. Where did a lord live? How did a lord live? He'd mentioned the name of his estate: Ridgely. How did it compare to the small cottage where she'd lived, a thousand years ago? What would he think of her home, he who had probably supped with the queen?

She snuggled deeper in his arms. "What was your house like in England?"

He was silent for several moments. "Old . . . old and full of history and memories. King Henry VIII slept there. So did George during your Revolution."

"Is it large?"

"Very large. When I was a young boy, I would get lost in the wings. The old part was once a castle, better than seven hundred years old. It was expanded, and expanded again to house whole armies. You walk through the halls and you can almost hear their voices."

He hesitated, and she rubbed his hand, silently urging him to continue.

"The family divided during the War of the Roses, one brother on one side, one on the other. One brother was even locked in the dungeon by the other for months. I used to go down there . . . I could feel the pain . . ."

His hand tightened around hers. "And the main hall . . . where dances were held . . . the music seems to still echo . . ."

"You loved it," she said quietly.

"More than anything in my life until—" He stopped abruptly. "Yes, I loved it. It was always my refuge."

"Refuge?"

"My father and I didn't get along. A second son was of no use to him, and all he cared about was people who were of use. The irony was that I was the son who cared about Ridgely, who would have preserved it."

"And your mother?"

"She died when I was young." His voice was curt.

"Your brother?"

"He always hated Ridgely . . . as much as I loved it. But because of English law, he inherited everything. And gambled it all away."

Lauren heard the pain in his voice.

"You would love it," he said. "There is a private forest with a fast-running stream. The fields are rich and productive." There was a terrible wistfulness in his voice. "I would like to show it to you."

"Who . . . owns it now?"

"A man named Rhys Redding. He won it from my brother. He's indicated he would sell it back for the right price."

The right price. Lauren felt the familiar sickening guilt inside. She remembered when, on the *Specter*, she'd asked him why he ran the blockade, and he had teasingly said it was the game. But it hadn't been. It had never been. Ridgely had simply meant too much to Adrian—he hadn't been able to talk about it. She knew that now as surely as she knew how painful it was to think of Larry. Yet he was finally sharing part of himself with her, though she couldn't do the same. She realized she had cost him the chance to regain his heritage. He would never forgive her. She wondered if she would ever forgive herself.

His hand tightened on her, tensing with suppressed emotion. "Ridgely's my legacy from the past . . . who I am. Cabots have lived there more than seven hundred years. For us to lose it now . . ."

"Your brother lost it—you didn't."

"But if I have a chance to get it back and fail . . ."

The defeat in his voice was almost more than she could bear. She cast frantically for another subject. "What is it like to be an English aristocrat?"

"Lonely," he said unexpectedly. "My father cared only about the name being carried on, not his sons as such. Though John, as heir, received attention, if not love. He had to be perfect, and he could never quite be that. So he resented everything about Ridgely."

"And you?"

"A nuisance barely tolerated, particularly when I got into mischief. But getting into mischief meant getting attention. So I was always doing that. I wanted Ridgely—I cared about Ridgely while my brother didn't—but there was never any chance of that, so I drowned my dreams in ale and disgraced my father by reckless gambling. At least it had the effect of making him realize I was alive." Adrian didn't know why he was telling her all this. He had never spoken of such things to a soul before. But Lauren's acceptance made the confession easier. He wanted her to know him, to trust him, to share the things close to her with him.

It was frightening how much he wanted that.

But he was answered only by understanding silence. A silence heavy with things left unsaid.

"And you, sweetheart?" he said finally. "How did you grow up as a doctor's daughter?"

With love, she wanted to say. But how could she when he'd obviously had so little? How could she explain that love had made her do things she ordinarily would never have done. Just as his lack of it had done the same.

She lifted her head, glad that the wetness of the night disguised the tears running from her eyes. I love you, she wanted to say, but she didn't have the right to say it. She would never have the right to say it, so instead she pretended a sleep that she was sure would be fraught with disturbing dreams.

But if she'd had dreams, she remembered none of them when she woke in Adrian's arms. Only the slightest gray peeped between the heavily laden trees. With her movement, she felt Adrian's and looked up. He was blinking, so she knew that he too had got a little sleep.

Socrates had found a place beside the two of them. He lay partly on Adrian, partly on her, in probably the driest spot around. No fool that monkey, Lauren thought with quiet amusement tinged with envy. Socrates's problems were minor ones, and he had a way of making the best of things.

She stretched out with Adrian, her hand touching a drenched, untidy braid. She could imagine how she looked. A drowned rat would probably benefit from comparison, and yet Adrian looked uncommonly attractive with his sleepy eyes and slow, languorous movements.

The rain had stopped, although water still found its way from the blanket above. The forest was shrouded in fog, a silver-gray mist that made the leaves sparkle with crystal drops. The heaviness was gone from the air, and now there was a sweet, fresh smell.

Socrates scampered off into a tree, and Lauren saw him lick moisture from the leaves. Her stomach groaned with emptiness, and her throat was parched. She moved and discovered that all of her was as stiff as a board.

Adrian's hands drew up the wet dress and rubbed her legs. He kneaded and rubbed until she felt life flow back into them.

"I think our first order of the day is food," he said as his stomach grumbled.

"What about finding the river?"

"I think I heard it last night . . . we can't be too far away. But we can't cross until nightfall."

"Where can we get some food?"

"Do you have any money?"

Lauren nodded.

"The Yanks confiscated all mine. At least that's what they called it," Adrian said. "But I have an account in Charleston, and I can get my hands on it in Wilmington. In the meantime, I suppose we'll have to use yours."

"It's sewn in my dress." Lauren liked the look of admiration she found in his face.

"I'll see if we can't find a farmhouse."

"Isn't that dangerous?"

"So is starving to death," he said with a wry grin. "But I'm thinking this area has been raided so much, almost anyone would be too grateful for money to raise an alarm." He put a hand to his head. The bandage had come off long ago. "Can you fix a new bandage for this addled soldier?"

"But . . . they're looking . . ."

"They'll probably be looking southeast of here. We've been traveling north, parallel to the Potomac. And I suspect most of the residents around here, being just across the river from Virginia, are Confederate sympathizers." He turned and looked at her. "You're from Maryland, aren't you?"

Lauren nodded, hating more and more each lie.

But he didn't pursue the subject. "A wife and her injured husband . . . Perhaps you can fashion a new bandage."

She did that, with part of her petticoat, and after a few uncomfortable moments seeing to their more intimate needs in the woods, they mounted again. He looked around with frustration. "I would sell my soul for a compass," he said. But compass or not, Lauren noticed he moved with assuredness, and it wasn't long before she heard the sound of rushing water.

Adrian found a path, almost overgrown, and they followed it for a long time, hearing the sound of the water growing louder and louder. The woods thinned out, and Lauren saw some fields. Like the farmhouse they'd left, these fields were trampled, and whatever food they'd once nourished had been stolen or destroyed. They went by a burned-out foundation and continued on, still following the path to where it once more wandered into the woods.

The mist had lifted, but the sky was still heavy with clouds and the air damp. Rainwater lingered on leaves, and another rain seemed not only likely but inevitable. Still, they traveled, her hunger growing sharper. Finally, Adrian veered off the path toward an almost invisible opening in the brush, and Lauren followed.

She saw him take the pistol from the saddlebags and tuck it in his trousers and then stop abruptly. As she looked beyond him, she spied a rough log cabin.

There was a sudden shout, and her horse shied.

"Stop right thar," she heard a voice say.

Adrian pulled up his horse, his hands reaching up where they could be seen. "We don't mean any harm."

"Who are you?" the disembodied voice demanded.

"Just a man and his wife . . . we need help."

"What kinda help?" The question was suspicious.

"Food . . . we can pay."

"Ken you now?"

"My wife is wet and tired and . . . with child."

Lauren started. *With child*. With Adrian's child. If she hadn't been so hungry and tired and wet, she might savor the idea. As it was, she hoped with him it would engender help and safety.

"Git down. Real slow like."

But Socrates, sitting hidden in the saddle in front of Adrian, apparently heard the threat in the voice, and he reacted as he had before to threats against those he considered his. He suddenly leaped, mouth open and paws outstretched.

The man yelled, as much in horror at the hairy beast coming at him as in surprise. The gun dropped, firing as it hit the ground, and then Adrian was down, grabbing for Socrates with one hand while taking out his own gun with the other.

Lauren looked around. The shot had gone wild, and the man, now on the ground, was eyeing Socrates with something akin to terror. The monkey, obviously feeling that he'd done his part, scooted several feet away and was thumping his chest in a self-congratulatory way.

Adrian held the gun loosely. "I mean you no harm," he said. "We just need some food, and we're willing to pay for it."

"What . . . what is that . . . ?" The man, a wiry white man with red hair, trembled slightly.

"A monkey," Adrian said easily. "He's . . . protective . . ."

"Gol damn, I ain't never seen anything like that!" The man looked at Socrates with wondering eyes. "And you ken put that gun down . . . now I see the missus. Cain't take any chances 'round here."

Adrian eyed the man carefully for a moment, then he stuck the gun in the waist of his trousers.

"My wife's cookin' some bread and fish now . . . You say you have money. Gold? Not that worthless Confederate stuff?"

"Gold," Adrian said, not quite sure where the man's sympathies lay.

"This way," the man said, and started to pick up his musket.

Adrian beat him to it, leaning over and taking it. "I'll

carry it for you," he said with a charming smile, though there was a warning edging it.

The man merely nodded, his eyes warily watching Socrates, as he led the way to a small cabin. Adrian laid the musket carefully against a log and then helped Lauren dismount, holding her protectively for a fraction of a second before a woman, tall and worn-looking, emerged from the doorway.

The woman eyed them both cautiously, and then her eyes softened at Lauren's bedraggled appearance. Lauren leaned against Adrian, trying to steady herself, but her legs weren't cooperating. She was too sore, her leg muscles too tired. She swayed, and he caught her in his arms.

"This way," the man said. "You ken bring her in." He saw Adrian eyeing the musket. "You don't need to worry 'bout that. It's to keep looters and riffraff away."

The man brushed aside the woman and waited for Adrian to follow. The smell of baking bread assailed Lauren as Adrian set her down in a chair.

"Our name's Cooper. Henry and Betsy Cooper. Used to tenant farm not far from here, but people who owned the land got killed, and we kept gettin' unwanted visitors. Seemed safer to move down here, out of everybody's way . . . lots of fish."

"You have a boat?"

Adrian's question was easy, but Lauren knew him well enough now to notice a sudden tension in his eyes.

"You Reb? Don't talk like any Reb."

"English," Adrian said. He'd decided it was useless to say anything else; his accent, he knew, was impossible to disguise. "I have some business on the other side."

The man's eyes narrowed speculatively, and Adrian could read the questions there. Spies? How much was it worth? Adrian concluded that Cooper's loyalties could be bought. He also thought he was probably not the first to buy them.

"How much is it worth to you?" Cooper said.

Adrian looked at Lauren. He had no idea how much gold she had with her.

"Our two horses," he said finally, knowing there was no way of getting them across the swollen river.

Cooper hesitated, sensing there was more to be had. "You said you had gold," he countered.

Lauren looked at Adrian. Her eyes told him that she was leaving the bartering to him.

"Just enough for food. I'll give you five dollars." It was an outrageous fortune, but Adrian wanted no trouble.

Cooper eyed them greedily. "Couldn't take the horses with you, no way."

"No," Adrian said, "but we could go farther upriver."

Cooper still hesitated.

"Another five dollars for some dry clothes for my wife," Adrian said, and there was a note of finality in it.

The man shrugged. "My wife has one other dress . . . ain't as nice as the one yer woman has . . ."

"If it's clean, we'll trade," Adrian said.

The woman nodded, her eyes enviously taking in Lauren's battered but mendable dress.

"And we can leave soon?"

"At dusk," the man said. "Too dangerous during the day."

Adrian nodded, turning his attention to the food now being placed in front of them by Betsy Cooper. There was fish stew and bread, and both Adrian and Lauren ate hungrily as their hosts darted apprehensive glances toward Socrates, now sitting peacefully on Lauren's lap.

When they finished, it was late afternoon. The two men went outside and Lauren changed into Mrs. Cooper's simple homespun dress. She asked for a needle and thread, since the dress was large, and she extracted the gold from her own dress and sewed it into the hem of the newly obtained one. Mrs. Cooper's dress was plain, ill-fitting, and threadbare, but it was clean. And best of all, it was dry.

When Lauren finished and emerged from the curtained changing area, there was an awkward silence. "We stayed in a farmhouse last night," Lauren said finally to break the quiet. "Not far from here. It was partially burned out."

"The Kendall place?" The woman's voice was surprised. "Folks hereabouts think it's hainted."

"Why?"

The woman shrugged. "People claim they hear crying. You hear any?"

Lauren shook her head. "Who lived there?"

"Man named Randall Kendall and his wife, Melissa."

"What happened?"

"Don't know much. Just know she wuz killed there. Deserters, some say."

"And her husband?"

"Fought with the Yanks. Not much sympathy for that 'round here."

"You and your husband favor the South?"

"Don't favor no one. One's bad as the other. Killin'. Destroyin'. We just try to live."

Lauren sat down in one of the chairs. The past few days were catching up with her, and now the warm food in her stomach and the deep weariness in her bones were dulling her senses.

"Why don't you jest git yerself some sleep," Betsy Cooper said. "You look plumb worn. And ain't no one going anyplace 'til t'night. You really with child?"

Lauren had forgotten that Adrian had said that. A whole new set of lies. So many now to remember. So very many . . .

She nodded and followed Betsy's suggestion, lying down on the corn-husk mattress in the corner. In minutes, she was asleep, her last thoughts about the mysterious Melissa Kendall.

Lauren didn't want to do this. She didn't want to do it at all.

She looked at the storm-swollen river, the rickety boat, and then back at Adrian.

Drat him. He didn't show the slightest apprehension. He stood there looking commanding as always and holding the saddlebags, which contained what little they could take with them. At the last minute, she had thrust the small book she'd found in the farmhouse into the bags. They also held some food prepared by Betsy Cooper, and the Deringer. The other gun was tucked into Adrian's trousers.

If anything, his grin was cockier than usual as he offered her a hand into the boat. Socrates, bless him, eyed the craft with the same suspicion that was in Lauren's heart. Only Adrian's coaxing lured him into Lauren's arms, and then he clutched at her neck as if his life depended on her.

Just as she wanted to clutch onto Adrian.

But she held her protests silent within herself. Nothing was more important than getting Adrian to safety.

"Patrols been light the last couple weeks," Henry Cooper said. "Hear tell of a big battle north of here."

Adrian nodded. "We heard about it too."

"Any news . . . who won or lost?"

Adrian shook his head.

"Guess it don't matter none," Henry said. "Folks still need crossing the river." Greed was back in his eyes, and Lauren knew he didn't care from which side the money came.

Cooper put the oars in the water, and the boat swung away from shore, Lauren holding on to Socrates with one hand and the side of the boat with the other as it rocked with the current. It was twilight, and a mist was floating up from the river. Nothing was visible on either side of the river, nothing but a green haze.

Socrates started rocking, making tiny keening noises, and Lauren tried desperately to quiet him. The noise mixed with the sound of oars hitting the water, moving them to the other side, to Virginia. The thought should have been comforting, but it was not. The other side was the Confederacy. Her enemy. Adrian's sanctuary.

She shivered, and the movement apparently made Socrates even more nervous. He suddenly made a leap past Henry Cooper, who reacted by shouting. One oar went spinning out of his hand into the water. At the same time, there was a shout from the Virginia side of the river, and a gunshot rang out.

The boat scraped the bottom of the river as she heard curses. "Bloody hell," came from the front of the boat. "Goddamn," came from the middle. Socrates was screaming.

"Get out," Adrian yelled at her, and she jumped into the river just as the boat was caught again in a current and swung back out into the river.

A hand caught her, guiding her to shore. "A friend," she heard Adrian call out.

And then they stumbled out of the river and were surrounded by a number of gray-clad men aiming pistols at them. Lauren held on to Adrian for everything she was worth. She felt a sticky wetness on her hand and looked down.

Blood was dripping from Adrian's shirt, a large red circle staining the blue shirt he had stolen from the Union soldiers.

CHAPTER 22

Socrates had jumped with Adrian, and now he scurried around his master, as if knowing something was wrong.

Several guns aimed at the animal, just as they were aimed at Adrian and Lauren, when a man with a distinct air of authority stepped up. His gray clothes were worn, and he, like the others, wore no insignia. But there was no question he was an officer.

His eyes skimmed over Adrian, then Lauren, and, amusedly, at Socrates, and finally back to Adrian. "Who," he asked, "in the hell are you?"

Adrian's hand had gone to his shoulder. He was starting to feel pain there, a fierce burning. "Adrian Cabot."

The officer's mouth twitched. "The blockade runner."

Adrian nodded as the pain started to spread, burning, weakening him. He had felt the blow in the boat, but not the agony, not until now. He nodded curtly.

One of the men in gray came up from the river carrying

the saddlebags that Adrian had lost in trying to grab Lauren. They were wet, as was the man who went in after them.

The officer held out his hand. "Captain Amos Kelly," he said. "I'm with Mosby. We've sorta been expectin' you. Thought you would be farther down river, though."

"Expecting us?"

"Yanks are goin' crazy, what with losin' you. Been burnin' up the wires we have access to. Big reward for you and the lady there . . ." He bowed. "Miss Bradley, I believe." His amused glance went to Socrates, who was now hanging on to Lauren. "And the monkey, of course. We didn't catch his name. We have orders to offer any assistance."

"Then why did you shoot?" Lauren asked angrily.

Amos Kelly had the grace to color. "Like I said, we thought you would be farther south, if you got this far . . . and then Cooper ain't that particular over who he brings across. And in this damned mist, it could have been a patrol boat. That ungodly scream startled one of my men . . ."

But all of Lauren's attention now was on the growing red circle on Adrian's shirt. "I've got to look at that."

"We have a doctor in camp," Amos Kelly offered.

"How far?" Lauren said tightly.

"An hour's ride. He can have one of our horses. We can double up."

Lauren shook her head as she saw blood puddle at Adrian's feet and his face set with pain. "I don't think we can wait that long."

The amusement fled the Confederate officer's face. He motioned the others to fade into the woods out of sight of the river. Lauren and Adrian followed, drops of blood trailing in his wake. Once into cover, Lauren looked about, finally finding a fallen tree trunk. Socrates was running around, his mouth working furiously with some monkey imprecations of his own.

Adrian sat, and Lauren unbuttoned the newly soaked shirt. A musket ball had entered his shoulder and had not exited. Blood was running from the jagged wound. Lauren knew a feeling of helplessness. She had watched her father extract bullets before, but she had neither the instruments nor the skill to do it herself here.

"Clean water," she said. "Does anyone have clean water?"

One gray-clad man offered a canteen. "Got some whiskey, too," he offered.

Lauren accepted both. She washed the wound as best she could, then rinsed it with the alcohol, wishing that she had been shot instead of Adrian as, despite his clenched teeth, a moan filtered from deep within his throat.

"Hey," the man who had given her the whiskey said, "I meant for him to drink it."

Lauren thought of the muddy Potomac water that had soaked into the wound and continued with her efforts, tearing a piece of material from her dress and binding it tight against the wound to slow the bleeding.

When she was through, she felt sick. Adrian's face was white, and the bandage of homespun was already darkening with blood despite her best efforts.

Captain Kelly already had some of his men mounted, and now he helped Adrian up onto one of the horses, then Lauren, who had to ride astride. But that didn't matter. Nothing mattered but Adrian. Socrates was with her; he had to be forcibly removed from Adrian, as the animal apparently sensed something was wrong and chattered worriedly.

She tried to calm him as they moved quickly, but her eyes kept going to Adrian, whose back was straight, too straight. He was usually so relaxed in the saddle. She closed her eyes. An hour until they reached a physician.

She knew it would be the longest hour of her life.

There was no morphine.

Lauren offered to help—she told the doctor that she had assisted her father, a surgeon—and the doctor finally agreed. He was getting ready to move out. What wounded he'd had from hit-and-run raids and skirmishes had been sent to Williamsburg. He'd been ordered north to meet the retreating Confederates.

Lauren had looked at him with horror when he said there was no morphine or chloroform. Whiskey was all he had.

The doctor shook his head. "Without men like him," he said, indicating Adrian, "we wouldn't have any medicines at all. Right now, all we have is in Pennsylvania, and God knows it's not enough."

He gave Adrian a cup of whiskey, and then another. Adrian's eyes started to glaze, but whether from the alcohol or the pain, Lauren wasn't sure. She only knew he was hurting. As she was.

But not nearly as much as when the doctor started probing for the ball, and she heard Adrian's smothered oaths. She cleaned the blood from the area, and Adrian's every agonized move made her tremble. After one muted groan, Adrian fainted. The doctor breathed a sigh of relief and dug out the musket ball, which was followed by a flood of blood.

Lauren watched as the doctor sewed up the wound. Adrian's eyes were closed, but his face was still lined with pain. Her hand reached out to touch his face, to try to smooth out the traces of agony. She wondered whether she could ever smooth them out of her mind.

"He should be all right," the doctor said, "if there's no infection. You wouldn't like to go with us, would you, missy? We can use another pair of hands."

Lauren looked down at Adrian. He would wake soon. The pain would be even worse with all the probing of tender skin and muscles. "No . . . thank you."

The doctor followed her gaze. "You don't know how much we need more of them . . . the blockade runners." He shook his head. "Amputating without morphine . . . if there's a hell, that's it."

Lauren bit her lip and took Adrian's hands in hers. It had been so easy in Delaware, so easy in Washington, to think her mission noble. Adrian's ship had been carrying cannon, but it had also probably been carrying medicines.

Had she, on top of everything else, sentenced men to agony? Was that what Larry would have wanted?

It was a thought beyond bearing. Nothing, she was discovering, was all right or wrong, black or white. There were so many shades in between.

She stayed with Adrian through the evening. The tent vanished, and so did the doctor, both piled in a wagon headed toward northern Virginia. Some of Captain Kelly's men went to escort him, but the captain himself was charged with scouting the banks of the Potomac, even now that the action was hundreds of miles away. There were still spies slipping across, as well as ranging bands of Yanks. And ladies to save, he added gallantly.

One of his men who, Captain Kelly said, had a special affinity with animals had taken temporary custody of Socrates. But not without mishap. Socrates bit his keeper once, and escaped into the medical tent before it had been dismantled. Recaptured, he later escaped again and found Adrian lying under a tree. With a pitiable cry, the monkey crawled next to him, laying his head on Adrian's leg.

No one dared approach the monkey, not even Lauren, after Socrates bared his teeth when he felt she might be trying to take him from Adrian. So Lauren let Socrates be, as she sat next to Adrian's head, washing beads of sweat from it, trying to keep him still as he thrashed in half-conscious agony.

"Adrian, what have I done to you?" she whispered once. She knew from the doctor, from her own knowledge, how prevalent disease and infection were, and she had nothing, the doctor had had nothing, to prevent them. She could only keep Adrian as cool and comfortable as possible.

Day faded into night, and she stayed at his side, as did Socrates. Adrian woke several times, his lips clenched tightly against the pain as he moved. He looked up once and smiled faintly. "An angel . . . I didn't think they existed."

She had swallowed down her denial. She was anything but that for him, and as soon as he was well . . .

Lauren was still awake, her back stiff, when he woke

again. Adrian and Captain Kelly talked briefly, and the captain said he would have a detail escort them to the next Confederate unit when Adrian was well enough. They were, he said again, to have every assistance. The Confederate Government held Captain Cabot in high esteem.

Adrian had tried to move, agony clouding his features again as he did so. But still his hand went down to Socrates, who looked at him beseechingly. Lauren had to smile at them. In the weeks she had known them—it seemed like years now—Socrates was constantly getting them in trouble. She wondered at a man who had the patience to continue loving such a beast.

She wondered if he would . . . could . . . do the same with her, for she had committed much worse atrocities than Socrates, and she didn't have the excuse of innocence.

Lauren erased the notions from her head, devoting herself instead to making Adrian as comfortable as possible. She had taken up a collection of food from the soldiers— Mrs. Cooper's food had been ruined in the river—and had made a broth of salt pork and wild onions and dried corn. It wasn't much, but at least it was hot.

She had to feed Adrian, since his right shoulder was now swathed in bandages that made movement difficult. She sensed his frustration at his helplessness, at yet another delay in reaching England and finding another ship.

But as always, he kept his feelings to himself. She often found his eyes on her, and she never knew quite what he was thinking. The blue of his eyes was so impenetrable. He kept his thoughts, and his pain, to himself.

His interest had flared briefly as Captain Kelly told them the war news. Adrian and Lauren had apparently just missed Jeb Stuart's troops in Maryland. Stuart had chased a Federal supply wagon nearly to Washington and captured 125 wagons, but it had made him late to Gettysburg. Garbled reports were still coming in from the battlefield there. Apparently there were enormous casualties on both sides, and Lee was retreating. Captain Kelly gave the accounts with a set face; he was obviously unhappy with orders keeping him on patrol duty.

Adrian finally sank back into sleep, his face still lined with weariness and pain . . . and some of the same sense of defeat that haunted the faces of their Confederate hosts.

It was the next afternoon, when he was sleeping, that Lauren remembered the book she'd taken from the farmhouse. The saddlebags had gone into the river with Adrian, but a Confederate soldier, not sure who they were or whether the saddlebags held any intelligence of importance, had grabbed them.

They had been returned to her, and she'd gone through them. The food was ruined, but though the book was wet she believed it salvageable. She'd set it out to dry, and now she went to it, picking it up and carrying it to where Adrian slept listlessly.

The book was a diary, much of the writing now running together, but a few pages still legible. Lauren turned to the middle of the book until she found a page she could read. The handwriting was neat, concise.

> June 12, 1861
>
> Tomorrow is my wedding day.
>
> I only wish with all my heart that my mother and father would attend, but I am, they say, no longer their daughter.
>
> And so I am staying with my future sister-in-law. Tomorrow I'll marry the man I've always loved, and I will become his alone. There is a sadness in that, but I can do nothing else. He may die next week, next month, next year. I will not miss this chance to love him, to share his life, to bear his child . . .

The writing ran then, the ink melding into the cream of the paper. Lauren started to pass those pages when she heard Adrian move restlessly next to her.

Her hand put down the diary and went to his. "How do you feel?"

He managed a twisted smile. "It's bloody inconvenient being shot by your own side."

The words sent a wave of distress through Lauren. He'd described what had happened to Larry. The irony was repeated over and over again. She could only nod.

His left hand touched hers. "I keep remembering seeing you . . . every time I . . . in my sleep, when I woke. You must be tired."

She denied it by a shake of her head as her fingers wove in between his. "I was worried about you . . . so was Socrates. I *do* think he cares."

"Bloody beast," Adrian said weakly. "Just worries about his banana supply." But his eyes went fondly to the monkey, who was now happily grooming himself with supreme indifference.

Adrian tried to sit up, but he fell back. "The doctor said you shouldn't move for at least five days," Lauren scolded.

"Five days, hell!" Adrian shifted again, this time bracing himself against pain and weakness. He sat up, his face drained of all color. "I want to leave tomorrow . . . I can rest later."

"Adrian!"

But he wore the stubborn look she'd seen before, and he asked a passing man to fetch Captain Kelly, who reluctantly agreed to pass him to the next unit if he felt well enough the next morning.

And he did, at least he said he did, despite the muscle working in his jaw as he was helped on a horse. Lauren also mounted, though she did so with bitterly mixed emotions. She had thought that she would leave him when he was safe, but now he wasn't safe, he was injured. He needed her.

At least that was what she told herself.

And where would she go? The fact that there was a reward for her told her that Mr. Phillips had no sympathy for what she had done. She could, of course, stay in the South, but she wouldn't feel comfortable with that either.

She no longer had a country. The thought was terrifying, and filled her with loneliness.

Captain Kelly had assigned them an escort of eight men. They rode until noon, heading toward Fredericksburg, Virginia. From that destination they would go the rest of the way by train: the Richmond, Fredericksburg and Potomac Railroad to Richmond, and then a train to Weldon, North Carolina, and, finally, a third train, the Wilmington and Weldon Railroad, to Wilmington.

The journey to Fredericksburg seemed endless to Lauren, who had to watch Adrian's obvious pain, but he would not stop, and when they rested he was the first to suggest they continue. By the end of the first day, he was swaying in the saddle, his mouth set tightly against the agony she knew he must be feeling.

She changed his bandages that first night, and the skin was bruised and discolored around the still-leaking wound. The stitches had torn loose, and again borrowing some whiskey, which alone seemed in ready supply, she resewed the wound and refused to move the next day. Adrian had to rest the whole day, she declared as stubbornly as he had insisted on moving the previous day.

It was indicative of his weakness that he finally agreed. Their escort did some hunting that night and returned with several rabbits. They were roasted on a spit, and Lauren and Adrian ate the tasty morsels with their fingers as Socrates found his own dinner in the trees. Adrian's eyes closed early, and much of the escort disappeared into the woods, setting up a cordon around them.

Using the firelight, Lauren took out the diary. She didn't want to have to think . . . not about Adrian and his obvious pain, not about her future.

June 20, 1861

A bride of one week, and I've already said good-bye to him. Randall's been called to his unit. They say there will be a battle soon. Dear God, I hope not.

My brother came by yesterday to tell me that he and my father are joining Lee's forces. I am so afraid they and Randall might meet on the field of battle. But I will never regret

*marrying him. I have loved him all my life, and I know he is
doing what he knows he must do, despite his family, despite
mine . . .*

*The fields are doing well, the corn growing, but there are
armies on both sides of us, and I fear we might be caught in
the middle. Sam and Lucas are working hard, but they too
miss Randall. He has been their strength as he is mine. It
was he who set them free, and they love him for it.*

*I know I have to be strong for him. I have to keep the
farm going. This land is Randall's soul. But . . . God help
me . . . he has been gone only a few days, and I am so
lonely . . . I feel my heart is missing.*

The light grew too dim to read by, and Lauren carefully
set the diary aside. She used the remaining flickering flames
to study Adrian's face. She didn't know if she would have
completely understood the diary three months ago, but
now her heart broke with Melissa Kendall's.

And she wondered whether she would ever have Melissa's courage.

Adrian woke painfully the next morning. A sudden
movement in his sleep had jolted him to full consciousness
as agony streaked through him. It had not been wise to
travel as far as they had yesterday, but he had not been
able to tolerate staying still.

Lauren. Ridgely. They haunted his thoughts, his
dreams. They were both so bloody damned elusive.

As each day went by, he felt further and further away
from Ridgely. And from Lauren. In some almost im-
perceptible way she was withdrawing from him.

They had been so close during their escape, during
those hours in the barn, but now the haunted expression
had returned to her eyes, and though she nursed him with
care and tenderness and stayed with him constantly, she
still gave him the impression of a bird poised for flight.

He silently cursed his weakness. Pain he could tolerate.

He had done it as a boy, as a young officer. But weakness was something else, something he couldn't control and therefore resented.

Lauren was not far away—sleeping now, at last. Though he had drifted in and out of consciousness the first two days, every time he woke, she was there. One of their escorts, a young lieutenant, had told him enviously how she couldn't be lured away from Adrian, no matter how much he and his companions urged her to rest.

Looking at her now, Adrian once more wished he could extract the truth from her. Honesty and loyalty were the two qualities he prized most highly. He knew he had not received honesty from Lauren, but she had certainly displayed loyalty in the past several days—that and much more.

But it wasn't enough. He knew as he looked at her face, soft and gentle in sleep, that he wanted her by his side forever, fighting with him, sleeping with him, sharing hardships with him. She challenged him, yet made him feel protective at the same time. Never had anyone so stimulated him, so excited him, so touched him.

He sighed and turned over, wincing as he did so, wondering at the turns his life had taken. But soon he would be going home—to England, perhaps even to Ridgely. He might as well make an offer for the estate.

And Lauren would be with him. One way or another, she would be with him.

CHAPTER 23

Fog, thick and heavy, limited Lauren's sight to a few feet. She couldn't even see the water below from the crowded deck of the ship, the *Sally Ann*. She could hardly see Adrian, who stood but inches away.

Lights barely flickered through the soup-like shroud that hid the city of Wilmington and the odd collection of other ships, many of which were also beginning to set sail.

Lauren felt a twinge of apprehension. She was sailing into immediate danger . . . and then into even greater danger.

Unpredictable, unknown seas. Bermuda . . . and then . . . She didn't know.

She looked toward Adrian, who stood stiffly, Socrates, who hadn't left his side since he was wounded, on his good shoulder. Adrian's other shoulder was protected by a thick bandage under a new shirt.

Dear God, it had been a long trip, and so terribly painful for Adrian . . . the endless ride on horseback to Fredericksburg, where they bought new clothes. She had wanted him to rest, but he wouldn't, and with official military papers they were able to board the first train south. The jerking and jostling over rough railbeds had kept Adrian's face tense with pain.

Still, he was insistent. There would be a new moon in three days, and most of the blockade runners would be leaving Wilmington in five to six days. They had to reach the port city by then, or else wait weeks before the blockade runners would return.

His determination, however, had cost him bitterly, and it had cost her in watching him. Twice, the train had stopped suddenly, and Adrian had been thrown against the side of the coach. Twice, she'd had to resew his wound, the shoulder red and sore and the area around it black and purple from bruising. It had been a nightmare journey of stifling heat and overcrowded train coaches for four days.

Even when they reached Wilmington, Adrian didn't rest, first visiting a bank, then the hotels frequented by the captains of the blockade runners. He found another Englishman, an acquaintance, who agreed to take them to Bermuda, where they could catch a clipper to England. The runners, built for speed, seldom made the long run to England and back themselves; they were designed for the quick sprint back and forth from Nassau and Bermuda to the American East Coast. This particular runner would leave the morning after next, after the cargo was loaded.

When Adrian had returned to the hotel where he'd engaged separate rooms for them, he'd been ill and exhausted, and she'd discovered that she was not with child as she had foolishly hoped.

They'd dined together almost silently, although their gazes often caught and held with longing, with questions, with quiet fire. He was still not well, and since the runners carried no doctors, Lauren had decided to go with him to Bermuda, to nurse him.

That was enough for both of them. For the moment.

After dinner she had helped him undress, and then sat

by him as he fell asleep. She stayed most of the night, just watching the way the thick lashes masked the dark blue eyes, the way his mouth gentled and the harsh lines of pain relaxed. She loved him so very much. If only she could do something to repair the damage she had done. Then, perhaps, they would have a chance . . .

But that was a ridiculous thought, an impossible dream, and she knew she must dismiss it from her mind. She looked over at Socrates, now sleeping peacefully on a blanket in the corner of the room after a very expensive dinner of fresh fruit.

She continued to watch, storing memories in her mind, until the wee hours in the morning. She wanted to slip into the bed with Adrian, but she feared hurting his shoulder further, and then she had her own indisposition. Reluctantly, she had finally gone to her own room, and the lonely bed within it.

And now they were to run the blockade again. As she had in Nassau, she wondered how the ships managed to avoid each other in the dark and fog, although they could still use lights here in the harbor. Once they were out in the Cape Fear River, once they were beyond the protection of Fort Fisher, the real risks, the danger, began.

Lauren instinctively moved closer to Adrian as the *Sally Ann* moved slowly from its moorings. She felt the warmth of his breath and smelled the clean scent of soap and bay rum. He had been to the barber this afternoon, and the bristles that had sprouted since a barbering in Fredericksburg were gone, taking with them the air of freebooter they had given him. It would still be days, she knew, before he could use his arm to shave again, perhaps even weeks.

She shivered with longing as she felt his good arm go around her. She leaned back against him, careful not to touch his bad shoulder but wanting the contact of his body. They would have three days till they reached Bermuda, maybe less.

"Do you want to be there . . . at the wheel?" she asked, indicating where the captain and pilot stood. The captain's name was Maximilian Abbot, she remembered.

"A little, perhaps," he said. "It seems strange not to be in control."

The ship shuddered slightly as the speed of the engines increased, and then they were sliding out of the crowded harbor, making for the Cape Fear River. Lauren leaned closer to Adrian as the *Sally Ann* moved down the river, past Fort Lee, Fort Campbell, and Fort Meares, which guarded the river, and then Fort Anderson. The guns from Fort Fisher would protect them on their final spurt through New Inlet and out into the open sea. Then they were on their own, and speed and luck would be their main defenses.

Just as they passed under the guns of Fort Fisher, all the lights on the ship were quenched, and even the soft whispers, born of tension, were stilled. Only the echo of the sounders could be heard, the soft drone of engines, the splash of paddle wheels against the water.

Lauren knew several ships had left earlier than they, and there would be a trail of them behind, just as there had been a parade in Nassau. From a distance, she heard the whine of shells, and through the fog she saw the diffused glow of an explosive.

"Why don't you go below?" Adrian said.

She shook her head, knowing that he would not, and she wanted to stay with him. She wanted to experience everything with him, every moment, every fear.

There was another explosion ahead. She wondered how anyone could see what was happening in the thick fog. Yet the ship plunged on, oblivious to the fog, the gunfire, the Union boats ahead. Lauren thought about Larry, what it had been like for him to wait there for enemy ships to make their run, to wait and then become caught in the crossfire. Her hands clenched around the railing as she realized her countrymen were now her enemies.

Still, she could not leave. She heard a throb of engines —not theirs—and her breath caught in her throat, but then she realized they must belong to another runner. It had the same sound and, like the *Sally Ann*, it carried no lights. The ship came so close, she saw its shadow and thought they must crash, but then the sound faded away.

Another cannon roared, and another. She felt as though she were blind, wandering in a field of fire, and her only safety was Adrian.

Her situation was so like Melissa's. She had not had a chance to finish the diary. She had always been with Adrian until the last few nights, and those few times she wasn't with him, she had fallen into exhausted slumber. She didn't know why she couldn't share the diary with Adrian; something always stopped her from doing so. She only knew it seemed meant for her, that Melissa had guided her to it for some reason.

The fog started to lift, and the engines speeded, gray smoke mixing with heavy moisture in the air. There were flares in different directions, smothered blazes in the sky. They were past the shoals, Adrian whispered. Now they would use the speed for which the ship was designed.

Caution no longer mattered so much. Coal was piled upon coal, maximum speed demanded. The ship sprinted ahead just as the fog lifted to reveal a black moonless night. Silhouettes were visible on the sea, but the *Sally Ann* was moving quickly. Lauren heard a shout from a faraway ship, saw flares and heard cannon splash far astern. And then the flashes and noise were farther away, and farther . . .

Several hours later, Lauren woke, still on deck, her head in Adrian's lap. Dawn had broken, and the *Sally Ann* was alone on the sea. She realized that she had fallen asleep on deck, and that, rather than wake her, Adrian had comfortably tucked them both between some cotton bales. He was watching her as she sat up against one of the bales.

She yawned, and he grinned. "Ready to go to bed?"

She nodded. Even if she wasn't, he should. And they were probably making a scandal of themselves out here. It was strange, though, how little she cared about that.

But Adrian needed rest.

They walked to their tiny cabins, Lauren all too aware of the unusual slowness of his steps. He kissed her lightly at the door of his cabin, his eyes again a mystery. His hand touched her cheek, and then he left.

Fully awake, Lauren paced the small cabin. It was permissible now to light the oil lamp, and she did that, then took out the diary.

> *July 26, 1861*
>
> *He's dead. Randall is dead. At a place called Manassas Junction. My brother died there too. And I wonder how I can bear it. Thank God for Sam. Lucas has gone, to look for Randall's body, he said. They grew up together as boys, one white, one black, but as long as I've known them, they've been like brothers. I think that's why Randall hated slavery so much . . . he saw men like Sam and Lucas enslaved. I never understood, not really, not until now, not until I saw the tears in Lucas's eyes. At least he could cry. I cannot. For I still can't make myself believe he's gone.*

But Lauren could cry. And she did. For Melissa. For Randall. For Lucas. And for herself.

She closed the diary, unable to read any more.

Bermuda was greener than Nassau, and its climate more hospitable. But the same sense of joie de vivre prevailed, an attitude that Lauren now had cause to suspect.

Unlike the *Specter*, the *Sally Ann* had several passenger cabins and, for propriety's sake, Adrian had engaged one for each of them. There were several other passengers, including two Confederate officials headed toward England. Their presence, along with the lingering pain in Adrian's shoulder, made Lauren and Adrian careful, Adrian for Lauren's sake, and Lauren for Adrian's. They talked together, they ate together, and yet they weren't together. And the distance was obvious to both of them.

In desperation, Lauren asked Adrian to teach her more about playing cards. The cards had been saved along with the diary, and Adrian and Lauren found a place on deck and vied with each other. Occasionally one of the other passengers would join them.

The game they played was always poker. Adrian was only too familiar with it because of the frequent games between the blockade-running captains. He declared it much simpler than the English games of chance, most of which took more than two players. And they wagered imaginary fortunes, Lauren delighting in besting him. At the end of three days, she was ahead by $25,000.

Adrian would watch her grin in glee, some of the sadness and secrecy fading from her eyes. He enjoyed watching her win so much that while he didn't lose purposely, neither did he bluff as much as he usually would. Her eyes fairly sparkled when she had a good hand, and he didn't have the heart to warn her against such signs. It was enough to watch her honey-colored hair blowing in the wind as her hands clasped the cards to keep them from blowing away.

And then they were in Bermuda, a pink gem in a turquoise sea, and Lauren exclaimed aloud she had never seen anything quite so beautiful.

"Wait until you see England in the spring," Adrian said. "And now, in late summer, it's so green it makes your eyes hurt. You will see it with me."

Lauren was silent. How could she go to England with him? She already loved him far too much for her own good. Nothing could come of prolonging their time together. Nothing but pain for her, and disillusionment for him. And yet he still needed her; his wound still required care.

Adrian took her silence as assent. They disembarked together, only to find themselves celebrities in St. George. They were greeted by Major Norman Walker, the Confederate representative, who'd been told of their prospective arrival by an earlier incoming ship.

"We're planning a dance in your honor," he told them. "And I've already made arrangements for you to stay at Hillcrest. This must be Miss Bradley. By Jove, you have to tell us all about your escape. The Yanks are beside themselves. And this must be that monkey we've been hearing about. Fetching little creature."

Adrian grabbed Socrates, who had taken the comment, or perhaps the way it was said, as an insult and was making ready to attack. The movement made Adrian wince, and Lauren took Socrates, a flush darkening her face.

"You have no idea what your escape did for our morale here," Walker continued. "It's the talk of Bermuda. The governor wants to meet you; the English are mad as hell, begging your pardon, miss, about the Yanks holding Captain Cabot in the first place. And you, Miss Bradley, are a *cause célèbre*. Like Rose Greenhow."

Lauren didn't listen anymore. She felt numb. She was quite aware of Rose Greenhow, a Confederate agent who had been confined in the Old Capitol Prison. And now, she, Lauren Bradley, was equally notorious. A Confederate heroine, when she was in actuality a Union spy! How had things ever become so twisted?

She felt Adrian's steadying arm on her. "I think," she heard him say, "that we both need some rest now. Can we talk about this later?"

"Of course, of course, Captain Cabot. Anytime. I'll take you to your lodgings."

"Are there any ships leaving for England shortly? We need passage as soon as possible."

The Confederate agent paused. "There's one sailing on tomorrow's tide, but surely . . . the dance . . . the governor . . ."

"I think the Confederacy would be better served," Adrian said shortly, "if I can get back to England and obtain another ship."

"Of course, but . . ."

"Will you be so kind as to see whether accommodations are available?"

Norman Walker's smile faded. "Certainly, if that's what you desire."

"It is," Adrian said shortly, "and now, if you will see us to our lodgings."

He tucked his arm into Lauren's, and she followed his

lead, almost blindly. Tomorrow. It was too soon. Too soon to give him up. Too soon to say good-bye. Too soon to make any plans.

Two rooms had been engaged at the comfortable guesthouse called Hillcrest. They were lucky, said the proprietor. The town would be flooded in the next three or four days with runners.

When they were finally free of the Confederate agent, Lauren sank down on the big feather bed in the middle of her room. Adrian was looking after their luggage. Unable to stay still, she went to the window from which, as in Nassau, she could see the harbor.

Could she go to England? And if not, where would she go? All she had in the world was the cottage in Delaware, and she certainly couldn't go back there now. Just their brief walk through St. George made her realize she would find no livelihood here. It was very small, and the only activity seemed to be in taverns. Perhaps in England she could find some way to support herself—as a governess, or a teacher in a girls' school. She had an excellent education.

And Adrian wouldn't be there long. He'd made that clear. Just long enough to locate another ship.

Excuses. Excuses. She knew the real reason. She wasn't prepared yet to give him up. Not until she knew his shoulder was well, not until he didn't need her any longer, not until . . .

She saw him alight from a for-hire carriage, one of their new portmanteaus under his good arm, his chestnut hair glowing in the Bermuda sun, his walk confident as he gave directions to the man next to him. Her eyes relished every inch of him, relished and coveted and hungered.

It seemed forever since he had touched her intimately, although his eyes did so frequently. She kept telling herself she couldn't, shouldn't, go with him to England.

But in her heart, she knew she would. And try as she might, she could not feel regret, could feel nothing but great joy that she and Adrian would remain together a little longer.

* * *

Unlike the brilliance of sparkling Bermuda, London did not appear very hospitable at first sight. The city was incredibly dirty on the waterfront, dirty and noisy. It wasn't at all as Adrian had described it.

Yet his eyes glowed when he first spied it from the deck of the clipper that brought them here. It was the first time in days she had seen that particular brightness.

She knew she had been looking for that hot blue flame in his eyes. And she occasionally caught glimpses of it, but now he controlled the fire as he hadn't before. He was polite rather than passionate. No, more than polite. Restrained was the word, she thought. Tightly leashed.

Once more he had engaged separate cabins, although she would have preferred to share one. He disappeared more and more during the day, into, she thought, the captain's cabin, or he joined the man at the wheel. She and Adrian usually joined the captain and the ten other passengers for meals, and took sedate walks around the deck, but there was no more of her going to sleep in his arms, and she missed it. How bitterly she missed it!

He had tired of her, she thought sadly. His eyes were masked, and he kept his hands close to his body.

Once when she had hesitated outside her cabin after dinner, he had only pressed her hand. Her eyes, she knew, pleaded with him.

"We have to be careful of your reputation," he said softly, his breath touching her with its usual exciting effect.

"I don't think I have a reputation left," she replied.

"Ah, but you do, Lauren. That of a heroine, and it will stand you in good stead if we do nothing to destroy it."

"I'm not a heroine."

"I would disagree."

"Adrian . . ." She saw him stop, pause, and wait, a strange sort of expectancy in his eyes. She couldn't go on. "Good night," she said, defeatedly.

Something like disappointment flickered in his face. Then he merely nodded and turned away, and she watched him reach his own cabin, hesitate, pass it, and go toward the hatch that led back on deck. She wanted to go after him, to stand with him against the wind, to taste all the flavors of life again, but something stopped her. She thought about the diary inside, but she dismissed the idea. She already knew too much about Melissa's pain. She didn't think she could bear more.

So the days had fallen into a pattern. They occasionally still played cards, but she felt him fade further and further away. Perhaps he felt that she would expect him to marry her, and was trying to let her down gently.

She knew she did not meet the requirements of a lord's wife. But it hurt.

Adrian directed the hired carriage to the town home of Sir Giles Gray, the man who had once been his captain, his mentor, and later his benefactor. He threw a glance at Lauren, who was looking discomfited in a muslin dress she'd purchased in Virginia before boarding the train to Wilmington. She was biting her lip, as she did when she was not entirely sure of herself. It was an endearing habit, and one he'd seen more frequently since crossing the Potomac.

If he did not know her so well by now, he might wonder that she was nervous about meeting Sir Giles when neither Yankee gunboats nor soldiers nor storms seemed to give her a whit of concern. He had known she was ready to bolt at any time, and he had used his wound shamelessly to keep her with him. Moreover, he had not given her any time to protest or plan, moving as he had so quickly from one place to another.

He most certainly was not finished with Miss Lauren Bradley.

Adrian had kept his distance from her on the ship, but found it extremely difficult, especially when she looked at him with those large hazel eyes. Yet he knew women, and he had recognized her indisposition in Wilmington. He knew she was not with child, and he was determined not to get her pregnant, not until they settled matters between themselves, no matter how painful it was for him.

And it was very, very painful.

He planned now to court her, slowly and respectably, and coax her secrets from her; to teach her to trust him enough so that he then could trust her. He knew he loved her, could never again think of life without the adventurous fillip she gave to it, but he longed for more than that; he wanted total honesty between them.

Sir Giles would help. Adrian had often stayed at his town house in London, since Giles knew that Adrian was saving his funds to regain Ridgely. Giles had a widowed sister who was kindliness itself, who managed the house and would provide a shield of respectability for Lauren. He had to offer her that, now that he meant for her to be his wife.

Lauren was nervous about meeting Sir Giles, although he'd explained that the "sir" was an honorary title, bestowed for his efforts in the Admiralty. Even less did she relish the thought of being forced upon strangers, but he patiently explained the mores of Queen Victoria's England. In answer, she merely clung tighter to Socrates, who was sporting a new pair of pants she had made for him on the voyage. Her list of accomplishments, Adrian often thought, was remarkable and apparently quite diverse: wrecking ships, planning escapes, nursing wounds, sewing trousers for small monkeys. The thought brought a smile to his lips.

The carriage pulled up to the Giles town house, and Adrian offered Lauren a hand, taking Socrates to his shoulder. The wound was four weeks old now, almost healed, though it still ached slightly at times. Lauren drew back slightly and then surrendered, walking with him up to the door. He knocked, and it was opened quickly, revealing a stern-faced man in austere black.

The man quickly broke into a wide grin when he saw Adrian. "M'lord, it's good to see you. Sir Giles had heard . . . well . . . that those heathens in America refused to release you."

"And so they did, Quigley," Adrian said, "until this young lady interfered. Broke me out of jail. Lauren, this is Quigley. And this is Miss Lauren Bradley."

The man gave her a bow. "Sir Giles will be most grateful. He's been very perturbed."

"Is Sir Giles in?"

"Yes, m'lord, and happy he'll be. If you will wait in the library." Quigley looked at Socrates. "And the little fellow. He made it too." But the butler didn't sound quite as happy about *that* salvation.

Adrian grinned. "You know what they say about a bad halfpence."

Quigley nodded. "Yes m'lord," he said dutifully, and disappeared up some steps.

Lauren looked at Adrian. "M'lord?"

Adrian winced. The title had seemed natural until he'd experienced American informality. Now, even to him, the title sounded pretentious. Even worse, it seemed to make Lauren more uncomfortable. "Meaningless," he said.

The old teasing light came back into Lauren's eyes, making them alive with humor. "Must I call you my lord too?"

He couldn't resist her then. He bent down, his lips whispering across hers. "Am I really? *Your* lord?"

Lauren's reply was lost in the magic that always flowed between them, its strength magnifying manyfold when they touched.

A cough interrupted them, and Adrian looked up to see a tall, distinguished man descending the stairs, a half smile on his lips.

"Quigley informs me that you and that obnoxious beast of yours bested the Yanks."

"With the help of this young lady, who, consequently, is now a fugitive with me. Lauren, this is Sir Giles Gray. Sir Giles, Lauren Bradley."

Sir Giles bowed deeply as a smile played around his mouth. "We owe you a debt of gratitude, Miss Bradley. We have missed Adrian, my sister and I. We heard the Federals refused to release you, although our minister in Washington tried."

Just then Socrates jumped from Adrian's shoulder to the floor and took Lauren's hand. Sir Giles's smile widened. "So you finally found a lady who could tolerate that impertinent little companion of yours."

"Miss Bradley is a very unusual lady."

Sir Giles's face, worn by weather and sea and responsibility, softened slightly. "Quigley said she helped you escape. I would very much like to hear of it."

"You will, sir," Adrian promised, "but I was hoping that Lauren might stay here several days . . . until I can find respectable and more permanent lodgings."

"Of course," Sir Giles said. "My sister will be delighted. My niece and her husband were visiting and left three days ago, and she's been moping ever since. This is just what she needs." He looked over to Lauren, the sharp gaze of his dark eyes meeting hers directly. "You are very welcome, my dear." He rang a bell, and Quigley appeared again. "Please ask Mrs. Featherstone to prepare a room and tell my sister we'll be having a guest."

"And now, may I offer refreshments while a room is prepared?" Sir Giles continued.

"I'll have to send to the ship for our luggage," Adrian said. "I'll engage some rooms nearby."

Sir Giles nodded. It would not be proper for two unrelated, unattached people to stay in the same house, even with Sir Giles and his sister in residence. And it was very obvious to Sir Giles that Adrian, for once, was concerned about appearances. It was singularly unusual for his friend, and thus very revealing.

When Quigley returned, he brought with him several bottles and glasses. Well acquainted with Adrian's taste, Sir Giles filled two glasses with port and then turned to her. "Some sherry?"

Lauren nodded. "Thank you."

Sir Giles poured her a glass and turned to Adrian. "What are your plans now?"

"I intend to see Redding. I thought I might make him

an offer. He might be tired of being a country gentleman."
The words were said with wry hope.

Sir Giles shrugged. "He might well be. He's been in
London this past month . . . frequenting the gaming tables. I saw him last week at White's."

Adrian stilled, tension invading his body. The estate
required constant attention, not an uncaring, absentee
master. "I'll seek him out."

"You don't have to," Sir Giles said. "I think I might
know where he's going to be tomorrow night."

Adrian felt the tempo of his pulse increase.

"Lady Caroline Sutton is having a party. It's one of the
few homes open to him," Sir Giles continued. "I think he
expected Ridgely would open many more to him, but he's
still considered little more than a soldier of fortune and
gambler."

Adrian looked surprised. "I wouldn't think Redding
would give a sniff for that."

"We were both mistaken in that regard. I think he cares
very much, though he pretends not to."

"Why is he welcome at Caroline's?"

"He is still a fine figure of a man, if not a gentleman,"
Sir Giles replied, but then his glance caught Lauren's fascinated face, and he looked momentarily chagrined. "I'm
sorry, Miss Bradley," he added, his face crimsoning in a
way that amused Adrian. If only he knew about Miss Bradley . . .

Lauren flushed prettily, making Adrian think again
what a fine actress she was. "Perhaps," he said slowly, "if
you can gain us an invitation, Lauren could attend too. I
assume that would be acceptable."

"Oh yes," Sir Giles said. "Caroline is still very much in
good standing; her family name and wealth assure that.
And I'm sure she would be delighted." There was a shaded
note in his voice that Adrian hoped Lauren didn't hear.
He, like many in the *ton*, had had a brief, and discreet,
flirtation with Caroline, who had a good heart and as a
widow for five years was often forgiven indiscretions that
would have tainted others. Her event would be a good

introduction into Society for Lauren; she was not cold and merciless like some other hostesses.

But Lauren had blanched. "I have no dress," she said.

Sir Giles appraised her quickly. "I think you're the same size as my niece. When Annalise married, she left some of her gowns here. My sister can help you choose one, and alter it if necessary."

"That's very kind of you," Adrian said, closing the subject.

"But . . ." Lauren started, only to be interrupted by the library door opening again. Now another stranger stood there, a slender woman with graying hair and a sweet face. "Adrian!" she cried with delight.

She turned and beamed at Lauren. "And this must be our heroine!"

CHAPTER 24

Lauren had never felt so much a fraud, or so uncomfortable.

She hated every moment of the evening at Lady Caroline's, including the gown, which was much too fussy for her taste. She was toasted, praised, and tittered over until she wanted to scream.

It was strange, because she had so enjoyed the Governor's Ball in Nassau, but that dance had been free and easy next to this event, where nearly everyone was a marquess, or viscount, or baron. There was even an earl. It was "my lord this" and "my lady that" and she couldn't get the titles straight; everyone, she was sure, thought her a barbarian. She did not enjoy being the center of attention, especially under such false pretenses.

She thought again of the dance at the Governor's House in Nassau, and how magical it had been. She should feel the same way now, the adventurous part of her enjoying the novelty of English nobility. But at the Governor's Ball, she hadn't yet learned the full extent of this terrible yearning for Adrian. And though he stayed close to her, a quiet, indefinable distance hovered between them, which seemed to yawn even deeper tonight.

He had engaged rooms away from her, and she had not seen him after their arrival at Sir Giles's town house until tonight, when he had called for her, and the four of them, Sir Giles and his sister, Adrian and herself, came to Lady Caroline's together.

This night Adrian seemed a handsome, reserved stranger bent on making her accepted here out of gratitude. His hand had done little more than brush hers. There was no hint of the kiss they'd started to share yesterday.

His reserve had been chipping away at her heart, piece by piece, during the last few weeks, and now she was near total despondency. No matter how many times she told herself she must make the break, the reality was almost beyond comprehension. She stood with a smile on her face while being introduced as a courageous friend who had assisted him, but his tone was impersonal and implied nothing more than gratitude and friendship.

And she understood. She felt awkward among these superbly dressed people with their precise accents and witty conversation. She would never, could never, fit in. She saw the appraising gazes even as complimentary words were said, and she felt the superficiality of the sentiments. She was a woman who had traveled alone with a man, and had none of the fine manners of those here tonight, nor a lofty background like theirs or great wealth. She was, quite simply, an oddity.

She was asked for dances and reluctantly accepted, for she did not wish to humiliate Adrian, but she had little to talk about with her partners, and merely tried to smile. It was a strained smile, one that belied her true feelings.

Late in the evening a man almost as tall as Adrian arrived, and he was so dominating in appearance that Lauren couldn't help but note his entrance. He was strikingly handsome, boldly so. His hair was black and his eyes almost obsidian, and a mocking smile played around his mouth as he glanced around the room.

She knew instantly that he did not belong in the room, and it was obvious that he also knew it. She felt a sudden empathy with him. His wandering glance seemed to catch hers, and it lingered for a moment before traveling on and finding the hostess, Lady Caroline. He moved with an easy quickness, not with the grace that Adrian did, but more like an animal in an unfamiliar place: wary but defiant.

He had come alone and, remembering the pieces of information she'd absorbed about the infamous Rhys Redding, Lauren wondered whether this was the man. She looked toward Adrian and saw him stiffen, and she knew it was.

The newcomer bowed low to the hostess. Then both of their glances turned to her, and they started in her direction.

At the same time she saw Adrian move toward her, reaching her side an instant before Lady Caroline and the newcomer.

Lady Caroline smiled slowly, her gaze going from Adrian to the man beside her. But all Lauren saw was her beauty, and she knew she paled beside it. Lady Caroline had the most lovely blond hair Lauren had ever seen, and huge violet eyes that had to be irresistible to men. She also had a nice smile, and throaty laughter, and intelligence.

"Miss Bradley," she said now with a friendliness that Lauren had no reason to doubt, "I've been commanded to introduce you to this scoundrel. Lauren, this is Rhys Redding, and Rhys, Miss Lauren Bradley. And of course you know the hero of the hour, Lord Ridgely."

Lauren felt tension radiate from Adrian, as his title was used in front of the man who now owned his estate, and she saw the mischief in Caroline's eyes. Lauren also felt all other eyes on them and realized that Caroline was making the meeting into an event for the amusement of her guests. Her liking of the woman receded, but when she looked up at Adrian, she saw only the smiling mask in place.

Adrian acknowledged Redding's presence with a slight

bow. "Redding. I was wondering whether you would join me later in the game room."

Redding nodded. "Later," he agreed curtly, then turned his attention to Lauren. "I understand you're somewhat of a heroine."

Lauren looked up at Adrian and wondered why his mouth tightened. Perhaps because the subject was being changed from what was so important to him? She turned back to Rhys's dark gaze. "I did very little," she said.

"Ah, modest too," Rhys said. "I wonder if I might have the pleasure of this dance . . . a waltz, I believe," he said as the first notes wafted over the room.

Lauren looked quickly at Adrian again, but his face was guarded, and he made no objection.

"I accept, sir," she said, and took his gloved hand as he led her onto the floor. Lauren leaned back slightly in his arms and looked up—at the man who had what Adrian wanted most of all.

His eyes were not black as she had first thought, but a very dark brown, as was his hair. His face was not classically handsome like Adrian's, but undeniably attractive in a harsh way. His expression was mocking, as if he found the world vastly amusing, and yet there was something hungry in it too.

"You are a very welcome addition to Society, Miss Bradley," he said.

"A novelty," she returned dryly. "I've never felt quite so out of place." Even as the words came out, she wondered why she was saying them to him. This man was Adrian's nemesis.

He chuckled. "I too am a novelty, Miss Bradley. Tolerated but not accepted."

"But you own Ridgely."

"Ah, so Lord Ridgely has told you about that," he said. "What else did he tell you?"

"That you are a gambler."

"And so I am. Does that bother you?"

"I'm the daughter of a country doctor. Does that bother you?"

"I think it's enchanting. But I suspect you are a lot of other things too."

"Do you like owning Ridgely?"

"Ah, back to that," he said, his gaze leaving her and going to Adrian, who stood watching them. Rhys's arm tightened slightly around her, and he swirled her around in practiced movements. Again she noticed the difference between the two men. Both were excellent dancers, but Adrian's movements had been easier, more natural. Again, she felt the essence of a man out of place, like a leopard she had once seen in a small zoo. Yet from what she'd heard, this one had stubbornly locked himself in the zoo. She felt a strong curiosity about him, and a return of empathy. It flowed between them, and she felt his hand curl around her fingers. She looked up at him, and their gazes met. She couldn't quite understand the feeling she suddenly had. There was nothing of the strong sensual and emotional attraction she had with Adrian, but something else, an immediate liking.

"Are you taken, Miss Bradley?" he said suddenly, and it took Lauren several seconds to understand his meaning.

She stiffened in his arms as she considered the question. She was. In her heart and soul, she was. But as her eyes went to Adrian, who was now talking to Lady Caroline, she knew she wasn't. Not from Adrian's viewpoint.

But she couldn't lie to herself, nor did she want to lie to Rhys Redding. She had lied far too much already, and it had brought her too much misery. "Yes," she said.

"Our Lord Ridgely?"

She nodded hopelessly.

"Does he feel the same?"

She shook her head.

He grinned cockily. "Then he's a fool. May I call on you?"

Lauren looked up at him miserably.

"Consider it," he said. "I have the strangest feeling that you too are a gambler, Miss Bradley, and we might have something to offer each other."

Just then the waltz stopped, and Adrian moved toward

them, his jaw set, and his eyes dark and unreadable. He reached for Lauren's hand, taking it from Rhys's grasp. "I think this dance is mine," he said.

Lauren's glance moved from Rhys's amused face to Adrian's. She wished she knew what he was thinking, whether he was jealous or angry, but his set jaw might have more to do with thoughts of Ridgely than of her.

The touch of their hands, as usual, ignited fires deep inside her. She felt her legs quake as another waltz started, and he pulled her close to him. Close but not close enough. Never close enough, never until their bodies joined again. At the very thought, sensations so strong and warm and liquid ran through her that her body instinctively moved closer to his, although her dress and its many crinolines necessitated a certain distance. She saw his eyes cloud and felt the sudden hesitation in his steps, and she knew he was feeling similar needs. No matter how hard he tried to keep a distance, he still felt them. Lauren felt a certain sense of triumph as well as a renewed desolation. She could take today, even if she couldn't have tomorrow.

Adrian had been unsuccessful with Rhys Redding. Lauren knew it the moment the two men emerged from the game room. She had been hovering near the entrance as much as possible, ever since the two men disappeared inside.

She had prayed that Redding would sell the estate back to Adrian. And then perhaps at least some of her guilt and regret would fade; perhaps then she could even tell Adrian of her deception. Perhaps then he could forgive her. Perhaps then . . .

So she had watched the game room with anxiety until the door opened, and Adrian emerged alone. She suspected no one else would realize he was bitterly disappointed, for his face showed little. But his shoulders were straighter than usual, as if he had taken a blow, and his eyes when they met her gaze had no elation in them, no laughter.

Lauren ignored the people to whom she was speaking and walked over to him, holding out her hand. He took it, holding it tight for an instant and giving her a wry smile. And then they were interrupted by a young dandy who asked her for a dance.

"Yes," Adrian answered for her, giving her no chance to decline. As the young man led her to the dance floor, she saw Adrian go through a pair of doors that led outside. Her heart, already wounded for herself, now cried for him, for the defeat in the stiff back. Still, it stung her that he had wanted to be alone, not with her, but alone.

She smiled a glittering smile as her dance partner asked whether she had ever seen an Indian in America. She continued to smile at the absurdity, but it seemed to be a common question tonight. War and Indians were all anyone wanted to know about.

"No," she replied brightly. She had never seen an Indian.

Adrian didn't return to Sir Giles's town house with them.

Sir Giles, his own mood heavy, relayed Adrian's apologies to her.

"Mr. Redding didn't agree to sell, did he?" she finally asked him.

"No."

"What will Adrian do now?"

"Go back to sea, to blockade running," the man said. "A friend of mine offered him a command of one of his ships, but Adrian wants his own. He can make a faster profit that way."

"Or lose even more," Lauren said softly.

"Oh, he can lose a great deal more. If the Yanks ever get him again, you can be sure they won't lose him a second time."

Lauren would have happily sold her soul that very moment if she could have reversed everything she had done, if she could, in some way, help Adrian.

And perhaps there was a way she could. Just maybe.

And her soul would be little enough price.

*   *   *

Lauren waited impatiently for three days.

She knew Rhys Redding would come. She felt it in her bones. He had issued a challenge, and he wasn't the type of man to back down.

Other visitors came in droves to the town house. Everyone wanted to meet Miss Lauren Bradley who had outfoxed the Yanks.

Adrian came by for supper on the third day, apologizing for not seeing her earlier but explaining that he had been combing the shipyards, trying to find a ship nearly completed. He didn't want to wait for the construction of a totally new vessel. With the disaster at Gettysburg, the war might soon end and, with it, any chance to win back Ridgely.

Socrates was with him. He had practically flown over to her, giving her great smacks on the cheek and apparently scolding her for her absence. It was ridiculous how much she'd missed the small animal. It had been the three of them those wonderful days in the woods.

Adrian grinned at her in the old, charming way as Socrates continued to hover near Lauren. "He bit me twice," he said. "His way of telling me he missed you."

Lauren could barely breathe for the lump in her throat. She had missed him so much, missed that smile that made her feel so wonderfully alive. She started to reach out, needing badly to touch him again, just to know he was indeed here. But she drew back, for she knew a mere touch would not be enough.

Sir Giles entered just then. "Any success?"

"I think so," Adrian said. "There's a ship that's pretty close to my needs. It was being built for a group of investors who are having second thoughts, now that only two ports are open."

"How long?" Lauren managed to ask.

"If we can come to an agreement, two or three weeks," Adrian said with satisfaction. "It's ready for a test run now."

The lump in Lauren's throat dropped to her chest. She didn't have much time.

"And you," Adrian said, his eyes meeting hers directly. "How are you faring in London? How do you like it here?"

"I . . . find it very different."

His brows furrowed together. That was not what he had asked her, but then he knew he had thrown Lauren into something entirely new. He had not meant to desert her so completely, but so much depended on his obtaining a ship. He could do nothing, say nothing, until his future was settled . . . and until he had the time to win her trust and her heart. The latter, he thought he had. But dear God, how he wanted the former!

They had supper together, the four of them, Sir Giles asking about the new ship, its cargo space, its speed. Adrian would have to secure a good crew to Nassau, where hopefully he could then find most of his old one. He didn't think he would have problems. The riches of blockade running were legendary; there were few sailors who would not take a few more-than-normal risks to partake of such wealth.

Lauren, however, felt her heart drop further with every word.

He would be gone soon, doing the same dangerous work, except now it would be worse. If only she could persuade Rhys Redding to sell Ridgely.

The thought, the means of accomplishing it, kept her occupied throughout the evening, until Adrian said he must take his leave. It was late, and Socrates had dozed off in her lap, his head lying trustfully against her arm.

Sir Giles shook his head. "You have a way with that creature, my dear. He never did like me."

Lisa, his sister, gave him a sharp look. "Because you never liked him."

Sir Giles sighed. "If I remember, Lisa, you had your own problems with Socrates."

"Well, I think he's a dear now."

Lauren bit her lip and looked toward Adrian, who was also trying not to smile. Socrates had lost him any number of friends, and Sir Giles and his sister were among the few who had tolerated the monkey. And even they were visibly relieved that Adrian had decided to take Socrates with him to his own lodgings.

Bidding Adrian good night, Sir Giles and Lisa took their leave, ceding the room to Adrian and Lauren. She walked him to the door, a reluctant Socrates moving between them.

In the foyer, Adrian accepted his cape and cane from Quigley, who kept a cautious distance from the monkey. Adrian thanked him and turned to Lauren, his hand reaching for her cheek, his fingers touching it lightly. "We need to talk, you and I," he said.

Lauren swallowed the words she wanted to say. *We need to do more than talk.* She nodded.

"As soon as I can complete this sale . . ."

Ridgely again. Always Ridgely. She chewed even more heartily on her lips. "Adrian . . ."

His gaze intensified, and she recognized the fire within, but was it for her, or Ridgely?

"Hmmmmmm?" he said, his fingers now fondling the back of her neck, and she couldn't say any more. She couldn't tell him not to go back to blockade running, because she knew he would. She couldn't give him an ultimatum, because she would lose.

"I miss you." His words were ragged, and she felt herself quake inside as his lips exploded on hers. His need was obvious; it signaled itself in hands that trembled slightly, in the way his tongue plundered at first and then gentled into tender longing.

"Be patient with me," he whispered so softly that she didn't quite catch the words. And then he moved away, his fierce blue eyes glinting in the candlelit hall.

Adrian walked back to his lodgings. He needed air. He needed exercise. What he needed was a cold swim.

Bloody hell, how he ached inside. He felt ready to explode. He had wanted to take her, then and there, in the hallway. He had wanted to steal her away. He had wanted to erase the sad, wistful look in her eyes when he'd talked about the new ship. He had wanted . . .

He wanted so many things. But for the first time in his life, he wanted to do things right. Lauren and Ridgely had become indelibly intertwined in his mind. He wanted it for her and wanted her for Ridgely, and he wanted everything right in every way. For most of his life he had gone his own way, swaggering into one disaster after another, until he had focused on Ridgely . . . and now Lauren. Both had become obsessions, and he knew it. And he didn't want to taint either. He didn't want Lauren to have to marry him because of a child, nor did he dismiss the possibility of capture again, or death. That meant he had to keep a distance from her.

If only he'd had a few more runs. If only ships could fly, he thought irreverently.

Rhys Redding had refused his offer of nearly a million pounds. The bloody bastard wanted a quarter again of that. After the cost of a new ship, the amount needed represented at least four runs, probably more like six. Redding did, however, promise not to sell to anyone else, and that was a great relief. Adrian trusted the man to keep his promise, though he wasn't exactly sure why.

Rain started spilling from the sky, and Adrian thought of another rain on a continent across the sea. Suddenly all the good the walk had done was gone.

The ache was back worse than ever.

The awaited card finally came two days later. Rhys Redding left it, asking whether he might call on Miss Lauren Bradley.

Lauren sent a note saying she would be delighted.

Lisa obviously disapproved, though she said nothing. Her guest was a grown woman, an American who had traveled by herself. Americans, it was well known, did not have the same . . . well, traditions . . . as the British. But Lisa's brows knitted together worriedly when Lauren informed her of her plan to go riding with Mr. Redding.

"Do you think you should, dear? Adrian . . ."

"Adrian," Lauren said, trying to disguise the hurt in her voice, "is too busy with his ship to concern himself." She had just heard from Sir Giles that Adrian had indeed opened negotiations for the new blockade runner. If she were to do anything at all, it must be soon.

"He's very fond of you, my dear."

Fond—what an altogether terrible word! But Lauren merely smiled at Lisa Tatterly, and went to change into her green muslin dress that brought out the green in her eyes.

Rhys Redding was very prompt. And Lauren knew if her heart weren't completely held by someone else, Mr. Redding could possibly pose a threat to it. He was dressed today in tight tan trousers, an almost cream waistcoat, and dark brown frock coat, all of which emphasized the darkness of his hair and the eyes that gleamed like freshly polished onyx.

He was the opposite from Adrian in coloring and, she thought, temperament. Adrian, although a private man who often kept thoughts to himself, was easy to be with. He was like the sun to her, the giver of life and warmth. Rhys Redding, with a sardonic curl to his lip and a kind of mocking amusement dancing in his eyes, was more like the night.

Yet Lauren felt no fear of him. She thought of her father's words again, that Larry was like the sunrise and she like twilight. Perhaps that was why she was so strangely comfortable with both the sun and the night.

But it was the sun she wanted.

The preliminaries were awkward. Lisa could not hide her disapproval, and Rhys met it with exaggerated courtesy. When he and Lauren were outside, and he'd handed her into what was a very gaudy carriage, he grinned at her. "You know, of course, that I'm not an *acceptable* escort?"

He looked so devilishly happy about it that she couldn't help but smile back. "So I've been informed."

"And Ridgely?"

"The lord or the estate?"

"The lord."

Lauren looked at him as he snapped the reins on two

very fine horses. She really didn't want to think about Adrian's reaction, or even whether he would have a reaction. Instead, she turned her thoughts to the vehicle in which they were riding, wondering about the bad taste of the carriage compared to her companion's excellent taste in clothes and horses.

"I like it," Rhys said suddenly.

Lauren couldn't help but look startled.

"The carriage," he explained. "You're wondering about the carriage. I saw one like it when I was a boy and thought it the most marvelous thing in the world. When I saw this one, I remembered a boy's dream and had to have it."

"And where was that?"

"A small village in Wales," he replied. "But you are avoiding my question. What would Lord Ridgely think of your ride with me?"

"I don't know whether he would think anything about it."

"Ah, Miss Bradley, I think you're wrong there. I saw his face when I was dancing with you. He didn't like it at all."

Lauren bit her lip.

"And I saw your face. I wonder why you are with me now."

"I want something from you."

He stared at her, then burst out laughing. "I've been told American women are different. I think you are the only young lady who has ever admitted she wanted something. First."

The "first" had an ominous ring to it.

"Are you going to tell me what it is, or do I have to guess?" Rhys Redding's voice was softly amused, but there was a note of warning in it.

Lauren had not planned the conversation this way at all. She had wanted to learn more about him first, to gauge how best to persuade him to sell.

"Then I'll have to guess," he said reflectively. "A matter of an estate, I believe. And since I don't think Lord Ridgely would send you on his behalf, you must have a proposal of your own."

Lauren could only stare at him, like a rabbit about to be swallowed by a wolf.

"Why, Miss Bradley?" he continued, his voice suddenly hard. "Do you want to be the lady of Ridgely?" The hardness carried a trace of contempt now. "It's not all it's reputed to be. Damnable nuisance."

"Then why don't you sell it?" she retorted.

"The simple matter of a bad bargain. I don't make bad bargains."

"What would you consider a good bargain?" The words left Lauren's lips before she thought them through.

His eyes moved away from the horses and traveled up and down her slowly, suggestively. "How do you plan to sweeten the offer?"

Lauren swallowed, realizing she had once more leaped into something before considering all the consequences. During her brief meeting with Redding at Lady Caroline's party, she had thought he might be a gentleman in behavior if not by birth. She knew now he was not. Words alone would never persuade him.

How *did* she plan to sweeten the offer?

Lauren thought of the way Adrian looked every time he talked of Ridgely. She thought of his face when his hands were being tied on the *Specter*, knowing he had lost everything. She remembered his look as he had left the game room the other night after talking with Redding.

She had an overwhelming premonition that if Adrian did go back to blockade running, something terrible would happen. And he *would* go back . . . within weeks. The whole Yankee fleet would be waiting for him, and it would be her fault. She knew from conversation that Union agents in London were fully aware Adrian was here, knew that he was trying to refit a new ship. There would be a cordon waiting for him, both here and along the Carolina coast.

She wasn't important, not anymore. She had lied and cheated and betrayed. But she had one weapon left, one weapon she could use in Adrian's behalf.

"I *do* have a proposal," she said finally.

CHAPTER 25

An arched eyebrow invited her to continue.

Lauren took a deep breath. She had thought about this, but she didn't know now if she could go through with it.

She had to!

It was the only way she could ever be free.

"You said I was a gambler, that we both were gamblers," she finally said.

His dark eyes glinted. "And that we might have something to offer each other. Do we, Miss Bradley?"

Lauren hesitated one more time.

"A game of chance," she said finally.

"So you *are* a gamester," he said with satisfaction. "Now what do you offer as stakes?"

She looked up at him, her eyes searching. "You said Adrian's estate was a nuisance. Why did you want Ridgely?"

There was a long silence. "It was offered," he finally said.

"But there's more," she charged, wanting, needing, more time. "You wanted more than you got."

"Are Americans fortune-tellers too?" Rhys snapped the reins on the horses, increasing the pace.

She laughed, but there was only wistfulness in the sound, not amusement. "I'm learning that sometimes when you win, you lose."

"And what did you win, Miss Bradley? And lose?"

They passed a couple in a phaeton as they entered Hyde Park, and Lauren remembered the faces—but not the names—from Lady Caroline's party. Their expressions were openly curious as Rhys touched his hat in recognition. Even in that seemingly polite gesture, there was mockery.

"They are wondering what you are doing with a scoundrel like me," Rhys remarked dryly.

"But I am an American," she said, "and apparently expected to do outrageous things."

"Not if you plan to stay among the *ton*, to be the wife of a lord—even a landless one," he replied, a half smile on his lips.

"I don't."

The words were said with such absolute finality that Rhys looked at her again. "Because he is landless? He won't be for long. He's quite wealthy, though not wealthy enough to purchase Ridgely. Not yet. But I suspect he will be. A very determined man, Adrian Cabot, Lord Ridgely." The last was said with something approaching a sneer.

Lauren stared at him. She had once thought Adrian cynical, but Rhys Redding was the embodiment of the word.

"No," she said simply.

"No, what?"

"That's not why I would not marry him, even if he did ask, which he won't."

"Was I wrong about those feelings the other night?"

Lauren was not going to lie any longer. "No," she said. "Not about mine."

"Nor," he said, "about his. And, forgive me for being dull, but why do you care about Ridgely's lands if you have no intention of marrying him?"

"Is that the only reason I should care?"

"It's the only reason most women would care."

"Do you think so badly of women then?"

"I think badly of everyone," he corrected with a smile.

Lauren's hands clenched in her lap. This was so much harder than she had expected. He obviously didn't care about the properties himself, and she had thought . . . She didn't know what she thought.

"Why?"

"Why do I think badly of everyone? I suppose because I've never had reason to do otherwise. I prey on weaknesses, Miss Bradley. I know them all."

"And you, do you have any?"

"Of course."

"What are they?"

"So you can prey on mine?"

Lauren had to smile. "I don't think you'd ever allow that."

"I might make an exception . . . you never did say why you are so interested in the Ridgely lands."

"It's not important."

"Oh, but it is. You interest me, Miss Bradley. You give every indication of . . . shall we say . . . caring about Lord Ridgely, yet you say you have no hope nor intention of marrying our good viscount. And you are here with me. As much as I would like to attribute such a delight to my charm, I'm not such an arrogant fool. I always like to know exactly what game I'm playing."

Lauren swallowed. She could delay no longer. "Is there any way I can convince you to sell Ridgely? Now."

Rhys's dark eyes grew even darker as he turned his harsh face toward her. "You mentioned a game of chance earlier. Exactly what are you prepared to wager?"

"I don't have much money. I do have a cottage in the United States."

"And what would I do with a cottage in the United States?" he replied.

"You could sell it."

"And how much is it worth?"

Lauren shook her head. "I don't know exactly. But you're a gambler," she challenged.

"But like any good gambler, I want to see the stakes. What else?" The question was merciless.

Lauren couldn't say "myself." There was no way she could speak the words. But she knew that was the only thing she had left. He probably wouldn't even want her. She was certainly no beauty, not like many of the women she had seen at Lady Caroline's.

"Yourself?"

Rhys had stolen her thought, her forbidden thought. She swallowed hard. Something in her died at the image of someone other than Adrian touching her. She wondered if the thought was reflected on her face, for she saw his face tighten, even grow cruel.

"Yes," she said suddenly, defiantly. Nothing mattered but Adrian now.

"You would agree to become my mistress . . . for as long as I require."

Require. Not *like.* Nothing tender. A pure business arrangement.

But she could win. She had to win. She'd won often with Adrian, and he'd said she had a real talent for cards. Talent and luck.

Adrian. I took Ridgely away from you. He would have had it by now, had it not been for her. It had been two months since his capture, which amounted to at least three runs for him, more than enough to meet Redding's price. She knew the economics well enough now.

"If I win, you'll sell Ridgely to Adrian?"

"For the price he offered the other night," Rhys agreed. "And if I win, you will be my mistress. *Willing* mistress," he added with emphasis. "And," he added generously, "I'll still sell him Ridgely."

Some of Lauren's doubt disappeared, though the pain remained. She nodded slowly. "But Adrian is never to know of the wager, and I can choose the game."

His lips curled up slightly at the edges. "Done."

Lauren felt her throat tighten, her heart become stone. She was committed now. "When?"

"Tomorrow," he said. "I will make the arrangements."

She nodded mutely.

"A little more enthusiasm, my dear," he said, "or I'll think it a bad bargain."

Lauren tried to smile, but she knew it was only a grimace, and his, in return, was the satisfied smirk of a devil who'd just won a soul.

Lauren kept looking at Melissa's diary, but she couldn't bear to read it. There were still several legible pages before the entries ended . . . before Melissa's death.

At the hand of deserters, she'd been told. Lauren wondered if anyone would ever know, or if there was a clue in the diary. She still had the feeling that Melissa had guided her to it, though she didn't know why.

But at the moment her own misery was too strong to share anyone else's. Instead, she put her hand on the diary, as if it were a beloved companion, one that would give her strength to do what she felt she had to do.

She looked out the window of the town house. The London street was still lively with carriages, the gaslights mixing with dust, extinguishing the stars which were so numerous and bright at sea. That's where Adrian was now, testing the new ship, preparing to ride his own lightning again. She clenched her teeth against the need that filled her, the need to be standing beside him, to feel the heat of his body, to smell the fine aroma of soap and bay rum. Her body pulsed with the thought of his body. But that was finished now.

If there had ever been any hope at all, she was ending it tomorrow.

But she would be giving him what he wanted above all in the world. And that was the most important thing of all.

She thought of the last time she had agreed to do something her conscience told her not to do, because of Larry.

Dear God, was she going to regret this as much as she ended up regretting that?

But as before, she was committed now. There was no turning back.

Adrian felt the engines of the ship hum beneath his feet. An English captain, an employee of the shipping company, stood next to him as Adrian guided the ship out the mouth of the Thames. Socrates was hovering nearby as he almost always did these last few days.

A United States Navy ship followed them, dogging the vessel's every movement. But Adrian knew it wouldn't approach, not unless it appeared that the ship was headed out of English waters. The ship was still under English registry, and was not violating the neutrality laws, yet.

But Adrian knew he would be under close scrutiny, on land and on sea. He would have to plan the ship's flight from England very carefully. He had already mentally named it *Specter II*.

There had been bitter protests lodged by the United States Government when Adrian appeared in London. There were even more heated protests when Union agents discovered he was seeking a new ship, a sleek new steamer.

For the first time, Adrian didn't feel the old excitement when he thought of running the blockade again. He didn't want to leave Lauren. He'd asked himself over and over whether Ridgely was worth the risk of death or capture now that he had found her. But now he wanted his ancestral estate as much for her as for himself. Adrian knew instinctively she would love it: the rolling hills, the neat fields, the woods full of game, and the stream full of fish. She belonged there, as he belonged there.

They would be out four days, running the steamer to its maximum speed, making sure of the durability and reliability of the engines, giving the Yankees something to think about.

He already had something to think about.

Lauren had to brave Lisa's silent disapproval, and even a certain grimness from Sir Giles, when she told them she planned to go riding with Mr. Redding again today.

She cringed inside at the prospect of their contempt if she lost today. They had been so kind.

But she couldn't lose. And if she won, she would soon be gone. Where, she wasn't sure, but she knew she couldn't stay this close to Adrian. Not and keep her sanity.

She was leaning more and more toward telling Adrian everything, and then returning home to Delaware. If that meant prison, then so be it. She was tired of running, both to and from things, heartsick because of the lies and deception that had made every day a nightmare. Anything, she thought, would be better than the accumulation of sins on her conscience.

But first she had to get through today.

Rhys Redding was again exactly on time, looking as dangerous and sardonic as he had on the other two occasions she'd met him. His eyes glinted with anticipation, filling her with dread. This was not a momentous event to him, but a game. A game that could destroy her.

She was wearing her most modest dress today, a blue day dress with long sleeves and a high neck, and she didn't miss the amusement in his face as he marked the challenge.

He helped her into his phaeton. They drove off at a quick pace, Redding adeptly avoiding the other vehicles in the road. He drove around the park and then to a secluded street where a closed carriage waited, and a strange, rough-looking man took the ribbons of his phaeton. Inside the closed coach, there was a long cloak and a hat with veil, the proper attire, she supposed, for a lady preparing for an assignation.

Rhys Redding had taken care of everything, as promised. There would be no gossip—unless, of course, she lost.

The coolness of the day penetrated the coach, and she shivered.

The closed coach drew to a stop. Redding alighted and gave her his hand, smiling slightly as she hesitated. "Come, my love," he said.

Adrian had twice called her "love." It had created little curls of warmth inside her then, but Redding's use only increased the chill. She gave him her hand and stepped out, looking about anxiously.

The sign outside the building where they'd stopped proclaimed it the Lion's Head, and it sported a great majestic profile of its namesake. Redding led her to a side doorway, holding it open with one hand while guiding her in with the other, as if he knew any small thing would send her skittering away.

An obsequious smile on his face, a rather thin man met them and greeted Redding as one might an old and valued friend, and Lauren couldn't help but wonder how many times Rhys Redding had been here, and not for a card game. The man nodded at her, his eyes avoiding her face as if he were used to entertaining women who did not wish to be recognized.

"I have your room ready," he said. "And a bottle of my finest brandy."

Rhys looked down at Lauren's veiled face. "Perhaps some sherry for the lady."

"Of course," the man said, and escorted them up a flight of stairs and into a room that left no doubt in Lauren's mind as to the main business of this establishment.

The room was small and luxuriously, if gaudily, appointed. It was dominated by a huge canopied bed. In a corner was a table with two chairs, obviously where cozy, intimate meals were served. A bottle of brandy and two glasses sat on it now, along with a plateful of food.

"I'll have the sherry shortly," the proprietor said as he opened the door and prepared to leave. "I hope everything is to your pleasure."

Lauren felt unclean in a way she had never felt with Adrian, even when they had lain naked in a barn, their bodies warm with each other's moisture. She knew what Rhys Redding would expect of her if she lost.

And as physically attractive as he was, she knew part of her would die if she had to fulfill her end of the bargain. Her heart and soul and mind were Adrian's, would always be Adrian's. Think of Adrian, she urged herself. Think of his joy at once more owning Ridgely. Lauren was grateful for the veil, for tears had gathered, and she was fighting desperately to hold them back.

But even that privacy was taken away from her. As the proprietor left, Redding lifted the cloak from her, and then the hat. His fingers touched her hair and her face. She couldn't help but flinch, and his hand moved quickly away.

"Are you sure you wish to continue?" His voice was light, challenging.

"If the terms are the same. Adrian gets Ridgely, win or lose."

"And yet you appear to dislike my touch."

Lauren looked up at him, afraid the tears in her eyes were visible. "It's just that . . ." She couldn't continue.

He did it for her. "You like Lord Ridgely's more."

Lauren stood still, fixed by his unblinking interest.

"Your choice of game, love," he said after a short silence.

"Poker."

"Ah, an American game. I'm afraid I know little about it."

"And I know less about English games," Lauren replied. "I'll teach you."

"Everything?"

"Everything," Lauren confirmed, quite aware of time going by. The longer she was gone, the more suspicious her hosts would become, and she dreaded the disappointment she knew she would find in their faces.

The play started then. Redding had brought several packs of cards with him, and some dice.

Lauren tried to remember everything Adrian had taught her, how to bluff, how to discard. She did not, of course, confide these finer points to her opponent, but he had an uncanny sixth sense about them. While Lauren won the first few hands, Rhys started to win the succeeding ones. They had agreed that the first to win five hundred pounds would be the winner, the money imaginary since nothing would count except the final result.

Rhys began driving the stakes of each game higher and higher. Lauren felt her body tense, and she was quite aware she was showing more and more emotion, and thus giving away her hand. But as her desperation grew, it became more and more difficult to hide her feelings.

"Three kings," he said when she thought she'd won with two pairs.

His luck was infernally consistent, and his grin even more so. For someone who claimed to know nothing about poker, he seemed a master at it.

Or else Adrian had lied about her own skill.

An hour went by, and then another, and she was down four hundred and eighty pounds.

"One last game." He grinned.

"Only if you win, Mr. Redding."

"I think it's time you called me Rhys."

Lauren took a sip of sherry as she studied her hand. She had one pair. She discarded two other cards, only to discover that he was discarding none.

They were at fifteen pounds on the table. If she quit now, his winnings would be only five pounds less than needed, but she had the one pair. Lauren said a brief prayer and bet five pounds on the draw.

Now she had three jacks. She called, and Rhys Redding laid down three aces.

Her heart sank, and she swallowed hard.

"Shall we talk about collection?" Rhys Redding's tone was lazy, even malicious, as he stood, taking her hand and drawing her to him.

CHAPTER 26

The lifeblood drained from her as his head came down and his lips captured her mouth.

Lauren didn't fight him, nor did she do anything to help him. Her lips remained still, her body unresponsive, as his hands went to her hair, pulling out the pins that held it up.

His lips were not harsh, but searching, seeking a response that wasn't in her. His arms held none of Adrian's gentleness, none of their warm security.

Rhys Redding was simply taking what was his. He made no attempt at anything else.

Lauren felt the chill in her spread, her limbs loose like the appendages of a rag doll . . . without life.

She had gambled everything. And she had lost.

She had only one satisfaction. According to the agreement, Rhys would still sell Ridgely back to Adrian.

Lauren tried to blank everything else from her mind. She closed her eyes as Rhys's mouth moved to her neck, to the soft column in the front and then to the back, seeking to excite some reaction. But there was none.

And then she was free, standing alone, and she opened her eyes again. Rhys Redding had moved away, his dark eyes almost black, a thoughtful expression on his face.

"The agreement wasn't for a corpse, Miss Bradley," he said, his hand settling over the back of a chair.

"I . . . didn't offer feelings."

"No, you didn't," he agreed with the look in his face becoming speculative. "You must care for Adrian Cabot very much."

Lauren remained absolutely still. She didn't want to think about Adrian now, or what he would believe when she became Rhys's mistress.

"You know," he said conversationally, "this is the second time I've won something Lord Ridgely wanted. And I think it's going to be every bit as unsatisfying as the first gain."

The words registered slowly in Lauren's numbed brain. "You . . . you will still sell him Ridgely?"

He nodded his head. "I don't understand why it means so much to you—enough that you would agree to bed someone who obviously . . . repels you, though it pains me sorely to admit that rather unflattering fact."

Lauren felt the tears that had been gathering behind her eyes, and held there only by the most enormous effort, begin to break through the control. Dear Lord, what a mess she had made of everything. "I'm sorry . . ."

"I see you don't disagree with my assessment," he said dryly, his hand going up to wipe away a tear that had worked its way free. "I've never had a woman in tears at the thought of bedding me before. The idea is usually quite agreeable."

Lauren couldn't speak. She had no idea what he was thinking, or even saying, now.

"Sit down, Lauren," he said, and there was a strange note in his voice. If she didn't know better, she would think it kindness. Startled, she sat.

"It's bloody wounding to think you might be the supreme sacrifice for another man," he said musingly. "You know, I've always disliked men like Ridgely, who always had everything handed to them, even charm." He grinned disarmingly. "I've had to work at mine, and now I find it wanting." There was something other than mockery in his words, a curious kind of surprise.

Lauren could only watch him, wondering at his mood.

"Tell me," he suddenly wheedled, "why you're ready to sell something that so clearly belongs to someone else? Why is Ridgely so important to you?"

His dark eyes bored into her now, and Lauren grew more and more puzzled at his strange attitude, although a seed of hope was sprouting somewhere inside—she didn't know why.

"Why do you want to know?" she asked.

"Because I think you owe me at least that much," he said. "This was your wager, not mine. I thought to win more than a cold body."

"You won't—"

"Go back on the bargain? Perhaps not if you tell me what I want to know. Mysteries interest me. You evidently love Ridgely, but you don't expect to marry him. You care desperately about returning his estate, but you won't share it. You care enough that you are willing to . . . God forbid . . . be my mistress. Yet I obviously hold not the slightest attraction for you." His expression was watchful, and Lauren thought she caught just a glimmer of amusement in his eyes, but then it was gone, and they were as dark and ominous as ever.

She was caught in his gaze. "I . . . wronged him."

"And does he know about this wrong?"

"No."

"And you can't tell him?"

"I've . . . wanted to."

"So you seek to right it by selling yourself. How do you think he'll feel about that?"

"He'll never know."

He looked at her without expression. "I know men like Ridgely," he said. "He would prefer to lose everything rather than accept what you've tried to gain for him to-day." His lips suddenly curled up in a wry smile. "I, on the other hand, would be flattered. Are you really quite sure you wouldn't prefer me?"

Lauren met his gaze steadily. "I made a bargain."

"And you will keep it, regardless of the pain to yourself," he said dryly. "However, I believe I will decline. I have never taken an unwilling woman. I don't intend to start with you. I will, however, uphold my end. I'll sell the estate."

It was Lauren's turn to question. "But . . . why?"

"It was an amusing afternoon, Miss Bradley. Not as stimulating, perhaps, as I'd hoped, but interesting. And to tell you the truth, I'm tired of the country life. I obviously was not born to be lord of the manor." Again there was a strange current in his voice, but Lauren couldn't decipher it.

His voice suddenly gentled. "I'll take you home before Sir Giles dispatches a search party." His hand went to her lips. "I envy Cabot. I really didn't think love existed until today."

Lauren couldn't take her eyes from his face. She tried to understand his words. He was freeing her.

"But one word of advice, Lauren," he said. "Tell Ridgely whatever there is to tell. I don't want my sudden . . . weakness to be in vain."

Lauren impulsively leaned up and kissed him quickly on the cheek. "You *are* very nice," she said with a break in her voice.

"If there is one thing I'm not, Miss Bradley," he said after a moment's pause, "it is nice. It's been a most . . . intriguing afternoon. I consider the entertainment fair return."

"You underestimate yourself, Mr. Redding."

"No," he said abruptly. "I'll take you home now and tell my solicitor to contact Lord Ridgely."

Adrian rode his borrowed bay through the London streets, impatient to reach Sir Giles's residence. Socrates was sitting in front of him, and Adrian sensed he knew they were going to see Lauren. The monkey had been impossible the last two days, and Adrian knew why. He could certainly sympathize.

He was returning early, his anticipation at a high pitch. Sometime during the past days, he'd decided not to complete the purchase of the ship. He kept remembering Lauren's face as he'd discussed it, the despair on it. He kept thinking how much he missed her, how long he would be away from her . . . six months, a year . . . perhaps longer if he was taken again.

And suddenly his obsession with Ridgely dulled. He would find another way. It might take longer. But if he invested wisely . . . After all, there were signs Redding was rapidly tiring of his possession.

What mattered now was Lauren. After the past week of intense loneliness and longing, he knew Ridgely would mean nothing without her. He had lain awake, heat suffusing through him as he thought of the barn, of the way she'd ridden with him through the dripping forest, the gentleness with which she'd nursed him. He thought of the humor in her eyes, the wistfulness, the challenge. And he knew whatever problem lay between them could be solved.

He stopped at a goldsmith's shop off a side street, one recommended by the officer which had accompanied him on the trial run, and found what he was seeking: an antique ring with a small but perfect emerald. As he left, his eyes were drawn to a man and woman who were leaving an inn, a well-known trysting place, across the cobbled road. The two were headed toward a closed coach, and Adrian immediately recognized one of them—Redding. Accompanying him was a heavily veiled woman. He smiled grimly, remembering his unsatisfactory conversation with the owner of Ridgely the other night, and the way Redding had danced with Lauren. He couldn't tell much about the woman with him now, her side was to him, and a cloak and hood all but covered her.

He shrugged. Redding was a well-known rake. Well, he,

too, had been a womanizer once. He had even used the same inn on occasion.

Adrian quickly mounted, the ring in his coat. He would talk to Lauren this afternoon.

But Lauren wasn't at the town house, and both Lisa and Quigley said only that she was "out," and they weren't sure where she was.

Adrian immediately assumed she had gone shopping. Her clothing was still very limited. "I'll wait for her," he said, and was mildly surprised by quickly exchanged glances between Quigley and Lisa.

"Why don't you get some rest and come back for supper with us tonight?" Lisa offered.

At that moment they heard the sound of a carriage stopping in front of the town house, and Adrian felt a wave of warmth roll over him. Socrates at his side, Adrian reached the door before Quigley, and threw it open, finding Rhys Redding handing Lauren down from his phaeton.

It was not the same carriage, nor was Lauren wearing the cloak and veil he'd seen earlier, but he knew it was she who had been with Redding earlier. He saw the guilt in her blanched face.

He stood in the doorway trying to comprehend. The implications were clear enough. And suddenly he wanted to kill both of them. He closed his eyes, hoping that the vision would be gone when he opened them, but it wasn't.

Lauren was standing at the side of the phaeton, her hair slightly mussed, as if hastily pinned, a red color staining her cheeks that had been white a second ago. And Rhys Redding's face was as inscrutable as it usually was.

"Adrian," Lauren whispered just as Socrates made a run for her, holding out his arms to be picked up. But Lauren didn't see the monkey. She saw only Adrian's face.

Anger seized Adrian. Anger and a sense of betrayal that dwarfed any other emotion he'd ever had.

"Did you find the Lion's Head as comfortable as I have?" he asked, every word loaded with soft menace.

He saw her tremble, her lips compress into a tight line so unlike her. "How . . . ?"

"I saw you, love. Or are you *his* love now?"

"Adrian . . ."

His eyes swept her with contempt. Contempt and fury and even something close to hate. Or perhaps self-hate. He didn't know how he could have been such a deluded idiot. He'd known deep in his bones that she had disabled his ship, but he'd thought—wanted to think—there was good reason for it.

There could be no reason for this.

"Why?" Even to him, his voice sounded strangled. Strangled and anguished. "Why . . . ?"

"I . . ."

"First the *Specter*, and now Redding. Is it Ridgely? Do you want that too? Bloody hell, why . . . ?"

Rhys Redding stepped closer, as if to protect her, and Adrian, his senses now maddened, aimed his fist, catching the other man's chin with his balled right knuckles. Rhys spun against the phaeton, falling to his knees. Adrian's other hand went up and seized the front of Rhys's clothes, hitting him again, sending the gambler to the ground. Socrates clung to Lauren, chattering in dismay.

"Adrian . . . don't . . . please . . ." Lauren's face was even whiter than before, her great hazel eyes glittering with tears, looking impossibly brilliant in the paleness of her skin.

"What a bloody fool I've been," Adrian said. "One betrayal wasn't enough. Damn you, Lauren. Damn you to hell. I *loved* you, God help me."

He swung around just as Redding was getting to his feet again and punched him one more time, sending him back to the ground. Adrian then grabbed a protesting, howling Socrates, mounted his borrowed bay, and rode away without a backward glance.

Adrian bought the English ship that afternoon and announced his intentions to sail immediately.

He didn't give a damn if the interior of the vessel wasn't completely finished. The ship's engines were working, and there was sufficient coal aboard because of the test run. He would have what remained to be done completed in Nassau.

It would be damned difficult to get a crew together, but he would manage. There were always sailors around, and his own crew should be waiting for him in the Bahamas.

At least the sea was honest, its dangers known. He would sail tomorrow on the late tide. The whole bloody damn Union fleet could be out there for all he cared.

Adrian knew about the *Specter*. He had known all this time and said nothing. He had known, and he'd said, "I loved you," not "I love you."

Lauren felt as if her heart had been jerked out of her body and torn apart in front of her. The anguish of his words echoed in her mind. *One betrayal wasn't enough. Damn you, Lauren. Damn you to hell.* She started to sway, and Rhys, who now managed to stand, barely caught her, lifting her in his arms and looking at Lisa helplessly.

"Bring her inside," the older woman said, her face a mixture of emotions.

Rhys followed her up the stairs to the room where Lauren was staying and placed her on the bed. He stood there uncertainly, rubbing his jaw. If nothing else, Adrian Cabot certainly possessed a powerful right hook.

"You may leave now, Mr. Redding," Lisa Tatterly said censoriously. "I think you've done quite enough today."

Rhys looked at Lauren. Her hair had tumbled down from the pins she'd used earlier, and her face was strained and white.

He looked at Lisa Tatterly, who had drawn up to as imposing a figure as she could, and said, "It isn't what you and Ridgely thought. Nothing . . . of any questionable nature occurred, I assure you."

Lisa's face cleared slightly at the sincerity in his voice, but her questioning eyes went from Rhys Redding to her young guest.

"She was trying to help him," Rhys said. "Trying to convince me to sell him back the estate. And she's accomplished that."

"You're going to . . . ?"

"Yes," Rhys said.

"Even now?" The question came as she studied his black eye and the blood dripping from his mouth.

"Even now, Mrs. Tatterly, if he will listen."

But Lauren knew he wouldn't. Unlike the other two in the room, she knew the extent of the disaster. There had never been trust between her and Adrian. She had killed his dream once, and then she had destroyed his faith in her completely. How could he trust her again? Adrian, who had made such a point of honesty. Adrian, who had somehow forgiven her first transgression, but could never forgive this one. "Please leave me alone," she whispered brokenly.

"I'll be near if you need anything, dear," Lisa said.

Rhys didn't say anything at all as he left. His mind was preoccupied with other thoughts, with the few cryptic words he'd heard. He, like so many others in London, had heard that Lauren had helped Adrian escape from U.S. authorities. It had been one of the things that had so fascinated him about her. He couldn't imagine a woman doing that, risking so much, and accepting nothing in return. He wondered over the words he'd heard Adrian say. He had mentioned his ship. *One betrayal was not enough.* He remembered Lauren's words at the inn: "I've wronged him." And because of that, she had been willing to do anything to help him. It soured Rhys that he had to place himself in the "anything" category.

But he felt much of this fiasco was his fault. He had been amusing himself, pure and simple, and now, for the first time in his life, he felt real guilt about something he'd done. He liked Lauren Bradley. More than that, he admired her.

Never in his life had he tried to do anything for someone else. Now, on his maiden attempt, it had turned out poorly.

It was ironical.

It was unfair.

It could not be permitted.

He rubbed his jaw again. Now where in the devil could he find Adrian Cabot, viscount of Ridgely?

Lauren couldn't sleep. Neither had she been able to eat. Fitfully, she lit the oil lamp at the side of her bed.

She paced the floor of the room for a while and then went to the window. The street lanterns cast an eerie glow in the mist. It seemed every London night included fog or mist or rain. The streets were empty, so it must be very late indeed. There were only shadows, cast by the diffuse light of the lanterns. It made her think of the house in Maryland, of the strange feeling of being guided, and suddenly she felt it again.

Or maybe it was the need for companionship, the companionship of a woman who had loved enough to give up everything she knew and loved.

Lauren had not been able to read the diary since that night on the ship. She had felt Melissa's pain and loss too deeply.

But now she reached down into her small trunk and found the volume, opening it slowly.

December, 1861.

It is Christmas Day, and there are only Sam and me to celebrate it. Lucas never returned.

Oh, and yes, and there is little Randall.

I am determined the child will be a boy . . . with Randall's dark hair and green eyes. A part of my dear husband will still be with me, and I am committed to holding this land, this farm, for him.

It is not easy. The number of marauders increases, and we have buried everything that is valuable, even my engagement ring that once belonged to Randall's mother. I have written my family about the child, but I have heard nothing. I pray that when this terrible war is over, they will come to accept my marriage and my child.

I loved Randall so much. I shall always love him, and I shall never regret what time we had. I tremble now when I think of those times I doubted him, and doubted my ability to defy my family and my loyalties. I know now that love is the most important gift one is given, and that it is a sin to throw it aside. Our few days together were worth a hundred years with anyone else. He has given me a joy I will always hold in my heart, and one day I will be with him again . . .

The entry ended, and Lauren wiped away a tear. She could almost see Melissa now, almost reach out and touch her. *Love is the most important gift one is given.*

Lauren thought over the past weeks, how many chances she'd had to confide in Adrian, to believe in the love she felt was there. But something had always stopped her, and now she wondered whether it had been memories of Larry, whether she hadn't always felt that talking about Larry would be the final betrayal of her brother. Or perhaps she'd felt that way because it meant letting her brother go.

Melissa had reached all the way for her Randall. And she, Lauren, had not. She had given half measure all the way, never truly giving Adrian all he deserved, always holding part of herself back.

But Adrian had known, and he had loved her despite it. He had been waiting for her to tell him. She knew that now, but that knowledge might be too late in coming.

I loved you. The words had been so desperately thrown out, a cry of anguish.

She knew his pride, and she had stripped him of it. She had to tell him why. She couldn't run any longer. Not from him. Not from herself.

There were other things she had to do. She had to go back to Nassau and talk to Jeremy. And she had to make things right with her own government.

But she would find Adrian first, explain everything. No more lies or evasions. He had to know her, to understand her, if he was to love her. She just prayed it wasn't too late.

Rhys Redding finally found his quarry in a dockside tavern.

Adrian sat in a corner drinking, his face lined with weariness and disillusionment.

Rhys sat down without invitation, meeting Adrian's hostile eyes.

"What in bloody hell do *you* want?"

Rhys reached into his very proper coat, which was very improper in this particular establishment, and took out some papers. He put them on the table and pushed them over to Adrian.

"You offered me a million pounds for Ridgely a few days ago. I'm accepting."

Adrian glared at him. "I don't have it anymore. I just bought a ship."

"Then I'll take what you have . . . and the ship. It's time for a new venture."

"I don't want anything from you, Redding."

"It's not from me. It's a debt due. A small matter of a wager, and I take that very seriously."

Adrian looked at him suspiciously. "What wager?"

Rhys rubbed his chin. It still hurt. He was inviting another blow, and he knew it. "Between your lady and me."

Adrian uttered a foul curse, and Rhys had the sickening feeling that a second black eye might soon grace his bruised face.

"She's not my lady," Adrian finally said, "and take your bloody damned paper and—"

"Don't be a complete ass."

"I've already been that," Adrian growled, a muscle jerking in his cheek.

"Miss Bradley offered to wager the only thing of value she had, a cottage in a place called Delaware, in a card game," he said, conveniently leaving out a few details.

"Delaware?"

Rhys shrugged. "Wherever in hell that is."

"Why would you do that?" Adrian said accusingly. "Why do you want . . . ?"

"I don't," Rhys said frankly. "But I must say the idea quite intrigued me—a lady willing to put up everything she had for someone else, without wanting that someone to know about it . . ."

"I've never known you to be altruistic." Adrian's tone was bitter.

Rhys leaned back and laughed. "Neither has anyone else. Believe me, generosity had nothing to do with it. I was tired of Ridgely anyway—never did see what you liked about it—and it was an amusing way to spend an afternoon. Of course," he said with a predatory gleam, "I would have preferred to spend it another way, but the lady would have none of that. Unfortunately she seems hopelessly in love with a stiff-necked ass."

A glimmer of interest shone in Adrian's eyes. "She won?"

Rhys raised an eyebrow. "My dear boy, of course she didn't win. I'm afraid you quite misled her about her skills at cards. Every little emotion shows in her eyes."

Adrian's eyes went to the paper in front of him. "Then . . . why did you change your mind?"

"I didn't sell you the estate before because I don't like you," Rhys said frankly. "I don't like anything you are. Thought I would let you stew a bit longer."

"Why, then?"

Rhys fixed an unblinking stare on him. "Because of all the 'ladies' I've ever met, your Miss Bradley is the only real one among them. I figured you couldn't be quite the ass I thought you were if she loved you that much." He shook his head. "And then, damn if you didn't go and prove you were."

Adrian scowled darkly at him, his mind working rapidly. There was no reason, absolutely no reason at all, for Redding to lie to him. And for all of the man's somewhat shady reputation, no one had ever accused him of being a liar or a cheat. He was a gambler who was merciless in his playing, in exploiting others, and Adrian would never forgive Redding for what he had done to his brother, drawing him in deeper and deeper.

"I don't believe you're doing this out of the goodness of your heart," he told Redding belligerently.

"That's your ill fortune," Rhys said, getting up. "I'll go after the lady myself. When she discovers what an arrogant bastard you really are, perhaps she'll be more amenable to my more . . . gentle ways," he said with a leering grin.

He didn't make it all the way to his feet. Adrian's fist hit him in his good eye, and he went tumbling to the floor, thinking that being a good Samaritan was a damned painful business.

And he was getting angry.

His hand shot out and jerked Adrian's leg, tumbling him to the floor, and he took great pleasure in landing a powerful blow on Adrian's chin.

Blow was exchanged for blow as the tavern exploded into noise, the fight igniting other fights until flying fists and legs were everywhere. Sometime along the way, Adrian was no longer fighting Rhys, but they both were fighting the whole bloody lot in the tavern.

Adrian felt a crashing blow on his head, and then everything went black.

CHAPTER 27

Lauren looked for Adrian everywhere. She sent messages to his lodgings. She went down to the docks, but there seemed to be hundreds of ships there, and no one knew the name of his new ship, or his whereabouts.

Sir Giles did his own checking and discovered that Adrian had purchased the ship a day earlier, and had informed everyone he was leaving shortly for the Bahamas. The ship was not moored where it had been, and he could only guess that Adrian had already sailed. Lisa had told him of the encounter with Redding, and Sir Giles was only too aware of Adrian's bitter past. That he felt the need to leave England was understandable, though disappointing.

Lauren was beyond comforting. That Adrian had left without seeing her was excruciating. Something in her had hoped, even expected, that he would wait for an explanation.

His silence, his leave-taking, meant that his fury had

not dissipated. She wondered if it ever would. Had she lost the most important thing in her life, thrown it away so carelessly?

She knew she had to go after him. But she had no money to do so. Her only asset was a cottage thousands of miles away.

Lauren swallowed her pride and told Lisa everything—about her brother, her role in Adrian's capture, about Rhys. Lisa told Sir Giles privately, and then he called Lauren into his study. She stood like a schoolgirl awaiting censure, but his eyes were uncommonly kind and sympathetic.

"Sit down, Lauren," he said. "I think we have a great deal to discuss."

Lauren sat and waited.

"Did Adrian ever tell you about a woman named Sylvia?"

Lauren's stomach tensed. She shook her head.

"Adrian thought he was in love with her, and she with him, but she was using him while she found a more . . . suitable husband. He never trusted a woman after that . . . until you, I think."

The tenseness in Lauren's stomach turned to an agonizing knot.

"Adrian," Sir Giles said, "never had much of a family. His father was a very cold man, even cruel, and his brother a weak libertine who cared for nothing but his own pleasures. After Sylvia discarded Adrian for a much wealthier man and his brother gambled away his heritage, Adrian never really allowed anyone to get very close to him. Oh, he's a very likable man, but I don't think he's ever been able to really care for anyone, not totally. Not until you. That's why he's lavished so much affection on that damned monkey of his."

Sir Giles's voice softened. "I think he . . . cares about you because he recognizes that you have the same strength he does . . . and a brave heart . . ."

"I've . . . made so many mistakes."

"But they've all come from the heart, Lauren, and I think Adrian will understand that."

"Will he?" she said miserably.

He nodded. "In fact, I'm surprised he has left . . . but he'll be back."

"I want to go after him."

"Of course," he said, smiling. "I know of a ship sailing for the Bahamas tonight."

She sat up straight in her chair. "If I could borrow passage money . . . I have property in the United States—I can pay you back."

He nodded, knowing she would accept no less.

"Thank you. Do you think he can . . . forgive me?"

Sir Giles looked at her kindly. "For caring about your brother . . . for loving him—oh yes, I think so. And now we'd better make the arrangements to get you on the ship tonight."

Rhys looked with disgust at the bulge underneath his shirt where his left arm was held in a sling. He sighed. Broken, it was, devil take it.

He heard a groan from his bed. Finally. He was beginning to think Adrian Cabot was going to die on him. The doctor had cheerfully said it was altogether possible if he didn't wake soon.

The man had been unconscious two days. Rhys had been out too, for a while. Apparently someone had bludgeoned them both and dragged them into an alley, where they lay God knew how long. When Rhys had finally stirred, all their possessions were gone, and he had an agonizing pain in his arm as well as his head. Adrian was absolutely still. And that diabolical monkey was running around demented.

Rhys had finally convinced someone to help them both to his lodgings. And then he'd called a discreet physician he knew. He was still feeling a curious responsibility, and he didn't trust hospitals.

They had to wait to see whether Adrian would wake, the doctor said while setting Rhys's arm. Send for him, he said, if there was any change. So Rhys had watched. Nearly two bloody days now. Two days of tending a man he didn't like and being subjected to the nastiest, most ungrateful, spiteful animal he'd ever had the misfortune to encounter. He looked down at the bites on his good arm.

"Lauren," Adrian whispered, and Rhys was surprised at the satisfaction the sound caused in him.

He poured a glass of water with his good hand and pulled a chair close to the large comfortable bed. "Ridgely," he said loudly, and Adrian's eyes fluttered open and tried to focus.

When they finally did, the blank gaze turned into a glower. "Where in bloody hell am I?"

"My lodgings and my bed. My only bed," Rhys replied pointedly.

Adrian tried to move, his glower growing darker. "Why?"

Rhys shrugged. "I didn't know where else to take you, except one of those charnel houses they call a hospital. I didn't think it wise to send you to Sir Giles—neither you nor I are in great favor there. And I didn't know whether you would live or not."

"You don't have to sound so bloody cheerful about the prospect of my death."

Rhys chuckled. "So you do have a sense of humor? I never would have suspected it."

"Not much of one right now. Socrates?"

"Is that the name of that incorrigible? He's a devil of a sight better than either of us."

Adrian's tightly drawn lips cracked as his gaze raked over Rhys's battered face, falling to the arm in a sling.

"Now *you* don't have to look so bloody cheerful," Rhys said.

Adrian had to summon enormous willpower to sit. "I was to sail tonight," he mused.

"You've been unconscious for two days," Rhys said.

"I've been here two days?" There was horror in Adrian's voice.

"I share your distress," Rhys observed dryly. "I not only

had to sleep in a chair, but also tolerate your ill-tempered friend."

"Why?"

"At the risk of repeating myself, I felt a trifle responsible."

Adrian groaned as he remembered the events leading up to this deplorable situation. "Lauren?"

"I don't know."

Adrian groaned again as he tried to rise.

"I don't think you're going far," Rhys noted with a slight grin.

"Did you mean everything you said?"

"Ah, you remember."

"Redding . . ." It was a threat despite Adrian's obvious weakness.

"If you mean the part about your being an ass, yes."

Adrian's glower turned ever darker. But as he recalled that conversation, he had to admit there was truth in Redding's words. He shouldn't have needed to be told there was nothing between Redding and Lauren, despite appearances. He *knew* Lauren. He loved Lauren. He should have trusted Lauren. But when he'd seen her with Redding, he'd remembered Sylvia. Lauren was nothing like Sylvia, however; Lauren was like no other woman. Bloody hell, what had he done?

"Will you send a message to her?"

Redding smiled sardonically. "With delight, if it means your imminent departure. And his!" He scowled toward the corner where Socrates sat glaring at Adrian as if everything was his fault.

And it was, Adrian acknowledged to himself. "I seem to remember," he said, "that you said you would sell Ridgely. Is the offer still open?"

"Yes." Redding stood.

"Did I tell you I bought a ship?"

"You did, and I said I would take it as part of the bargain."

"It's built for blockade running."

"Remember, I'm a gambler."

"You know nothing about the sea."

"I know a little, and I can learn the rest if you help me find the right people."

"You're a lunatic."

Rhys glanced over at Socrates. "*You* have that animal, and you call *me* a lunatic?"

There was some wisdom in that observation, but whatever liking Adrian was developing for Rhys Redding, it was quickly dispelled by the man's next words.

"And I've discovered I *do* like American women."

Lauren looked out the window from Jeremy's house in Nassau, just as she had months ago. The harbor was nearly empty, at least in comparison to several days earlier. The new moon had arrived three days ago, one day before the ship carrying her had docked. It, too, was a steamer, but not one meant for the blockade.

The blockade, the captain had told her, was growing much too dangerous now. More and more companies were withdrawing from the trade.

She had hoped Adrian would arrive before her, and now she worried that he had been captured on the way from England.

Lauren could not stay away from the window. She haunted it when she wasn't down on the docks, staring into the water, willing a new ship to appear, waiting to see Adrian standing on the deck of his ship once again.

Jeremy and Corinne had been wonderful. She had thought he might not want her to stay after hearing what she had to say, and she'd been prepared to find cheap lodgings in a boardinghouse and find some way to make her own livelihood. But he would have none of it. One can't choose whom one loves, he'd said, and she had more than fulfilled her bargain. Yes, he had heard she would be arrested if she returned to the United States, but he thought he could convince Phillips otherwise. After all, Phillips did get the *Specter*. Jeremy's optimism did nothing to soothe her spirits; but she stayed, hoping that Adrian would come.

Lauren watched as a new ship entered the harbor, a

steamer. A lean silhouette, just like the *Specter*. She didn't remember seeing it before, and her heart fluctuated madly until she told herself to cease being such a fool. She saw figures on the deck, but she couldn't identify them. For a moment one looked vaguely familiar. Then she told herself it was only wishful thinking. Do something useful, she said. Help Jeremy in the store. Don't tantalize yourself like this.

Jeremy, apparently sensing her restlessness, asked her to check the stock, especially the tobacco items. When the blockade runners came in, they would be clamoring for such.

She stooped down. While checking the humidors in the cases, she heard a running noise, and felt a breeze from fast movement. Suddenly a furry thing hurled itself at her, and she found herself being smacked in the face by two enthusiastic lips.

Lauren fell back against the wall as Socrates chattered excitedly, and in his excitement bit her. His greeting completed, he leaped for the counter and grabbed a stick of licorice.

A tanned hand reached down for her, grasping hers with the lazy strength that was endearingly familiar. She looked up into wonderful deep blue eyes as Adrian pulled her up so easily. For the first time in nearly three miserable weeks, she faced him.

His eyes devoured her, though his face remained rigidly set as if he didn't know what to expect. The heat that always circulated between them, the magnetism that had bound them together almost from the very first minute, cloaked them with its own mysterious power as he searched her face. There was suddenly no one else in the world but the two of them, and it was as though there had been no treachery, no distrust. There was only now, only this minute . . . and the other priceless moments when they had loved so intensely.

"I've missed you," Adrian whispered fiercely as his arms went around her, pulling her close against him, seeking to hear the beat of her heart.

Unbelieving, Lauren lifted her head so her eyes could

meet his, and she lost herself in their smoldering depths. He seized her lips with his, and the world caught fire, filling her with a miraculous glory.

When his lips finally released her, Lauren looked up, her wide eyes welling with brilliantly shining tears. "I love you," she said aloud for the first time, though she'd said it so many times in the silence of her thoughts.

His hand went to her cheek, quivering slightly in suppressed emotion before moving lovingly along its contours, as if reassuring himself that she was there.

"Would you like to go for a sail, Miss Bradley?" he said.

He was asking much more than that, and Lauren knew it. "Yes," she said simply.

The small skiff skimmed through the water.

Lauren knew now that Adrian had just come in on the ship she had seen from the window, and she wondered at how swiftly he had come to her, and how he had obtained this skiff so quickly.

She knew without asking that they were returning to that wondrous island where they had started falling in love with each other, where there would be privacy, complete and absolute . . . except for Socrates, who refused to leave either of them.

Lauren couldn't take her eyes from the striking man who so confidently handled the sail and tiller. She remembered thinking months ago how appealing he was as he moved with such agility, how at ease he was with the sea and the sun and the wind. She supposed she had loved him even then, though not like she did now. Not with her whole soul and heart and mind. Then, her heart was divided.

Now it belonged wholly to him, if he would take it. But there was still so much she had to confess to him.

For the moment, however, she rejoiced in watching him. As before, he had pulled off his polished black boots with a boyish smile, yet there was nothing boyish about the snug trousers and open shirt that revealed his powerful chest. The wind ruffled his chestnut hair, and she ached to run her fingers through it. He smiled at her, slowly and sensuously. That smile was as intimate as a kiss, as full of tenderness. As full of promise.

The small craft turned, spraying cool water on her, and she felt the contrast of Bahamian sun and water. Every sense was heightened now, and her body was stretched as tightly as a bowstring as she watched Adrian's body move gracefully, his hands competently.

And then he was picking her up, carrying her to the unblemished smoothness of white sand washed by sea. She was barely aware of Socrates, who had swung up on Adrian's shoulder for the brief ride to shore but climbed quickly down as soon as they reached the beach and ran off to find a tree.

There was only Adrian now. The closeness of him. The thunder of being in his arms, the lightning of lips touching. The storm when he laid her on the sand and knelt beside her, his hands moving along her body, caressing it, loving it.

The storm whipped into a hurricane as their bodies came together, neither of them able to touch enough, to convey enough, to express enough. Frantic because of need. Not mere lust, but so much more, the need to envelop each other, to become one again, in spirit as well as body. They had been so very far apart . . .

"I love you," Lauren whispered as he entered her, their bodies joining in mutual longing and need and love. Gently at first, and then with all the wild, desperate fierceness born of loss and fear and emptiness. The fierceness turned to exquisite sweetness, then to driving need, and finally to exploding splendor.

They lay together, their clothes scattered around them, discarded in ways neither knew how, nor cared to know. They felt the sun bless them, the cool wind dry the wetness of their skin and the tears on Lauren's face, and both felt an overwhelming sense of peace. Lauren's hand ran down the length of Adrian's chest, lingering only slightly at the wound inflicted in Virginia. She leaned over and kissed it.

She felt the beat of his heart, which was also the beat of hers.

And then she met his eyes, knowing it was time now to open every part of herself to him: the secrets, the lies, the terrible truths.

"There is so much I must tell you," she said.

Adrian's lips touched hers, hushing them. "I think I know it all, love. Lisa told me some—Redding the rest."

"And you still . . . ?"

"Love you?" He had a funny smile on his face, sad and regretful and even guilty. "Dear God, I love you. I have from the beginning, ever since, I think, you curtsied to Socrates." His lips nuzzled her neck. "I knew it without doubt when you came to the jail, holding Socrates and telling that ridiculous story about a deformed baby." He chuckled, his teeth nibbling along the side of her cheek so she could barely comprehend his words.

"Life," he added, "would be incredibly dull without you."

"But—"

"I know about your brother." The nibbling stopped, and his eyes met hers steadily. "I'm sorry, Lauren. I'm so damned sorry. I didn't know at the time, and if there was any way I could bring him back, I would. But I can't."

Lauren saw the deep pain in his eyes, the regret, and she knew he meant it. She felt the last residue of guilt and anger leave her. She would always remember Larry, but now she could let him go.

"The *Specter* . . ." she started.

"I know about that too," he said. "Somehow I knew you were responsible from the beginning. But I thought you had to have a good reason, and I wanted you to tell me, to trust me . . . it was so bloody important to me."

"I wanted to," Lauren whispered, "but . . ."

"But what?"

"Jeremy told me about a bet you had with Clay."

Adrian groaned. He was beginning to understand so many things now. Her sudden reticence on the *Specter*, the times she had drawn away from him. She had reason to mistrust him. That damnable stupid bet.

"It was a stupid spur-of-the-moment thing I'd agreed to after I'd just met you," he said. "We were accustomed to betting on everything. We decided to call it off almost immediately, but Clay went ahead with . . . with the dinner."

Lauren felt a sense of relief. She hadn't realized until now how much that bet still bothered her. The relief must have reflected in her face because he halted what she was going to say with a kiss so gentle, her heart sang with the promise of it.

"I didn't realize," he said very slowly afterward, as if he were explaining it to both of them, "that I was judging you for something I, too, was guilty of. I didn't trust you enough to tell you what I suspected, to ask you why. I put it all on your head, and I almost lost you."

Lauren started to protest, to say that everything was her fault, but he put his fingers to her lips and hushed her. "I haven't known how to trust for a very long time, Lauren, but I'm learning. Be patient with me."

Adrian's voice was low and quiet and pleading in a way Lauren had never heard before. In so many ways, he had trusted her, she mused, so much more than she'd allowed herself to trust him.

Trust. Such a precious commodity. It shouldn't be a fragile thing, but they had strengthened it today, and she vowed to herself there would never be secrets between them again.

Yet there was one more secret, she admitted silently, one more obstacle between them: Rhys Redding.

With that sensitivity he seemed to have about her, he knew what she was about to say, and how painful it would be. He stopped her words again. "If I'd had any doubts about what an ass I'd been, Redding made it painfully clear," he said with a strange smile. "He told me about the wager . . . said of all the ladies he'd ever met, you were the only real one."

Lauren's eyes widened.

"He also said I didn't deserve you, and speculated that his 'gentle ways' might eventually win you." He said the words in a teasing voice, but there was a question in them nonetheless, an uncertainty that made her ache.

Her hands tightened on his, and she said the words he'd been waiting a very long time to hear: "I love you, Adrian. I love you so much I hurt with it . . ." Her voice trailed off, the truth of her words evident in the raw, ragged sound of them.

Adrian's hand stroked her face, touching the corners of her eyes where tears were now hovering. Tears of so many emotions. Grief. Regret. Hope. Happiness. His heart, which piece by piece had been stolen by her, became completely Lauren's.

"I tried to come after you in London," he said, wanting her to know. "But you had left."

She looked at him wonderingly. "I was told you had gone. I was coming after you. I was so afraid I had lost you . . . I had to explain . . . And then you weren't here . . ."

"Redding and I had a . . . rather painful encounter," Adrian continued, a gleam of amusement in his eyes. "We both ended up somewhat the worse for it. I was unconscious for two days, and his arm was broken." He grinned at Lauren's startled, horrified expression.

"He took care of me, much to the surprise of both of us, I think, and when I finally regained my senses, I went after you only to find you gone. Rhys and I entered a . . . partnership of sorts . . . to find you."

"Rhys?" Her shock was obvious.

"I gave him the ship I bought as partial payment for Ridgely, and in turn he gave me a free ride to Nassau."

It was too much for Lauren to comprehend. She remembered Rhys lying on the street, the open antipathy of the two men, even at the dance. "Rhys is here?"

"He's going to run the blockade . . . Most of my crew's here, and I'm retiring, so he'll have the best. He says he enjoys a good game. I *did* try to warn him," Adrian added.

Lauren had to smile. He looked well satisfied with himself, like a boy who had talked an unwary friend into doing a despised chore by intriguing him with the joys of it.

"You didn't," she accused, but there was laughter in her eyes.

He only smiled. "Rhys Redding is entirely capable of taking care of himself," he said. "Now you, on the other hand . . ."

She looked up at him, slightly insulted.

". . . need a husband," he continued smoothly.

Her eyes grew even larger, and her mouth pursed too irresistibly to ignore. His lips met hers perfectly, his tongue pleading his case quite well. When he completed his delightful task, he paused long enough for her answer.

"Must I be 'm'lady'?" she asked cautiously.

"My lady," he replied, nibbling her ear.

"And can I play cards and break people out of jail?"

"Perfectly normal behavior for a Cabot," he said, grinning. "After all, you don't have an ill-mannered monkey."

"I do now," she said, her eyes shining as she gave her hand, her heart, and her soul to Adrian.

And so engrossed were they in each other that neither one was aware of a wise little face beaming from a tree.

EPILOGUE

"The war's over."

Clad in a sturdy cotton shirt and tight breeches, Adrian read the letter that had just arrived.

He had ridden in from the fields for his noon meal, and his shirt was plastered against his skin despite the coolness of May in England.

He hadn't spared himself, and the fields were now showing the result of seemingly endless work. Ridgely had lost tenants during years of mismanagement. They were short-handed. Slowly over the past eighteen months, Adrian had lured good workers, and the estate was finally showing signs of prospering. Money remained tight; almost everything Adrian had earned had gone into the repurchase of his ancestral lands, and bankers did not yet trust the Cabot name again. But slowly they were producing order out of chaos, and every improvement was a major victory.

And they were doing it together.

He continued to read Sir Giles's letter. "No news of Rhys," he said, "but I think we would have heard if anything had happened to him. We know he got away from the Yanks. Damned if I know how—he didn't have Lauren."

Lauren giggled. "A wager with an unwary guard, perhaps." She moved over on the bench in the garden where she had waited for him. She loved this place, with its profusion of roses.

The house was now bright, sunlight streaming through the curtains she herself had made with the help of one of the two servants who remained. And Socrates was a very contented monkey. There were enough trees to keep him in leaves and bark forever, and he had dozens of rooms to explore. The cantankerous side of his nature was well satisfied in making life miserable for Mary the housekeeper and Simon the butler.

Lauren felt the loving pressure of Adrian's hand on hers, and the quiet joy his presence always brought her. Still, she couldn't escape a certain melancholy. The war was over, but its impact would last for generations. She thought of Melissa and Randall; of Clay, who had finally been captured on one of the last runs into Wilmington; of the Confederate captain she had met in Virginia—was he still alive? Finally she thought of Mr. Phillips, whose manipulations would now come to an end.

The war was finally over for some—including Lauren, on whose behalf Jeremy had interceded with Mr. Phillips, who had agreed to drop all charges against her. It would never be over for others. Lauren thought again of Melissa, whose diary she had recently shared with Adrian. One day, she knew, she would send it to Melissa's family. They should know the agony she had suffered because of her love for Randall.

She smiled as Adrian put his hand on her belly, his mouth creasing into satisfaction as he felt a mighty kick.

It had to be a boy, with that kind of power.

Adrian, however, said no one but a daughter of hers could have that determined a will.

She looked at his face, the strong bronzed face that she loved more than life itself, and watched the slow, lazy smile break the solemn line of his lips. His eyes shone with accomplishment, his laughter with happiness.

She loved him more each day.

She still thought of her dead twin. Adrian had already suggested that their child, if a son, be named for Larry. Her brother would like that, she knew. And he would understand. He had always understood love.

She looked up at the blue sky. Laurence, her father said, had been like the first bright glow of the morning sun, and Lauren like the gentle twilight of evening.

Lauren would always look for that first bright glow, but Adrian had filled her days with another kind of brilliance, one that allowed sweet memories along with tumultuous storms and the lightning that had raged between them from the beginning.

Adrian's lips caught hers in understanding, and that lightning flashed anew. Lauren put her hand in his, and together they disappeared inside the manor, both forgetting the letter that had closed a chapter in their lives and allowed them to start a new one, unfettered by the past.

If you loved
LIGHTNING
don't miss Rhys's own spectacular story in
Patricia Potter's
NIGHTHAWK

Coming from
Bantam FANFARE
Spring of 1993.

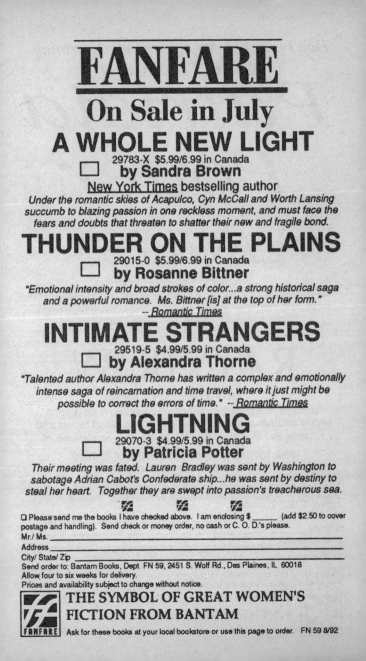

FANFARE

On Sale in August

DAWN ON A JADE SEA

☐ 29837-2 $5.50/6.50 in Canada
by Jessica Bryan

bestselling author of ACROSS A WINE-DARK SEA

She was a shimmering beauty from a kingdom of legend. A vision had brought Rhea to the glorious city of Ch'ang-an, compelling her to seek a green-eyed, auburn-haired foreign warrior called Zhao, the Red Tiger. Amid the jasmine of the Imperial Garden, passion will be born, hot as fire, strong as steel, eternal as the ocean tides.

BLAZE

☐ 29957-3 $5.50/6.50 in Canada
by Susan Johnson

bestselling author of FORBIDDEN and SINFUL

To Blaze Braddock, beautiful, pampered daughter of a millionaire, the American gold rush was a chance to flee the stifling codes of Boston society. But when Jon Hazard Black, a proud young Absarokee chief, challenged her father's land claim, Blaze was swept up in a storm of passions she had never before even imagined.

LAST BRIDGE HOME

☐ 29871-2 $4.50/5.50 in Canada
by Iris Johansen

bestselling author of THE GOLDEN BARBARIAN

Jon Sandell is a man with many secrets and one remarkable power, the ability to read a woman's mind, to touch her soul, to know her every waking desire. His vital mission is to rescue a woman unaware of the danger she is in. But who will protect her from him?